PRAISE FOR

Engraved On A Heart Of Flame

"Claire's lush prose transports readers to a diverse world where 'blessed ones' attempt to find their place."

—Austin Valenzuela, @valenzuela.au

"The perfect read for fantasy lovers who value inclusivity, spice, action, and character development!"

—Sarah Madden, @lucidthenovel

"This story just keeps getting better! Exceptional world building paired with beautifully written characters that draw you in and win your heart."

—Aiden Murray, @aidenmurrayauthor

"Engraved on a Heart of Flame is perhaps Claire's best work yet!"

—H.P.T., beta reader

PRAISE FOR

The Threads of Destiny Series

"Devastatingly powerful! What started as a quest to save the day, ended with the fulfillment of some of life's most precious gifts: love and peace."

—R.J. Castille, author of Goddess

"Fantasy, adventure, romance, and even a little spice! What a journey!"

—Becca Longi, @beccasbookishlife

Use QR Code to View Full-Color HD Map:

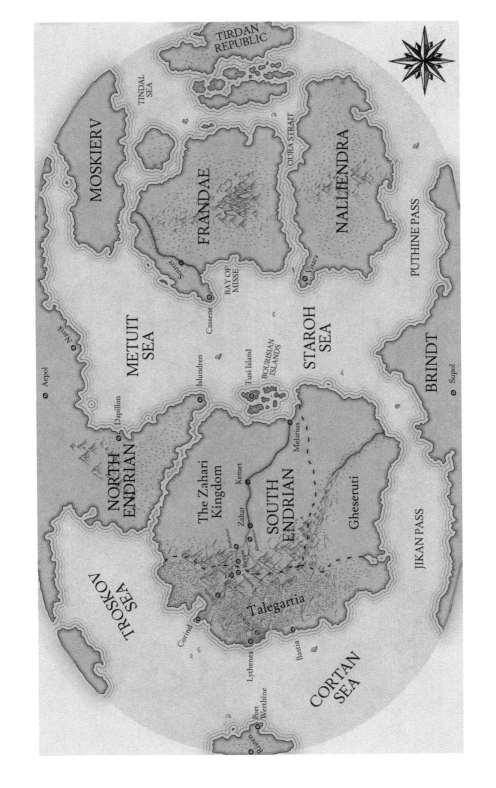

Novels by Claire E. Jones

Engraved
On
A
Heart
Of
Flame

CLAIRE E. JONES

THREADS OF DESTINY BOOK 3
CLAIRJOYANCE PUBLISHING LLC

Published by Clairjoyance Publishing LLC

www.claireejones.com

Copyright © 2024 by Claire E. Jones

Cover Art by Carlos Ortega-Haas

Map by Claire E. Jones

ISBN:

979-8-9888028-5-3

Library of Congress Control Number:

2024913233

Hardcover, Paperback, eBook editions / October 2024

For all of my hopeless romantics out there,
may we find the love that transcends everything.

DAY ONE

Rakhmet attempted to focus on the unnecessarily detailed explanation his guard Rami was giving him, but his thoughts were going in a thousand different directions. He was trying to keep track of everything that needed to be done in the next fifteen hours because come dawn, he would be leaving his home behind and leading a dozen of his trusted guards into a secret war against an enemy that always seemed to be ten steps ahead of them. It didn't help that his eyes kept straying to the corner where Hara silently stood watch either.

She'd been there for hours, keeping a careful eye as one person after another came to confirm the final numbers with him before their departure. It had been a constant stream of guards, accountants, advisors, and sailors, and his brain felt like it was starting to overheat. But every time his gaze slid to her, his shoulders relaxed a fraction.

It was a relief to be in her presence again. Sure, they had fought on and off over the years, but she had always come around after a few days, putting her duty to the Crown above their petty squabbles. That was why he had been so desperate for a truce by the time she had shown up in his rooms the day before with that message from Sennuhotep. The two weeks she had avoided him had nearly reduced him to begging for her understanding. For her pity.

This expedition to the sacred plant temple was his chance to prove that he wasn't a waste of space, that he wasn't a coward who all too deftly avoided the responsibilities his birth had bestowed upon him. After the disaster at the fire temple had left him disfigured and humiliated, he was determined to do everything in his power to not fail again. And it had cut him deep when Hara had refused to see that.

He frowned as expectant silence filled the room. Glancing back at Rami, he realized that the guard was waiting for an answer from him.

"Sorry, what was that?" he asked, clearing his throat.

"Your Highness, I was asking if you were willing to approve the proposal to reduce the rations to 30 days' worth due to the recent change of plans?" Rami repeated, his tone polite, but Rakhmet could see the teasing gleam in his eye from catching him with his attention wandering.

"Fine." Rakhmet smirked, only slightly annoyed at how comfortable the guard had become with him after a couple weeks of being Hara's substitute, and waved his hand to dismiss him.

"Yes, Your Highness." Rami bowed, half mockingly, then shot a grin over his shoulder as he left.

Rakhmet huffed and rolled his eyes, leaning back in his chair to pinch the bridge of his nose. It had already been a long twenty-four hours and he still had a full docket of responsibilities that needed his attention before he would be able to get some rest. His lids fell closed as he massaged the tightness around his brow and temples, but the sound of more footsteps approaching had him straightening and putting on his best prince face as Uma, the royal manager who kept them all in line with an iron will, entered his office.

His mask instantly dissipated, breaking into a genuine smile.

"Good afternoon, Your Highness." She beamed at him. From the moment he was born, Uma had practically raised him herself and, although she was technically his inferior here at the palace, he cared for her just as much as he cared for his actual family.

"Good afternoon, Uma," he greeted her warmly.

"I have come to let you know that the farewell dinner will be starting in an hour."

"Oh shit, is it that late already?" Rakhmet glanced at the gilded clock on his desk, rising from his chair.

"I'll leave you to it, Your Highness." Uma gave him a look that clearly said *what would you do without me?* and then disappeared to continue with her never-ending list of duties.

Hara instinctively fell into step just behind him as they left the overly wrought quarters he had been provided for official matters, with the hammered gold accents and elaborate family crest that hung behind his desk, and headed toward his much more subdued personal chambers

3

so he could clean up and change. As they passed burbling fountains and lattices crowded with colorful flowers and vines, their matching steps echoed through the polished stone halls and the sound settled over him like a soothing balm, as familiar to him as his own breathing.

He glanced over his shoulder and gave her a small smile, silently conveying how thankful he was that she was back. Her deep brown eyes met his briefly before training ahead once more, the slight dip of her chin letting him know that they were back on neutral ground.

They often spoke in this hidden language of theirs, a shared physical vocabulary they had developed over eighteen years. Volumes could be conveyed in just a look, which was why she usually avoided him entirely when she was mad at him. If he could only see her, he could catch glimpses of the machinations plotting his demise behind her dark gaze. Luckily, he hadn't spied that telltale lip curl since yesterday morning.

He was calling it a win.

Reaching his chambers, he slipped into his bedroom as Hara waited for him in the parlor and went to take a quick bath before dressing. It was a shame to rush it really, considering it was likely the last chance for a relaxing soak he'd have for a long while, but the afternoon had gotten away from him in a blur of inventory counts and route adjustments.

They had initially been planning on turning southward once they reached the fork in the Aswa River at the bustling trade city Khemasaru, with the idea that they would start closer to the center of the western coast of South Endrian in their search for the temple. But, now that the Rutrulans, through Sennuhotep, had let them know that they would likely find it to the southwest of the coastal city Lythenea, it would be more expedient to take the northern fork and then enter the Terra Cotta Mountains via the Shiran Pass. This would force them to go through Renpet, a town situated at the mouth of the pass where the river became too shallow to sail farther.

It had necessitated major changes to the estimated timing as well as a need to quickly research new arrangements for lodging along the way. They would be taking Captain Aidu's ship to Khemasaru and then split into two smaller vessels for the thinner river that would take them to Renpet. There wouldn't be enough room on the secondary boats for sleeping so they would need to dock and secure quarters overnight at least once before reaching the pass.

There had been a flurry of activity to adjust accordingly, and the tension headache behind Rakhmet's forehead was only growing despite his attempts to convince his taut muscles to release as he dried off and strode into his bedroom to find a suitable tunic for the event. He grabbed one in an ivory silk with gold borders and threw it on, folding and tucking it into a belt of shimmering red until he was satisfied. The bright fabric contrasted against the deep brown skin on his right as well as the scarred skin that now covered the majority of his left side. After three months of special care from the royal physicians, the tender red burns had settled into warped splotches of muddy brown like a watercolor left in the rain, and it was all he could do not to wince every time he caught a glance of the ruined flesh.

Turning to his vanity, he grabbed a wide comb to pull through his wet black curls as he stared at the empty wooden back of the mirror attached to the table below. He had instructed the servants to turn it toward the wall after the accident at Furaro's temple, also making sure to take note of where other mirrors were set throughout his sprawling home so that he could avoid them like the plague. Seeing the twisted skin on his left arm as he used it throughout the day was enough of a reminder of his ineptitude. He didn't need to see the full breadth of damage that had been inflicted on his body reflected at him at every turn.

Everyone at court had been quick to return to their complimentary ass-kissing, and his mother never ceased in her constant praise and encouragement, but he knew the truth. His appearance finally revealed something he had always known he was: a disgrace. He could no longer hide his incompetence behind a dazzling smile and roguish charm. His defects were exposed for all to see.

Sighing, he tossed aside the comb and slipped on a pair of leather sandals before rejoining Hara, who was leaning against the door leading to his private courtyard with her arms crossed. She glanced at him and straightened as he approached and stopped short a few feet away.

It was a comfortable silence as he studied her studying him. They hadn't had much of a chance to talk after their ceasefire the day before, too busy with the subsequent discussions and meetings, and he had needed to take in everything that had changed since he had anxiously watched her retreating figure disappear into the desert to clear the fire temple with Nasima and Cas. She had returned with vicious scars streaking up her arm and it carved open something inside of him, making him feel simultaneously helpless and incensed beyond belief.

His fingers itched to touch the rippled skin, to trace the ridges and memorize them.

A knock sounded at the door, and Uma peeked her head around the edge with a smile. "Your Highness?"

"Yes?" Rakhmet hid his flinch, moving away from Hara.

She simply tapped a finger to her watch then continued on her way as Rakhmet cleared his throat, grabbing his dagger holster off a side table. He secured it around his waist and headed out into the hallway with Hara close behind. They reached the royal family's dining room in silence, the guards outside the double doors letting them in without so much as a glance.

He was early, as attendants rushed to finish the final touches on the table that had been extended with multiple leaves to accommodate the royal family, Hara, Nebehet, and the dozen guards that they had selected to go on the trip with them. Traditionally, they would host a ball to celebrate those who were to march off to battle, but the more dangerous aspects of their goals for visiting the plant temple had been strictly kept secret from everyone who didn't need to know the truth.

The court at large simply believed that the guards were coming along to safeguard him as he located the plant temple, so they knew nothing of the underlying reason to find it: defeating the monstrous beings they were likely to encounter there to clear Tabriara's sacred land of corruption. Thus, the king had decided to host a private

7

farewell dinner in lieu of a warrior's ball to maintain the ruse of a nonviolent expedition.

Rakhmet approached his mother, who stood at one end of the table giving instructions, and leaned in to kiss her on the cheek as she gave him a smile that only wavered for a moment and pulled him into a tight embrace.

"My dear boy," she murmured. She had taken his determination to seek out the temple badly, crumbling when they were alone under the weight of her grief. It made him feel immensely guilty, especially so soon after his sister, Esare, had been married off to Prince Kiran down in Gheseruti, an arranged pairing in the name of political alliances. Queen Ishya had set the date for when Esare turned twenty, a little under two years ago. Their mother, Oyah, had been clinging to Rakhmet ever since the wedding, and now he was leaving her on a potentially deadly mission.

He squeezed her back, taking a moment to enjoy the hug before other people started arriving and they would have to put on their unfazed masks of royal authority. With a shaking inhale, she finally leaned away and trailed his features with her worried gaze. She pressed down his sideburns and stroked the edge of his jaw, attempting to smooth away the slight tremor in her fingers.

Catching her hands in his, he brought them to his mouth and dropped a light kiss on her knuckles before tucking one into the crook of his elbow and turning toward the table. "The room looks beautiful, Mother, and you look gorgeous in your dress. You have outdone yourself as per usual."

Her crown glittered in the flickering light of the chandelier, highlighting the streaks of gray in her locks as she tipped her head back to smile at him and patted his arm, grateful for the shift in tone. "Always the charmer, Rakhmet."

He returned an easy grin, slipping into his role for the evening, just as the door opened to admit his father with his two personal guards, Karim and Tariq. The king spotted them immediately and a flash of cheer broke through the heavy brow underneath his own crown as he crossed the room.

"Rakhmet," he greeted and then leaned in to kiss his wife on the cheek. "My love."

"Father." Rakhmet nodded in response as his mother murmured her hellos.

"Are you all set then?" his father asked him, slapping a broad hand onto his shoulder and giving him an appraising glance.

"As much as I can be," Rakhmet replied, striving to keep his tone confident.

The king offered him one more searching look before giving a satisfied pat and gesturing for the three of them to take their places on one side of the door to greet the guests as they arrived. Hara had recommended twenty out of the fifty royal guards that made up the entirety of the palace's force and then had, with the king's and prince's input, narrowed the ranks to just twelve that would accompany Rakhmet, Hara, and Nebehet to the temple.

Nebehet had volunteered to join them immediately following the initial announcement that Rakhmet would take a group to Talegartia, but Rakhmet had made a point

9

of speaking to him privately in the subsequent days to impart the true risks they would be facing. His friend's face had paled when he had recounted the horrific stories he had heard about what had been found in both the water and the fire temples, and Rakhmet had even encouraged him to speak with Hara as well to hear it firsthand. But Nebehet had been undeterred, choosing to join them, knowing full well that he could possibly be heading toward his death.

It was a decision that had both comforted and stressed Rakhmet in equal measure. They had been close friends since childhood and were practically brothers by that point, with Nebehet the younger by a few years. It almost felt selfish to bring him along on such a dangerous endeavor, so Rakhmet just had to pray that they would have the advantage of numbers by bringing as many of the guards into the fight as possible.

Their dinner companions started filtering in and he shook himself from his circling thoughts, fixing a bright grin and offering his hand to the forming line. Well-wishes and words of encouragement fell from his lips, burning the tip of his tongue as he swallowed any hint of fear or doubt. He settled into the cadence of smile, greeting, clap on the shoulder, personal reassurance, then onto the next one until they had all found their seats, his hand tingling by the time he sank into his own chair to the left of his mother.

Hara had been seated across from him next to Nebehet, who was on his father's right, and she briefly met his eyes with a slight raise of her brow, asking him if he was okay. He tipped his wine glass toward her, a signal that all was fine. Without responding, she slid her attention back to Layla, one of her closer friends in the guard force, and Rakhmet took the cue to engage Amasha next to him in a conversation about their shared love of daggers.

He was too tense to do anything but rely on his carefully bred manners to carry him through the dinner, and the evening wore on as his parents shone in their element and the guards enjoyed their fill of a luxurious feast before leaving behind the comforts of city life. It would be about one day to Khemasaru, another two to Renpet, and then they would embark on the arduous trek through the mountains to the rainforests of Talegartia. They estimated that it would take around twenty days to hike the whole way to Lythenea, but they were hoping to find a river route once they got closer to the coast. The steep and unpredictable elevations of the jungle landscape would make the journey difficult, though.

All in all, he expected to be roughing it with these guards for the next two months and he was sure that he wasn't the only one considering hugging his pillows tonight in a tearful goodbye. Not that he would admit that to anyone.

Eventually, his father stood to give a rousing speech at the end of the meal. He said something about king and country, fighting for love, the usual themes his father gravitated toward. But Rakhmet hardly listened anymore, having grown up with the same pronouncements year after year. He could practically recite them in his sleep, which would serve him well once he took the throne.

If he lived long enough, that was.

The thought brought his attention back to Hara, who was obediently listening to his father's words and raising her glass at the expected moment. He caught himself and jerked his hand up to drain his wine like everyone else, the usual response to a royal cheers or speech. She caught his eye as she set down her empty glass, her dark gaze flickering in question at his delayed reaction, and he tensed his jaw, letting her know he didn't want to talk about it.

The king clapped his hands together and officially ended the dinner, inviting those present to retire early and enjoy their time with their loved ones before their departure at dawn. It was about an hour after sunset, and Rakhmet sighed longingly, already anticipating the quiet of his chambers where he might be able to finally get rid of his headache. But first, he followed his parents to the door where they gave gracious farewells to each and every guard until the only ones left were Hara and Nebehet.

His friend draped an arm around his shoulder and grinned. "Well, Your Highness, care to have a drink with me before we ship off into the sunset? Er, I guess, sunrise?"

Rakhmet let a genuine smile crack through his weariness and wrapped his arm around Nebehet to drop a hand on his other shoulder. "I think I can pencil you in."

His father and mother shook their heads at the exchange, saying their own goodbyes before turning and disappearing down the hallway toward their private chambers, and Rakhmet released Nebehet as the three of them headed to his own.

"I'm sorry I couldn't meet you earlier. I was stuck in last-minute business deals with some of the viceroy's partners in town," Nebehet apologized as they walked. "I didn't see your note until I came home to dress for the dinner."

"Don't worry about it." Rakhmet waved him off. "Just thought you'd want to know about the change in plans."

"Yeah, that's great news. We have somewhere specific to start the search now."

"Yeah." Rakhmet puffed out a tired laugh. "Now we don't have to waste weeks wandering around the rainforests like dumbasses."

"Hey, I'll take the win." Nebehet grinned over his shoulder, reaching to open the door to Rakhmet's chambers.

There was a screech and a blur as something bowled into Rakhmet just as he stepped over the threshold, knocking him against the doorframe with a thump. He instinctively reached out to grab onto Inenekah's arms as they wrapped around him, saturating him with the overpowering scent of rose water and orange blossom oil.

"Rakhie! My love! Oh, how I will miss you! Whatever am I going to do?!" She reached up and planted her hands on either side of his face, peppering his forehead and cheeks with kisses as he attempted to disentangle himself with a laugh.

"Ine. **Ine.**" He grabbed her hands and pried them off as he glanced over her shoulder to see Khenti grinning at him lazily from one of his couches with a spread of wine, desserts, and a hookah before him. "Good gods, you relentless fiends."

"I told Khenti we just **had** to send you off in style, my lovie!" Ine's smile was thirty percent cunning, fifteen

13

percent genuine, and fifty-five percent sticky, saccharine sweetness.

Rakhmet rolled his eyes and gently pushed her away as he approached the other couch and fell against the glittering pillows with an only marginally annoyed huff. He should have expected his friends to seek him out before their departure, plying him with their favorite vices: alcohol, sugar, tobacco, and incessant flirting.

Nebehet dropped down next to him, leaning forward to pour them both some wine with an amused smile as Rakhmet glanced over at Hara, who was lingering by the courtyard door and pointedly ignoring them.

"Want to join us, Hara? A bit of celebration before we ship off?" he asked, hoping for an answer he was pretty sure he wasn't going to get. Even if they were on speaking terms again, he had a feeling it would be a while before things returned to normal between them.

Her dark eyes met his, half an expectant second passing as he held his breath, but she nudged her chin to the side. "No, thanks. I need to be sharp in the morning."

"Ever the paragon of propriety and judgment." Khenti scoffed, rolling his eyes as he turned his attention to Rakhmet and Nebehet. "You two are looking a bit worse for wear. Have you not been sleeping well? Maybe the time away will be beneficial for your . . . stamina?"

Rakhmet smirked at Khenti's usual delivery, an artful balance of insult and innuendo, as Ine squeezed her way in between him and Nebehet. "Trust me, being tired from suffering through a dozen meetings today has nothing to do with my stamina."

"I hear that my Rakhie here has absolutely no issues in that regard, isn't that right?" Ine countered and fluttered her eyelashes, leaning into Rakhmet so that her full breasts pressed against his side as she passed him the hose to the hookah.

She was always the first to jump on a new trend and had heard about this new type of water pipe in the Tirdan Republic, a country on the other side of the Cortan Sea that had a much larger smoking culture, about a year ago. They were the only ones in the Pyrantus palace who used one, but Rakhmet did enjoy the occasional indulgence even if it left his throat raw the next day.

"Now, where did you hear that from?" he asked with a raised eyebrow, accepting the hose and taking a pull before passing it to Khenti. He had made a point of never involving himself with anyone connected to the court after a very awkward conversation he had been forced to have with his father as a teenager when he had been caught fooling around with the Ghesruti ambassador's daughter.

Ever since then, he had sought out company in the city proper. It was how he had perfected the art of sneaking outside the palace walls, thanks to all the late-night visits to a wide range of cafés and halls. He had become close friends with merchants, intellectuals, and artisans over the years, who, in turn, invited him to gatherings where he could discreetly meet courtesans and other unattached individuals around town. Engaging with women, men, and everyone in between, he kept his affairs casual and completely separate from his more princely duties, yet he was still the target of a constant barrage of offers and advances from court families.

"Oh, you know, **around**." Ine batted him playfully. "Just because I don't want the stress of being queen doesn't mean I don't call first dibs whenever you get over this ridiculous vow of yours to never fuck anyone from court."

She snaked her hand across his thigh and shifted so that her chest, straining against the top of the strapless red dress she wore, spilled over his forearm as Rakhmet caught her hand and gently guided it away.

"**Ine**," Khenti snapped as he handed the hookah hose to Nebehet. "Leave the poor man alone and come cuddle with me. Let him prepare to go die in the jungle in peace."

He lifted his arm and she huffed, yanking her hand free and standing to move to the other couch. Pouting, she tucked herself into Khenti's side and nuzzled into his neck as he pulled her in and took a sip of wine with a smirk. She slipped her hand inside his tunic, absentmindedly caressing his abs as he let her.

"What about you, Nebbie?" Ine asked, smiling again now that she was getting attention from someone. "How's your stamina doing these days?" She wiggled her brows for emphasis.

Khenti scoffed before Nebehet could answer. "For gods' sake, Ine, we all know that little **Nebbie** here is too hopelessly noble to jump in the sack with just anybody. He has to have that certain spark, no?" He pinned Nebehet with a knowing look.

"Fuck off." Nebehet scowled at him, a blush crawling across his cheeks.

"Whatever," Rakhmet interjected as he accepted the hose from Nebehet, tired of the topic. "Our sex lives are going to be the least of our worries in the coming months."

"I would imagine not, what with the lucky prince having his two favorites well within arm's reach." Khenti's grin was a hundred percent shit-eating as Rakhmet furrowed his brows.

"What the fuck are you even talking about?" He huffed. His eyes darted to Hara across the room and then to Nebehet next to him, who was gulping down a mouthful of wine to hide his grimace.

"**Any**way," Ine interrupted in a singsong as she straightened in her seat. "Who wants to play Mehen?"

"I'm in," Nebehet agreed quickly, eager for the change in conversation.

Khenti smiled as if he had won whatever contest he had been setting up as Rakhmet nodded, breaking the strange tension that had been building.

They soon lost themselves in an hours-long board game that was popular in court, with Ine creating new rules that involved drinking at various intervals, but once again, Rakhmet kept finding his gaze straying to the figure that sat apart from them in a chair facing the windows. She was idly fiddling with her new dagger as she stared out into the night, the divine weapon that had been gifted to her by the Fire God in gratitude for her service in clearing his temple of corruption.

It was certainly an object of power. Both he and his father had immediately picked up on the energy vibrations that emanated from it, and Rakhmet had been spending quite a bit of the last couple weeks in the royal library, looking for any mention of daggers in their bloodline histories. All of the scrolls and tomes that held information about the elemental crowns had been sealed long ago in a chamber deep underneath the temple in Kemet dedicated to Furaro. Sennuhotep, the allegiant cleric there, had been elated when Rakhmet had reached out to him and asked him to assist them in unearthing the ancient records. He had since proved himself to also be an invaluable midway point for the messenger pigeons that flew to and from Tusi Island.

But Rakhmet still hadn't had the chance to ask how Hara was feeling about it all. She hadn't just come back with scars. Literally overnight, she had become an extremely visible target due to the two divine weapons that now hung at her waist and it tugged at him, urging him to keep her near.

He blinked, trying to remember where they were in the game, and glanced back at Ine and Khenti to find them casually making out on their couch. Rolling his eyes, he looked at Nebehet to share a laugh at their expense to find him fiddling with the hose where it connected to the base of the hookah. He was squinting with his tongue peeking out the side of his mouth in concentration, just inebriated enough to be making it worse rather than better as water started dripping onto the table.

Rakhmet chuckled, shaking his head and clapping his hands together once. "Alright, you fiends, party's over."

He stood, waving his hands in their direction in a shooing motion, and Ine blew out a huff of annoyance as she climbed out of Khenti's arms.

"But Rakhie . . . ," she whined as she followed him to the door before throwing herself on him again. He braced an arm to catch them on the doorframe, wobbling off balance, as the other circled her waist to prevent her from falling farther.

She pressed up against him, her curves adhering to his torso and hips as she wrapped her arms around his neck and started nibbling her way up his throat. "I'm going to miss you."

He sighed as he broke her embrace and stepped back, holding her at arm's length. "Ine, I'll miss you too."

She sniffed. "Don't die in a jungle, okay?"

"I promise." He smiled softly at her hidden soft side. She didn't show it often, but when she did, he was reminded of her inherent goodness that was always there, lurking underneath the carefree facade she showed the world.

"Yes, please do take care of yourselves out in the wilds. I'd hate to be forced to summon some tears at your ostentatiously royal funeral," Khenti drawled as he reached them, tucking Ine under his arm once again as he drew her toward the door.

He wasn't the hugging type unless he was interested in getting in your pants, and Rakhmet had thwarted his flirtatious overtures enough over the years that he no longer attempted to lure him into his bed like he did with everyone else who caught his fancy. A surprisingly large number of palace visitors, staff, and members of the court had fallen for his charms over the years, in addition to the trail of lovers he left in his wake whenever he ventured into the city.

Rakhmet had once enjoyed the chase. There were too many nights to count where he and Khenti had wasted away their future inheritances on companions, drink, and other more illicit substances. They'd lived the life of unbridled privilege, with the ability to toss coin at every new, shiny, thrilling, and salacious experience without even making a dent in their coffers. He had gradually stopped accepting invitations to those types of gatherings ever since his blessing had begun waning about three years ago, but he still enjoyed Khenti's company when he wasn't busy being an entitled brat.

Smiling, Rakhmet clapped him on the shoulder and nudged his chin in Ine's direction. "Take care of her for us, alright?"

"Of course. You know I'll take care of our girl." Khenti squeezed her closer with a sly grin, and Rakhmet chuckled as they sauntered away. The two of them had started their affair when they were teens, falling in and out of favor as they grew older and each indulged in their uninhibited thirst for entertainment and pleasure. He was pretty sure they'd end up married someday, though, considering they were the only ones who were suitable for each other and could tolerate each other's company for more than an evening. Even if neither of them would admit it just yet.

"Well, see you first thing in the morning?" Nebehet asked, coming up at his side and slinging an arm over his shoulders.

"Yep." Rakhmet pulled him into a hug, patting him on the shoulder before letting him go. "Onward and outward?"

"May the gods guide us all." Nebehet nodded, staring at Rakhmet for a long moment with his usual fondness. He then pressed his lips together and dipped his head, disappearing into the hallway.

Rakhmet let out a long exhale and closed the door before walking back over to the table to put out the coal feeding the hookah with his blessing, immensely grateful that it had been restored, and then grabbed the pipe's base to dump it out in his sink so that it didn't get the chance to leak all over while he slept. It took him a minute to return to the sitting room, finding that Hara had moved toward the door. She stood there, watching him as he placed the base back on the table and met her eye.

His feet carried him to her, and his gaze dropped to her scarred arm. She stilled as he reached for her elbow without thinking, brushing his thumb across a swell of ridged skin. It was quiet, only their soft breaths filling the night air as he studied the wound and imagined, not for the first time, the terror and pain she must have felt as she had fought for her life in the fire temple. His heart twisted as he tried to read her expression.

"What changed your mind?" He asked the question that had been bothering him since they had made peace the day before, and there was a long pause as she considered her response.

"I just . . ." She shrugged a shoulder with a look that told him there were too many answers burning in her throat to pick just one.

He hummed, understanding the feeling. The sense that there were unspoken depths between them had been becoming more and more obvious in the last week. While she was no longer giving him the silent treatment, her stoicism was certainly more apparent than it had been before their fight. She still hadn't forgiven him completely, and there were things she wasn't telling him. He couldn't pretend that he wasn't hiding anything from her either, though. He just had to trust that they were both doing it for the right reasons.

"I'll be doing last-minute counts at the ship in the morning, but I'll send Rami to escort you to the dock," she added, using her guard persona to hide the questions that smoldered in her eyes.

Nodding, he released her elbow and stepped back to respect the space she was evidently asking for. He wasn't going to push her so soon after getting her back.

"Rest well," he murmured.

"Rest well, Your Highness." She nodded formally and then turned to open the door, looking over her shoulder at him once before leaving him with his searing doubts and fears.

DAY TWO

The winter sky was a bright blue, the sun shining down on the excited faces of the crew and guards as the *Abydir Sedjet* cruised westward along the Aswa River. While the sailors were under the impression that this was a standard royal excursion to a neighboring country, each guard that had been handpicked to accompany them had been secretly briefed and trained in what to expect and how to best fight the horrors they would encounter at Tabriara's temple.

Throughout the day, Rakhmet made a point of seeking each out individually to express his gratitude for their loyalty and discretion, but he saved Nebehet and Hara for last. He was having trouble finding the words that would adequately convey what their support truly meant to him. The often repeated words of encouragement and bravery that he bolstered the guards with were easy enough. The role of charismatic leader was something that had been purposefully ingrained in him from an early age.

Genuinely vulnerable words of appreciation for his two closest childhood friends? That was proving to be a much more difficult task.

It wasn't until after dinner had concluded that he was finally able to approach Nebehet as everyone gathered for celebratory drinks on deck. Finding his friend staring out over the water at the bow of the ship, he handed him one of the two tankards he had filled from the barrel being passed around.

Nebehet accepted the ale with a smile, pulling Rakhmet in for a side hug before releasing him and propping his elbows on the railing. "I was wondering when you'd get around to me."

Rakhmet huffed out a laugh. "Am I that obvious?"

"You're a good leader, Rakh." Nebehet gazed at him thoughtfully and nudged his chin in the direction of the guards scattered across the ship. "You care about them and they know it."

"Thanks," he murmured as Nebehet nodded and turned back to the river.

There was a long but comfortable silence as Rakhmet considered his next words. Nebehet held a special place in his heart, a brother that he never had, and he could remember when they were much younger, chasing each other through the palace on one imagined adventure or another. They had often been the thorn in Uma's side, disrupting her carefully laid plans by charming the laundresses into lending them billowing sheets that he and his friend had used to transform one of their bedrooms into a fort that they had bravely defended against enemy armies. The resulting carnage had been of ripped fabrics, broken chairs, and shattered pitchers. If only the fight they were now heading toward would be that bloodless.

"I just wanted to . . . thank you, for everything," he finally admitted. "It means a lot to me that you wanted to come with us, even after you learned the truth of the dangers we face."

"Of course." Nebehet met his eye again. He seemed to want to add something but shook his head, deciding otherwise. "Speaking of, I've got something for you."

Rakhmet's brows rose in surprise. "For me?"

"Yeah, I'll go grab it." Nebehet nodded with a smile then pivoted, walking to the ship's stairs and heading below.

He reappeared a few minutes later with an oblong bundle of fabric in his hand and offered it to Rakhmet, grinning as if he were the one receiving a gift.

Rakhmet glanced at him curiously before handing him his tankard so that he could unwrap the object, finding an intricately engraved leather dagger sheath with a shining pommel sticking out the top of it. He drew in an appreciative breath as he slid the blade out of its case, unveiling the stunning weapon that had been shaped to look like a pillar of flickering flame.

There were striations in the polished metal that replicated the texture of fire, and the sharpened edges curved in and out organically, stretching about ten inches from the hilt before ending in a slightly forked point. The grip itself was decorated with embedded fire opals and mother of pearl in shapes that also referenced the power of his blessing.

It was the most beautiful weapon he had ever been gifted, and he was momentarily speechless as he thumbed the sharp curves. He looked back at Nebehet, gaping at his friend, whose bright eyes were drinking in his reaction with delight.

"Neb, this is—it's gorgeous. Thank you," he stuttered.

"I'm glad you like it. I figured you needed something a little more wicked to face the monsters." Nebehet chuckled.

Rakhmet returned his smile, blown away by his generosity. An idea struck him.

"Want to try it out?" He jerked his chin in the direction of where the crew and guards were gathering around Amon, who had started plucking out some shanties on his lute. "I'm sure they'd all want to watch the crown prince and his loyal companion in action."

He had been trained in a wide range of skills as the heir to the throne: history, politics, linguistics, the arts, biology, economics, industry, the medical sciences, as well as martial combat. But his private instruction was wholly separate from the exercises that the Nesu Medjay, the title for the head of the guards, Rahim Jabbar, set for the palace's forces, so most of his practice had either been with Hara, Rahim, or Rahim's right-hand woman, Nesu Sesemet Amina Nasri.

Plus, with his father's mostly peaceful reign, he hadn't had much of an opportunity to show off his combat abilities, particularly now that his divinely blessed status was public knowledge. After the news had broken, he had made a point of practicing his unusual blend of fighting styles with both Rami and Nebehet in preparation for the trip, but he figured it would be worthwhile to familiarize the rest of the guards with them as well.

"Sure." Nebehet grinned as they turned and approached the group.

"Friends!" he called. "Who here wants to see what a true Pyrantus prince can do?"

A round of cheers went up as tankards were raised, and the mixture of gathered crew and guards moved to make space for them in the middle of the deck while Rakhmet's gaze found Hara's in the crowd, her lips hooked in a smirk as she took a sip of ale. They both knew that she could beat his ass in hand-to-hand combat, but she had been the first, and only besides his immediate family, to see the true extent of his powers after she had become his oathed guard at age sixteen. After training for the position for several years, she had formally pledged herself to his Crown, which in turn meant that she had also guarded the knowledge of his blessing with her life.

But that didn't stop her from wiping the floor with his face from time to time.

He rolled his eyes at her knowing look and turned away, positioning himself opposite Nebehet, who had retrieved his own shortsword and dagger. Unsheathing the dagger he usually kept at his side, he held one in each hand and crossed them as he mirrored Nebehet's bow. He then set his feet shoulder width apart and bent his knees, leaning his weight forward as he waited for Amon to signal.

Those gathering around quieted as a tense pause echoed around the ship, and Nebehet tightened his grips, locking eyes with Rakhmet in a friendly challenge.

Amon hit a crescendo of notes, shouting, "Begin!" as they both lurched forward.

Nebehet met Rakhmet's first swipes, the sounds of scraping metal drowned out by the yells of encouragement around them, and he parried as they started circling each other. Blocking and slashing, they swerved and ducked as if they were improvising a choreographed dance. They weren't ruthless enough to draw blood but were breaking a sweat as the fight wore on, their blades flashing in the torchlight.

They were pretty equally matched, but Rakhmet eventually knocked Nebehet to the ground, sweeping his feet out from underneath him with a well-aimed swipe of his leg. He loomed over him, forcing him to yield as the crowd burst into a swell of cheers. They chanted his name to the stars above as he smiled and offered a hand to Nebehet, pulling him up to clap him on the shoulder while they caught their breath.

His grin stretched across his face, and he searched for Hara again as her glittering, dark eyes met his. She unfolded her arms from where she had been leaning against the railing and clapped her hands mockingly, as if she were humoring him and his victory, her brow cocked to let him know that she wasn't exactly impressed.

He huffed and jutted his chin in her direction as a challenge, daring her.

She rolled her eyes in response, scoffing as her smirk widened.

He looked her up and down, planting his feet and gesturing with the tip of his dagger for her to take her place opposite him.

She heaved a sigh, as if he were grossly inconveniencing her, before ambling over to the center of the deck where he waited. Locking him with her gaze, she dipped her chin as she drew the gleaming, otherworldly zulfiqar and dagger from her holster, and the crowd around them grew even louder as they realized that they were about to see the real showdown.

The grin on his face turned sly, his heart picking up in his chest as anticipation flickered through his veins. This would be the first time he revealed his own blessing to the public, a secret that had been forced to the light when Nasima had returned from the fire temple crowned as the new Water Queen by Furaro himself only fifteen days ago.

There had been no way to officially acknowledge her sovereignty without admitting the validity of the gods' interference in mortal political structures. Which meant that his father had had to own up to his and Rakhmet's statuses as blessed ones, those select few that wield the inherited elemental gifts of the gods. Luckily, Nasima, Cas, and Hara had freed the fire temple of corruption and defeated the entity that had cut off his and his father's access to their blessings so the king could adequately demonstrate his powers in front of the court when they had asked.

If their secret had been exposed while they had been dampened, they would've been screwed. Accused as liars and madmen.

He and his father had thought they were being punished for lack of faith when their blessings had started dwindling a few years ago, after keeping their powers as hidden as possible for their entire lives. They had been afraid that the gods had finally turned their backs on them, fading away bit by bit until there had been a vacuous chasm where his divine connection had used to live. Losing grip on something so fundamental to his being had caused him to retreat, spending more and more time in his rooms, desperately praying for forgiveness.

But tonight, he felt the tingles of flame licking through his limbs once again and was perhaps a bit too eager to show the world at large what he was capable of.

Crossing his blades again, he bowed as Hara mirrored him then shifted to the balls of his feet as Amon played to the visceral expectancy that clutched the crowd, an excitable hum that fell into the background as Rakhmet trained his gaze on Hara. Time slowed as he watched her chest rise with a deep inhale, and Amon's lute rose to another crescendo, calling for them to begin.

The only warning she gave him was a twitch to the side as her zulfiqar, the double-edged sword with a curved, forked tip, erupted in flame, and she lunged forward, swinging the blade up in a move that forced him to dart away. He responded in kind, slashing in succession to push her back as he drew his blessing to his fingertips and latched onto the fire surrounding her blade.

He yanked on it, pulling the entire flame off her zulfiqar and leaving it bare as the blaze rose above her head in the night air. The guards and sailors gasped, their astonishment palpable.

Scowling, Hara whipped her arm out with a snap that relit the blade, and Rakhmet chuckled, seeing that he had caught her unaware with the move. They hadn't had a chance to spar since she had been gifted the weapons from Furaro and he was relishing in the fact that her zulfiqar's flames were as pliable to him as any other. Before she could attack again, he threw the ball of fire at her feet to drive her back a few steps in a flash of light as it impacted against the deck, leaving a scorch mark in its wake.

She rolled out of the way, spinning in a fluid movement to swipe both blades at his side and pressing him toward the stern as the crowd around them shifted to make room. They shuffled and slashed across the ship, Rakhmet ducking once then twice before reaching out to entice the flame off her blade again.

This time, he coaxed it to grow, circling her in a swirling wall of burning heat, but he wasn't fast enough to trap her as she swiveled away at the last second. She leapt over a barrel, using the momentum to meet his blades with a sharp clash and urge him farther back.

The blaze dissipated in a puff as Rakhmet twisted to swing his elbow into her temple, both hating and loving the satisfying thud as she jerked away with a grunt. They had spent plenty of time dueling each other over the years, practicing their moves, and every time he was equal parts pained and proud (even if he lost more times than won).

She gritted her teeth with a snarl and knocked one dagger out of his hand with a wide swipe, then she spun and drove her knee into his side, knocking the air right out of him.

31

Folding over, he tried to suck in a breath as he lurched forward and shouldered her in the stomach. His weight forced her to the ground as their blades clattered away and they wrestled, both vying for control.

They punched and kicked until Hara managed to gain the advantage by wrenching his arm behind his back and pressing his chest to the wooden deck, effectively immobilizing him. He pushed with his free arm, rising in a one-armed push-up as she straddled his back, but her foot hooked around his elbow and knocked him back down.

He grunted heavily at the collision, his cheek smashed and the taste of blood on his tongue as he panted, and the crowd went wild. It was a clear defeat on his end, and in front of so many people, it was a risk, but he trusted that his guards and sailors wouldn't see it as a personal failing of his. Over the years, he had come to realize that they were hard-working, salt of the earth kind of folk who preferred to know that there was something more beyond the untouchable royal facades. Too much arrogance and pretension made them skeptical.

The eyes at court were the ones he was more worried about at the end of the day. They were the ones that could take even the slightest hint of weakness and turn it into a damning indictment. They may pay lip service to him face-to-face, offering compliments like it was their job, but he knew that behind closed doors, the rumor mills and snide comments could seriously interfere with his ability to rule effectively.

Darius, the ship's beloved cook, pushed forward and dropped to his knees beside them. He pounded three times as he counted it out, declaring Hara as the victor and grabbing her hand to pull her up. He held it above their heads, starting a chant in her name as she grinned and swiped the sweat away from her forehead with her other.

She glanced down at Rakhmet, who was holding his side and trying to catch his breath as he got to his knees with an obliging smirk, and her eyes glinted with triumph. They betrayed a flash of anger at him that had seemingly been appeased with the beatdown, and his grin widened at the sight. He would gladly serve as her punching bag if it meant he could be there to read the silent messages that were hidden by the mask of royal guard she usually wore. He called it a win whenever he could catch a glimpse of her true thoughts behind the facade.

Her attention shifted, and she noticed his reaction as her gaze softened with the briefest touch of sympathy as she reached out a hand to help him up. A tankard was shoved into his grip the moment he found his feet, and the crowd surged forward to clap them on the shoulders, a cacophony of shouted admiration and consolation. He laughed, wiping the trickle of blood off the side of his mouth as he was embraced by his people.

They eventually let him go, returning to their drinks and side conversations as he dropped down on a stack of crates to rest his bruised body, and Nebehet slumped next to him, clinking his tankard against Rakhmet's.

"Good show," he said with a delighted smile.

"Thanks." Rakhmet laughed as Hara and Layla moved to join them.

"The win was inevitable, but I do admit your little trick threw me for a moment there." Hara knocked Rakhmet's arm with her elbow.

"Serves you right for trying to play with my element." Rakhmet huffed. "You may be the owner of the blade, but its fire will always belong to me."

"Humble as always." Hara rolled her eyes and looked away, taking a sip of her ale.

"I don't know. I think it's pretty awesome." Nebehet shrugged at Hara. "You've both kept it under wraps for years and years, but I only learned about all this stuff a couple weeks ago."

He turned back to Rakhmet. "What's it feel like? To control flames?"

Rakhmet snorted in surprise. He didn't think he'd ever been asked that before. His family, and even Hara, had never liked talking about the fire blessing much, always afraid of unseen eavesdroppers. It had been a secret to keep at all costs.

As heir to the throne, his every move had been carefully watched and analyzed by those around him since before he could remember. Any side comment or remark could be misquoted and any handshake or hug could be misconstrued, so he had been thoroughly trained on how to act appropriately in all that he did. Especially once his blessing had started developing.

He had become a chameleon, always shifting from one mask to the next depending on who he was around. Among his guards, he donned one persona. Among the court, he wore another. Out in the city? Someone else entirely. Employing every manner of smoke and mirror to hide the fire that burned inside, he had felt hidden and unseen until he had met Hara. Besides his sister, she was the only peer of his who had been allowed to peek behind the curtain.

It had been a revelation the day he had first been given permission to spar with Hara using the full breadth of his abilities. He had successfully completed his initiation ritual on his sixteenth birthday, but it hadn't been until a year later, when she had officially become his oathed guard, that he had been allowed to show her his blessing. Back then, he had still been learning how to wield the flames, and more times than not, they had both ended up with soot marks on their limbs and errant scorch lines on the ground. Nowadays, it felt like a second skin, and it took a few moments to come up with how to best explain it.

"Well, I—" he started. "I don't know how to describe it, but I feel like there's this constant flickering heat that sort of . . . rolls . . . under my skin. Usually, it's pretty mild. Barely there. But when I want to use my blessing, I focus on pulling it to my fingertips and it grows stronger. I start to feel the burn of it. Then I sort of imagine what I want to happen and release it."

"Wow," Nebehet breathed, his eyes widening a bit.

"I can't produce flame spontaneously. I need an external source to draw it from." Rakhmet set his tankard down and held out his hands. "But that's why I have these rings."

He pointed to the one on his right middle finger. "This is embedded with flint." Then he pointed to the one on his left. "This with steel. I can use the spark to create the flame."

35

When he swiped his hands together to demonstrate, the rings struck one another and a small ball of flame formed in the space between them. He then drew his hands wider to grow it to the size of a head before snuffing it out with a flick of the wrist.

"Or I can take it." He reached out toward one of the torches lighting the deck and plucked the fire off, letting it flicker in midair before replacing it to a smattering of applause from the surrounding crowd. He gave them an embarrassed salute, feeling a bit exposed. It was something he would have to get used to.

Layla whistled low next to Hara. "Well, damn it if I'm not impressed. Can't say I've ever seen anything like that before."

"Right?" Nebehet answered her excitedly. "He's wielding a divine power that hasn't been witnessed in centuries. It's incredible! This is history in the making here."

He laid a hand on Rakhmet's shoulder. "**You** are history in the making."

Rakhmet huffed, rubbing the back of his neck. "Oh, I don't know about that."

"Come on, the secret fire heir adventuring to find the long-lost plant temple? There will be ballads written about this. Am I right, Amon?" Nebehet called out to the bard, who cheered in agreement and toasted his tankard to them.

Rakhmet cleared his throat, flustered by the adoration in his friend's gaze, and took a sip of his drink. His attention landed on Hara leaning against the stack next to him, but she was saying something to Layla, who threw her head back and laughed in response. The last time Hara had offered him a smile was when she had been recounting her experiences in Furaro's palace shortly after returning with Nasima and Cas, and the noticeable lack of warmth between them since then had left a persistent knot in his chest.

"Yeah, it's—" Rakhmet answered quietly. "It's been nice to have it back."

He took another gulp of ale then turned and clinked his tankard against Nebehet's to subtly signal an end to the topic. He was beyond tired, the kind of weariness that weighed down the very center of his being, although he was reluctant to show it. The world outside of their merry ship was confusing and hostile, and the full impact of what they were undertaking was still something he carefully avoided thinking about for too long.

Yes, he had his powers back, but he had still lost much. Hara's scarred arm moved into his periphery as she took a sip from her own tankard, and it was too much of a reminder that there was a lot at stake here.

If Nebehet held a special place in his heart, Hara took up an entire wing of it. He had certainly known Nebehet for longer, but the bond that had developed between him and his guard was something that seemed to surpass even the connection his father had with Karim and Tariq. Only the king was allowed two oathed guards, whereas the queen, prince, and princess each had one, but Rakhmet would be required to choose another once he took the throne. He rarely let himself dwell on that, though, because whenever he tried, it just didn't feel right.

His parents had been increasingly adamant that he select an additional guard to join his training sessions in order to start getting used to them, similar to how he had been tutored alongside Hara for years before the official oathing ceremony had taken place. They were actually quite relieved when Rami had been chosen to stand in as Hara's replacement in recent weeks, and Rakhmet almost felt guilty, knowing that it would be a great honor for Rami, but he couldn't bring himself to confirm the choice.

Even though he and Hara had been on the outs quite often in the last four or so years, she knew him in a way no one else did. She had seen every side of him, both the good and the bad, and could almost always predict what he was going to say and do, penetrating beyond the facades he showed everyone else. He even remembered times when she could anticipate his need to escape a situation before he had been able to form the thought himself.

There was once when he had been out drinking and carousing with Khenti into the early morning hours and somehow had ended up in the back parlor of a greasy-haired man who was running an illegal gambling operation under the noses of the city's authorities. In order to assure the prince and his friend's silence, he had been more than willing to ply them with drinks, companions, and anything else he could get his hands on, and they had readily accepted his offer.

They had spent the next few hours sometimes winning, sometimes losing at several rounds of cards alongside some of the owner's buddies and a couple of merchants who had seen better days. They had joked and heckled, the atmosphere balancing on the edge as amenities had been passed around like fruit platters and everyone had taken their fill. As the night had worn on, Rakhmet had gotten the impression that they were probably being shaken for all they had on them, but he had been enjoying himself, his worries long gone, and Khenti had been too preoccupied to give a shit, his hand firmly wrapped around the breast of the giggling woman who sat in his lap and picked his cards for him.

It wasn't until one of the merchants had lost his third consecutive round that things had started to turn sour. His frustration had become a palpable thing, causing the hair on the back of Rakhmet's neck to stand as the man's eyes bulged. The sheer desperation rolling off him had momentarily overwhelmed Rakhmet, sparking the embers of his own ache that he spent every waking moment trying to ignore. Rakhmet had understood the ravenous hunger in the man's bloodshot glare all too well, painfully aware that a similar yearning for more burned in the back of his throat day and night.

Slamming a calloused palm onto the table, the merchant had demanded another round to win back what he had lost, but Rakhmet had suddenly lost his appetite for the evening's activities. He had been too inebriated to react, though, his hands fumbling as new cards were dealt to him. Furrowing his brows, he had blinked at them in confusion and let them drop to the table.

His bleary gaze had sought out Hara in the corner, where she had been keeping a dutiful eye on everything, as he had tried to push his chair back and stand, but he had pitched to the side, unable to right himself. She had already been striding across the floor and reaching for his arm before he could even get a word out, pulling him up and steadying him as the angry merchant took offense, thinking that Rakhmet was depriving him of his chance to win the round.

The man's complaints had barely reached him, though, as Hara had waited for him to catch his breath. She had looked him dead in the eye, no judgment, no shame, no reprisal in her expression. She had simply offered a lifeline right when he had needed it and made sure that he had been clear-headed enough to stand on his own before she had grabbed Khenti by the collar and hauled him to his feet too.

The girl in his lap had protested, gripping onto Khenti's arm as they had both been tugged across the room to the door, but Hara had just rolled her eyes and thrown a coin purse at her. She had then pushed Khenti outside with one hand, maneuvering Rakhmet with the other as she had led them through the slums and back to the palace. By the time they had made it to his rooms, his heartbeat had calmed and he had slumped onto one of his couches as Hara had pushed Khenti onto the other.

Rakhmet had hung his head in his hands, the room spinning until Hara had pressed a damp cloth to his face. He had sat back in surprise, apologies starting to form on his lips like ash, but she had just shaken her head and told him it was okay. She hadn't even had to ask him what had happened or why he had felt the need to lose himself in the first place. She had understood the pressure he had been under without him having to say it.

That was why it had been so jarring when she had refused to see his need to prove himself at the plant temple, when she had yelled at him for being impulsive and rash. It would be okay as long as they were in it together, right? That was what he had always believed. But he knew that he was toeing the line. The razor-thin boundary that separated success and failure, victory and utter devastation. He just had to pray that he had learned enough lessons to pass the test.

DAY THREE

They reached Khemasaru a couple hours after sunrise the next day, disembarking from the *Abydir Sedjet* and saying goodbye to Aidu's crew before boarding the two smaller vessels that would take them to Renpet. Rakhmet was placed on the first with Nebehet and half of the guards, while the others went with Hara on the second. Still reluctant to be separated from her, he spent the day distracting himself from the clench in his chest by sparring with each guard to test their readiness for the temple.

He wanted to make sure that they were as prepared as possible, having absolutely no desire to see any of them return to Zahar scarred and maimed. He, and now Hara, had had enough of that to go around, and the abject fear he felt for all of them charred his insides every time he let his mind drift to the countless what-if scenarios that plagued him.

The initial accident at Furaro's temple, the only time his beloved element had been his enemy, had felt like it was inevitable karmic payback for all the years he had spent fucking around and not taking his duties seriously, so he had tried to accept it with as much dignity as he could summon. He knew that, on some level, he had deserved it, but he'd be damned if he let anyone else suffer from a similar fate.

It pained him enough to know that Hara had been unjustly injured in the second journey to the temple, and the blaze of regret that he hadn't been there by her side for it was what kept him up, tossing and turning, most nights. So he was giving his best, putting in the work to equip his guards with as much practice as possible without knowing for sure whether or not it would be sufficient. Only fate knew what was in store for them.

The sun had just started to set by the time they reached Ankhebari, the town roughly midway between Khemasaru and Renpet where they had arranged for lodging at an inn before they continued on, and Rakhmet was more than looking forward to the chance for a filling meal and comfortable bed after a long day of sweating under the relentless sun. Nebehet strode ahead to speak with the innkeeper as Rakhmet waited for Hara and the rest of the guards at the dock, anxious to have her close by again. After the beatdown the night before, he was willing to bet that he had a good chance of winning her back to his side sooner rather than later.

"Hara!" he called, waving at her above the crowd of guards. She was the last to come ashore, keeping a careful eye on everyone else as they filtered through the many people who littered the dock area.

Ankhebari sat at another fork in the rivers that flowed from the Terra Cotta Mountains and combined to form the Aswa, so it was a common byway for ships heading east and west. Its central market opened right onto the docks, forming a large square with one side dominated by the Surinat Inn, another holding a few cafés, and the third a mixture of stores, a perfect place for travelers to rest and restock.

She caught his eye and nodded, heading toward him as her keen gaze watched for any hint of threat in the mass surrounding them. The divine weapons hanging at her sides caught flashes of the fading sunlight as more and more noticed her and stepped aside, caught gaping at the unusual sight. They whispered to one another and pointed, recognizing her from the rumors that had spread like wildfire through the kingdom, but they all scurried away once Hara gave them a sharp look.

Her expression was hard by the time she reached him. She was clearly annoyed by all the attention she was getting, but it only intensified once people noticed that her companion was Rakhmet, the scarred Crown Prince of Zahar.

"Come on," she ordered, grabbing his elbow and pushing him toward the door of the inn.

"What? You're mad that folks can see how much of a badass you are?" Rakhmet jokingly prodded as they

45

walked, but she just huffed and clenched her jaw, glaring at everyone around them in challenge as they passed.

They found Nebehet finishing up their transactions as they entered the massive, whitewashed, plaster structure with dozens of rooms on the upper two floors as well as a tavern hall that stretched the length of the building on the bottom. It was bustling with activity, his guards easily doubling the number of people staying there as they headed to the bar area to order food and drink.

Rakhmet and Hara moved to join them as Nebehet fell into step and handed Rakhmet a rolled message. "Here, this was waiting for you at the front desk."

Rakhmet unfurled it as they wove through the crowd, aiming for an empty table in the back corner.

To His Royal Highness, Prince Rakhmet of the Honorable House of Pyrantus,

Blessings be upon you. I am afraid I have some troubling news to impart since my last missive, Your Highness. I have received word from my scouts that a local warlord who has been conducting illegal raids on neighboring villages in recent years has heard of your intentions to travel through Renpet with a host of guards on your way to Talegartia. He has been quite vocal in his disapproval of the king's and your newly reclaimed statuses as blessed ones, and it seems as though he has plans to confront you upon your arrival here. In response, I have increased security around my manor and can assure you that we will do everything within our power to protect the blessed crown prince and his guards throughout your

*stay. There will be an armed escort waiting for you
at the docks. May the gods guide us all.*

Your Humble Servant,
Seshetu Hapimose, Lord of Renpet Manor

Rakhmet sat down heavily as they reached the table,
rubbing his brow as he absorbed the news. They had
reached out to Seshetu when plans had changed at the
last minute, seeking shelter at his manor before they
headed into the Shiran Pass. The lord had responded very
favorably to the request as one of the titled landowners
who had immediately renewed their vow of support for
the royal family after hearing of the reclamation of their
elemental crowns. Now, Rakhmet was putting them in
direct danger as a result of that support.

Sighing, he accepted the tankard of ale Nebehet placed
in front of him and took a long drink as he handed the
message to Hara. Her brows furrowed as she read, Nebehet
looking over her shoulder.

"Shit," she muttered, giving the piece of parchment
back to Rakhmet.

Nebehet sat back in his chair, his lips pressed into a
line, and tapped his fingers on the side of his tankard as
he thought.

"I don't think there's anything we can do about it now.
We'll just have to see how bad it is once we get there,"
Rakhmet said, the uncertainty burning a hole in his gut.

"He should have a fairly large force at his disposal."
Nebehet ran the numbers in his head. "The Hapimose
lands are the largest in the region."

"We can't plan off 'shoulds.' We need to know for sure," Hara interjected. "We need to gather more intel. See exactly what we're up against."

"That would give them more time to prepare, though," Rakhmet countered. "We need to slip in and out before they get a chance to do anything about it."

"But we don't even know who this warlord is. We have no idea how many people he's conscripted. We could be walking into a bloodbath," Hara argued.

"We'll make our visit as short as possible," Rakhmet urged, his expression telling her that he wouldn't hear any argument against it. "We should reach Renpet a little after sunset tomorrow, so we should head immediately to the manor, eat, rest, and leave at sunrise."

"Should we warn the guards?" Nebehet asked, glancing around the room where they had settled in with their own refreshments.

"Yeah, we should arrive in armor just in case." Rakhmet frowned, discomfited by the fact that they could be facing enemies much sooner than anticipated.

There was a long pause as Hara stared hard at Rakhmet, her jaw working in displeasure.

"Fine. I'll let them know." Hara stood to convey the orders. As she disappeared, Nebehet took her empty chair next to Rakhmet and placed a hand on his shoulder with a look of understanding.

"They're well trained, Rakh. We'll be able to handle it."

"I certainly hope so," Rakhmet agreed, his frown deepening.

"Between your blessing and Hara's new blades, no one would dare think they could best us."

Rakhmet huffed, his friend's unwavering faith in him turning the ale in his stomach sour just as a barmaid approached with their meals. She smiled at them shyly, curtsying and fluttering her lashes as she placed the plates full of roasted meats, charred vegetables, and buttered flatbreads in front of them. He murmured his thanks, and she looked at him as if his mere presence were the greatest thing that had ever happened to her, which only stoked the flame of unease that was flickering through him.

Nebehet cleared his throat as he watched her trail back to the bar for her next order, casting hopeful glances at them over her shoulder.

"Maybe you should, you know"—he seemed to choke on the words for a moment as he nudged his chin in her direction—"distract yourself for the evening. You deserve a break from the stress."

Rakhmet huffed again, noting the awkward tension that rippled through his friend's shoulders. "What's it to you?"

"Well, you haven't, you know." Nebehet winced at Rakhmet's hard stare. "It's been a while since you've . . . at least, from what I've heard. I may be wrong, but . . . I just, you know, didn't know if there was a reason why you haven't . . . ."

Rakhmet raised a brow at his friend's uncharacteristic fumbling. "What are you getting at? Why is everyone so interested in my sex life lately?"

Nebehet's cheeks colored as his eyes dropped to his plate, and he picked up his fork, prodding at the food in front of him. "I just . . . We care, you know? You haven't necessarily been your usual self in the last few years, and I thought that, maybe, since you got your blessing back,

49

it would . . . change things. But you seem, ah, stressed. Still."

Rakhmet let out a long exhale and leaned forward, clapping his friend on the shoulder. "Thank you, Neb. Really. I appreciate it. But I'm not—I've got other things occupying my mind right now. I've spent too many years being a fuckwit. It's time I started taking things seriously."

It wasn't uncommon for barmaids to react to him like that; he was the crown prince after all. There was a target on his back as large as a building, advertising his availability as a bachelor who could make many a lover's dreams come true. That was exactly why he had kept his rendezvous secret with no strings attached. It didn't really deter any of the hopefuls, but it at least helped him establish expectations up front. He didn't want to break any hearts when he was simply looking for a fun diversion.

The playboy mask was a role that people could easily accept of him, as well as one that was easily played on his end. Carefree indulgence was the name of the game, and there was never a lack of people who were willing to encourage it. But the allure of the lifestyle had fallen flat once his blessing had started fading midway through his twenty-eighth year. Losing access to such a vital connection had caused him to realize that he had been investing too much time and energy into the empty attachments he used to distract himself.

What truly mattered were the blood bonds that made him who he was at his core. Everything else was dispensable. The meaning and purpose he had been searching for all along was actually within him, but he hadn't realized it until his blessing had been threatened. By then it had been too late.

That was why he had jumped at the chance to investigate the fire temple with Hara the first time around and had offered to seek out the plant temple now. It was his chance to show that he had learned his lesson, to prove that he did know what truly mattered.

If that meant giving up the playboy role and turning into a chaste knight determined to earn redemption, so be it.

"Of course." Nebehet's worried gaze darted over his face. "I just want to make sure you find the happiness you deserve, too."

Rakhmet gave him a thin smile and nodded, knowing that his friend was simply looking out for his best interests. "I'll be okay, I promise."

Nebehet dipped his chin in return, hearing the unspoken dismissal of the topic, and turned to dig into his food as Rakhmet caught sight of Hara leaning over a table near the center of the room. She was speaking to a group of guards, and they listened to her with intent expressions on their faces, their respect for her obvious.

He let himself stare for a moment, the gold bands around her biceps and bun glinting in the tavern's torchlights. All royal guards were fitted with a band on each arm, and those specifically oathed to the members of the royal family wore another on their heads, but Hara now sported an additional one on her right bicep to indicate her recent promotion to Nesu Sesemet and it suited her well. Her skin was a shade or two darker than his, and he had always admired the way it shone against the bands, the metal bringing out the warm undertones.

She looked good in gold.

Shaking his head, he urged the thought to burn away as he focused on the meal in front of him, and Nebehet filled the silence with observations on what he knew about the region surrounding Renpet and the Hapimose lands. It was one of the westernmost townships that lined the Terra Cotta Mountains, marking the border between the Zahari Kingdom and Talegartia. Known for its trade in timber and clay gathered from the many creek beds that snaked through the foothills, it was a relatively prosperous area that had seen a lot of conflict over the centuries as different parties fought to lay claim to the wealth produced from its natural resources.

It had been one of the more prominent battlegrounds during the war that had brought about the Endrian Coalition of Rulers Treaty when his father had been a child due to its tenuous location on the border. After peace had been won, Seshetu had been assigned as the land's protector by the late King Diemani, and he had been mostly successful in maintaining his control over the subsequent years. The discontent had certainly decreased, but it wasn't uncommon for there to be lingering hostilities among some of the communities there—especially in the out-of-the-way rural areas. According to the missive, it seemed as though the recent reveal of his and his father's intentions to reestablish the elemental crowns had further incited their anger.

Nebehet was finishing his dissertation as Hara rejoined them, giving Rakhmet a look that told him the guards had been notified and all were prepared to fight upon arrival in Renpet. The tightness in her expression had him reaching out to squeeze her arm, as he could see his own fears reflected at him, but he didn't let himself linger, all too aware that there were many pairs of eyes watching them across the tavern.

He refocused on his food as Hara started a discussion about the estimated numbers of Hapimose's forces with Nebehet around mouthfuls of her own meal. It was proving difficult to determine whether the lord's defense plus Rakhmet's guards would be enough of a match without knowing anything about the enemy. They would simply have to trust that Seshetu was well-informed and well-resourced enough to prevail.

This would be the first true test of his abilities as a leader. He had never led people into a fight before, and everyone would be looking to him for guidance, authority, and confidence. All the things he had trained for his entire life. All the responsibilities he had dodged for years.

He couldn't let them down. He had to be the one to bear the consequences this time. Him and only him.

The thought made his fingers twitch around his fork, clenching until the metal bent ever so slightly as the cold edges pressed into his heated skin.

Hara's eyes dropped to his hand, then she met his gaze with a question as she finished whatever she was saying to Nebehet. Clenching his jaw, Rakhmet grasped for an answer that would both satisfy her and hide the truth of his deep-seated fears that were scorching through his throat. She remained trained on him, waiting and watching as

Nebehet answered her, unaware of the silent conversation happening without him.

Rakhmet attempted to swallow, but the burn was too much. He broke Hara's gaze and reached for his ale, downing the rest of it in a large swig. Swiping his mouth with the back of his hand, he looked around the room aimlessly. He couldn't bear to meet Hara's knowing stare, so he caught the attention of the closest barmaid and signaled for another round of ale, his pulse becoming a loud pounding in his head.

He absently watched as their ale was poured and brought over, stuffing the doubts deep down inside until he could turn to Nebehet and Hara with a mild expression once again. Hara quickly noted the change, her eyebrow twitch letting him know she wasn't buying it. She would let him have this one, but they would need to have it out one of these days.

Even though he had hoped that they would go back to normal once they had made up, the potential list of things that they needed to talk about between the two of them was just getting longer and longer by the day. But there hadn't been any time.

They had been moving from one thing to another for days now, running from each other while standing side by side.

He cleared his throat and focused on Nebehet, clapping a hand onto his friend's shoulder. "How about it? A third ale won't make us too useless to fight tomorrow, eh?"

Clinking his tankard into Nebehet's, he raised it and drew half of it down in two deep pulls. He then dropped it onto the table, grinning at Nebehet with a dare.

His friend's returning smile was quick as it stretched across his face and his eyes lit up, but he bit his lip and looked at Hara to judge her reaction before answering.

"Come on, we won't get to Renpet until sunset anyways. We can nap it off," Rakhmet doubled down, pulling Nebehet into a side hug and slugging his chin.

Per usual, his friend's reluctance faded away in the light of his enthusiasm and he chuckled as Nebehet reached out to touch his own tankard to Rakhmet's before tipping it back.

Rakhmet watched as Nebehet's throat bobbed, his neck fully exposed as he drank the whole thing in big gulps, and his grin widened. His gaze darted to Hara, who had sat back in her chair with her arms folded, observing the scene in front of her with a mask of indifference. Only he could see the slight feathering of her jaw muscle, the weight of her brows. She was annoyed but wasn't going to show it.

Her respect for and loyalty to the Crown kept her from even hinting at her displeasure at him in a crowded room, and he knew full well that he was only egging her on with his behavior, but he couldn't help himself. He wasn't ready to fully admit to some things, but as long as she was still by his side, everything would be fine.

By the time Nebehet dropped his empty tankard back onto the table, Rakhmet had his own in hand once again and nearly finished. Done, he twisted and hailed the barmaid for another round, her smile brighter and brighter each time he acknowledged her.

She was enticing, he had to admit, and he certainly took longer than would be proper as he watched her hurry toward them in the crowded bar with newly filled tankards. She was wearing a simple white dress and faded blue apron that fell in graceful drapes to her calves. It swished to the sway of her hips, rocking gently as she approached. A hint of her flushed skin winked at them at the edge of her neckline, and he slowly licked the foam off his top lip as he momentarily wondered how she would feel pressed against him and panting eagerly.

His fingers instinctively curled and brushed against warm fabric, the sensation startling him out of his reverie as he realized that he still had his arm slung over Nebehet's shoulders. He turned to find his friend's gaze darting curiously between him and the barmaid so he shifted, leaning away as he lowered his arm to the back of Nebehet's chair before refocusing on the girl as she set the drinks on their table.

"Thank you," Rakhmet drawled, and she blushed prettily, her lighter skin turning to the color of red clay. "What's your name?"

"R-Raia, Your Highness," she stuttered, dropping into a curtsy and peeking up at him through her lashes.

"Raia, a beautiful name," he murmured and reached for his tankard just as she lurched forward to push it toward him. Their fingers brushed as he took it from her, and he felt the tremble go through her as her cheeks turned even darker.

He gave her a warm smile and sat back as she dipped her chin and retreated like a little mouse. Glancing at his two companions, he found Hara pointedly ignoring him as she took her time sipping on her first ale and Nebehet reaching for one of the new tankards with a determined look on his face.

"Here's to our inevitable victory!" Nebehet cheered with an enthusiastic grin, tapping his ale against Rakhmet's.

Rakhmet laughed as he returned the cheer, both of their heads tipping as they drank together, and his doubts quieted into the pleasant numbness that blanketed him. It was much easier to present the facade of unfazed assurance with a bit of liquid courage in his veins. He let Nebehet's joviality buoy him as the evening wore on, but eventually, Hara bullied them into retiring for the night, glaring at them silently as Nebehet guided them to their assigned rooms.

Hara's was the first at the end of a block set aside for the guards, the closest to the more luxurious rooms Nebehet and Rakhmet had been given around the corner, but she still insisted on trailing them to Rakhmet's quarters so she could check them over for threats first. As she exited, she didn't say a word but gave Rakhmet a pointed look before disappearing down the hall.

He rolled his eyes at Nebehet, getting a chuckle in return as his friend smiled at him with a goofy grin. He was leaning against one of the bedposts with his arms crossed, attempting to look more sober than he was, and it made Rakhmet's smirk widen. Neb had always been the one to follow him into anything and everything, like a loyal puppy, just excited to come along for the ride.

Clapping both hands onto his shoulders, he laughed as he pulled his friend in for a hug and let his affection melt into him. Nebehet instantly relaxed, falling into Rakhmet with a sigh, and his arms wrapped around Rakhmet's waist.

"My friend, how good you are to me," Rakhmet rumbled as he pulled back, holding him at arm's length. "How will I ever repay you for your undeserved devotion?"

Nebehet's eyes were soft as he gazed at him, his teeth pulling on his bottom lip. "It's an honor, Rakh. Truly."

"No, the honor is mine, my dear Neb." He grinned at him, his elbows slackening a bit as his gaze dropped to where Nebehet had started chewing on his lip again.

His friend's hands clenched briefly where they still sat on his waist and a question started to form. "Could . . . Could I ask you something?"

"Of course, what is it?" Rakhmet watched as Nebehet licked his lips and leaned in slightly for whatever he was going to say.

"Have you— Would you ever—"

"Oh." A soft noise sounded at the still open door as Rakhmet glanced over Nebehet's shoulder to find Raia frozen mid step behind them. Her hands twisted in her apron as her eyes bounced between them.

Rakhmet moved back from Nebehet, dropping his arms as he cleared his throat. "Do you need something?"

Raia took a tentative step forward, a blush spreading across her skin as Rakhmet tracked its progress, and then another until she was next to them. She took in Nebehet's confused frown and Rakhmet's stiff posture.

"Your Highness." She turned to Rakhmet and pinched the end of her pinky with a nervous smile. "I–I wanted to . . . make sure you were taken care of. For the night."

She glanced between them again, her cheeks impossibly red. "In case you needed . . . wanted, ah, any company."

Rakhmet inhaled, caught off guard, and opened his mouth, but she rushed on.

"You seem to be, ah . . ." She licked her lips as her gaze landed on Nebehet. "I wondered about— I mean, I'm not . . . I don't have any qualms about, you know, being shared. If that's what you . . . prefer."

She refocused on Rakhmet, her bright eyes shining with eagerness to please him, and he suddenly found it difficult to breathe. His inebriated mind tripped from one thought to the next, absorbing the meaning behind her offer. He felt a part of himself light up at the idea, the promise of a pleasurable diversion and satisfying release too strong as an unconscious groan escaped him. It was a temptation he would've accepted without any hesitation in the past.

Nebehet had been right. It had been over a year since he had last gotten laid. He had been just drunk enough the night of his sister's wedding that he had found a willing stable hand to fuck discretely in a hidden corner of the elaborate Gheseruti palace grounds. The copious amounts of wine he had consumed during all of the wedding cheers had allowed him to temporarily forget the pain of losing access to his blessing, and he always had more than his fair share of eager hopefuls to choose from.

The stable hand had been the quietest throughout his stay at Queen Ishya's court, surreptitiously watching him out of the corner of their eye whenever Rakhmet had walked past the stables. Rakhmet had sought them out in the still darkness of the night, hoping for a respite from the overwhelming festivities going on indoors, and had been received with calloused hands that were surprisingly gentle as the prince took what he needed.

59

He wondered about another set of hands as the memory of Nebehet's lip getting squeezed between his teeth just a moment ago filled him with unexpected heat and it turned his attention to his oldest friend. Nebehet's eyes were wide with disbelief, worry, and the barest hint . . . a tiny, almost imperceptible sliver of hope.

His head reeled at the realization, his eyes flicking back to the blush disappearing into the neckline of the barmaid's dress. He sputtered, attempting to find the words, and his balls tightened in response to the wide-open offer in her expression.

"Y—you're not being pressured to . . . be here, are you?" He had never, ever taken advantage of anyone who found themselves at his bedroom door, especially those that came from the working class of his kingdom. He knew that there were far too many reasons why someone would seek his influence, and he would rather pay them off than take what was offered with any hint of reluctance.

"No, not at all." She stepped closer, placing one hand above his heart where it pounded beneath his ribs, and took Nebehet's hand with the other, placing it on her waist as she moved between them. "Please, Your Highness, I want to be of service to you."

He drew in a tight breath, grasping for a single thread of logic, but she started gently twisting her hips so that his rapidly hardening length brushed against her warmth. His hand instinctively reached for where Nebehet's sat on her waist and squeezed, watching his friend's mouth part with surprise over Raia's shoulder.

As Rakhmet stared at the plump edge of Nebehet's lip and felt Raia press herself against him, he knew there were reasons why he shouldn't let this happen. He just had a hard time putting a finger on them at the moment. The tension was building and his mind circled around the sensations that momentarily blinded him.

Raia's breasts rubbing against his chest. Nebehet's hand gripping her waist. Breathy sighs that reached down into him and stoked the fire within.

He shuddered as his thoughts spun away from his control. He was imagining things he had never had before, and yet sourness burned in his stomach.

Raia probably had a family counting on her. Working as a barmaid wasn't the sort of position that easily paid the bills and he knew that, if he asked, there would be a similar story that he had heard from many of his citizens: a story of struggle and strife, of barely making ends meet and working to the bone just to ensure that there would be food on the table.

Sure, she might be there willingly, but come tomorrow, he would become just another what-if fantasy she used to keep her candle of hope burning when the days were hard and the nights long.

Not only that, but his dearest friend would still be by his side the next day and the one after that. There would be no running away from the knowledge of what lust and too much ale compelled them to do during one night of bad decision after bad decision. He couldn't let his lack of impulse control ruin one of his oldest relationships.

"I don't think—" He forced himself to reach out and grasp Raia's shoulder in a gesture of grateful but firm refusal.

Rakhmet's eyes met Nebehet's over her shoulder, and he could see the sting of rejection starting to bleed into his expression. It made him jerk backward, extracting himself from Raia and belatedly slamming down his boundaries. This was why he had to be very careful about who he got involved with. The repercussions of mixing business and pleasure were never worth it. His cock ached but he rapidly swallowed the urge and put on his serious prince face.

"No, thank you. It is a kind offer that I must decline," he said roughly, steadying himself on the edge of his door and sweeping his hand out to dismiss them both. "Good night."

He didn't even spare a glance as they shuffled out and shut the door behind them, locking it and standing there for a moment as he calmed his breath. His skin was crawling, itching for release as he stumbled over to his bed and he braced himself on the bedpost.

The heat of embarrassment and disappointment was a blaze inside of him, only igniting the inferno of want even further as he battled with himself. It would be a long night, but he'd be damned if he let the monster within win.

DAY FOUR

He was one of the last people to come down for breakfast the next morning, too ashamed to face them all in the clear light of day. He paced around his quarters for as long as he could before forcing himself to open the door and don the mask of confident prince. With his head held high, he strode to the rear of the tavern hall where Hara and Nebehet sat at the same table as the night before and gave them a forced smile.

"Good morning," he greeted them as he sat.

"Morning," Hara returned, looking at him with a thousand questions in her dark gaze.

He winced internally, turning to Nebehet, who was valiantly trying to hide his own embarrassment, and he immediately regretted it.

"Good morning," Nebehet answered, his voice slightly lower than usual.

Clearing his throat, Rakhmet nodded and then swept his eyes across the room. He studiously avoided both of them and waved at the closest barmaid to bring him a plate of food, specifically choosing one who wasn't Raia, as he spied her speaking with another table on the other side of the room. Quickly turning around, he refocused on his two companions, who were still staring at him with heavy looks, and let out a long exhale.

"What?" he finally demanded, too irritable to play the guessing game.

Nebehet dropped his eyes to the empty plate in front of him, choosing not to engage, as Hara crossed her arms and leaned back in her seat, giving him an appraising glance as if to say *you brought this on yourself.*

"I did not," Rakhmet grumbled, looking away as his plate was deposited in front of him by the barmaid. He grunted his thanks and picked up his fork, bringing one of the sausages to his mouth. Biting down a bit harder than necessary, he chewed and glanced up to find Raia staring at him from the other side of the table next to them. She had just picked up a couple of empty tankards and plates, balancing them in one hand as she brushed a towel across the surface.

They locked eyes and he froze, the fork halfway to his plate, as she blushed that same earthy red.

Hara noticed his reaction and turned to see what had caught his attention as Nebehet also glanced up to find her standing there, which made her cheeks go pure scarlet.

She flinched away, scurrying back to the kitchen door and disappearing behind it.

His guard slowly pivoted to give him a scrutinizing look, then noticed Nebehet's paling face and her brows slammed down as suspicion flamed in her eyes. She studied both of their expressions, Rakhmet daring a peek at his friend to find a familiar sting creeping over his countenance.

"It's not—" He glanced back at Hara. "We didn't—"

Her jaw tightened and she puffed out a small exhale. It would have been a scoff if she had put any force behind it, but she knew that he knew what it meant.

"For gods' sake, I'm not that stupid, Hara." He huffed, smoothing his hand over the top of his curls.

Nebehet shifted, the barest of flinches, away from him.

Rakhmet frowned as he glanced at his friend, his heart squeezing as one of the cherished few who had supported and cared for him from childhood onward cringed at his words. Nebehet's shoulders were slightly hunched as he stared at the plate in front of him, trying to stay out of it until either he or Hara backed down. It was his default whenever they had quarreled over the years, after learning too many times that his efforts at peacemaking between the prince and his guard often made things worse.

Looking around the room, Rakhmet found a handful of curious faces watching them and cleared his throat. He squared his shoulders and met Hara's dark gaze.

"If you want to ask me something, then ask it. Otherwise, you need to stop staring daggers at me in front of everyone," Rakhmet gritted between his teeth low, so only she and Nebehet could hear him. "You can yell at me in private for whatever sins you think I've committed, okay? Out here, you are **my** guard."

It was extremely rare that he used his rank against her in arguments, and he watched as the cut landed, her eyes flashing with blazing anger before she was able to snuff it out and don the impassive mask of her station.

"Yes, Your Highness," she answered automatically, her appeasing tone in stark contrast to the fire he knew lit up her ribs.

He sighed, hating himself as he started eating his breakfast with all the dignity of a prince but barely tasting it. It was just fuel for the physical form that barely contained his screams of frustration, desperation, and fear. They licked at his insides, instantly turning the meal to ash.

This was not a good omen for their trip, to be passive aggressively fighting with his personal guard in front of everyone. They hadn't even managed to get out of the country before the tensions between them flared. He should have made a point of talking to Hara before they had left. He should not have drunk so much the night before. He should have retired early, alone.

Gods, what was he doing?

Who was he to think that he could hold up the facade of competence, tricking all who followed him into thinking he knew what he was doing. He ruined everything he touched, and now he was leading them to their deaths.

Not much more was said between the three of them as the guards eventually rallied to head to the docks, and soon they were separated once again on the two ships sailing westward. Rakhmet gave instructions, telling them to rest and prepare in the hours leading up to their arrival. They would armor up once they were roughly two hours away, ready and vigilant for any and all potential threats.

After the message was conveyed, Rakhmet sequestered himself at the bow of the ship and stared out over the water in stormy silence. He hated everything about the situation he currently found himself in. It was awful enough to be acutely aware that they were mere hours away from potentially meeting enemy forces, but he had also somehow managed to estrange the two people closest to him in one fatal swoop. It was all he could do to keep from wringing his hands and pacing like a madman as the sun journeyed across the sky.

Dipping over the mountains that were becoming clearer and clearer in the distance, the sun reached its final quarter and Rakhmet gave the signal to arm. Expressions were hard and contemplative yet determined as they pulled on thick leather bracers and leg guards, chest plates and shoulder pauldrons, their blades reflecting the last rays of sunshine.

Samira, the Nesu Pawat under Hara that had been assigned to his boat, finally approached to let him know all twelve guards were armed and ready and Renpet was estimated to be about an hour and a half away. He nodded, dismissing her as he turned back to the river in front of him, and tightened his own grip on the two daggers at his sides.

The surrounding land out here was much emptier, more sparsely populated than the towns and cities to the east. Small homesteads with plenty of room for agriculture and animal husbandry sat next to the occasional village square or simple, whitewashed temple. It was quiet too, the faint sounds of clucking chickens and snorting pigs carrying on the wind.

Every now and then, one of the inhabitants would stop and watch them pass, their expressions unreadable from afar. But eventually, the river thinned further and a small town nestled into the very foothills surrounding the towering mountain range came into view. The landscape elevated quickly, the river ending in a waterfall spilling from a crack in the cliffside about a quarter of a mile west of the various small shops and homes clustered on either side of the water.

The main docks were secured on the northern bank, and Rakhmet could see a large group of guards and townsfolk gathered there. He squinted, trying to count the guards separately from the plain-clothes individuals, and came to around ten. Maybe more, maybe less. It was hard to tell from a distance.

Hapimose's guards unsheathed their blades and readied crossbows as the two ships approached, ushering everyone else to move aside, and Rakhmet could hear a few grumbles and complaints rise above the crowd. He gritted his teeth, stalking to the side railing as he carefully surveyed everything. Nebehet was next to him before he even realized it, Samira stationing herself on his other side, and he let his lifetime of training take hold.

Sheathing his plain dagger and keeping the other clenched close to his thigh, he raised his empty hand in a wave as the boat bumped into its mooring.

"Greetings, respected people of Renpet. I am Prince Rakhmet, Crown Prince of Zahar, and I arrive to visit with your most gracious lord. We wish to reaffirm our warmest relationship with this region of our great kingdom and thank you from the bottom of our hearts for your kindness and hospitality. May the gods grant you a bountiful harvest and prosperous year. Gods willing."

His voice echoed across the docks, and his guards instantly returned "gods willing" as Hapimose's guards joined in half a second later. There was a smattering of applause among the townsfolk and a few cheers, and Rakhmet's shoulders relaxed a fraction. He had passed the first test: no one had attacked yet.

A small win.

He cleared his throat and nodded to Samira, who signaled Layla. The younger guard helped the ship's crew unload the gangplank and get everyone disembarked, Rakhmet and Nebehet waiting to be the last from their boat as the rest of his guards formed a human shield on every side of him.

Hara was at his right in a heartbeat, Nebehet shifting to take his left, and Samira fell behind him as Hapimose's guards led them forward, taking a packed-dirt road leading away from the river. The lord's manor soon came into view as they rounded the last few homes hugging the edge of town, an impressive stone estate that backed into the forest that clung to the mountainside, and it didn't take long to reach the heavy front gates in tense silence.

Rakhmet didn't sheathe his dagger nor breathe easy until they were all inside the lord's cavernous front hall and both the gate as well as the reinforced front doors were locked securely, a thick post of iron sliding into place with a resounding thud as the guards finally parted to let Seshetu approach Rakhmet and bow. He touched his fingers to his forehead, lips, and chest in a gesture of reverence, showing his loyalty to the elemental Crown without hesitation.

Dipping his chin to the lord, Rakhmet asked him to rise and greeted him warmly. They had only met a handful of times over the years, whenever Seshetu would come to Zahar to take part in political negotiations, but what he had seen of him was trustworthy. He forced his heartbeat to slow, praying they were safe here.

"Your Highness, it is an honor. I welcome you to my humble home with the utmost pride." Seshetu opened his hand, inviting Rakhmet to join him, and turned to the hall on the right.

Samira stayed behind to discuss logistics with the captain of Hapimose's guards, but both Hara and Nebehet followed Rakhmet closely as the lord led them to a large dining hall lit up with dozens of candles. There were three long, wooden tables in the room, the center more decorated than the others as Seshetu led Rakhmet to the seat of honor at the head of it.

The lord bowed again as one of his attendants scurried forward to pull out Rakhmet's chair, and the prince nodded in gratitude as he sat. Seshetu positioned himself to his right, inviting Nebehet to sit on his left as Hara took up her guard position behind Rakhmet. He had to give the lord some credit. So far, his eyes had only wandered twice to the divine weapons hanging at Hara's waist, and the sharp gleam in them told Rakhmet that he was admiring but also appropriately intimidated by them.

Engraved On A Heart Of Flame

The confidence lent by the two blades (not to mention the woman wielding them) helped Rakhmet settle into his role for the evening, holding his chin high with a warm smile as Hapimose's family filtered into the room accompanied by their own collection of guards. His wife, Nefara, his daughter, Amunet, and his son, Khaemwaset, performed the expected honorifics then settled into their own seats around the central table as about a dozen guards took up spots lining the walls. They were in full metal-plate armor, and Rakhmet eyed them appreciatively as the lord's family started asking him all the usual polite questions about their trip.

He didn't fail to notice their attempts to deck themselves in the family jewels and gold. Amunet, in particular, wore an elaborate headdress of shimmering chains and hammered phoenixes. It wasn't unusual for noble families like the Hapimoses to parade their daughters in front of him like mares with their tails and manes brushed until they shone. His mother had a list miles long of all the young noblewomen in the kingdom who aspired to wear the crown alongside him one day, not to mention a list half as long full of young men and others who wouldn't mind sharing the prince's bed with a courtesan or two that could bear him an heir.

His parents had never much cared how the blessing was passed on. As long as he could secure at least one successor with the power of fire, it didn't matter who the mother was—queen or no. There had to be a stable spouse to help rule from the throne, but he could make heirs however he wanted. He was honestly grateful for the freedom it provided him, but his mother had been increasingly persistent when it came to choosing someone to marry ever since Esare had left for Gheseruti. She wanted him to pick someone from the Zahari Kingdom, settle down, and never leave.

Another expectation of him that he had been failing to fulfill.

Eventually, most of his guards filled the tables on either side of the room and dinner was served: countless courses of roasted birds, whole suckling pigs, herbed vegetables, and pillows of rices and flatbreads offered to him in a never-ending procession of food. Occasionally, a guard circled through and stopped at Seshetu's side to whisper updates into his ear, and Rakhmet kept a close eye on both of their expressions. The lord seemed to want to determinedly maintain his cheer, but the guard was hard to read.

His eyes deliberately avoided the prince, and it did nothing to ease Rakhmet's tense mood, but he kept telling himself to trust that his guards and Hara would be enough. They had to be enough. They had to get to Lythenea in one piece. This was only the first step of many.

What would his people think of him if he couldn't even safely get out of the country? How could he instill confidence in them if he couldn't handle a domestic threat, let alone an international one? He would have no right to the throne if that were the case.

The guard disappeared into one of the back doors and was gone for a handful of minutes as Rakhmet tried to convince himself to relax. He was just about to glance at Hara to see if she was thinking the same thing when a commotion suddenly sounded in the hallway leading to the rear of the manor. Rakhmet flinched, his already frayed nerves lighting up in alarm, and a shout went up as a different guard came running into the dining hall, tripping over himself as he bellowed, "THE MANOR HAS BEEN BREACHED! PROTECT THE PRINCE!"

Rakhmet's stomach dropped as the room erupted into motion and they all pushed themselves to their feet. Chairs clattered to the floor, drowned out by the screams of the Hapimose women and the dozens of unsheathing weapons as Rakhmet drew his blades and backed away from the table. Nebehet and Hara instantly flanked him, their eyes darting everywhere as a group of guards pushed forward to surround Seshetu's wife and children and herd them to a door in the rear corner.

There was a clash of metal on metal as curses and grunts started echoing through the stone room and a mess of fighting guards spilled into the dining hall. They were being harried by a number of unfamiliar soldiers wearing dark tunics underneath their armor, their faces masked so that only their angry eyes were visible.

Rakhmet swore loudly, moving to place himself between the retreating figures of the Hapimose family and the crush of guards who descended upon the soldiers with fury, but a piercing cry went up behind him just as a second group of soldiers burst through a different door toward the rear of the room. It was the one the attendants had been using whenever they had fetched platters or pitchers throughout the meal, the same that one guard had exited through not too long before.

Amunet and her mother were now trapped in the corner, the lady clutching onto her adolescent son and using her

73

own body as a shield for him as the soldiers turned to them and lifted their swords. The women wailed in pure terror, and Rakhmet lurched forward, reaching for them as the guards that had been nearby threw themselves at the intruders.

Purely out of instinct, he pulled for the flames that were flickering on the torches circling the room and threw them at the soldiers. They stumbled back in surprise, their arms rising to protect their faces from the heat as Rakhmet tried to create a barrier of fire between his guards and the attackers, but the swarm of figures was too tight, too condensed. His own guards were also forced to cringe back, the blaze licking their armor and starting to smoke.

Hara held Rakhmet back, her arm wrapping around his waist as he instantly doused the flames, too afraid of hurting his own people. Slipping in front of him, Nebehet took the opportunity to latch onto Amunet's arm to pull her away from the fight, tears streaming down her face. Her headdress slipped off and got crushed under her feet as she scrambled to Nebehet while Nefara fell forward, also grabbing onto Nebehet's shoulder as Rakhmet shrugged Hara off and opened his arms to catch them.

Amunet immediately clung to him, burying her face in his neck as the lady wept, praying to the gods for protection in an endless stream of panicked breaths. He held onto them, swiveling his head and trying to see over the mass of bodies surging around them as Nebehet and Hara did their best to fend off anyone who got too close. But what he saw was not encouraging, with sprays of blood now decorating the fine tapestries on the walls and people falling left and right.

Some wore dark tunics that seemed to be an intensely deep shade of plum, some Hapimose burgundy.

"Fuck!" He cursed again, "Fuck!"

Amunet whimpered against him and all he could do was wait as he watched for an opening, his hands burning with the need to contribute more.

Samira carved a passage through the fray, heading in his direction, but he almost lost his dinner as he witnessed Layla take a sword to her neck just behind the Nesu Pawat. He cried out in anguish as his guard fell, Samira glancing over her shoulder in horror and Hara spinning around at his alarm.

Rakhmet tried to reach out and stop her, his movements hindered by the two women clinging to him, but was too late as Hara realized that her friend had been killed. Time slowed as her features twisted, a slow ripple across her face as her brows rose for a tremulous moment. The rumble of her bottom lip as her jaw dropped open in shock was the barest of signals that only animals could sense before an earthquake hit. That eerie pulse that locked up the muscles for a fraction of a second just before their flight instinct kicked in. He sensed, more than saw, her free-fall into fury as her emotions struck flint, and he was instantly drawn toward her heat. Like a moth to a flame.

The fire inside her erupted with an enraged howl, her eyes flaring as she whipped her arm out to the side and lit her zulfiqar. Wheeling her two blades in a perpetual revolution of scorching destruction, she was no longer on the defensive. She actively pursued with an insatiable hunger.

Over and over again, she moved with blind purpose and the intruding soldiers fell before her until there was a clear path to the kitchen door.

"Go! I'll bar the way," Samira ordered as she reached them, jerking her chin toward the back hallway. She had smears of blood across her cheeks and was panting, but her hard expression made Hara nod and sheath her zulfiqar, putting the flame out and grabbing Nefara's arm to pull her forward.

Amunet continued her wailing as Hara led Rakhmet, Nebehet, the two women, and young Khaemwaset out of the hall and into a darker passage lit with flickering torchlight. The door thumped closed behind them, only slightly muffling the noise of battle on the other side, but they came to a stunned halt as they stumbled upon the slain bodies of attendants that were slumped on the ground before them, pools of blood leaking across the tiled floor as Nefara dry-heaved at the sight.

Rakhmet clenched his teeth, willing the threatening bile back down as Hara turned to Nefara.

"How do we get to the bedchambers from here?" she demanded, rapidly assessing their situation.

The lady gasped for breath, her hand pressed to her stomach. "Th-that way."

She raised a shaking finger toward the western end of the hallway, and Hara pushed them forward, keeping her dagger out as they half-ran, half-shuffled due to the paralyzing fright that held Hapimose family in its tight grip.

Rakhmet spared a glance at Nebehet over the top of Amunet's head and found his friend looking back at him with wide eyes, his sleeve torn and hanging open from a tussle with one of the plum soldiers. He was panting, his lip was swollen and split from where he had been punched, and there was an almost manic energy pouring from him that raised the hairs on the back of Rakhmet's neck.

He swallowed thickly and refocused ahead of them, where they had reached the foot of a spiraling stone staircase. As they climbed, Rakhmet's mind flicked from one plan to the next, but the sounds of continued fighting carried to them through the hallways, and his hope was fading by the second. He trusted his guards, but he had already witnessed one fall and had no clue how many plum fighters were out there.

It was entirely possible that they were outmatched two-to-one, even four-to-one.

He had no fucking way of knowing.

Flames rippled underneath his skin, called forth by the raging fires of uncertainty and desperation. The heat was building and it felt like puffs of smoke leaked from his nostrils as they reached an elegantly furnished hallway with several wooden doors on either side. Their boots sunk into the plush burgundy rug stretching the length of the hall as Nefara nervously pointed out the rooms.

"This one was s-set aside for you, Your H-Highness. This, for your trusted companion. O-ours are on the floor above," she stuttered.

"Nebehet"—Hara turned to his friend—"take the lady and her children to their rooms. Lock them in. Meet us back here as soon as you can."

She reached for Amunet and pried her from Rakhmet, depositing her onto Nebehet as he nodded and started tugging them back to the stairwell. Then Hara threw open the door leading to what was supposed to be Rakhmet's room and strode inside, her sharp eyes instantly searching for something. He followed her in a daze, gripping onto his daggers now that his hands were empty again.

"What's the plan here?" he asked roughly, his blessing begging for release.

She didn't answer, though, and instead grabbed his pack that had been brought to the room and placed it next to his dresser. She yanked it open and quickly cataloged what was inside before starting to open drawers and grab fistfuls of clothing that she shoved into the pack. Moving to a trunk on the other side of the room, she opened it to dig through the piles of rations that they had been planning on distributing among the guards before heading into Shiran Pass.

His fists clenched and unclenched around the pommels as he watched her in silence, his overheated brain incapable of following what she was doing. They had to get back out there. They needed to fight.

She stuffed several packages of rations into his pack, drawing the straps tight as she secured the whole bundle and slung it over her shoulder. Repeating the process with another pack that she found in the trunk, she added another set of clothes and rations before securing that one too.

Running footsteps echoed outside the doorway as they both spun toward the sound with weapons drawn, but it was only Nebehet rushing into the room with his own blade at the ready.

"They're locked in," he told them as Hara tossed the second pack to him.

He caught it with his free hand and looked at her with a question in his eyes.

"We're running," Hara said, eyeing Rakhmet and Nebehet for any sign of disagreement.

"What?" Rakhmet started as Nebehet simply nodded, instantly accepting her order.

"We can't—" he tried again but was interrupted by the sounds of a group of people charging into the hallway outside the room. The aggressive shouts immediately told them that it wasn't their guards, and Nebehet lunged to shut and lock the door just as a flash of plum was seen hurtling toward them.

The soldiers collided with the closed door, banging on it and shouting as Hara ran to the other side of the room and tore open the heavy window dressings. She hurriedly unlatched the window and pushed it open as the room's door started cracking under the heavy impacts. Throwing her pack out the window, she waved Nebehet and Rakhmet forward, and Nebehet threw his out too.

He climbed up onto the windowsill and slung his legs out over the ledge, looking down at the ground a story below them for just a moment before taking a deep breath and jumping. Landing with a grunt, he bent his legs and rolled to the side to soften the hit just as Hara urged Rakhmet to go next.

He mirrored his friend and leapt from the window, using the momentum to roll a few times before springing up into a defensive position as he looked around to see where they were. It seemed like they were on the western edge of the manor, next to a mostly rusted, closed ground-floor door that looked like it hadn't been used in decades, with the forest standing about a hundred feet or so in front of them.

Hara joined them, her and Nebehet grabbing their packs just as the door next to them creaked open with a protesting groan. A Hapimose guard came stumbling out, his face bloodied and eyes wide with fear as he spotted the three of them.

"Your Highness," he cried with alarm and fell forward to clutch at Rakhmet's shirt. "There are too many. They—"

He was cut off by a pair of plum soldiers emerging from the door after him, their swords already slashing toward the guard as they all lurched out of the way. Unfortunately, the guard was not fast enough as the blade caught him in the gap where his breastplate met his hips.

Crying out, he fell as Hara whipped her arm to the side and lit her zulfiqar. She moved without hesitation as Nebehet positioned himself in front of Rakhmet and blocked the attack of one of the soldiers. Blades clashed and his friend and guard grunted as they threw themselves at the plum figures.

Rakhmet held his daggers out, circling around Nebehet's side to slip one into the side of the soldier's neck just as they swerved out of the way to avoid a swipe from his friend. He forced it into their flesh, gritting his teeth as he twisted it to snap the neck before jumping back just as a third soldier dropped from the open window above them.

Looking up in horror, he watched as three additional plum soldiers each leapt from the window, joining them on the ground. Five soldiers, one dead, and the three of them.

"Fuck!" he screamed, throwing his arm out to latch onto the flame of Hara's sword. He didn't wait as he ripped it off the blade and heaved it toward the plum figures to drive them backward, but one managed to latch onto Nebehet's arm and yank him with them as they fell back.

Hara relit the sword and was attacking the one holding Nebehet in the next breath, successfully cutting through the man's armor down to the bone of his forearm. The spray of blood burned into nothing in the heat of her weapon as she dislodged it and brought it up for another slice, the soldier jerking away in pain.

Nebehet took the opportunity to spin, punching his fist right into the jaw of the soldier with the blunt end of his pommel and then kicking him onto his back. He impacted hard just as the three other soldiers each went for Nebehet, Hara, and Rakhmet, effectively separating them as they swung their swords in wide arcs.

Meeting hers head-on, Hara pressed forward as her flames licked at the figure's face covering. Nebehet managed to dance out of the way, forcing his opponent to stumble off balance in a feint, but Rakhmet sheathed his daggers and snarled like a wild animal, striking his hands together and letting flame explode from his fingertips to engulf his soldier in a bonfire as he stoked it higher and higher.

The plum figure screamed in agony, falling backward onto the ground as they attempted to roll and put the fire out, but Rakhmet only renewed it with a growl as Hara finished off her soldier and turned to find Nebehet

81

wrestled to the ground by two plum fighters. She lunged toward them, grabbing the back of one of their chest plates to try and pull them off Nebehet.

"Rakhmet!" she yelled as she managed to roll one of the soldiers away, kicking and punching him as they slammed into the dirt.

His body moved without thinking, using his still flaming hands to grip the other soldier around his collarbone. Planting his feet, he tried to haul them off Nebehet as the smell of burning flesh filled the air.

"Gods above," Nebehet choked out as he tried to get up, but the plum figure had a vice grip on his ankle and wasn't letting go. He stretched for his dagger that had fallen to the side just as Rakhmet glanced up to see six more plum fighters appear around the far eastern corner of the manor and start booking it toward them.

He swore a colorful string of desperate curses as he tugged again on the soldier holding onto Nebehet, the individual's flesh covered in more and more burns, but they didn't yield as Hara struggled to subdue the figure she was grappling with a few yards away.

Nebehet's eyes found the plum fighters rapidly approaching and swung back to Rakhmet, making an instant decision. His fingers gripped his dagger, and he used it to slice the strap of the pack he was wearing, freeing and throwing it at Rakhmet.

"Go!" he shouted.

Rakhmet gaped as it hit him in the chest and fell to the ground, his palms immediately losing their heat and breaking out in a cold sweat. "What—"

Hara gave a frustrated grunt as she finally managed to slit her opponent's throat and pushed to her feet, grasping Rakhmet's arm. "We need to go."

"What the fuck?!" Rakhmet objected, leaning forward to try again to free Nebehet of the plum figure on top of him. "Neb, we can't—"

Two plum fighters broke from the head of the group running toward them, slightly faster than the others as they drew closer and closer.

Nebehet slugged the soldier in the chin, continuing to wrestle for control as he glanced up at Rakhmet with a look of firm resolve. "Go! You're the crown prince! There is no other!!"

Bending down, Hara wrapped the severed strap of Nebehet's pack around one hand and fisted it tightly before tossing it over her shoulder. "Rakhmet, we need. To. **Go.**"

She wrenched Rakhmet away from Nebehet with her other and started dragging him toward the forest line, his feet faltering underneath him as everything in him screamed to turn back and save his friend. But when he looked over his shoulder, he could see the two soldiers gaining on them with their swords out as they charged.

Moving out of instinct, Rakhmet twisted to pull Hara's zulfiqar out of the holster at her waist and flicked his hand out to light the blade like he had seen her do. It immediately rose to his call, the glow incredibly bright as he swung it behind him in a smooth arc. He launched the flame to impact right at the plum figures' feet, helping him and Hara put some distance between them as they sprinted toward the trees.

He gasped, the tightness in his chest unbearable as he caught a glimpse of Nebehet swarmed by two plum soldiers just as a group of guards emerged from the nearby door. One wearing burgundy and two wearing heavy leather royal armor met the remaining two with a clash of blades, but Rakhmet was forced to draw his attention back to the soldiers pursuing him and Hara as one aimed a crossbow at them.

The bolt released, whizzing by his head to impact with a thud in the trunk of a tree just as he and Hara finally reached the edge of the forest. Hara immediately dashed into the foliage, starting an evasive pattern as she wove her way through the trees in order to avoid further bolts.

Seeing one last opportunity for a clear shot, Rakhmet hurled a final fireball at the two soldiers to push them even farther away, then he and Hara laid on the speed.

His heart battered his ribs, thrashing from one emotion to the next. He couldn't believe he was leaving Nebehet behind. Everything was screaming at him to turn back, but his legs had a mind of their own as he was pulled behind in Hara's wake. Her grip was like iron on his wrist, as if she could also hear the war going on inside him.

He was failing again. He was failing everyone, yet she still wouldn't let him go.

They leapt over downed trunks and dodged around overgrown bushes, climbing higher and higher into the foothills while the sounds of their pursuers diminished and eventually disappeared entirely. But they didn't dare slow down as they mounted boulders and ascended up and up until the true mountain landscape began, an expanse of sheer cliff faces and outcroppings all in a dusty red color.

There were patches of vegetation here and there, mostly concentrated around the creeks that carved through the rock, and the mosaic of muted greens and browns was growing harder and harder to make out in the falling twilight as stars started to peek out of the sky. But eventually, Hara slowed and stopped in the middle of a clump of tall trees.

Glancing around, she put a finger to her lips then gestured up the tree.

His brows furrowed as he desperately searched her shadowed face for any sign of her emotional state. Their breath was ragged, their chests heaving from the adrenaline. He was bursting at the seams. What was going through her mind?

She shook her head, a silent refusal of the question he didn't voice, and pointed up the tree again for emphasis.

He clenched his jaw, swallowing his burning rage, and moved to start climbing the tree. Carefully, he made his way to a midway branch that was thick enough to hold both of them and straddled it. He scooted backward and pressed his back to the trunk, making room for Hara as she quickly joined him.

Pushing the two packs to her front so that she could balance better, Rakhmet wrapped an arm around her waist and held her there while his other hand grasped her unlit zulfiqar against his chest in an effort to hide the gleaming metal between them.

She looked over her shoulder at him, silently urging him to not make a sound until she said so. Her hard gaze conveyed that she would answer his questions later and he was damn well answering hers too.

Biting his lip with a harsh exhale, he leaned back.

Too annoyed.

Too livid.

Too heartsick for this.

They sat for an hour like that, straining to hear any sign of pursuers as the moon rose in the east and bathed the forest in soft light.

And he spent the entire time seething.

At himself. At her. At the plum soldiers. At Seshetu. At Nebehet.

Nebehet.

Brave, loyal, dear Nebehet.

He choked on the memory of his friend's eyes pleading with him to go. To save himself.

He swore internally, an endless tirade inside his head as his teeth ground together. What a total and utter disappointment of a prince he was. The whole thing had been a complete fucking disaster.

As Rakhmet slipped into his twentieth cycle of self-loathing, Hara finally stirred and moved to stretch her legs out. She huffed a bit at her stiff muscles but gritted through it as she slung the packs to her back once again and started to climb down to the ground.

He groaned, following her as his limbs protested, but he soon dropped next to her with only one stumble as he caught himself against the trunk.

"Now what?" he bit at her, the words burning his tongue.

She glared at him for a second, then turned and walked away toward a rock formation to the north of them.

"Hara," he practically growled. When she didn't acknowledge him, he growled again and stalked after her.

She picked her way across a rocky ravine in the cold moonlight, still not saying a word.

"**Hara**," he said louder, grabbing at her ankle as she leapt from one rock to another above him. Missing, he cursed and hefted himself up after her.

She continued around the edge of the larger cliff face where it opened up into a path as it wove its way farther up the mountain. It seemed to be old and unused, but it flattened out enough that Rakhmet was able to jog ahead and finally catch Hara's arm.

"Fuck, Hara, talk to me," he demanded, forcing her to turn toward him.

Her brows were drawn tight as she glowered, her eyes impossibly dark. They stood in the shadows and breathed heavily, each waiting for the other to break first.

"Come on," Rakhmet urged. He ran his free hand over his curls and chewed on his cheek, looking down at her telltale lip curl as fire swirled in his gut.

"Look, I'm fucking devasted here!" he pleaded, his voice rasping and raw. "Nebehet, you just let him—"

"Fuck off, I'm devastated too!" she yelled, a little too loud.

He flinched and her shoulders dropped, rolling back as she tried to get a rein on her temper.

"I didn't 'just let him,' Rakhmet. He told us to go. He knew what he was doing," Hara bit at him, her teeth bared. "We **both** lost people, but we have to. Keep. Moving."

"Hara—" he started.

"No, what we need to do right now is find shelter. We don't have time for your sad, self-centered sack of shit act," she interrupted, yanking her arm from his grip and continuing up the path.

He huffed, stinging from her harsh words in the wake of what had just happened but following her nonetheless. What else could he do? She still carried both of their packs, and at the end of the day, he trusted her completely, even if he didn't always want to. The invisible bond that connected them always overruled and they both knew it.

They trudged on in stony silence until Hara spied a cave tucked into a pile of boulders that would protect them for the night. She insisted on checking it out first before letting him crawl through the triangular opening. It had just enough space for them to each stretch out flat as well as store their packs at their heads. Too cautious to risk lighting a fire, they set up their bedrolls and Hara passed him a ration.

Chewing on the dense biscuit, he searched for a way to open their overdue conversation as Hara studied her hands.

"I didn't sleep with Raia or Nebehet," he blurted, wincing at himself.

Hara glanced up at him, her face giving away nothing. "I know."

"Then why are you mad at me?"

"I'm not—" Hara started, but Rakhmet shot her a look.

She glanced away. He could barely see her in the dark, just the occasional flash of white teeth and gold bands, but her voice was thick with emotion.

"I'm mad about a lot of things." She sighed, her breath catching. "I don't . . . I didn't think you were taking any of this seriously enough. Rushing into plans. Not considering the risks."

He closed his eyes against the pain as she gently stoked his doubts, her voice soft yet piercing.

"You were acting like an ass last night and you know it," she grumbled, still not looking at him. "So, yes, I was mad. Am mad. Because tonight . . . I saw my fears come true."

Her words echoed in the space around them, and he tried to swallow the knot in his throat but failed as the ration suddenly became much too dry. He coughed, the half-chewed bits falling to the ground.

His words of defense fell flat before they even stood a chance because she was only confirming what he already knew.

It was him. He was the ruination of all that he touched.

Setting the biscuit aside, he didn't answer but let Hara think he had fallen asleep as he slumped there and gritted his jaw against the searing, undeniable truth.

DAY FIVE

Dawn rose morose and bleak, a light fog nestled into the base of the red mountain where their lonely cave sat tucked away. The sharp edges of Rakhmet's anger had been ground down by a night of little to no sleep, his thoughts circling endlessly as he listened to the sound of Hara's uneasy breaths. He didn't have to see her bloodshot eyes to know that her night had been as restful as his.

Begrudgingly chewing on his leftover ration, he waited for her to say something as she packed her bedroll away, but couldn't help himself as he exploded.

"We have to go back," he demanded.

Hara continued what she was doing without looking at him. "We can't."

"Are you fucking mad? We have to go back!"

"No."

"Hara, for fuck's sake!" He stood from where he had been hunched on a small boulder by the mouth of the cave, throwing his ration to the ground. "We can't just leave them!"

She finally met his eye, straightening and placing her hands on her hips. "It's obviously not safe there. We have no idea if our guards survived and what state the Hapimose forces are in. If we go back, it will be us versus who knows how many soldiers in plum."

"Then we go to another town, gather more forces," Rakhmet argued.

"The warlord's fighters could very well be made up of people from neighboring towns. I said we needed more information. I said we needed to wait until we knew more about him . . . but here we are. We have to work with what we've got." Hara bit the words out, each syllable dripping with blame.

"Oh, fuck off with your 'I said this' and 'I said that.'" He mimicked her in a high-pitched voice. "You act like you're some fortune teller or something!"

She scoffed, rolling her eyes at his mocking tone. "No, I'm just smart enough to ask for help when I need it."

"Great, now you're doubting my intelligence?" He glowered at her.

"Yeah, after some of the shit I've seen you pull just in the last few days, let alone the last few years, I think I've earned the right to question if I was in my right mind when I chose to oath myself to your worthless ass for life."

He winced at the force of her blow and shot back at her, "Fuck you, I'm trying here! I'm trying to do the right thing!"

"Might I remind you that **I'm** the one that went to Tusi and found us the information and allies we needed? That **I'm** the one that went to our temple with them and cleared it and got your powers back? That **I'm** the one the Fire God granted his boons to?" She jammed her finger into her chest for emphasis then pointed it at his face. "And yet you still don't listen to me!!"

"What are you talking about? I was fucking injured for all of that! Or don't you remember the godsdamn explosion that turned me into this . . . this . . . disaster of a human being?!"

"Right, like you were doing all that much with your life before. What with all the moping around and moaning about losing your blessing. You weren't doing jack shit about anything, just hiding in your room all day! Then we get word from the Rutrulans about the temples being corrupted and suddenly you're all gung ho about it because you finally get the chance to be a hero?" Hara threw her hands up in frustration. "Well, surprise surprise, you managed to fuck it all up again!"

Rakhmet staggered backwards, stunned by the vitriol in her expression and hurt by the accusations. "I wasn't—"

"No," she interrupted him. "You're not allowed to have a say anymore. Out here, it's just you and me. No one else. And out here, what I say goes because you obviously cannot be trusted with making decisions for us anymore. People are dead because of you. Layla is—"

She choked, unable to finish the sentence, and turned away to wrap her arms around her torso. Her shoulders shuddered for a moment as she attempted to gather herself, his own insides falling to pieces from her barbs.

Their chests heaved, their harsh breaths moving wisps of the fog that surrounded them, and Rakhmet struggled in vain to find the words. Her accusations were terrifyingly accurate, and he couldn't summon a shred of defense against them.

She eventually cleared her throat, turning her head to the side to address him without looking at him directly. "We are better off heading farther into Talegartia than wandering the border. I don't want to take any more chances."

"We could get help," he tried again, his own voice wavering from the doubt burning through him. "We can send word to Zahar, ask them to send support."

"Almost all of our resources are going to the Staroh coast right now for the fight against Nalliendra. They won't be able to spare anyone without leaving themselves vulnerable. That's why we specifically chose royal guards to accompany us—not military." Hara sighed long and hard, her own anger abating in the face of their immediate problems. "Plus, where would we find a pigeon station? The nearby towns aren't safe. News of the attack will have spread by now, and the capitol will hear of it soon anyway."

She unfolded her arms and rubbed at the back of her neck, staring out across the blanketed forest in front of them. "The warlord didn't get to you, which was probably his main target. He likely wanted you for ransoming or negotiating with the king. It would've given him a massive amount of leverage."

"But now they have Nebehet." Rakhmet followed her reasoning, a nightmare unfolding in front of him.

"If he's even still . . ." She didn't finish the thought, but they both knew what she was thinking. The warlord would have Nebehet for leverage now, if he was still alive.

He buckled and sank back down to the boulder, bracing his elbows on his knees and dropping his head into his hands. He was absolutely heartsick thinking about what fate could have befallen his childhood friend. Glimpses of his smiling face and eager gaze flashed through Rakhmet's mind and twisted the knife in his gut further. His throat clogged, his eyes watering from the force of emotion as he moaned his grief.

Nebehet. Poor, dear Nebehet.

And Layla.

And all his guards that had thrown themselves into the fray without hesitation.

All of the people that he was responsible for.

All of the promises he had made to their families.

Was Samira still alive? Or the cheerful, teasing Rami?

A few tears escaped and splattered on the dusty ground in front of him as he fought for control.

It was all his fault.

The silence was tense as he wrestled with his demons, trying to swallow back the inferno of hurt and guilt that blazed within him, but Hara spoke first.

"We'll take a less-traveled path, one of the animal trails." She had softened her voice, speaking to him as if he were a skittish horse that might bolt at the first sign of threat. "We'll stay away from the pass, but we'll have to keep an eye out for predators. It's not uncommon for wayward travelers to die by beast out here."

She waited for him to contribute to her plan, but he kept his face buried in his hands, salty wetness seeping through his fingers.

"As much as I have a deep respect for our fellow countrymen, I trust the apolitical mountains, trees, and waterways more than the questionable loyalties of the people in the surrounding region right now," Hara continued after a few moments. "I'd rather fight a couple of rabid wolves than a warlord's army."

She cleared her throat, a sign that she, too, was struggling to keep her emotions at bay as she reasoned through a tentative plan. Rakhmet could sense her hard gaze but still couldn't bring himself to meet it.

"We'll aim for a border town on the Talegartia side. We need to stay inconspicuous, but we can restock our supplies and find a pigeon to send to Zahar." He heard movement as Hara fastened her pack. "I've removed the royal crests from our armor and I'm not going to wear my bands anymore."

That was what made him finally look up, noticing for the first time that morning that her hair was not in its usual sleek top bun but instead in a long braid that lay heavy across her shoulder. He scraped at his face to remove any remaining signs of tears and considered the impact of what she was saying.

They had no idea how many people were out there right now looking for a runaway prince and his royal guard, and they would have to remain as anonymous as possible until they could get confirmation of safety. He glanced down at himself, feeling oddly exposed yet almost liberated at the removal of his princely trappings, but his attention caught on the mottled skin on the back of his left hand.

"You'll have to cover your scars with a cloak, but I don't imagine we'll be seeing many people until we cross over into Talegartia," Hara added, sensing where his thoughts had trailed. He nodded absently, his head sluggish. A cottony numbness started filling him and he blinked up at her slowly, trying to string together a suitable response.

"Okay," he finally managed to croak.

Her brows creased, her own pain flickering in her dark gaze as she looked at him with a mix of pity and anger. She was very obviously not happy with him, but she hadn't left him to die either. He couldn't even summon up the optimism to call it a win.

When she sighed again and picked up her pack, he instinctively mirrored her and stood to strap his own on his back. Then, he followed her silently as she set a course up a steep path to the north, like a kit following its mother.

She was survival. She was life.

So he followed.

Minute after minute, hour after hour, they trudged through a landscape of towering red rock formations that dominated all they could see with their jagged peaks and steep cliffs, casting dramatic shadows that matched his mood. In the deep ravines, layers of sedimentary rock revealed the passage of centuries. Each stratum featured a different shade of red or orange, creating a mesmerizing contrast to the flat desert lands they had grown up in, and as they gradually ascended, the fog dissipated so that the panoramic views could unfold even more, revealing valleys, canyons, and distant peaks bathed in the cold winter sun.

The air was crisp and clean, tinged with the earthy aroma of mineral-rich soil, and the wind whispered through narrow crevices, but Rakhmet hardly noticed. His head was full of noise, his heart weighted to the pit of his stomach. How could he have let everyone down so utterly, totally, and irrevocably? How had he ended up in this hell?

The accident at Furaro's temple had been his final transformation, the consummation of his destiny.

A monster he had truly become.

Inside and out.

Every decision that had laid his path in stone mocked and taunted him now.

Even before the incident, he had known that he needed to change. He had been well aware of the fact that he couldn't keep on going like he had been, in a never-ending cycle of avoidance and distraction. He had always thought that the problem was outside himself, that there was something else behind his misery, but getting burned half to death had put it all into stark clarity. He was the true rot.

Hara had been the one to carry his ruined body back to the palace by herself after doing as much temporary on-field wrapping and mending as possible. She had been the one to step up and take charge in an emergency, just like she had at the Hapimose estate.

All he did was make things worse, just like he always had.

There had been too many nights to count where he had been a drunken mess, too high on whatever he could find and whomever he could fall into bed with, if there had even been a bed to be found. He had fucked people in alleys, on roofs, in front of complete strangers he had happened to stumble upon, cheered along by Khenti and the lovers that trailed behind him like the pied piper, each one more eager than the last to get a piece of the playboy prince and his hedonist friends.

He had always made sure to take preventative herbs to avoid siring any unwanted heirs in the process, but that was the bare minimum he could do as he had spread his seed far and wide. In mouths, in asses, on faces and breasts. He had left lovers strewn about like used tissues, draped over furniture that had been overturned in their flashpan passion and forgotten just as quickly. And Hara was always the one to pick him up and drag him back to the palace.

One night had been the worst, though, when he had been introduced to a new sort of drug, one that had made him hallucinate things that hadn't been there. The walls and floors had simply melted away, leaving only a sea of naked bodies undulating before him. At first, it had been exhilarating. He had fallen upon them with ravenous excitement, sucking and licking at every inch of skin available to him. Wet, warm slits and thick, proud staffs. Deliciously round hips and pounding thrusts that had his back bowing with intense need.

The sensations had become a riot of vibrant colors that had dazzled him, leaving him moaning and gasping for more as hands had trailed along his limbs and tongues had lapped at his skin, but a door had crashed open and the party had suddenly been interrupted by some very angry

CLAIRE E. JONES

individuals. To this day, he still didn't know whether they were hired guards or aggrieved landlords or scorned spouses, but he had reacted out of instinct, drawing his blessing to his fingertips without a thought.

Hara had tackled him immediately, not even caring about the state of undress he had been in, and had even knocked over a candelabra in the process to explain the unexpected burst of fire that had emerged from him. There had been heat and screaming and the sounds of people panicking as he had fought against her weight, but she had held on like a bull rider, pinning his arms to his sides and wrestling him toward the open courtyard door.

She had murmured in his ear like a soothing lullaby as she had pulled him away, calming him until he had realized that it was her and suppressed the flames that had been licking up the sides of the room all on their own. Luckily, everyone else had been able to get out before things had gotten really bad, but the damage to the house had ended up being in the range of tens of thousands of gold pieces.

After getting Rakhmet home and into a cold bath, where he had sobered up quickly, she had explained everything that had gone down, and the next day, he had anonymously sent the hosts enough money to cover it all as his own penance. That had been one of the only times that he had seen the disappointment clearly written on Hara's face as she had made sure he had gotten into his bed before retiring to her own.

But the look on her face now was ten times worse, and once again, he only had himself to blame. He was the shit on the bottom of her boot, the bloodstain that refused to wash out, the monster that curled around her shoulders and left burns in its wake. People were cold and dead because of him.

They trekked into the mountains in grim silence, trail running when they could. They only slowed when they came to sections of cliff face they had to scale carefully, opting for speed just in case the warlord sent soldiers after them.

Rakhmet let his scorching self-loathing drive him forward, keeping his eyes trained on Hara's back as she led the way. It seemed like they had each made an internal decision to stay the accusations of blame that were swirling inside both of them, and Rakhmet suspected it was because Hara was feeling just as fragile as he was in the wake of losing everyone. They had no idea what had happened to his guards, the Hapimoses, and the rest of their people who hadn't been slaughtered immediately.

Layla's and Nebehet's faces, in particular, plagued him ceaselessly, and he knew he wasn't the only one haunted by ghosts. He could see the strain in Hara's eyes, the puffiness of her skin, the tension in her shoulders. Both knew that their hurts, angers, and animalistic needs for revenge were still too sharp to let fall from their lips in the light of day. To admit to the relentless burn would cause their precious grasp on a plan to go up in flames.

What they would do once they reached safety was a discussion for another time. They had to focus on getting through the mountains first, which was a more than treacherous endeavor in itself, so they hustled on and on into the chilling heights, taking smaller trails to the north instead of the wider and more popular pass. The air was biting cold this far up and their cloaks flapped in the rushing wind, but they kept their leather armor on just in case, adding an additional tunic underneath to keep their sweating bodies just warm enough. It took everything within him to just keep going mile after mile, his hope for redemption slipping away piece by piece.

DAY SIX

I t was a particularly rough day, their cheeks stinging and breaths coming in sharp pants as they ascended a steep ravine. Snow was all around them this far up, piled in the crevices and growing thicker the farther they climbed. Having grown up in the dry heat of the desert, it was a type of weather that they were not particularly familiar with, and Rakhmet's hands had started to crack in the seeping cold.

Yet, his turbulent emotions were more than enough of a distraction.

Seemingly in staunch opposition to the furnace of angst that burned within him, flurries started around midday and fell gently from the gray sky as Rakhmet and Hara eventually crested the cliff, finding themselves in a sheltered cranny between two towering peaks.

Rakhmet begged for a brief rest, coming to a stop. His body was really not happy with him after running on a diet of rations and restless sleep on the chilly ground. Heart, body, and soul groaned in protest.

"Hara, please," he rasped.

She halted, her chin dipping in silent agreement as she braced her hands on her hips and caught her breath but didn't meet his eye. She stared into the distance, her face hard, and Rakhmet's already bruised heart rattled louder in his chest. His grief overpowering him, he sank to his knees and let his pack fall to the side as his head hung like a sack of flour from his shoulders.

His chest heaved, partially from the exercise and partially from the onslaught of frustrated tears that clogged his throat. He swallowed and swallowed again, forcing them back.

"I'm just . . . so tired." He moaned, the edge of desperation leaking into his voice.

Hara huffed drily and dropped her pack next to his, refusing to acknowledge his pity party.

He looked up, taking her in as she stood above him with an almost menacing expression. Her brows were drawn and she scowled at him exactly as he deserved, the telltale lip curl now a permanent feature. They both knew the truth: he was the fuckup. Always was and always would be.

His mouth opened to appease her, the instinctual need to have her on his side again a fierce, starving hunger.

"Don't start," she gritted out, interrupting him. Her eyes blazed with fury, all of the emotions from the past week threatening to erupt in her too.

"Please, Hara . . . ," he whined, unable to help himself. He had lost everything and needed her forgiveness almost as much as he needed air to breathe. He knew he had no right to ask for her grace, yet he ached nonetheless.

"**Don't**," she repeated, the harsh exhale brooking no argument.

"You can't do that," Rakhmet argued, struggling to his feet. Senseless fury burst from him as he advanced on her, his finger pressing into her shoulder. "You can't shut me down anymore. We have to get this out."

"Get what out, Rakhmet?" Hara shot back, shoving against him. "You want to talk about it? Fine, let's talk about it. Let's talk about the fact that I fucking warned you about all of this and you didn't do shit about it!"

Rakhmet winced. "You didn't—I didn't . . . There was no way we could have known, Hara. It's not like I **wanted** any of this!"

"You never listen to me!" Hara got up in his face again, her teeth bared. It was the same accusation she had lobbed at him the night his father had announced Nasima's crown. The fight that had caused her to avoid him for two whole weeks. "You never have! I told you that you were rushing into things and yet you DID IT ANYWAY!"

It was her turn to poke him in the shoulder. "We could've waited, gathered more information. But no, you wanted to be the hero! Your godsdamn pride has blinded you!"

"My **pride**?! Fuck that," Rakhmet snarled. "You know as well as I do that I don't have any fucking pride, that this was my one chance to prove that I wasn't a total waste of space! And as per usual, it all went to absolute and utter shit. I'm the failure I've always been. People are dead and Nebehet is gone! All because of ME!!"

He shouted the last word, and it echoed across the stone surfaces around them, throwing it back into his face.

"Well, at least we both know who is to blame here . . . ," Hara growled, her pain obvious, and Rakhmet fell back, astonished at the naked statement.

It pierced him to hear her say it in such stark terms and he groaned without realizing it, his arm coming to cradle his stomach as if he had been physically wounded. Swaying and stunned, he watched as regret flickered across her face and her anger burned away, leaving deep sadness in its wake.

She took a soft breath and reached for him. "Rakhmet . . ."

"No, I—" he started to refute but stopped midsentence as the sound of low growls echoed around them. They both whipped their heads around and spotted two massive snow cats prowling toward them, trapping them on either side.

Hara breathed out a string of curses, unsheathing her weapons as Rakhmet mirrored her. They instantly turned their backs to one another, each focusing on a cat as they slowly circled. This was exactly a situation they had been hoping to avoid. With steep drop-offs on either side, there wasn't a lot of room, but he and Hara instinctively kept the two cats separated and distracted.

The creatures struck first, swiping at their legs to test their reflexes as Hara and Rakhmet broke apart to engage their targets. Rakhmet kept his daggers tucked close to his torso, only lashing out once he got an opening at the cat's flank as he dodged its initial attacks. He barely saw Hara dancing and weaving out of the corner of his eye as he was chased across the cranny in a sideways shuffle.

He jabbed once then twice, slicing into his cat's thick white fur before getting thrown to the ground by one massive paw. He impacted with a grunt and its claws dug into his side as he gritted his teeth. It pounced on top of him, eager to press the advantage as he braced one arm against its neck while the other batted away its swipes at him, but he wasn't entirely successful as he felt more gashes score into his forearm and bicep.

Luckily, his armor was thick enough to keep it from piercing through to his torso, but its heavy body weight was keeping him pinned in place as he struggled beneath it. He heard Hara grunting and panting as she fought with the other and his frustration doubled. Switching tactics, he sheathed his daggers and blindly reached out for the flame he knew would be on Hara's blade.

Finding it, he latched on and drew it to his hands then shoved the flaming digits into the beast's face to momentarily blind it. It cringed away, and he rolled to a kneel, spreading his hands wide to lock around its neck. He couldn't reach around the entire thing, but he got enough of a grip on the furry folds to wrench it backward as he pushed to a stand. The cat screeched and reared back on its hind legs, seeking distance from the heat as the smell of burning hair and flesh filled the air. At its full height, Rakhmet was startled to discover that it was a head above him, but he gritted his jaw and kept going.

He shoved it farther and farther, slamming it to the ground as he muscled it onto its back. It was yowling loudly now, doing its best to squirm away from his hot grip as he straddled it. Using a leg to hold down one of its front paws, he released one of his hands from its neck and palmed Nebehet's gift from his waist. He brought it up in a tall arc before sinking it into its neck all the way to the pommel, twisting and pulling it out through the side in one brutal movement.

The cat spasmed, its lifeblood spurting out onto the ground in thick bursts as Rakhmet turned in time to see the other cat lunge and bite Hara in the hip, just below her armor. Its fangs sliced through her, leaving two long, ragged tears in her flesh, and her cry was pure agony, ripping from her throat and causing Rakhmet's blood to run cold.

He scrambled across the space, his legs churning to get there as the cat fell upon her, and managed to shove his still flaming hands into the fur on its back right as its head reared up again, sharp white canines flashing red. Gripping tightly, he urged his heat to burn into it and tackled it to the side as it violently protested and tried to buck him off. They rolled and rolled, each fighting to get on top, but Rakhmet caught them by jerking out a leg to brace against a boulder as he realized that they were heading for the edge of the cliff, abruptly halting their bruising tumble at the last second.

Hollering, the cat twisted this way and that, trying to get at Rakhmet, who held onto its back with his red-hot hands buried in its singed fur. The smell was absolutely awful, choking him as he wrestled for control, but he finally managed to pin it down with his other leg and palm his dagger once again.

With a wrenching motion, he shoved the blade deep into its ribcage and cleaved its side open. It tried to cringe away, sounds of panicked desperation coming from its throat, and it gave Rakhmet enough leverage to plunge the metal into it again, this time in the throat as its cries turned into gasping gurgles. Instantly letting go of it, he spun to where Hara was slumped on the ground surrounded by a pool of blood and fell forward, trying to get to her.

His knees landed painfully, sharp rocks cutting into him as his feet tangled with the still twitching paws of the dying creature underneath him, and his rapidly cooling hands sizzled as they reached the edge of liquid leaking out around Hara. She tried to push herself up, her face pinched and elbows wobbling as she strained, and he extracted himself, rushing to her. He threw his dagger to the side and cupped her cheeks streaked with tears, blood, and dirt.

"Shh, shh, it's okay," he tried to soothe her, his voice shaking. "I've got you."

He glanced down at her wounds, eyeing the two bloody tears stretching from her left hip to the middle of her lower back. The teeth had cut through the fabric of her clothing and the blood was soaking through the majority of her outfit. She groaned and collapsed, giving up on her struggle to sit up.

"Shit, shit, shit," Rakhmet muttered, rapidly running through their options in his head. He had to get that wound cleaned and wrapped up. There was no way they could continue until she was taken care of.

His mind raced through his medical knowledge. Thank the gods he had actually paid attention during all those lessons with the royal physicians when he had been younger. Field medicine was something he never thought he would need, but he had found the subject a fascinating change of pace compared to the hours and hours spent on memorizing obscure historical and political facts with his other tutors.

He had even had the forethought to brush up a bit on the subject before leaving, knowing that he would be spending quite a few weeks on the road with his guards. Of course, he had assumed that he would have access to helping hands and plenty of supplies, but he knew, at the very least, they needed hot water, sterile wraps, and a way to stitch her up. As soon as possible.

Rakhmet looked around. He could certainly use the snow, but he would need to melt it, which meant he needed a fire. And he didn't want to do this out in the open. Gods knew what kinds of other creatures were lurking out there. He had a feeling that the cats' corpses would draw the other carnivorous animals out, the ones that would see him and Hara for exactly what they were: injured prey. He had to find shelter, fast.

"Wait here, don't move," Rakhmet ordered Hara, squeezing her hand once before standing. She let out a strained huff in response, the exhalation turning into a lingering groan as her fists clenched open and closed.

He hurried over to the cat corpses, grunting as he gripped them tightly and hefted them over to the cliff edges, then he pushed them over one at a time, watching as they rolled to the bottom and making sure they landed far enough away. There were still massive smears of blood everywhere, but at least the meat was now farther away from them.

Quickly sheathing his dagger and gathering their packs, he strapped both to the front of him then kneeled in front of Hara, who was still gritting through the pain as she fought to keep her breaths even.

"I'm going to have to carry you, and it's going to hurt. I'm sorry."

He waited for a response as she slowly craned her neck to look him in the eye. There was a moment where he watched her try to grasp a thread of logic, some sort of contribution to this plan he was presenting, but she failed as the burn of pain coursed through her. She relented with a slight nod, her body going loose as she gave control up to him.

"It's going to be okay," he murmured as he turned around and started to pull one of her arms up onto his shoulder. She whimpered as the movements stretched her wounds, and he continued the soft thread of encouragements and reassurances as he situated her onto his back with her arms looped around his neck and shoulders. He stooped a little so that her feet dangled, bearing her full weight, then started toward the boulders to the southwest that would get them up to the next section of the trail they were following.

He gripped her forearms tightly, and she held on as best as she could as he picked his way across the rocks, moving as swiftly as he dared and keeping an eye out for caves hidden in the cliff faces that surrounded them. It took a while, nervous sweat dripping down his temples as Hara pressed her face against his shoulder and groaned with every jarring step he took. Her breath kept hitching, speeding away from her in bursts before she was able to rein it back in as she fought the throbbing discomfort.

Eventually, Rakhmet spied an opening that was just above them and let out a rough exhale as he hustled toward it. He had to scale the side of a boulder and climb over an outcropping of red cliff, grimacing as Hara objected to the jerky movements, but brought them into a relatively protected recess that widened into a cavity in the mountainside that was about six by eight feet across. The ceiling was low enough that he wouldn't be able to stand at his full height, but that was the least of his concerns at the moment.

He shuffled inside, gently dropping to his knees to shift Hara from his back to the ground and set the packs to the side. Immediately, he studied her wounds again as she settled on her stomach with another strained sigh and checked to see if the journey had torn anything else open.

She was still bleeding, but the flow seemed to be slowing. That was a good thing, right? He thought so. He hoped so.

Reaching out, he sent a silent prayer to his god and held her cheek for a moment as she panted. His thumb brushed along her jaw and tilted it so that her bloodshot gaze met his. "It's going to be okay."

Her eyes squeezed shut, but she managed a tight nod that reassured him enough to turn back to their packs. He focused on breathing deeply, willing his hands to stop shaking as he pulled out a blanket and laid it flat. As he lifted Hara onto it with care, she twisted her head to the side with a groan and found a position that gave him easy access to her back.

"There's—" she croaked, her voice breaking in the cold quiet of the cave. "There's medicine . . . in the med kit . . . for pain. Brown glass."

He located the bottle easily, his hands steadier once given instructions, and held it up to her. "This?"

Her chip dipped. "R-redan flower."

Ah, right. He remembered the bright yellow bloom from his textbooks. The petals were crushed and distilled to create a potent extract that was used for pain management. Ingesting one drop of the liquid provided mild relief, two drops produced an effect similar to heavy intoxication, and three would knock a patient out for five to seven hours. The vial he held was small, the dropper necessary in order to dispense the exact amount needed.

Digging through the pack again, he found one of their tin cups and a waterskin. He carefully poured an ounce of water into the cup then set it on the ground as he unscrewed the vial of redan flower extract. He added two drops of medicine, choosing not to put her to sleep just yet since he still needed to collect some firewood to melt snow for sterile water and didn't want to leave her alone and completely unconscious.

"Here." He kneeled in front of Hara and held the cup to her lips, using his free hand to guide her chin so that nothing spilled. She drank it in one gulp then eased back down, her lids shut tight as she waited for the relief.

It didn't take long for her breaths to slow, her face slackening as her body relaxed. She let out an extended exhale and almost smiled as her eyes blinked open. The barest of smirks told Rakhmet that she felt a sense of triumph over the racking pain that had been harrying her, and he couldn't help but return it as her sluggish gaze found him. His own breath eased, some of his anxiety melting away with hers.

Pressing two fingers to the pulse in her neck, he waited for a few moments as they stared at each other in silence. He counted the beats of her heart as it neared a normal pace, and even though they weren't speaking, her dark eyes bored into his. Somehow, it seemed like they were saying more to each other than they had for years. Apologies and explanations that were truly overdue flickered into the empty space between them like a welcoming blaze filling a fireplace long gone cold. Too much time had passed since they were completely honest with each other.

When they had been younger, everything had been shared between them. Toys, food, armor, weapons, books, friends, secrets, dreams, fears. Everything.

But that had all changed once his parents had started pressuring him to get serious about the Crown. They had been perfectly willing to let him have fun in his youth, but they had eventually grown impatient when his bawdy extracurriculars had continued year after year. Because up until that point, he had been very pointedly unserious about it all. He had spent the entirety of his teens and early twenties gallivanting around town with Khenti and the other ne'er-do-wells they had picked up along the way. And Hara had followed every step.

As his oathed guard, she had trailed after him in taverns and manors, brothels and slums, anywhere he could seek out heat, excitement, and distraction like a moth. Whenever he had snuck out of the palace, she had been right there beside him. Whenever he had ended up in someone's bed, she had been waiting outside the door. Whenever he had been riding the high of drugs and liquor, she had been watching over him.

It was her duty and she performed it willingly, although it had earned him quite a few eye rolls and scoffs over the years. He had even considered it a secret game of his, trying to get a reaction out of her with his antics. The rare moments he was able to break through her facade and make her laugh, even if it was at his expense, were dearly cherished, stored away in the depths of his being like jewels coveted by a dragon.

Then, on the eve of his twenty-seventh birthday, his parents had informed him that they were calling on him to step up to his rightful place. He was now expected to attend all court meetings and start holding formal office hours just as the king did, actively participating in the palace's political dealings. The new schedule had severely limited his ability to get out into the city, but he had made it work, his leisure activities becoming a sort of therapy for him in order to cope with the increased demands. It also meant he had had to start keeping secrets. He had begun sneaking around, leaving Hara behind in favor of being invisible, and at first, she had let him stay hidden. She had seen how much his royal responsibilities weighed on him and understood why he sought relief in the night.

But his and his father's powers had started fading a year later and the pressure had only intensified. Their biggest secret of all had been coming unraveled at the edges and there had been nothing any of them could do about it. The royal family had done their best to present a unified front to the court and public at large, but tempers had flared when they had been in private.

As he had withdrawn more and more, Hara had tried to keep him grounded. He pulled and she pushed. He pushed and she pulled. She wanted to tether him; he wanted to escape.

The night of the big storm, the one that had stolen his powers entirely, had broken his will and shattered him. So much so that poor Hara had been left guarding a pile of jagged pieces. A talented, loyal, respectable guard reduced to the keeper of an empty husk of a man. He had felt like a walking corpse, haunting the halls of the palace in blind search of a purpose. A mute puppet—the strings had moved his limbs for him, but no awareness had been behind his eyes.

It hadn't been until they had received word from the water blessed regarding the corruption of their temple that he had finally roused out of his stupor. That nudge had been the catalyst for everything, reigniting the embers one by one. It was what had led them down this perilous road they now walked, and he could only pray that it wouldn't lead to what he feared most in this world. A fear he only recently realized was nestled deep within him like a bur. One he couldn't yet voice.

Once he was satisfied that Hara was stable, he leaned back and dug through the packs for the two small camping pots they carried and moved to the mouth of the cave. He looked back once, his nod letting her know that he would be back soon, and exited into the biting mountain air.

The snow was picking up so he didn't dally as he located enough wood to start a fire and a pile of clean white powder to scoop into the pots. He hurried back to the cave and fell into a meditative state as he watched his hands from afar, carefully building a makeshift rock oven of sorts and stoking a fire underneath it. He then pulled out a block of soap and cleaned his hands and forearms thoroughly before grabbing whatever bandages they had packed and tearing one of their extra tunics into strips. Once the water was boiling, he took the pots off the flame and immersed his instruments in them to sterilize.

Moving to Hara's side, he gently removed her top layers and folded her pants down a few inches to give him clear access to her wounds. He left her bandeau on and grimaced at the smears of dried blood across her taut brown skin, grinding his jaw at the two deep cuts. It looked as if the cat's teeth had pierced deepest in the middle of the slash, tearing through the muscle that sat just above the back of her pelvis bone.

He glanced back up at her face, studying the glaze in her eyes as she absently stared at the fire. Patching her up wasn't going to be a painless task, but it had to be done.

"Hara?" he ventured softly as her gaze moved to him with the languid crawl of molasses. "I'm going to give you another drop of the extract. You don't want to be awake for this. Okay?"

There was a pause and then she nodded, closing her eyes as she submitted. He quickly measured out another mix in the tin cup then held it to her lips, and she accepted the liquid without complaint. A few minutes and she was out like a light, her chest rising and falling evenly.

117

Rakhmet cleared his throat then got to work.

First, he poured a bottle of tonic over the whole area and rinsed it out as much as he could, then scrubbed his hands with soap once again. Pulling his now sterile instruments out from the pots, he settled next to Hara and began the awful process of sewing her closed—one bloody slash at a time.

She had been the one to care for his wounds after the incident at Furaro's temple, but now he was the one to attend to hers. It took forever since he kept having to rinse the needle and his fingers clean whenever her blood made things too slippery to grip, which meant he had to scrub down with soap each time. The blanket beneath them was soon soaked with red and pink, the torn knees of his pants staining as he hunched over her. He used as much of their supplies as he dared, all too aware that they might be screwed if either of them was injured later on in their journey.

After what seemed like an eternity, the wounds were finally sealed up and he slumped backward, giving himself a breather before moving onto the cleaning and wrapping stages. The stitching was uneven, but he had done his best, singularly focused on the woman in front of him. He vaguely wondered how much time had passed, attempting to calculate how much longer he had before she woke up again, but her bloody and unconscious body was all he was aware of as his heart pounded through him.

His breaths hitched nervously as the tremors came back to his hands and he shook his head, unwilling to let his emotions get the best of him until he was finished with his duty to her. He used some more of the sterile water to rinse her off then washed the blood off his hands once more.

Finding a container of antibacterial salve, he gingerly spread it over the cuts then layered the clean bandages on top. He finished by wrapping the tunic strips around her waist, holding everything in place. Their bedrolls were laid out on the other side of the cave, and he tenderly moved her to them so that he could take care of the mess he had made. Folding her arms into his last clean tunic and tucking her in with the remaining blanket, he took the soiled one and her bloody clothes outside the cave with the leftover water to rinse and scrub until most of the discoloration was gone.

He gathered more snow to melt then came back inside and finally attended to his own wounds. There was one deep slice in his right deltoid and one across the top of his left forearm, so he sewed them up as best he could at the awkward angles. His knuckles were starting to crack open, stinging in complaint as he washed his hands again, but he couldn't stop just yet. A few more applications of the slave and he wrapped himself in some bandages, his mind utterly blank beyond getting the job done.

More time passed as he gathered enough firewood for the night and snow to refill both of their waterskins, and then, as the sun started to set over the mountains, he melted one last pot full for dinner. He doubted she would be able to tolerate solids, so he broke up and dissolved a block of rations into the water to make a thick porridge, stirring it until the consistency was relatively smooth.

He filled a cup for himself, and only then did he allow himself to finally fall back against the wall in exhaustion, sliding to the ground with a ragged sigh as he waited for her to wake. Shoveling the sustenance into his mouth, he fought the shivers that were threatening to overtake him. It wasn't that he was cold. No, his blessing kept the fire warm enough to keep them protected from the snow outside. It was the bone-deep worry that rattled him, the fraying edges of his resolve that had been powering him through.

Staring intently at her face, he watched for any signs of discomfort. She was his sole lifeline at the moment. The light that shone at the end of the tunnel. There was no way he would be able to get through this journey without her.

She had said that her fears had come true at Seshetu's estate, but here—now—his worst nightmares were rearing their ugly heads.

She stirred and he lurched forward, dropping his empty cup to the side as she groaned softly.

"I'm here, Hara. I'm here." He scrambled over to her, taking her hand in his.

Her face tilted toward his voice, her body shifting slightly as she came to. She groaned again as she became more aware of her injuries and her brows furrowed.

"It's alright. You're alright. Don't move too much," he murmured, stroking a hand on her hair. Some had come loose from the braid and he absently tucked a few sections back in, tidying it a bit as she slowly blinked her eyes open.

He tried to smile reassuringly at her. "How are you feeling?"

She groaned again, this one clearer and more pointed as she reached up to scrub at her face with her knuckles.

It took another moment for her eyes to find his, and she cleared her throat before she could find her voice.

"Thanks," she rasped.

"Of course." His response was immediate. "Of course, Hara."

"It—it's not too bad," she ground out, twisting to relieve some of the stiffness in her body as a few of her joints cracked.

"Don't move too much," he repeated, laying a hand on her shoulder. "Are you hungry? We should get some fuel in you."

She settled into a more comfortable position and nodded. "I think—I think I could eat."

He reached up, smoothing her hair back once more before shuffling over to the pot to grab a serving for her. Bite by bite, he slowly spooned it into her mouth, and she dutifully swallowed it down. She had to take a few pauses near the end but managed to get it all, slumping back to the ground with a heavy sigh as soon as they were done.

Rakhmet was quiet as he took the cups and pot outside to rinse before returning, finding that Hara's eyes had closed again. The wrinkle in her brow was coming back which told him that he needed to give her another dose of the extract.

"Hara, how much pain are you in?" he asked gently, pulling out the vial.

She squinted at him and a low grumble rolled through her chest. "Some. . . I-I suppose quite a bit."

"Two drops? Or do you want three?"

"Two . . . Let's just stick with two." Her voice was weak, but her tight gaze told him everything he needed to know:

she was raw flame on the inside. Turning to ash from the heat of her sensations. But she didn't want to be left entirely unaware of her surroundings.

He nodded, swallowing the thickness in his throat, and measured out the dose with water. Helping her, he poured it down her throat then sat back to keep an eye while it took effect.

Her whole body soon went loose, her tight jaw softening as her mouth popped slightly open and glazed eyes found his. They both breathed, gazing at one another as the tension between them dissipated after too many days and weeks and months of arguments. He almost cried from happiness at the release, his breath catching as he finally found forgiveness and understanding in her expression.

"Rakh-met," she breathed shakily. "I'm— Sorry."

"No." He leaned in and brushed his fingers across her cheek, cupping her jaw like a delicate flower. "No, I'm sorry."

"I-I know . . . you are try-ing." She stumbled over the syllables, her heavy tongue slurring. "I know . . . your heart."

Her words punched him in the lungs as he fought for breath. "Hara, I-I–"

"I was . . . scared," she murmured, the sound so soft that he pitched even closer in order to catch it. Instinct drew him forward as he lay down beside her on the bedrolls, angling toward her and folding one arm under his head. He reached out with his free hand, weaving his fingers through hers.

"*Dearest Hara*," he whispered. Pulling their entwined hands to his face, he turned them so that he could lay the back of her hand to his cheek and held it there as he drank in the sight of her.

"I'm so sorry I led you into this. This—this was never the plan." He rushed to explain himself. "I hate to see you hurt."

Her gaze drunkenly read his features. "When you hurt . . . I hurt . . . my prince."

The last word was a puff of air so slight that he would have missed it if he hadn't been watching her lips as she murmured to him, catching each breathed vowel and consonant as if they were the most precious of gems, and her well of gravity pulled on him until his forehead pressed against hers.

"*My Hara.*" His whisper fluttered the stray hairs resting on the side of her neck and he felt them sweep across their linked fingers, still clasped to his cheek. "*I can't lose you.*"

"*I'm right . . . here,*" she whispered in return, her nose stroking the side of his as if she were soothing him, and the small movement made his diaphragm tighten and twist. He almost groaned at the sensation, the force of it tilting his head so that their lips were almost touching, but he stuttered to a stop at the last moment. Her heavy lids closed, the vulnerability stealing the air from his lungs, and his body strained in vain.

"*Gods above,*" he prayed as his overwhelming need clarified within him. This intense inferno of righteous want was nowhere near the appropriate response, but he could taste the sweet exhalations coming from her, mixing with his nervous pants, and his blood was boiling with vivid certainty.

He trembled, holding himself in place as he wrestled for control. She was injured, compromised, and definitively not sober. Not only that, but she was his guard, his childhood friend, his responsibility. Sure, there was a history of court members hooking up with palace guards from time to time, but Hara was oathed to him for life.

If things went wrong, if this was a mistake . . .

He couldn't even let himself finish the thought. There was nothing he wouldn't do to spare her the embarrassment and shame. He would rather cut off his own leg than make things irreparable between them.

But he was too slow to move and her lips landed on his, sealing his fate before he managed to tug himself away. A moan rumbled through his throat as she pressed in and he was consumed by her. She was soft and firm, yielding and asking in equal measure, and he eagerly matched the ebb and flow of her fire.

Time ceased to exist as he explored her mouth, memorizing the ridges of her teeth and the contours of her tongue. He untangled their fingers and curled his hand around the back of her neck, angling her just how he wanted as her breath caught and she fisted the front of his tunic, tugging him.

She tasted like his salvation, the soft sounds she was making causing his hips to twitch in anticipation, and he wrapped her braid around his hand to pull her closer. As she arched into him, there was a sudden shudder as her side twisted and she cringed back, her sharp inhalation breaking his daze as they broke apart.

Her pain was clear as day, and he dropped her like a hot coal, instantly moving away to give her space as she squeezed her eyes shut and breathed through the ache.

"I-I'm sorry. I didn't mean to . . ." He tried to get his bearings. His eyes caught on her swollen lips, red and juicy from his kisses, and his heart pounded out a riotous beat. His ribs were breaking open as it fought to reach her and terror flashed through him, stark fear seizing him as he waited for her to respond.

He clutched his chest, attempting to keep the shards in, and teetered on the precipice as her breath steadied, her bleary eyes blinking open to find him.

"It's okay," she croaked. "I'm okay."

Her lids lowered again, exhaustion weighing her down as Rakhmet tried to find the words in the haze of his panic. "Hara . . . I . . ."

"Is . . . okay. Just . . . need sleep," she murmured, the words protracted and delayed as she drifted into a deep slumber.

He could almost hear the wind whistling by his ears as if he were out on one of those mountain peaks surrounding them, a steep drop before him. Realization had hit him hard, and he struggled against the novel awareness kindling inside him, the spark of insight that he couldn't unsee.

Without a doubt, he was hers.

Utterly, irrevocably, and most ardently hers.

She was the brightest light in his life, yet all he brought her was slums and scars. All he had to offer her was ashes, falling in the wake of his ruin.

DAY SEVEN

The pale morning light filtering into the cave did nothing to lift Rakhmet's spirits as he started moving about after another restless night and got ready to cook them breakfast. Hara had woken him up once, asking for another dose of redan extract before slipping back into unconsciousness. He, on the other hand, had tossed and turned, unable to ignore the pit of dread in his stomach.

He had no idea what he was going to say to her when she awoke. Would she want to talk about what had happened? Would she even remember it? Did he want her to? As countless questions circled, it was all he could do to pull himself together and dip outside to gather more firewood and refill their pots with snow to melt.

He was stirring another heated mixture over a fresh fire when her eyes finally cracked open, landing on him from the other side of the space. Chewing on his bottom lip, he stayed still as her gaze sharpened and her faculties solidified. Silence stretched for a moment, but his breath caught and the words he had considered burned away as her features shifted, the remembrance of their evening activities becoming visible in the crinkle of her eye and the crease of her brow.

Studying everything her expression was telling him, he knew the exact moment she shut him out and his heart plummeted. She was going to deny him, deny any possibility of what had been given so freely the night before. He knew it without her ever having to utter a single syllable. His eyes dropped to their meal, shoulders slumping forward at the bite of the rejection even though he agreed with the decision.

Nothing good would come of it, and they were both fully aware of that fact.

She was probably the only person who had any clear idea of how many lovers he had left behind over the years, of how many mistakes he had made, of how much of a fuckup he was at his core. She was the only one who recognized who he was behind the facades. This whole journey was a joke, a fanciful illusion of redemption that he had painted in his head with gilded naivety.

He should have left the clearing of the temples to people who actually knew what they were doing. Who did he think he was? A hero?

Gods, he was a fool.

And Hara knew it.

Sighing, he turned to their packs and fished out the bottle of extract. He then poured a bit of water into a cup, pausing with the dropper poised over it.

"How many drops do you want?" he asked, his tone flat as he avoided her eye.

She cleared her throat. "One, for now."

Glancing up in surprise, he caught the message loud and clear: she would rather grit through the pain than succumb to the intoxicating effects with him there. She didn't trust herself around him, and he didn't know what to do with that information.

"Uh, okay." He stalled for a second before catching himself and focusing on the cup in front of him. Adding a drop, he then carried it over to her and helped her get it down before returning to the pot over the fire and pouring out portions for the both of them.

He didn't bother making conversation as his mind tripped from thought to thought, and she stayed quiet, too, as she shifted into a more comfortable position. Sitting down next to her, he carefully monitored as she spooned the porridge into her mouth, and he ate his. Her hands shook ever so slightly, but as to be expected, the weakness from her injuries were no match for her gritted determination.

She had always been the strong one between them, even when she was the damaged party. It made perfect sense. She was and would always be the better of them.

Rakhmet cleared his throat. "I was thinking I would try to hunt something down to eat. I counted our rations and we won't have enough if we keep going at this rate, now that we have to wait for you to heal before we can carry on."

He waited for her response as he gathered up their cups and the pot to take outside and was almost at the mouth of the cave when he heard a short, "Okay," from behind him. He only stopped for a breath before he continued without a glance. If she was going to construct her iron-walled boundaries, he was going to respect them. It was the least he could do.

His mind was spinning through all the small moments between them over the years. The shared jokes and giggling fits when they had been younger, the pleasant ache that he was left with only after a sparring session with her, the way his eyes always found her no matter what room they were in or whom they were with, the agony he was flattened by whenever she avoided him.

It was all too obvious now. He hadn't ever given his heart to someone before because it hadn't been his to give. It was already spoken for, had been for over a decade.

He returned with the cleaned items and set them to the side before grabbing his cloak and daggers. "Will you be alright? I'll try not to take too long."

Hara's expression had eased a bit with the small dose he had given her, but her body was tense as she fought to keep the aches in check. She nodded tightly. "I'll be fine."

"Yell if you need me . . . as loud as you can. I'll stay close," he couldn't help but add as he hesitated.

Hara only nodded again, her dark gaze flickering with passing emotion before it was gone just as quickly.

Dipping his chin, he turned and breached into the harsh wind. It was colder, the snow having piled up overnight, and the gusts were whipping through the mountains at a breakneck pace, but it suited Rakhmet just fine as he tucked his face into his hood. It was relatively easy to keep his own blood warm thanks to his blessing. Plus, the weather seemed to be as bitter as he was at the moment, and he almost smiled at the unlikely companionship he felt.

He chewed over his realizations as he circled the mountain and searched for burrows and dens that could be home for midsized, rodent type animals, the kinds of herbivores that couldn't take a bite out of his flank if he dared to have it for his dinner. He didn't know if he would survive another encounter with the snow cats in the shape he was in.

His head was reeling. No wonder he hadn't given two shits about finding someone to share his throne. Some part of him had to have known that there was no way he would be able to honestly step into a marriage with someone who hoped for his heart along with the crown. It would've had to be an impersonal arrangement, the contract between two people of power that too many royal relationships were.

He had almost been resigned to that being the inevitable, without ever being able to articulate why he believed that. Which was why he had stalled and avoided and conveniently "forgotten" all those years.

It was because he was hers and only hers.

He let himself imagine for a moment what it would be like to go to his father and mother and tell them that he wanted Hara to share his throne. He wanted Hara by his side, day and night, not as his oathed guard but as his partner, his wife, his one and only. He imagined the faces of the court when he revealed that he was raising a royal guard to the station of queen.

His gut twisted. They would see it as impertinence, more evidence of his ineptitude. He was supposed to select someone who had the background and experience to be a suitable leader of the country, they would say. The children of court members, ambassadors, and titled landowners were educated with care, intentionally imbued with the knowledge and skill development it took to participate in negotiations, diplomacy, and public policy.

Yes, Hara had worked her way through the ranks of the royal guards, proving herself to be an invaluable asset. But the ability to handle a sword and defend a member of the royal family were not the usual prerequisites for queens.

It hardly mattered anyhow. It was beyond clear that Hara would never let these imaginings of his ever come to life. She didn't want him.

As he grimaced at the harsh truth, his eyes caught on a small indentation in the cliff face just below him and to the side. He stopped, carefully shuffling to the edge to peek over. It seemed to be a burrow stuffed with leaves and other dried debris that blocked the howling of the wind, telling him that something inside was concerned about heat and comfort.

Eyeing the area, he determined that he could remain upwind and be within reaching distance of the opening if he scaled a few boulders down the mountain, so he positioned himself appropriately then unsheathed his larger dagger. He clutched it in his right hand and held still, listening for sounds of movement within the leaves.

He had to close his eyes, blocking everything out, but eventually, he heard the faintest rustle coming from inside.

It was enough to convince him to wait it out, perching there ready to pounce the moment he saw anything emerge. And wait he did, his fingers growing stiff and cold in the unrelenting rush of air across the peaks. He flexed them every few minutes, clenching and unclenching to get the blood moving as his mind carried back to the woman waiting for him in a cave.

She had refused to take two drops of the extract and it gave him pause.

She also hadn't worn that curl in her lip that told him she wanted to gouge his eyes out with melon ballers. She wasn't mad. She was . . . afraid.

That would make sense. She had admitted to being scared the night before, right before he had lay down next to her and curled his fingers around hers. But with two drops of extract in her system, she had trusted him. She had unfolded like a flower opening to the sun, the softest touch of her nose against his seared into his memory.

The feel of her lips, the sounds she had made for him rolled under his skin like a wild blaze, keeping the mountain chill out as his heart ached in his chest. So why would she deny him in the sober light of day?

Because she had come to her senses. She knew that to let herself be intoxicated by the extract would be opening herself to his rot, his bad influence. He was nowhere near deserving of her and they both knew it.

She was right to be afraid of him. He had nothing good to offer her. He couldn't offer a crown or safety; he couldn't even offer freedom. He was the monster to which she was chained. The fire that burned her at the stake.

But flames were supposed to be his to influence and direct, were they not?

They were his to leash and release, urge and entice.

Something lifted away inside of him, revealing a possibility that had been hidden under a black mourning shroud. He almost turned his head in surprise at the mental image, startled by its sudden yet not entirely unexpected appearance. It was a proposition that had been creeping around the edges of his consciousness for a while now, a vine that persisted no matter how many times it was burned back.

Change. Redemption. Hope.

Could he change? Did he even have a chance after all the sins that had fallen from his hands? All the names of people he had disappointed that were carved into his ribs like epitaphs?

A louder rustle reached his ears as the leaves started shifting in front of him, and he homed in on the burrow, starting to see bits of debris fall away from the entrance. One white paw then another emerged, pushing this way and that to clear a passage as a round head with pert ears followed.

Rakhmet didn't hesitate. Darting in with his left hand to grab the scruff around its neck, he yanked it up with a quick move and plunged the dagger toward its exposed chest. Its squeal was short-lived as it died away in its throat, red dripping down the soft fur on its belly and into the nest below it.

It seemed to be some sort of snow badger, and Rakhmet glanced around to see if anything else had heard their struggle. He wouldn't put it past the larger creatures to come investigating after catching the sounds of dying prey. The cliffs seemed quiet, though, so he quickly drew his dagger back and moved a little bit away to start the process of skinning and gutting it.

He wasn't going to risk having entrails leading other animals near their cave, so he rushed the hack job out there, away from Hara, and stripped everything that wasn't worth keeping. Never having butchered his own kill before, it was a mess. But he knew what a roast was supposed to look like, having seen a pig turning on a spit in the throne hall on occasion, so he gave it his best shot. The results looked like something out of a nightmare, but at least there was enough meat for the both of them.

Satisfied, he scrubbed everything with some clean snow and resheathed his dagger before hustling back to their cave. He ducked inside, clearing his throat as he entered, and found Hara laid out close to the fire, trying to keep near the low flames as the last of their wood burned.

"Oh, sorry, I'll go—" he started as her enigmatic eyes found his. He stopped short and held out his kill. "Here, ah . . ."

She didn't respond, and in the awkward silence, he cleared his throat again. Sighing, he looked down at the mangled body dangling from his hand. He would have to hang it up somehow while he went and found more firewood for them, so he turned and rifled through their packs until he located one of their pitons, a hammer, and some string. Wrapping the creature's feet, he tied it off,

135

tapped a piton into the cave wall, and hung it up as he finally met her gaze again.

She was watching him, her discomfort evident in the crease of her brow, and he took a moment to really study her. He traced the exhaustion in the puffiness of her eyelids, the white knuckles of her fist on the blanket next to her, and the broiling frustration that ground the muscles of her jaw.

She was suffering because of him.

His lungs seized and he made his exit rapidly, not wanting to see the shiver that clenched her shoulders. He needed to find a way to fix things between them, and the first step was making sure they didn't freeze and were fed appropriately. Basic survival needs.

There was no reason to waste energy ruminating on the questions that would still be there once they made it out of these godsforsaken mountains. Those were problems for future Rakhmet.

Tonight, he just had to focus on keeping them alive and helping her heal. Which meant staying away from her. No touching beyond what was necessary, he told himself. A clinical distance.

He gathered up an armful of wood and hustled back to the cave, lighting his hands on fire to get the blaze going as he dropped in three new logs. He kept his hands on the wood until it started to turn red and then withdrew, giving his attention to the creature as he used his dagger to separate the limbs and ribs. He then clumsily washed them and waited for the surface of his makeshift rock oven to heat.

His traitorous eyes wandered to Hara in the following quiet as they listened to the small pops of burning wood. She had shifted back from the fire and was lying on her side against their packs.

"Do you need any water? More drops?"

She nodded, the movement stiff. "Yeah—can I have another?"

"Are you sure?" he couldn't help but ask. "I can tell you're in a lot of pain, Hara. I don't want you to suffer on my account. I won't . . . I'll just sit over here. I promise."

Her eyes slid away, hiding her reaction from him. "It's fine. One is fine."

"Alright." He sighed, keeping his comments to himself. Her backbone was made of pure steel and it wasn't bending for anyone. Pouring out the mixture, he handed it over and she gulped it down like a shot.

After a minute, her posture released a fraction and some of her prickliness abated as she stretched out her tight muscles. He settled back on his haunches, crouched by the fire.

"What'd you find?" she asked, nudging her chin toward the pieces of meat piled in the pots next to him. Caught in his thoughts, the effort at conversation took him aback for a second as he stared at her, and she pressed her lips together as if she were trying to pretend the tension between them didn't exist.

"Uh." His mind caught up to her question. "It's some type of snow badger, I think. The burrow was to the northeast of here."

"I'm impressed." Her comment was dry, but he sensed the olive branch behind it.

He smiled wryly. "I left quite a mess behind."

She curled her mouth in return, an attempt at a polite smirk, and his grin widened for a second, but it soon faded, his attention falling back to the stone oven in front of him. He tested the temperature with a few drops of water then arranged the pieces on the hot surface, listening to the sizzle of meat.

It filled the silence as the enticing smell started to surround them, the heat of the fire comforting and the promise of a satisfying meal smoothing the edges of their desperation. He never knew he would be so grateful that his particular blessing was fire-based. The heat of the desert had always made it seem as though his powers weren't quite necessary despite how helpful (and dangerous) they could be at times.

But on top of a frozen mountain? Fire was one of the best things you could hope for, and it alleviated some of his worries to know that at the very least, they wouldn't freeze to death. As long as he could keep tracking down small prey and provide a safe environment in which Hara could properly heal, they might just make it to Talegartia in one piece.

After a while, the meal was ready, so Rakhmet scrubbed their pots with some soap and divided the spoils between them as Hara pushed herself into a semi-sitting position. The strain on her back was making her frown, but she managed to hold herself up so that she could use both hands to strip the cooked meat from the bones.

Rakhmet slowly cleaned up then returned and sat with his back against the wall opposite Hara. Folding his hands over his belly, he closed his eyes so that he didn't have to watch her as his body worked on digesting their large lunch.

Or was it dinner?

He had no concept of time in this liminal space between coming and going, between the real world and this little pocket of stasis they existed in that was neither here nor there. But he couldn't help but catch the soft groan that Hara exhaled from across the cave.

He cracked one eye open and watched as she struggled to find a comfortable position on the bedroll. Sitting up had strained her back and it seemed like every position she tried just aggravated it more. Her brows were knit together and there was a faint sheen of sweat on her forehead.

"Hara," he grumbled. "Just take another drop, you're in pain."

She stilled, her frustrated movements halted by his words as if she had been caught doing something she wasn't supposed to.

He held up his hands in surrender. "I'm not going to try anything, I promise. You're in charge here."

She eyed him, the grimace creasing her face, and he lowered his head like a scolded dog. He was submitting to her, trying to fold into himself to appear as nonthreatening as possible.

After a minute of wrestling with herself behind her carefully blank gaze, she relented and dipped her chin. "Fine, one more."

He quickly complied, pouring her another dose, and she took it without any more complaint. Settling back against the wall, he watched as the drug eased into her system and her breaths grew longer. She melted into the bedroll, her lids blinking in slow beats, and he let himself breathe along with her, the very air becoming lighter on his shoulders.

Her attention stayed on the fire, though, not daring to lift it in his direction, and that was more than fine with him. It gave him space to consider the dark lashes that fluttered as they shifted, the slight dimple that appeared when her mouth fully relaxed, the graceful twist of her neck from reclining against the pack.

"Do you want me to brush your hair?" The question was formed and voiced before he could take it back, a knee-jerk reaction to the tangled sections that lay across her shoulder.

Her inebriated eyes found his and there was a pause as she considered him.

"It's just . . . your braid is all messed up and I figured it would make you feel better," he offered in explanation. "But if you don't want—"

"No," Hara murmured. "That . . . would be nice."

His brows went up at the unexpected response, his heartbeat starting to pound in his fingertips. "Oh, uh. Yeah, okay."

Clinical, this was merely clinical. He just needed to help his patient find comfort, like any other physician or field nurse.

He wiped his palms on his pants and then shuffled over to his pack to find a comb. Approaching Hara from the side, he moved to her head. He figured it was better to stay out of her line of sight, so he sat where he could fan her hair across his lap.

His touch was gentle and slow as he untied the end of her braid, then he laid out the sections and started running the comb through them. He started at the bottom, working through the tangles one at a time, and took care not to tug on her scalp.

After a few extended exhales, her taut shoulders relaxed and Rakhmet smiled to himself. He had always marveled at how smooth and straight Hara's hair was, having come from a family of notoriously frizzy offspring. He was one of the lucky ones to have loose curls that were relatively easy to manage, unlike his sister's tighter texture that required hours of upkeep and all sorts of conditioners the dry strands eagerly sucked up.

But Hara, her hair was like liquid night when taken care of well. She usually hid most of it in that top bun of hers, but he had caught a few glimpses of the full length over the years. When loose, it hung all the way to the middle of her back, and now, he delicately worked his way through every inch.

The strands went from dull and crimped to shiny and sleek under his hands, the sheen catching in the firelight as he finished his last few swipes from the roots all the way to the tips. When he was satisfied, he separated it into three sections and started folding them together.

He had learned how to braid with his sister years and years ago, when he had begged their governess to teach him so that he could also weave flowers into little Esare's hair. They had been sitting in one of the courtyards and the woman had been humming as she had tucked blooms into the tight plaits on his sister's head, and Rakhmet had been in his I-want-to-do-everything-myself phase.

Over the years, it had turned into one of their sibling bonding activities: him and his sister lounging in the relative quiet of their gardens as he had decorated her hair with vibrant colors. Hara had never let him touch her hair, though. Maybe she had considered it to be something he shared only with Esare, but to be honest, he had simply never considered it before.

Hara's shimmering lengths were like her secrets: she couldn't entirely hide them from him, but there was a silent agreement that he would never touch them directly.

Until now.

His fingers trembled for a moment as he fumbled with the ribbon that tied around the end of the braid, but he managed to knot it securely then eyed where her wounds were hidden by the blanket covering her.

"Hara?" he asked softly, wondering if she was still awake.

"Mmm?" she hummed groggily.

"I should probably check your stitches and refresh your bandages." Rakhmet shifted to where she could see him, although her eyes were closed as she nodded slightly and mumbled in the affirmative.

He got caught for a second, watching the firelight flicker across her serene face, but shook his head and retrieved what he needed from their packs. A quick trip outside and he had another pot full of snow that he brought to a boil over the fire. He immersed some cloths to use as a warm compress, then returned to her side and tenderly folded her blanket and tunic to the side. Some blood had seeped through her wraps, but not a lot, so he took that to be a good sign as he quickly scrubbed his hands with soap.

Carefully unspooling her, he removed everything from her stitches and then laid the compresses over the jagged seams as she sighed at the comforting heat. He let them sit for a few minutes then softly wiped her skin clean with the lightest of touches, doing as much as he could not to pull at the tears. The antibacterial salve came next, and then he sealed her up once more with a set of clean bandages.

He had spent so much time as a patient himself that the whole recovery routine was old hat for him by this point. Triage? On the field treatments? Rapid blood loss? Not so much. But healing slowly, hour by hour and day by day? He knew the dance by heart. It only seemed appropriate that he was now in the position to give back a fraction of the care that had been given to him.

He tucked her back in and cleaned up his things, dutifully scrubbing the used bandages with soap and making sure they could reuse as much of their supplies as possible. Waste not, want not and all that. While the domestic activities were certainly not something that he was accustomed to performing, there was a sort of innate logic that drove him forward. He knew how to calculate cost analyses, inventory counts, and project timelines. He was painfully fully aware of the cold, hard facts of their situation, so he did what he needed to do to keep them alive.

Which apparently meant lathering and rinsing strips of fabric with a cake of flaking soap and a dented pot of melted snow on top of a mountain gods knew where while the injured woman who held his heart pointedly ignored him about ten feet away. The person he had been only two days ago felt like a ghost from a long distant past, a character from a history book. Truly. If that wasn't an indication he was actually capable of change, he didn't know what was.

He finally finished up and moved to his own bedroll behind her, lying there for a while as he watched her chest rise and fall evenly. Her head was turned to the fire on the other side of her, but the movement lifted the plait lying across her shoulder, the reflection of the flames sliding up and down it like a slow metronome.

His heart beat in his chest with a steady rhythm, and he counted her breaths but kept his hands tucked into the crooks of his arms. He would give her the space that she had requested without words. He would give her anything she entreated of him because that possibility he had stumbled across outside the small burrow in the mountainside had at last been given shape and meaning.

He would do what she asked him to at the very beginning of all this.

To listen. To wait.

He would dig deep into himself and pull out every shred of patience he possessed.

For her, he would listen and he would wait.

DAY TWENTY

The second morning after Hara's injury, he had awoken with her hand curled loosely around his bicep, but he had gingerly set it to the side before she had come to and begun what would soon become their usual routine while they remained in the cave and waited for her to heal. He had cooked them porridge for breakfast, given her a dose or two of extract, left without saying much, and hunted down a meal. After returning to fill the cave with the scent of grilling meat, he had gone through the whole cleaning-and-rewrapping routine and had then dozed until the cycle started anew.

The third morning, her hand had been there on his arm once more. But the temporary bridge that her sleeping body had made to his, the unintended point of connection that had warmed his soul for the barest of moments wasn't to be seen again after that evening, when she had started insisting on only taking one drop of extract at a time.

She had stretched her limbs and taken shambling steps around the cave on the fourth day, making her way to the outside of the cave on the sixth. Buoyed by her own progress, she had pressed him to continue on their journey the very next morning, and Rakhmet, unable to tell her no, had simply gone back into the snow to find her a suitable walking stick first.

They hadn't gotten far that first day, with Hara alternating between using her stick for balance as she had shuffled along as quickly as she could manage and begrudgingly letting Rakhmet carry her weight whenever their path had become too precarious. But they had slowly traveled from cave to cave as the days had worn on, some nights finding a space large enough for both of them to lay out and some where they had to make do with a barely sheltered outcropping of rocks.

On the tenth day after the cat attack, he had carefully removed their stitches. On the thirteenth, the snow had stopped. On the fifteenth, they had run out of rations and Rakhmet had started hunting for all their meals. But on the sixteenth, they had managed to locate one of the many mountain streams that cut through the dusty rock and had solved a few of their looming problems.

Rakhmet's unbridled joy at having found a valued resource that would keep them both fed and hydrated, from the plants gathered along its edges to the promise of prey that would also be drawn to its waters, had even brought a slight smile to Hara's face after too many days of her brows drawn in gritted determination. Every mile they traveled was a challenge for her, and it took every last reserve of his to practice patience.

But on the eighteenth day after his eyes had been opened to a new thread in his path, they had finally scurried down the last of the boulders that made up the mountainside and had stepped into the lush rainforests of Talegartia. After weeks of being surrounded by nothing but red rock, white snow, and gray skies, the vibrant greenery had been overwhelming.

Massive trees reached toward the sky and their branches formed a dense canopy, filtering sunlight in a dappled mosaic on the forest floor. Exotic flowers bloomed in a myriad of colors, and thick vines created natural curtains between the trees as Rakhmet and Hara had breathed deeply, gorging on the scent of damp earth, moss, and the sweet tang of blossoms. There was a hint of decay from the fallen leaves and organic matter, intermingled with the freshness of undiluted chlorophyll, and it was a stunning contrast to the dry desert air they were accustomed to. Each breath carried a rich fullness of biodiversity that the palace gardeners only wished they could emulate.

Melodic calls and whistles filled the air and insects produced a constant background hum, giving both of them a much-needed sensory distraction after weeks of being stuck in their own heads. The occasional rustle of leaves indicated unseen creatures moving, but much was drowned out by the rush of waterfalls that dotted the landscape. The terrain was steep and unpredictable, their particular stream occasionally tumbling over ledges or bending this way and that to find its path.

Following it farther to the northwest, it had taken them another two days to find the first signs of civilization: a small village nestled into a clearing that hugged a curve of the stream where it widened into a shallow pool about twenty feet across. There were a handful of children playing in the cool mountain water and laughing unreservedly as they splashed at each other, the sight and sound so foreign to Rakhmet and Hara that they both stumbled to a halt in astonishment.

They stood frozen in the tree line, still obscured by the dense rainforest flora as they watched the scene in silence. There were maybe a dozen or so buildings clustered around each other, and on the other side of the clearing, a road could be seen leading away from the remote homesteads. Large carts were lined up here and there, obviously awaiting some sort of load, and a couple of oxen stood hitched to a sturdy post. Smoke trailed from chimneys and chickens pecked around for bugs.

It was like any other idyllic rural village, and it brought tears to Rakhmet's eyes as he fought to catch his breath. The past few weeks came back to him in a rush, sensations and memories flickering like a flipbook. So much had happened to them, and yet the world had still gone on. While they had been struggling to survive, babies were born, lovers married, crops harvested, and deals made. All without any concern about two errant runaways lost and injured in the mountains.

He reached out for Hara without thinking, his fingers wrapping around her wrist, and she let him as they stared in bittersweet awe. He wondered, not for the first time, what his parents were doing at that moment. Were they pacing the halls of the palace, desperately waiting for word about him? Had they sent soldiers to Renpet to save the Hapimoses? Did they believe him to be dead?

That was the first item on their list for whenever they managed to reach a pigeon messenger station: sending word to Zahar and providing sign of life.

"Do you think they'll have one?" he asked quietly, still watching the scene in front of them.

"It's hard to say," Hara murmured, her own eyes glued to an older man who was hanging laundry on a line behind his cottage. "Most of Talegartia is well-developed, but not every village has a station."

There was a long pause, but neither of them made to move, his fingertips gently pressed against the jumping pulse in her wrist. He let himself hang on for as long as he dared and then dropped his hand, clearing his throat.

"Ready?"

"Remember the plan."

He squared his shoulders and took a deep breath, centering himself as he adopted the demeanor of a slightly worried but hopeful and hard-working, salt of the earth kind of guy. Luckily, they had taken turns bathing in the stream the night before and had composed their appearances so that they were reasonably put together, but he still made sure to hide most of his scars under the folds of his cloak. His approach was firm yet respectful as he led the way into the village, aiming for the gruff but honest-looking man who looked to be in charge of the oxen.

They caught a few eyes as they neared him, but Rakhmet kept a polite smile on, giving off as much easygoing energy as possible, and the man looked up at them in surprise as

149

he straightened from picking something from one of the ox's hooves.

"Please excuse us, my good man," Rakhmet greeted him warmly. "My sister and I . . . well, I'm sorry to say we seem to have gotten lost in the forest and are looking for some assistance."

The sister fib was an idea that Hara had proposed a few nights prior, giving them a suitable alibi without having to pretend they were a married couple. He had rolled his eyes when she had suggested it but had humored her, knowing that the further from truth their cover story was the better. They had no idea whether the rainforest's border towns would be welcoming to a foreign prince on the run with his guard and had hidden anything that would give them away deep in their packs.

The man eyed them speculatively. "Sure does seem like you've found yourself in a situation, if you don't mind me commenting. How did you manage to wander your way to these parts?"

Rakhmet could do nothing to hide his more Zahari accent but did his best to match the rural inflections and cadence as he responded, "You know, I hate to admit it, and you bet she will be right glad to confirm, but it might've been my fault. You see, we were traveling through Orentha and my sister, she wanted to see some of the waterfalls in the area."

He named the town that sat on the other side of the Shiran Pass from Renpet, the town they would've traveled through with the rest of the guards had everything gone to plan. They had no way of knowing how far off track their mountainous paths had led them from the original route and he needed to subtly mine for some information while he chatted up the villager—without raising his suspicions.

The man's eyebrows raised slightly at the mention of the larger town, and Rakhmet forced out a good-natured chuckle. "The innkeeper recommended we take a guide with us, but I insisted that we'd be fine on our own. But famous last words and all that, am I right?"

Rakhmet kept his shoulders loose, appearing as if he were a simple man with simple problems. After a tense second, the man's face relaxed and he let out a rumbling chuckle in return, his heavy, callused hand coming up to land on Rakhmet's shoulder consolingly.

"Ah, a fair rub that is. You seem to have gotten yourselves into a situation indeed, haven't you now?" He wagged his square finger at Rakhmet, then Hara. "Orentha is all of a dozen miles to the south of here. You've tarried quite a ways out. This here is the village of Agart. I hope those waterfalls were worth it, ha!"

"Twelve miles!" Rakhmet feigned dismay. "Good gods, I've done it now. There's no way we'll get back before nightfall."

He glanced over his shoulder at Hara, who stood by quietly, trying to seem as unassuming as possible, and she met his eye with a knowing look. Turning back to the man, he stuck out his unscarred hand.

"I'm so sorry, where are my manners? What is your name, my good man?"

"Kippren, Elbus Kippren at your service." The man clasped his palm in a firm grip and grinned, the skin around his eyes crinkling like a rug that had gotten caught between a door and a wall.

"Well met, Kippren. I am Tanam Yagal and this is my younger sister, Kona."

"Well met, Yagal. Well met." Kippren gave his hand a hearty shake then stepped back, pointing toward a larger building on the other side of the village. "See the yellow roof over there? That's old Grandel's place, a tavern and place to stay. He'll set you two up for the night."

"Oh, thank you," Rakhmet responded with a grateful sigh, lighting his expression up with hope and relief. "You've been so kind. We thank you."

"Of course, of course." Kippren grunted, waving them off with a small smile. "I better get back to it now."

Rakhmet nodded respectfully and turned to usher Hara to the building the older man had indicated. He kept his arm around her like a protective older brother as they walked, other villagers casually watching them pass as they went about their business. Hara's muscles were tense, but her expression was reserved and showed no opinions.

The heavy wooden doors of the tavern opened easily, the hinges worn smooth after many, many years of use, and they were immediately greeted by a middle-aged woman standing behind a long bar on the other side of the large room. There were four round tables with a scattering of chairs toward the rear and a curving staircase at the front. The bar ran the entire length, and the woman was in the middle of wiping it down as she called out to them.

"Ah, hello! What can I do for you two?" Her thin gray hair was piled in a knot on the top of her head, and she gave the impression of someone who had spent decades kneading dough and scrubbing tables, her thick forearms disappearing into the rolled-up sleeves of a faded yellow dress.

"Good afternoon!" Rakhmet greeted her with a smile. "Kippren sent us your way."

"Kippren? Is that so?" She tilted her head with the smile of someone who smelled gossip.

"Yes, we are the unlucky wandering ones who found themselves lost in the jungle and needing a place to stay for the night."

Her grin widened. "Well then, that old coot sent you to the right place! I'm Adema, and Grandel'll be around at some point."

"Ah, thank you, Adema. I'm Tanam Yagal and this here is Kona, my sister." They approached the bar and Rakhmet leaned against it. "How much for a room with two beds?"

"Well met, you two." Adema patted both of their hands affectionately. "We don't have any rooms that big, but I can offer the two singles we have left. They're a gold each."

"Done," he happily agreed as Hara reached into her pack and drew out the necessary coins. They had had the forethought to exchange some of their money into Talegartian currency before leaving Ankhebari and had roughly ten gold between the two of them. They would have to be careful in stretching it out as much as possible, but he was positive that Hara was craving a good sleep in an actual bed with a pillow and a blanket as much as he was.

"Lovely! I'll get those rooms ready for you. How about some food and drink while you wait? Another gold and that'll cover both of you—tonight and tomorrow." Her wink was the practiced move of someone who knew how

153

to upsell, and Rakhmet smirked but nodded, glancing at Hara, who withdrew the additional coin.

They found a table and she soon brought them a pitcher of mead, two glasses, a loaf of bread, a chunk of cheese, and some dried sausages. She then left to do whatever she needed to, and they fell into silence, each savoring the taste of real food again at last. They took big bites and drank deep, both on their seconds within minutes.

As the alcohol hit and their pace slowed, they sat back in their chairs with tandem sighs. Hara closed her eyes and tilted her head back, swiveling her head side to side to crack her neck and relieve some of the pressure, while Rakhmet watched her lazily.

The thought that he should be careful about how he looked at her flickered vaguely in the back of his mind, but he was too relieved and satiated to care. So he drank her in, studying the soft curve of her jaw and the stretch of the muscles in her neck as she twisted it. He sighed with her as her shoulders dropped and body loosened, but the calm was too soon interrupted as Adema swept down the stairs.

He straightened and flicked his eyes away as she bustled about, humming under her breath, and cleaned up their empty dishes before heading back behind the bar to a door that presumably led to the kitchen. Disappearing again, she left behind another heavy silence as Hara braced her hands on the table to stand.

She jerked her chin toward the stairs, and Rakhmet followed obediently as they found their rooms at the end of the upstairs hallway, both doors cracked open with the keys in the locks. They were opposite each other, and

154

it ignited a brief flare of panic in Rakhmet's gut as he realized this would be the first time they'd be separated since they first arrived in Renpet. She had been his sole and constant companion for nearly a month, and tonight he would fall asleep in absolute silence, alone.

Suppressing the shiver, he strode into the room on the right and dropped his pack at the foot of the bed. It was a simply decorated space, with a medium-sized wooden bed, armchair, dresser, and nightstand. A window overlooked the rear of the tavern, showing a fenced-in yard that seemed to hold a small vegetable garden and chicken coop. He could hear the cluck of the birds from there, even with the window closed, and it eased his anxiety a bit, knowing that at least he could have them for company in the night.

Hara entered his room without knocking, and he glanced over his shoulder at her. Her expression was carefully blank, but he could tell she was about to say something that she suspected would make him mad.

He raised his brows, curious to hear what it was, and waited as she stopped in the middle of the room and crossed her arms.

"I want to go out and see if I can buy some supplies," she said, eyeing him for a reaction.

"Okay," he replied, shrugging.

"You . . . have to stay here. I don't want to risk people recognizing you."

He shrugged again. "Fine by me."

She pressed her lips together. She had been expecting him to push back, but he wasn't going to fight her. He didn't want to. Too many of his decisions had led to disaster and it was time that he listened to her for once.

"Okay . . ." She stalled.

"The bathtub's calling my name anyhow," he joked, hitching his thumb toward the metal tub that took up one corner of the room. The Talegartians considered themselves to be the most civilized of countries and adored their inventions and modernizations. There had been numerous governmental projects over the years installing public utilities throughout the entire countryside, and they had a robust system of advancement measures that ensured continual improvements in efficiency and productivity. It had rubbed on his father's nerves over the years, always being a step behind them.

But Rakhmet had never been as grateful for their obsession with innovation as at that moment, the whispered promise of a hot bath too urgent to ignore. He almost groaned from the want.

Hara huffed dryly, understanding the need but still unnerved by his compliance. "Alright, well, I guess I'll see you in a bit. Do you want me to grab you anything in particular?"

"Pants, I really need a new pair of pants. And more bandages and salve. Rations if anyone has them." Rakhmet ticked off the priorities on his fingers.

Hara nodded and crossed over the threshold of his room, looking back once before turning down the hall. He closed the door behind her and sighed, kicking his boots off and flexing his feet.

The village of Agart. He brought up the map of Talegartia in his head as he turned on the faucet embedded in the wall above the tub. Playing with the knobs until he found the right temperature, he disrobed and watched it fill. He didn't remember seeing the village marked on the map he had studied leading up to this trip, but he definitely remembered where Orentha was.

If they were a dozen miles to the north of the pass town, they were northeast of Lythenea, and since they were only a couple days out from the mountains, they were likely a bit farther from the coastal city than Orentha would have been. That meant they either had to find a direct waterway from Agart to Lythenea, veer south and go through Orentha first, or set a triangular route and hope to intersect a river that connected Orentha and Lythenea.

There were pros and cons to each approach. There may or may not be a direct waterway from Agart to Lythenea, there may or may not be people looking for them in Orentha, and there may or may not be dangers lurking in the jungle if they footed it to find another river. All he could do was wait for Hara to come back, hopefully with some information gleaned from the folks she talked to.

Turning off the tap, he slipped into the hot water and let out a long moan as his skin prickled at the change in temperature. It felt like heaven, and for the first time in a very long time, his circling thoughts slowed and settled. They were relatively safe for now. Both of their wounds had healed well. Their bellies were full, and tonight they would be clean and warm in real beds.

He would almost call it a win, but he didn't want to jinx their luck by overthinking things.

He washed leisurely, thoroughly enjoying the washcloths and the scent of their herbal soap. By the time he was done, he finally felt human again. No longer a monster, but a man of flesh and bone, rebirthed.

Putting on the only other clean tunic they owned, he wrapped a towel around his waist then worked on scrubbing his dirty clothes. He draped them over the arms of the chair to dry then lay out on the bed, sinking into the mattress pad with an extended exhale.

It wasn't long until he drifted into sleep, and it felt like hours later when Hara knocked on his door, opening it to hand off some of the things she had purchased. She startled to a stop in the middle of the room as she realized that he was still wearing a towel around his waist and her gaze darted around, avoiding his as she took in the drying clothes and the dripping washcloth hanging on the side of the tub.

"Ah, here," she said, dropping a bundle on the dresser.

"Thanks." His voice was thick with sleep, and he rubbed at his eyes as he sat up.

She backed up to the door and nodded.

"Wait." He held out a hand to stop her. "Tell me what you've learned."

She cleared her throat, her eyes going to the window behind him. "It's a remote village, specializing in lumber and woodcraft. Population estimated to be around a couple dozen, maybe thirty. Goods are cheap. People, friendly. I was able to restock everything, but no pigeon station."

Her gaze landed on him again and stayed on his face as he shifted to sit on the edge of the mattress, his bare feet on the worn rug.

"How far to the closest one?" he asked.

"Orentha, but we would have to hike through the jungle to get there. The road will take us west to Rosha, a town that sits at the fork of two rivers where we could catch a boat to the coast. But it takes us to Corind, which is the next major city north of Lythenea."

"Rosha has a station, though?"

"Yes."

He considered their options for a moment as he watched Hara on the other side of the room. She hadn't bathed yet and was still wearing her stained clothes under her cloak. He could see the area where she had stitched together the tears in her tunic from the cat's teeth. They hadn't been able to scrub the blood out entirely so there were discolored patches that had seeped out from the wounds.

"Did you get yourself a new shirt, too?" he asked.

"Uh." She glanced down at herself and shifted uncomfortably, crossing her arms. "Yeah."

"Good." He nodded then paused. "How much did it all cost?"

"Another gold total." She waited as he did the math. Six gold left for who knew how many days until they could get their hands on more.

He huffed and rubbed his face, his circling thoughts back with a vengeance. "Go take your bath. We can decide what to do over dinner. Alright?"

Hara paused, searching for something in his expression, but she apparently didn't find what she was looking for as her brows twitched down. She shook her head and lifted a shoulder to say *whatever* then exited without a glance back.

Rakhmet stood as the door snicked closed behind her, moving to the things she had left on the dresser. He found a pair of pants, three rolls of bandages, a tin of salve, and a pouch of ration blocks. Drawing one out, he found they had a different color and spice profile from the ones typically made in the Zahari Kingdom, but he was honestly a bit relieved to have a break from the dry cakes that had kept them alive during their frantic trek through the mountains. He'd be a very happy man if he never saw one of those square packages again.

He rolled his shoulder, dismissing the immediate tension that rose at the thought, and slipped on the pants before packing away the other items. Lying back down on the bed and folding his arms behind his head, he listened to the sounds of the village moving around them. The chickens clucked and there was an occasional shout of joy from a child, mixed with the sounds of people working and talking.

It was surreal after so many days of nothing but wind, and the simple mundanity lulled Rakhmet into another doze until the smells of dinner started to waft up from the kitchen below them. Voices started filling the tavern, their mixed pitches rumbling through the wooden floor, and Rakhmet decided to go check on Hara.

Peeking into the hall, he glanced around first then locked his door before crossing to hers and knocking softly. There was a rustle of movement on the other side, then it opened to show Hara with her wet hair draped over her shoulder and a new linen tunic and pants that were of a more Talegartian style. They preferred a much more structured look, with clean lines and sharp angles, compared to the billowing Zahari silhouettes. It didn't look half bad on her.

She stepped back, allowing him to enter before shutting the door and leading him to the table in front of the bed.

Her room was bigger than his, with an additional chair and nightstand.

"Check it out, how's it feel to have a nicer room than me for a change?" he joked, nudging her with his elbow.

She huffed another dry laugh and rolled her eyes as she sank into one of the chairs and crossed her arms. "I ordered us dinner. She said she'd send it up."

As if on cue, a knock sounded at the door, and since he was still standing, Rakhmet turned to open it. An unfamiliar young man was on the other side, holding a large tray that carried two covered dishes, a loaf of bread, a pot of butter, a jug of mead, and two glasses. He smiled warmly and accepted it from him, but the boy didn't stick around, heading back downstairs quickly to continue his duties for the evening.

Rakhmet kicked the door closed and set the meal on the table, taking the remaining seat and dividing up the dishes. He could feel Hara watching him, just as she had when they had first met all those years ago. But ever since their kiss, he'd been picking up a different energy in her study of him. She was wary and uncertain, eyeing him as if he were about to make a sudden move any minute that would trigger her defenses. It was the same look she had whenever they were sparring, keeping an eye on every twitch and trying to anticipate his next attack.

As much as he had tried to not directly acknowledge whatever had happened between them, it followed their every step like a ghost who refused to pass on, and Rakhmet had almost grown attached to the invisible presence. It helped keep him focused on the promise he had made to himself, reminding him that there was something between them that was worth changing for.

But he had to tread carefully. They had both been through hell in the last few weeks and had been quarreling for far longer than he cared to admit. His chest constricted as he recalled all the words they had spoken in anger at one another over the past four years, ever since he had started hiding things from her. That was when his rebellious behaviors had truly tipped the edge from harmless fun into self-destructive animosity.

She hadn't minded the former, but also hadn't beat around the bush when voicing her thoughts about the latter. He had been willfully blind, though, not realizing how much her opinion of him mattered until he had been faced with the threat of losing her. First at Furaro's temple, then at Renpet, then again after the cat attack.

His gaze landed on her forearm as she started spooning the thick stew into her mouth, the ridges of her scars catching the flickering candlelight, and he had to clear his throat.

"How are you feeling?" he asked.

"Alright," she answered, tilting her head side to side. "Sore, but it's not bad. I think it's more from hiking for an entire month than from the injury."

He chuckled, grinning at her. "Gods, can I understand that."

There was a comfortable pause as they ate and drank.

"It almost feels like I'm dreaming," he murmured. "It's hard to believe we're on the other side of it all."

"Yeah." She nodded, eyeing him. "We still have a long way to go, though."

She sounded kind of sad, and he frowned down at his bowl of stew. "I think we should go to Rosha next and catch a boat to the coast. It'll be faster than trying to cut distance by going on foot."

Hara nodded again. "I would agree."

"Plus, I'm fucking tired of walking," Rakhmet joked, a wry grin stretching his lips.

"Also agreed." She smiled then went back to her meal.

He finished his and sat back in his chair, watching her as she mopped up the last bits with a hunk of bread. Cleaning off the spoon, she set it to the side then reached for her glass of mead and took a long drink before meeting his gaze, as if she had been waiting for him to break the quiet.

"I'm sorry." He let the words hang between them as she took him in with an almost philosophical tilt to her chin, like he was a theorem that she was trying to solve.

"I'm sorry that we got to this place between us. This place where there is mistrust and things left unsaid and hidden." He continued on, the long-overdue explanation falling from him. "All I wanted to do was the right thing.

"You know how it was, after we lost our blessings. I was—I was not in a healthy place at all. It felt like I was just waiting around for death to come call my name." He leaned forward and drew a line on the table between them, as if he were underlining it. "Then we learned about the corruption and there was finally something I could do about it."

He glanced up at her. "And you were just as eager as I was to go investigate our temple. We both thought it was the right thing to do."

163

Her face was passive as he spoke, but her eyelids fluttered and told him a different story, a tale that whispered of her reactions to his words. She blinked once, letting him know that she was hearing him, that she knew the truth of his assertion.

"But then . . . well, we both know how that ended." He grimaced. "I was stuck in bed for weeks and you left for Tusi without me. And then, once you came back, you were only there for two days before you left again."

His chest tightened but he forced himself to say it. "And you came back with scars, Hara, and this story of blood and glory and not only one but two fucking divine weapons from my god. I-it ripped me apart."

"Your god? Like only you can pay respects to the Fire God?" She scoffed, crossing her arms.

"No, no," he rushed to say. "That's not what I'm saying. I'm saying—ah, he was my god and now he's yours too. Even more so than before. It just strengthens the connection between us. Right?"

Her shoulders relaxed a fraction as her anger abated, but she didn't uncross her arms as her silence encouraged him to continue. "So . . . so I volunteered us for the plant temple."

She tensed again and he knew he had to be careful; that night was one of the biggest arguments they had ever had.

"I thought, you know, since it was so painful . . . I really did not like watching you go off to the fire temple without . . . I was so worried and just wanted to be there. It was like there was this gaping hole. Then you came back with the . . . and it seemed like that was all the proof that we needed to stick together. Blessed Furaro rewarded you all and Nasima was crowned and it made sense that another blessed heir was needed. That I was needed." He laid his hand on the table, palm up. "I thought we could handle it together."

She let out a tight exhale, turning her head to the side as she considered what he had said. That night, she had called him impulsive and rash. She had said that he was rushing into things and putting lives in danger. Which was exactly what had happened after all.

"I'm sorry," he repeated. "I am well aware I fucked everything up. I made the wrong call and should have listened to you."

Sighing, she looked into the distance for a few moments, and he waited for her to say something. Right when he was about to call it quits and retreat to his bedroom like a shamed pup, she turned to look him in the eye.

"I didn't want you there," she said softly, the words harsh but the tone gentle. His brows furrowed, but she continued before he could respond. "I didn't want you there, in the temple. When . . . when I was in the middle of that nightmare, all I could think was 'gods, I'm glad Rakhmet is safe at home.'"

Sadness bled into her face as she looked at him. "I prayed, Rakhmet. I prayed my way through that entire fight. 'Gods, please take care of him. Gods, please restore his blessing and make him whole again. Gods, please make my death worth it.'"

His chest constricted and he choked at the unveiled emotion in her piercing gaze, held rapt by her attention.

"My duty, my whole reason for being is to keep you safe. And Rakhmet, what I saw in that temple was the

165

complete opposite of that," she gritted out. "You are too important. Too important to your family. Too important to our country."

She paused for a fraction of a second, almost as if the words were slipping past her filter and she couldn't pull them back in time. "Too important to me."

Rakhmet sat back in his chair, stunned by the admission. She hadn't been afraid **of** him; she was afraid **for** him.

When she had said her fears had come true at the Hapimose estate, it wasn't because of Layla's death. It was because he, Rakhmet, had been put in danger.

"Our fears aren't all that dissimilar then," he murmured without thinking. She feared losing him and he feared losing her. The clarity rang inside his skull like a loud gong, vibrating his brain matter to the very stem.

She was quiet, her slight frown telling him that she had said more than she wanted to and wasn't liking the look on his face either. He tried to contain his wonder but knew he was failing as he dropped his attention to his hands. They were white-knuckled, grasping onto the edge of the table in front of him, and he consciously unclenched them, tucking them in his lap and stretching them out.

That was why she had gotten so mad at him, because he was running headfirst into a dangerous situation with no regard for himself. She had urged him to slow down and prepare more, but he had ignored her, thinking that she was trying to hold him back, not help him. But she had been doing that all along, hadn't she?

She had never denied him his diversions or outlets. She had just wanted him to go about them with more finesse and tact and strategy. *Don't jump in with both feet, test the waters first. Learn, gather information, create a plan.*

"I'm sorry," he said again, looking up at her. "I hope to— I plan on doing better."

She gave him a soft smile and it loosened the tension in his chest, easing his breath. Even if her full forgiveness wasn't going to come soon, the small flame of optimism grew brighter inside him. He drew the moment to himself, clutching it like a jewel and storing it deep down. A treasure to be cherished.

But her smile soon faded to a look of gentle refusal and she moved to stand, pushing back from the table. "It's time I head to bed."

Rakhmet cleared his throat and pushed back as well. "Right, of course."

Reaching for the doorknob, he glanced over his shoulder as he opened it and drank her in. The heavy hair still loose on her shoulder, the unfamiliar clothes, the shaded eyes that he knew he would see again in his dreams.

Oh, but it was the most delicious ache.

"Sweet dreams," he murmured. A ghost of a smile curved her lips in response, and he turned and exited, closing the door behind him with a low click.

The soft sounds of chickens were the lullaby that soothed him to sleep that night, nestled in bed with his arms wrapped tight around the pillow. He buried his face in the softness, breathing deep and slow and imagining shimmering lengths, breathy sighs, and eyes that burned.

DAY TWENTY-FIVE

After a quick breakfast the next morning, Rakhmet and Hara had paid another gold to hitch a ride on an ox cart heading westward out of Agart, and it had taken five days to reach the bustling river town of Rosha. The journey had been equal parts boring and intriguing, the novel landscape soon losing its appeal after days and days of the same vibrancy and overstimulation, and they had made sure to keep to themselves, being kind and friendly to the logger that had escorted them but not providing too many details about their backgrounds. Somehow, they had managed to both keep up their sibling ruse as well as hide Rakhmet's extensive scars.

But eventually, they reached the much larger byway town that reminded Rakhmet of Ankhebari. Instead of dusty sand blowing through the streets, however, there was a startling abundance of plant life that dominated public and private spaces alike.

Massive boughs stretched over roofs and alleys, sheltering inhabitants from the bright sun, and every building was a harmonious blend of human innovation and natural beauty. Designs reflected both functionality and aesthetic appeal, and suspended wooden walkways connected different parts of the town, allowing easy navigation above the gentle flow of the river.

Colorful market stalls dotted the riverbanks, showcasing local crafts, freshly harvested produce, and fragrant herbs and spices. Occasionally, the smoky aroma of grilled fish wafted from open-air restaurants as Rakhmet and Hara wandered through, looking for an inn near the docks. It wasn't difficult to find, a sign welcoming travelers hanging proudly on a large wooden building just next to the market.

They entered the front doors to find an older man sitting behind a worn hostess stand, his haywire eyebrows giving him the look of someone who spent a lot of time rubbing their forehead in frustration. He accepted their story with a grunt and informed them that there was only one room left available, but as it would only cost them a gold between the two of them for both room and meals, they couldn't complain as the innkeeper handed over the key with no hint of amusement in his furrowed expression. Down to four gold and counting, Rakhmet ground his jaw as they took the stairs up and located their door on the third floor. He was realizing that they had been taken advantage of at the tavern in Agart, Adema apparently marking them as naive travelers who hadn't even bothered to barter, and he vowed not to make the same mistake again.

It would be a day by boat to get to Corind, then another to get to Lythenea. Finally, they would be able to get back to the real reason why they had hauled their asses over hundreds of miles, hand and foot: to find and clear out the plant temple. It almost felt like going back to square one, but Rakhmet couldn't let himself think that way or else he'd lose his already tenuous grasp on a plan.

He shook his head as he dropped his pack at the foot of the bed, turning to find Hara looking at him with an unreadable expression.

"What?" he asked flatly.

"I'm going to go out and find the pigeon station." She crossed her arms and looked at him like it should have been obvious. Right, because that was the point of all this. Focus, you idiot, he told himself.

"I'll be right here." He forced some cheer into his voice, lifting his arms to indicate the room. It was honestly a bit bigger than he was expecting, with a separate sitting area in the corner and a privacy screen hiding the bathtub.

She gave him a smirk, letting him know that she wasn't buying his false optimism, and shrugged one shoulder. "I'll be back in a bit."

He just nodded and waved her off, the door closing behind her. Flopping back on the bed, he stared at the plain plank ceiling as the sounds of the town filtered in through the open window.

One minute, he was certain she would forgive him and they would be able to move on. The next, he was doubting everything. Maybe he wasn't capable of change. Maybe she

171

saw through every pathetic attempt of his. Maybe they would be stuck in this impasse for years and years to come.

Yes, she had seen the absolute worst sides of him and he truly had no pride left when it came to her. He was the playboy prince, after all. What could he offer her that wasn't soiled beyond redemption by his despicable deeds? He cringed thinking about all of his shortcomings she had borne witness to over the years. How could she stand to be around him after all was said and done?

She had admitted to fearing for him, for his safety. That it was her reason for being to keep him safe, but was she simply doing what was expected of her? Or was she doing it out of the goodness of her heart? Was it because she was dutiful, or did she truly care for him?

There had been a time in his life where he would've been able to answer that question without hesitation: of course Hara held him in high regard. He had known that without a doubt, after all the hours they had spent together as younger versions of themselves, training until they had dropped from exhaustion, staying up into the early hours imagining what it would be like once he was king, or getting lost in the deepest parts of the royal library devouring any passing mention of his blessing's history.

They had both been so convinced that he would easily be able to rise to the heights that was expected of him with her by his side, but that had started to erode once puberty hit and hormones did what they did best. First, he had gotten caught fooling around with the ambassador's daughter. Then, Ine and Khenti had gotten him drunk for the first time ever. Then, before he knew it, they had been sneaking out, diving straight into the seedier sides of Zahar.

When he had started to become aware of the poverty, addictions, and inequalities that plagued the people of his great nation, he had begun to realize how protected his childhood had been, that he had been taught to turn a blind eye to the true depths of suffering that existed out there in the world. He had begun to realize that all of his princely trappings were an empty joke.

He wasn't expected to lead his people with compassion, understanding, and integrity. He was expected to be the same type of king his father was and his father before him, one that stood on the shoulders of tradition and the status quo and kept everything exactly the way it had always been. He was supposed to just do what he was told.

The door opening broke him out of his thoughts, and he looked over as Hara entered the room, glancing at him with a light in her eyes that he hadn't seen in too long. He sat up at the small flickering flame of optimism staring back at him, and he couldn't help but smile as she shut them in and tossed a bundle to him.

"What—" he started to ask as he automatically caught it. It was a hard, rectangular shape underneath the fabric, and he let it slide to the side to reveal a leather-bound tome. The font engraved on the front cover proudly declared: *A Complete History of the Talegartian Council.*

Snorting through his nose, he looked up at her for an explanation.

"So you don't die of boredom." She chuckled, crossing her arms with a look of triumph.

He smirked. "Thank you, but you truly didn't have to spend money on—"

"Let's just say that I got it on sale." The curl of her smile gave him pause.

"What exactly does that . . ." His brows shot into his forehead. "Are you telling me that you **stole** this?"

"What do they call it?" she mused. "The five-finger discount?"

"Hara!" he exclaimed, his jaw dropping. His loyal, respectable, duty-bound Hara? Stealing things for him? He couldn't believe it.

The only other thing that she had ever lifted was a very expensive sword from the palace armory when he had been about fifteen or so. It was balanced to perfection, a stunning example of the palace smithy's craft. She had had her eye on it for weeks, but the Nesu Medjay at the time had told her that she needed to work on earning the right to wield it. Together, they had hatched a plan to sneak into the armory one night and remove the sword without anyone noticing.

Problem was, after the sword had been securely tucked away in a hidden compartment in Rakhmet's bedroom, she had been stricken with deep-rooted guilt that Rakhmet hadn't been able to talk her out of. She had gone to her superior the very next day and confessed their crime, unable to stay silent. She had been suspended and he had been disallowed all extracurriculars beyond his required studies for an entire week.

Yet here she was, smirking at him with a lightness that disarmed him.

"What has gotten into you?" He laughed, unable to hide his stunned amusement.

She shook her head good-naturedly as her smile faded a bit and she sighed. "It's nothing. I just . . . figured you'd need it."

"Well, thanks." His own grin lost some of its enthusiasm. "Did you send the message?"

"Yeah." She paused. "I addressed it to Rahim, from a Tanam and Kona Yagal in Rosha."

He nodded, understanding why she still kept their identities secret. It would have been a big red flag to send a pigeon directly to the King and Queen of Zahar. They had chosen the pseudonyms Tanam and Kona because those were names of the top two palace cooks, a husband-and-wife pair that were respected members of the staff. Anyone who lived or worked in the palace would be able to easily identify them.

"I also tracked down a hookah bar as well as a drink hall. I'm going to see if I can pick up any news," Hara added. "Do you need anything?"

He waved the book at her. "I think I'm good, thanks."

Once he was left in silence once more, he stood and walked to one of the chairs, absently flipping through the aged and slightly yellowed pages before catching on one that held an older map of the entire South Endrian continent. It was dated about a hundred years before the revolution that crumbled the elemental crown political structure, and Rakhmet was drawn into the adjacent explanation of how the Talegartian Council was formed in response to the fall of a monarchy that considered themselves to be guardians of the land.

The plant monarchy.

There was no mention of divine blessings, all talk of anything supernatural having been written out of the history by a culture that prided themselves on their intellectual and scientific approach to life's conundrums. But he read on, taking in the details of how the council set laws and regulations, forcibly determining what the future economy and culture of Talegartia would look like.

He had certainly studied this nation before, as was expected of the future ruler of a neighboring kingdom, but the specifics had grown fuzzy over the years and it was interesting to read about it all from the perspective of the Talegartians. He remembered his education being mostly Zahar-centric and, within the royal family at least, they knew the real reason behind the council's rise to power.

It seemed as though in Talegartia, they were taught that it was a peaceful transfer from monarchy to council, but Rakhmet was well aware that it had been a bloody fight to the end. His own family had had to disown the reigning Fire King at the time, going as far as beheading him and his two young sons in a public execution before the throne was transferred to a lesser-known branch of cousins. The story went that the fire blessing had been wiped out at the end of that previous family line, never having developed in the newly crowned king and his children.

What the public didn't know was that Rakhmet's ancestor had kept his blessing hidden for the rest of his days, teaching his children to do the same.

That was eighteen generations ago.

Eighteen kings who had followed the same script that had been written for their fathers. Eighteen half-lived lives. Eighteen lifelong lies.

That was what Rakhmet had been fighting against all those years. The rehearsed role that he had been stuffed into since birth like a tunic that was two sizes too small. Be a king, lead the nation, but never tell the truth.

Never, ever, ever, ever let people see the real you.

That was, until Nasima had come back from the fire temple crowned as the new Water Queen by Furaro himself.

To say that Rakhmet had been surprised when his father had announced his intention to reinstate the elemental crowns would be a gross understatement. He had reasoned from Hara's story of what the Fire God had told them that someone would need to go clear the plant temple too, but the broader implications of his father admitting to as well as demonstrating his blessing in front of the entire court were something he was still wrestling with.

They had been in meeting after meeting after meeting with the court, trying to hammer out the details of what the reinstatement would look like, but nothing solid had been decided yet. Tales of what had happened had spread to every corner of the kingdom within the week and there was a mixture of reactions.

Some immediately repledged their allegiance to the Crown, and some grumbled about how it might affect the economy. There was even a small portion of people who emigrated, choosing either Talegartia to the west or Gheseruti to the south. An even fewer number went to North Endrian to avoid any and all potential conflict, especially with news of the effort against Nalliendra rumbling through the countryside too.

Change was afoot, was it not?

Rakhmet leaned back in his chair, tapping his thumb on the spine of the book.

He had to admit that he wasn't entirely happy with his father's rule. Up until this point, it had been relatively unremarkable. No major wars, no economic disasters, no sudden plagues. His father had simply followed the path that had been laid out for him step by step by step. He carried on the same traditions, gave the same speeches, griped about the same old arguments.

Generation after generation, king after king. The same song over and over.

It had been a shock to see his father so willingly step up to publicly claim his blessing, but it had been a defensive reaction to Nasima letting the cat out of the bag with the mere presence of the silver crown upon her head. Even his father's intention to challenge Nalliendra had been a reactionary move. They had threatened a Zahari ship first.

But what alternative could Rakhmet possibly propose?

An offensive stance? What would that even look like?

There were far too many moving pieces for him to see a clear way to position the Zahari Kingdom better. And what did "better" really mean anyway? Wealthier? More powerful? To what end?

World domination was not something he was interested in by any means, but he couldn't deny that there was room for improvement. He had seen too many of his people starving and suffering, in rotten circumstances with rotten luck, and they would all be his duty one day.

If he lived through this.

He sighed, pinching his nose against the headache that was forming. Glancing out the window, he realized that night had fallen and stood to look down at the town below when the door opened behind him. Hara's footsteps approached, and he caught a whiff of tobacco smoke as he turned to greet her.

"What news?" he asked, watching her as she shucked her cloak and quickly washed her hands and face in the water basin. She stretched her neck side to side as she patted her face with a towel and then tossed it aside, taking one of the chairs at the table.

"You'll probably want a drink first." She smirked.

"That bad?" He grimaced and she shrugged.

He started to pull out his own chair but was interrupted by a knock on the door. It was a young woman and she handed over their dinner, a tray with bread, butter, and the works. They had quickly learned that the cuisine of Talegartia was not the flavorful, spicy rainbow in your mouth that Zahari dishes were, but the stocky stews and thick breads did their job and did it well.

Depositing it on the table, he poured himself a glass of mead and waited. He swirled his drink in her direction as if to say *see?* and she rolled her eyes as she poured her own.

"First off, there's talk of the war all over town," Hara started, taking a long drink. "Folks are complaining about how it's going to affect the price of imports and exports, saying that Zahar should be focusing on the Somansian Canal, not sending their forces to the Staroh Sea."

She named the canal that separated North and South Endrian on the northernmost border of the Zahari

Kingdom. It allowed trade to flow from the Metuit Sea in the east to the Troskov Sea in the west and it was vital to Talegartia's economy. Of course they would want Zahar to ensure their flow of wealth and goods more so than protect Melatius and the eastern coast by giving the Bourisian Islands back up.

"That's not entirely surprising," Rakhmet remarked drily.

"Right," Hara agreed, taking another deep pull from her glass. "The other thing is that you've been turned into somewhat of a folk hero."

He sputtered, his own drink spewing as he sat up in his chair and started coughing. "Excuse me?"

"It's all over, news of this legendary fire prince who managed to escape from a kidnapping attempt, saved two noble ladies from certain death, took down a dozen men at once, oh, and saved a babe from a burning barn." Her delivery was wry, and she read his reaction with a cynical brow arch.

"Are you shitting me right now?" Rakhmet asked, his eyes wide.

"Gods' honest truth." She held up her hand like she was swearing in a court of law.

"Oh gods." He groaned and rubbed his face. "What the fuck?"

"They will spin up any kind of story to explain what actually happened. You know how the gossip mills work." Hara sighed, seemingly exhausted by the topic.

"Do we at least know if anyone made it out?"

She shrugged. "Hard to say. Some say all of the royal guards were killed; some say it was the other way around."

He groaned again, dropping his face into his hands with his elbows braced on the table.

"Moreover, no one knows where this prince is now," Hara continued, ignoring his sounds of pain.

He looked up at that. "No guesses?"

"One story said you turned north, one south. I heard one guy say that you disappeared into a puff of flame. He was also shouting about the end of times, so, you know, reliable source."

He sat back in his chair and stared into the distance, trying to absorb the information.

"People are saying, though, that the Crown sent soldiers in when the news broke," Hara added a bit softer. "Whatever happened seems to be concluded now, but no one knows the specifics."

She paused then started dishing out their meal, setting his stew in front of him with a hunk of bread, and waited for him to process. The silence lengthened as he absently spooned the pieces of meat and vegetables into his mouth, chewing through his thoughts.

A folk hero, of all things.

He was being presented in a positive light by the public. It wasn't considered a disaster at all. The mystery of his newly reclaimed status as a blessed one had somehow conflated the story of what had happened into a mythical tale, and he had no idea how that would affect the perception of his right to the throne.

"What's your vision for the future?" he asked suddenly, turning to her.

"What?" Her eyes widened.

"Your vision . . . for what you want to happen after all this is over." He waved his hand. "Granted that we somehow survive this and clear the plant temple and get back home and, I don't know, win the war. What's after that? What do you want the future to look like?"

She leaned back and considered him for a long moment. "You haven't asked me that in years."

He shrugged a shoulder. "I'm asking now."

"I—" she started, unsure. "I guess I haven't thought about the larger picture in a long time, at least seriously. I've just focused on the immediate day-to-day. My guard salary allows me to keep my father comfortable, and most of my time nowadays is spent chasing you around town, so I gave up on thinking about the long-term a while ago."

Her father was a retired royal guard himself—both her parents had been, but her mother had died in a skirmish with some smugglers when Hara had been very young. It was part of why she had been so determined to join the guard force, as a way to honor her memory. Loyalty ran in her blood.

The last few years had been difficult, though, after her father had started suffering from mental and physical degeneration. After so many decades of staunch, reliable stoicism, he had fallen into a fog, sometimes knowing who Hara was and sometimes forgetting entirely. She had had to set him up in a group home, where he could get around the clock care and attention. It wasn't cheap and the palace helped some in gratitude for his years of service, but it often drained whatever was left from her pay at the end of the month.

"There's nothing else you want for yourself? For Zahar? For the kingdom?" Rakhmet questioned, his mind turning.

She looked down at the table, thinking. "I've been . . . grateful to have been able to step up in the last few months. When everything started . . . and with how things have gone . . . it's an honor of a lifetime to serve in my full capacity. I never thought that I'd get a chance like that. I mean, who would? This is all so new.

"I don't know what I would add . . . Winning the war, yes. Securing the temples, making sure everyone is safe and happy. I . . . I suppose I would like to see something done about the, ah, wealth inequality . . . ."

She hesitated and glanced at him to watch his reaction.

"Tell me," he urged.

"It's just that . . . it's a bit obvious that the palace, the Crown, has a lot of material wealth and resources. It's no secret that your home is one of the most well-decorated buildings in the kingdom. No expense is spared when it comes to displaying the full power and influence of the house of Pyrantus: the precious metals, jewels, fabrics, gardens, ships, food, drink, everything really."

He nodded, understanding. "I can't deny that."

"There are some in the kingdom who believe that the money should go to better things, more . . . constructive things."

"Like what?"

"Public works, health services, libraries, academies . . . institutions and organizations that would help those with less . . . wealth and opportunities."

He certainly saw the sense in that. He had been in enough slums to know that there were missing pieces, social supports that could improve the lives of many, and it was certainly a view of life that not many in the palace got to see. Most of the court stayed within their prescribed social networks, only meeting and mingling with those of their own socio-economic class. He and Khenti were some of the few that had made a point of sampling all the flavors that life had to offer.

He nodded again. "We could do something about that."

Her brows raised. "Really?"

"I've been thinking . . . about how I might want to rule someday if I get the chance. I want to do something different, break the pattern." He tapped his finger on the table. "For eighteen generations, we've been doing the same thing, talking the same talk, walking the same walk. King after king after king. But I have a real opportunity here to do something good, enact change that can create a better future."

She was quiet, surprised.

"What if we could create a kingdom where everyone is supported, where the sciences and the arts and the pursuit of knowledge is just as revered and valued as my elemental crown? As our connections with the gods?"

"That would . . . Many people could benefit from that," Hara murmured, taken with the vision he was painting.

"I don't want it to be an either/or kind of thing. Religion or science. Blessed or secular. I want to harness the advantages of both. I want to push the envelope, see what we can truly achieve." Rakhmet leaned forward, the flame of hope growing brighter as he watched it reflect back to him in Hara's gaze.

"I've been chasing after something for years and years now, but I think I was chasing after the wrong thing," he admitted. "I was looking for an answer, some way to break the pattern, and now we've been handed the opportunity to do something about it."

"What do you mean?" she asked, her expression turning worried.

"The elemental crowns, this mission we're on." He tried to find a way to explain this amorphous idea that was taking shape. "It's an opportunity for me to . . . see what truly matters and gain the experience I need to change things. To change myself, my future, the country's future.

"I was chasing novelty and excitement when I really needed to be focused on . . . impact and . . ." He searched for the word. ". . . meaning."

Her brows had relaxed midway through his explanation, and now there was an almost impressed look on her face as she studied him.

"What have my experiences meant? I once assumed that all the people we came into contact with, the artisans, merchants, intellectuals, even the courtesans were . . . bystanders, just average people that represented the populace I was meant to lead one day."

He grimaced. "I didn't see them as individuals, as whole people who had their own dreams and fears and needs. I saw them as actors, filling a role just as I was. I thought that was simply what everyone did: play the part that they were assigned whether they actually wanted it or not. But the last few years, the last few weeks have stripped everything away. Everything I thought mattered . . . My eyes have been opened. So what could these experiences mean?

"I'm starting to understand now that there's so much more to life, to the individuals that inhabit it. I've been seeing what actually matters."

"And what's that?" she asked, her head tilting.

"Those I love, my country, the people I'm responsible for . . ." He bit his lip, not knowing whether he should finish the thought, but she was sitting there in that chair, her posture poised and regal, and he couldn't help but see the imaginary crown on her head.

Oh, how good she would look on the throne. On his throne.

"You, Hara," he confessed. "You matter to me."

The soft inhale was subtle, but he caught it as her lips parted and her brows twitched upward at the unexpected declaration.

His lungs tightened as he waited for her response, her eyes bouncing between his to gauge his level of sincerity. He poured everything he could into that look, his heart burning in his gaze, urging her to see that he meant every word and so much more.

"Rakhmet, I—" she started but gave her head a small shake, as if trying to sift for the right response.

She opened her mouth to try again, but he stopped her, reaching out to grasp her wrist. "Please."

There was a moment of heavy silence and he swallowed thickly. "Please, don't—"

He cleared his throat and couldn't continue, her eyes still darting between his to search for answers to questions she wasn't asking, but he couldn't maintain eye contact as he dropped his attention to where his fingers rested on her pounding pulse. Sliding under her palm, he lifted her knuckles to his lips and brushed the softest of kisses across them. He glanced up just as he neared the edge of her pinky and caught the expression of shocked want on her face, but there was still uncertainty lingering that speared his gut.

His lids fell closed at the sting and he moved her hand so that it cradled his cheek. He nestled into the warm skin and sighed out a deep, long breath. They sat like that for a few moments as he memorized the sensation, but he didn't let it drag on too long before he forced himself to open his eyes and sit back, laying her hand back on the arm of her chair with care.

"Apologies." He cleared his throat again. "It seems I should head to bed."

He dared meet her eye and found that she had also attempted to gather herself, a more reserved facade clumsily falling into place. She was shimmering before him, a mirage that whispered of his greatest dreams and deepest fears. And yet, there was something holding her back, and he couldn't bring himself to hear the self-protective rejection he knew was building behind her lips.

Standing, he moved to the bed and kicked his boots off. Without a further glance, he lay down on one side and draped an arm over his eyes to block out the light as he had sometimes done when they had been cave-hopping. It was a subtle way to give them both privacy if isolating physically wasn't possible, and he sensed that they both needed the space now.

He kept his other arm casually folded across his stomach and let his breath slow and deepen to feign sleep. Listening to her measured breaths, he imagined her palm on his cheek until he truly started dozing sometime later. He didn't know how long it had been, but eventually the mattress pad dipped next to him and he felt her body heat as she lay down beside him.

They didn't touch, pretending to sleep. Their controlled exhales set a careful rhythm in the dark, and Rakhmet drifted off once more, focusing on the slightest whiff of charcoal that betrayed the inner burn.

—

The next morning, he awoke to find her warm hand curled around his bicep once more and let it sear a brand into his flesh. She pulled away moments later when she started to shift and wake, but that small touch was enough to keep him going.

DAY TWENTY-SEVEN

They spied the shining beacon that was the city of Lythenea on the horizon just before midday, and within a few hours, they reached the cultural behemoth that dominated the coast in all of its grandeur. They hadn't even bothered staying the night in Corind, choosing to immediately pay for passage on a different ship heading south the previous evening. Officially down to five lonely silver pieces after all was said and done, they disembarked into the biggest city either of them had ever seen.

Lythenea was a pinnacle of intellectual culture and innovation as one of the five academy cities of Talegartia. They stretched along the western coast from north to south and each was home to a sprawling complex of libraries, laboratories, and lecture halls to which students from all over the countryside flocked to study and push the boundaries of knowledge.

Accordingly, the cities were full of theaters, museums, bookstores, intellectual salons, debate halls, society groups, and galleries showcasing their rich cultural heritage, with performances, exhibitions, and events every week. But that wasn't the first thing visitors noticed when they entered Lythenea's harbor. Instead, they were greeted by a marvel of urban design.

The city was built on a mountainous bay, the roads and buildings shaped into a series of ascending concentric circles that rose gracefully from the docks to the towering peaks at Lythenea's heart, where the academy was located. The meticulously crafted stone buildings, adorned with intricate carvings, shimmering mosaics, and elaborate orreries, reflected the city's reverence for knowledge as lush, terraced gardens cascaded down the slopes, filled with exotic plants and sparkling fountains, and created a sparkling tapestry of precision and control.

Rakhmet and Hara quickly disappeared into the crowd surrounding the docks, the ports teeming with ships from all over the world. Enormous trading vessels adorned with sails of all colors unloaded exotic goods and rare treasures, fueling the city's thriving commerce. The Talegartians specialized in exporting their advanced inventions and fine crafts, their market squares brim with stalls selling textiles, tools, instruments, books, and art. They were so confident in their work that it was rather uncommon for vendors to shout out the expected proclamations of quality, like they did in other markets, and their aloof stares took some getting used to as the two of them wove between the stalls.

As they ventured farther in, they aimed for the higher circles of the city where they knew they would find the pigeon station at which Hara had instructed Rahim to leave a message. It was the closest to the inn that Rakhmet had intended to visit with Hara, Nebehet, and the guards as they searched for information about the plant tribe, but with the five coins feeling much too light in his pocket, they were painfully aware that they were not in the position to foot any bills for such accommodations. They would be lucky if they could afford dinner.

The city's architecture also reflected its social hierarchy, with the elite classes residing in the upper circles, where grand palaces and opulent estates offered panoramic views of the bay and surrounding landscape. But closer toward the docks, the buildings were modest homes and simple taverns. If there wasn't a message waiting for them at the pigeon station, they would likely have to backtrack and return to the docks to find somewhere to settle for the night.

They focused on their mission, though, pushing through the masses into pristine streets that felt like the corridors of a museum, decorated with finesse and gently ascending into the bright blue sky. Walking under towering arches that were polished to shine and larger than life statues who held their wreathed heads high, Rakhmet and Hara were soaking it all in quietly.

There had been a shift in the energy between them since his confession, and Rakhmet was nervously waiting for Hara to give him some kind of response, but she hadn't been keen to be direct with him. Instead of her usual guarded attentiveness, she was now subtle in her study of him. On both ships, he had caught her watching him out of the corner of his eye, but when he had turned to acknowledge her, she had pretended that she was focusing on something else.

Her eyes would flick to the side, casually passing over him as though he were part of the landscape, but he always saw a peek of her hand clenching and unclenching at her side. She did that when she was chewing over a problem in her head, seeking a solution to a riddle presented to her. It was almost as if she were tightening her hand around the pommel of a sword, planning her next swipe.

So he gave her space, letting the silence between them be enough as his heart rattled around in his chest. He was nervous about the state of most everything at the moment. Restless and eager and frustrated. It felt like they had moved mountains to get to this point and it wasn't even the main event. They still hadn't done enough.

Yet, he kept reminding himself. They hadn't done enough yet.

New eras were not built in a day, and he reached down deep to search for patience in the ashes of his gut, finding just enough to keep his feet moving forward as he followed Hara up and up.

Eventually, they located the modest sign of the station, advertising a safe and secure way to send messages and conduct business, and they almost broke into a run as they neared. Hara held out her hand and stopped him two storefronts away, scanning her piercing gaze over him to check that his cloak was still doing its job hiding his scars and they both had their unassuming masks firmly in place. When her eyes met his, they flashed, but the fire was quickly hidden once more, veiled from sight.

He cleared his throat and nodded, letting her know he was ready, and then they proceeded to the door. Walking in with purpose, they approached the elegant waist-high counter behind which a young woman stood wearing a tidy apron with big pockets. Her dark hair was drawn into a demure bun at the nape of her neck and her hands were delicate as they organized a box of scrolls. She looked at them with a warm and polite smile, her manners finely trained as she greeted them.

Hara took the lead, succinctly asking after a message waiting for a Tanam and Kona Yagal, and the station assistant dipped her head in confirmation, the flare of relief making Rakhmet's knees quiver for a second before he was able to lock them back in place. His unscarred hand numbly set the two silver required for payment on the counter, and he couldn't help but stare as a rolled missive was deposited in Hara's hand. He was astonished at how small the object seemed considering how much import it carried.

Before he knew it, they were outside the shop once more and Hara was guiding him to the closest alley to find a bit of privacy. She led him halfway down before ducking into a recessed doorway and moving aside to make room for him in the shadowed space. Her hand came forward and opened between them, palm up, as she met his gaze.

The paper that could answer so many of their circling questions sat there, waiting for him, but it took him a moment before he could drag his attention from her face. There were flickers of emotions dancing across it: her brow twitching up then down, the crease next to her mouth deepening than flattening, her lashes fluttering in a staccato rhythm. He could watch the show for hours, lost in the expressiveness she so valiantly tried to keep under wraps.

But he broke his focus and reached for the message, turning so that she could read it along with him. His fingers shook as he unrolled it, then Hara's hand was suddenly there, supporting his, and the tremors stilled.

To the dear Tanam and Kona Yagal of Rosha,

Your long-awaited message was received with much joy and relief. Your families and the people of your home are filling the halls with jubilant celebration at the news. We all hold you in our highest regards and have been praying for your health and safety. Praise the gods for their guidance in these troubling times. Arrangements have been made for you at the previously discussed inn with the help of a friend of the family and all will be provided if you give your name to the front desk. We eagerly await your next report.

Your Eternal Ally,
Rahim Jabbar, Nesu Medjay of the Royal Guards
Zahar Palace

Rakhmet slumped against the wall. The message was annoyingly but understandably vague. Some of his worries had been soothed, but there were still too many choking his lungs for comfort. His arms fell to his sides as Hara read the message twice and then three times, the paper crinkling from the force of her grip on it. It was both satisfying and supremely frustrating to realize he was steps away from reintegrating the facade of prince, and his fingers curled protectively around the three coins sitting in his pocket.

He stretched his neck and squared his shoulders, putting on his game face, then held out an inviting hand to Hara. "Ready?"

She met his eye again, and there was a charge that pulsed for the briefest of moments before it was gone. Sliding her gaze away, she nodded but didn't take his hand. She tucked the message in her pocket and then motioned for him to lead, falling back into her just-a-step-behind guard position. It turned his stomach, making his grim mood even worse, but he hid all that away.

They strode forward and emerged into the thoroughfare, no longer the unassuming tourists that had ducked into the alley minutes before. Still wearing the same cloaks and packs, their whole demeanor had shifted and morphed into an air of importance that not only matched but superseded the upper echelons of the best that Talegartia had to offer.

His chin was tipped with arrogance and her gaze was a challenge to anyone who dared glance their way, and the people around them did. Before, they had been invisible. Another set of anonymous pedestrians. Now, they were a prince and his guard.

The whispers followed them as they circled a handful of blocks and found the Aerie Auberge, the luxurious inn in the center of the Aerie District. It was the part of the city that was home to the richest merchants and intellectuals in Lythenea, and the inn was famous for its opulent sitting rooms where people came to discuss, debate, and deal. But their steps only grew more confident as they approached the leaded glass doors that proudly reflected the crisp sunshine.

With the two doormen immediately coming to attention, they were swiftly welcomed inside a plush vestibule adorned in rich hues of burgundy and gold. Intricately woven tapestries depicting scenes of scholarly pursuits and bustling marketplaces lined the walls and a crystal chandelier hung overhead, casting a warm glow upon the polished marble floors. Underfoot were intricate mosaics depicting constellations interwoven with symbols of alchemy, and there was a grand staircase to their right that split halfway up, leading to the second-floor galleries that overlooked the cavernous inner hall.

On their left was a series of archways beckoning guests into intimate alcoves and private chambers, but they aimed for the grand reception desk, where two women waited with attentive smiles. They wore matching uniforms, simple black silhouettes that only highlighted the material wealth surrounding them. Their youthful beauty was an undeniable, and likely purposeful, addition to the warm embrace of the establishment.

Rakhmet sighed, the overwhelming softness of everything starting to make him feel like he was wrapped in cotton, but threw back the hood of his cloak as he approached them. Their eyes widened as they took in his bearing and the force of his stride before landing and catching on the rippled skin trailing down the side of his face and into the neck of his shirt.

The scarred Crown Prince of Zahar, found at last.

He wouldn't even have to give his name, it seemed. With impeccable courtesy, they dipped into identical curtsies and fluttered their big brown eyes at him.

"Your Highness, welcome to the Aerie Auberge," the one on the left said with a lilted accent. Her smile was sweet and inviting as the other hurried to select a key from the board behind them and collect a long, fat envelope from a drawer.

"Thank you," he rumbled. "A beautiful establishment, my compliments to the owners and staff."

"How kind of you, Your Highness. Thank you very much." Her blush was quick and powerful, turning her cheeks into pink apples. "Would you like anything to drink? Wine? Tea? Water?"

His throat was dry, but he declined, shaking his head. "No, thank you. I was told accommodations were made for my guard and me?"

"Of course, if you please." She swept her hand to indicate the stairs. "Follow me."

The other woman handed her the key and envelope, then the first took off at a brisk pace, leading Rakhmet and Hara up to the gallery toward the front of the building. They headed to a set of grand double doors in the northwest corner, and she used the key to unlock one. Swinging it open, she stepped to the side and curtsied again.

"Thank you," Rakhmet repeated, taking the items from her and giving her a close-lipped smile before entering the room. Hara closed the door behind them and signaled for him to wait as she surveyed the suite. There was a small foyer that led into a well-appointed parlor matching the decor of the rest of the building. A door on either side of the room presumably led to bedchambers, and he broke the seal on the envelope as Hara searched one, then the other.

His brows furrowed as he realized what he held. It was a stack of scrolls that had been pressed flat, there must have been at least half a dozen tucked into the envelope, and there was a piece of stationery with a familiar family crest on the top.

To my dearest nephew, His Highness Rakhmet Pyrantus,

It is with a full heart that I welcome you and your staunch guard back into the fold. Your families have missed you dearly. The attached is evidence of their joy as well as an explanation of answers I am sure you are seeking. The king and queen contacted me immediately upon receiving your message and entreated me to intervene on your behalf, assistance I am more than happy to provide. I have my own rooms at the Aerie Auberge and wish to invite you to dine with me once you have settled in. In the meantime, my attendants will be bringing you some things to hopefully make your road a touch more comfortable going forward. Blessings be upon you, my boy.

Your Other Uncle,
Otani Rekandran

It was his mother's younger brother who lived in Bastia, the next major city to the south on the coast. There was also an academy there, and it was where they had originally planned to start searching for information about the plant temple before they had received the tip about Lythenea. His uncle was the head of an influential merchant family there and conducted business from his sprawling estate just outside the city. He must have jumped on the first ship and headed north, securing them rooms at the Aerie Auberge and ensuring that they would have a safe place to land upon their arrival.

Behind his message was a collection of notes from Rakhmet's parents. They must have sent a flurry of pigeons back and forth with his uncle, planning and arranging it all. The Rekandrans had their own coop and provided a much more secure mode of communication than a public messenger station.

The first scroll was from the queen, gushing about how relieved and happy she was to have received word about him and Hara. It was smudged with tear marks, obvious signs of her tumultuous emotions, and his heart ached in his chest for her. The second was from his father, expressing some of the same sentiments but in much less flowery language. It was all couched in his usual stately reserve, and Rakhmet suppressed an eye roll.

Next was a very brief report, having only so much room to use on a piece of paper light enough to be carried hundreds of miles by a small bird, of the casualties at the Hapimose estate. His breath stuttered to a halt as he read the names: Layla Azhar, Temino Farouk, Ziah Hamdi, Fatij Khalitep, and Omat Faisana.

All talented and respected guards that he had known for years. Dead because of him.

He gritted his jaw as he forced himself to read on, searching for one name in particular. It explained that the palace had immediately sent a battalion of soldiers to Renpet upon hearing word of an attack involving the prince and his guards. They had already been on the Aswa headed to Melatius, so they had simply turned around and made it to the pass town within forty-eight hours.

Somehow, the remaining Hapimose forces and Rakhmet's guards had managed to expel the warlord's soldiers from the manor and barred themselves in, but it was the next sentence that caught his eye: it had been in large part to Nebehet's leadership that they had been able to turn the tide. Then the battalion had arrived soon after and driven the plum fighters out of the town, freeing those in the manor.

Rakhmet's legs gave out and he sank into one of the armchairs in the parlor and closed his eyes, sending a prayer to the gods for both his friend's safety and the lives of those lost. His poor battered heart was throwing itself against his ribs in vain, so much of his being calling for him to return to Zahar at the first chance. He wanted to confirm that his people were okay, that Nebehet was okay. His fingers itched to touch him, feel the solid mass of his shoulders and assure himself that his dear friend still breathed.

But they had things they needed to do.

He let out a rough exhale then moved on to the next scroll, Hara finally finishing her inspection and handing him a glass of water poured from the pitcher on the table. Exchanging the drink for the scrolls he had already read, she settled into the couch next to him as he perused the remaining ones.

The fourth was an explanation that his parents had instructed Otani to subtly ask around for information on the plant tribe, hoping to save Rakhmet and Hara some time since they were now a week behind schedule. A week that had felt like a year. Apparently, Kelah, the newly crowned Moon Queen on Tusi Island, had had a vision about the plant blessed soon after Rakhmet had left Zahar. Ohn Rutrulan had written to his father about three months ago, telling them that Kelah had visions of some sort of tapestry corridor and she had seen a vision of the water tapestry prior to visiting Tusi's temple. She had also seen a vision of the fire tapestry after Nasima had left the island to come to Zahar. These visions were one of her gifts from her goddess, an ability to see between the veils, and it was a needed confirmation that they were on the right path if she had had a vision about the plant tapestry.

The fifth was more of his mother worrying about his health and safety, agonizing over the fact that Rakhmet and Hara would be heading into the dangers of the plant temple after having suffered so much in their efforts to get there. It mentioned a request for his uncle to outfit him and Hara with new clothes and supplies, noting that most of the things they had packed for the journey had either been used in the Hapimose standoff or returned to Zahar with Nebehet and the guards. But she had also

201

included a small note that Hara's father had been notified of the incident and the staff of his group home had kept a candle lit for them, offering prayers to the gods at least once a day.

Rubbing a hand over his curls, he glanced up to find Hara frowning at the report on casualties. He couldn't imagine what it was like for her to see the names of her fellow guards listed, people with whom she had trained, worked, and lived. There seemed to be more anger than sadness there, although most of her grief was secreted away behind her stoicism.

When she realized he was studying her, the hardness in her gaze told him that she would need an outlet for her frustration sooner rather than later. He considered offering to be a punching bag and spar with her before they left for the temple, but he could also see the usefulness in helping her hold the anger in so she could unleash it fully on the nightmares he knew they would encounter there. They would need all the advantages they could muster.

He gave her a sympathetic look and handed over the last two missives as a knock sounded at the door. Rising, he answered it to find two young men with wheeled carts stacked high with expensive-looking trunks. He stepped back, waving for them to enter, and watched as they unloaded them into the parlor.

Shaking his head, he huffed at the piles. His uncle had been overly excessive in his gifts, and the attendants handed over another sealed envelope before exiting. He broke the seal, finding a short note that told him to take what he needed. The rest would be returned later.

He finished off his water then opened the first trunk, a large rectangular one that had metal filigree on its corners. It was filled to the brim with weapons and armor: daggers, shortswords, crossbows, breastplates, shin guards, bracers, anything a fighter could want. And it was all of the highest quality, the polished metal and leather mirroring his face as he bent over the bounty.

Digging through, he grabbed some armor to replace his worn leather pieces as well as another pair of daggers, a crossbow, and a sword. He then left it open for Hara as she stood to look over his shoulder and moved onto the next one. Trunk by trunk, he discovered a horde of Talegartian-style clothes, boots, medical supplies, rations, flint and steel, navigation instruments, stationary, camping kits, tools, jewels, coins, and even some fire starters and explosives.

Those had been critical in their success at the fire temple, Hara had told them. Both the water and the fire temples had been covered in some type of sentient caustic substance. She had described it as veins that took over the floors and walls and stung like a bitch if touched. It was vulnerable to flame, however, and they had planned to pack as much fire power as possible. A quarter of the dozen or so trunks of supplies they had originally packed for their journey had been stocked with flammable liquids and powders.

He was also well aware that his blessing would most likely be taken away once he entered Tabriara's sacred lands. It had happened on Tusi as well as in Zahar. Nasima had later described it to him as feeling like a sort of drunkenness, as if something had blanketed her senses. A numb buzz. He wasn't looking forward to it and made sure to set aside the trunk of flammables to divide between their packs. Perhaps it would be a good idea to get a pack animal for the trip to the temple, he realized as he eyed his quickly growing pile.

It took the rest of the afternoon to select the items they needed, repack their bags, take baths, and make themselves presentable in their new outfits, but he couldn't help but stash those last three silver coins in his pocket when he was done. Yes, it was true that they were now stocked with more than enough Talegartian currency to travel around the entire continent five times over, but he was unable to let those three pieces go. They burned in his pocket, reminding him of everything they had suffered as well as everything they had triumphed over. A win to remember.

His gaze was intense, somehow older, as he straightened his jacket in the mirror, the pressed linen fitted snugly across his broad shoulders. He had chosen a suit in an off-white with a bloodred pocket square, leaving the collar of his white tunic unbuttoned at the top. It helped him breathe a bit easier, the trappings of a Talegartian aristocrat feeling a bit too constricting for his tastes. Pulling his cufflinks taut, he gave himself one last glance then headed into the parlor to find Hara waiting by the window.

She was wearing a guard outfit that consisted of fitted pants underneath a long tunic that reached mid-thigh. There were high slits on either side of it to give her freedom of movement, and for the first time since the cat attack, she had her shining dagger and zulfiqar harnessed at her waist. The leather breastplate strapped on top and the gold bands around her biceps and top bun completed the look. Royal Guard Hara Gamal was back in action.

A pang in his gut ached for the long black plait, shining in his hands, but he swallowed the sensation and cleared his throat. She turned and there was a flash of light, the sun shining in the window to illuminate her from behind like his very own vision between the veils. He choked on whatever he was going to say, his throat closing up of its own accord.

Instead of standing there awkwardly staring at her, he pivoted and headed to the door, knowing she would follow. He had sent a note to his uncle before dressing, asking to meet him in the inner hall for dinner, and figured they might as well keep marching forward with their plans. When he heard the soft pad of her boots on the carpets behind him, his breathing settled as they descended the stairs and turned toward the clusters of sitting areas that filled the center of the inn.

The massive three-story hall was capped with a glass roof, letting sunshine filter into the cavernous space, and all over people sat and conversed with one another. Nearly every eye turned to him as they entered, and he grimaced internally at the reminder of his now even more notorious reputation. The mantle settled on him uneasily, like a new pair of leather boots that were still stiff and rubbed his heels raw.

But he kept his slight smile firmly in place and scanned the room for his uncle, locating him just as he strode out of one of the side alcoves and raised his hand in greeting. Otani was a barrel-chested man, a tall, dark figure adorned in a sharp green suit who commanded respect both professionally as well as physically. He was certainly not above decking someone if the situation called for it, but he preferred the more gentile ways of business.

On his face was a broad smile and his eyes sparkled with happiness as he pulled his nephew into a bear hug, rapping him on the back with his thick palm.

"Ah, my dear boy. How good it is to see you whole." His deep baritone rolled through Rakhmet, giving him a dose of home that he had been craving.

Rakhmet almost lost his footing but locked his knees as he patted his uncle's shoulder and pulled away. "Good uncle, you are a sight for sore eyes."

"Yes, and it is quite the journey that has brought you here!" Otani clapped him once more then stepped back to give Hara a friendly smile and wink as well. Her mask cracked for a moment as she gave him a grateful nod, then he turned and started leading them to the alcove he had reserved. It was an intimate space, a round table with four armchairs grouped around and a delicate chandelier giving everything a soft glow. He invited Rakhmet to sit with a wave of the hand and started pouring him a glass of wine from the pitcher, the liquid bubbling with effervescence as it filled the crystal.

Hara took up her usual position behind Rakhmet as he raised his glass to Otani. "Thank the gods I was blessed with an uncle who can swoop in to save the day with such flair."

Otani laughed, the sound full of mirth. "Ah, yes. What else would all my riches be good for except coming to the aid of the great fire prince?"

Rakhmet groaned, subtly rolling his eyes. "Please don't tell me you believe the stories."

"Well, the truth is always somewhere between fact and fiction, is it not, my dear boy?" He gave Rakhmet a knowing look and he leaned in, lowering his voice. "There has been a lot of news coming out of the kingdom lately and there will always be folks who seek to twist the stories to suit their narratives."

"And what narrative are you spreading, uncle?" he asked.

"One that will do a lot of people good, Rakhmet." Otani's gaze went to the many pairs of eyes that were subtly watching them from all over the hall, then he flashed him a quick smile and wink. "And line my pocketbooks, of course."

Rakhmet sat back in his chair and took another sip of wine, thinking. This was not the place to get into details. There were far too many potential eavesdroppers and they had to be careful about what they said.

"You sure worried your poor mother." Otani wagged a finger at him. "My pigeons were flown until they dropped."

Rakhmet sighed. "Yes, I am aware, and it does pain me. Things got . . . out of hand."

"But you handled it, Rakhmet." His voice grew serious. "As we all knew you were capable of, you have triumphed. Greatly."

"Yes, but—"

"No buts," his uncle cut in. "You have risen in the eyes of many, in quite a few different ways, and the success of your mission here will secure much for you."

"Nothing is guaranteed." His heart clenched at the surety in Otani's gaze.

"That is true, but the gods bless us immensely. They have given us the tools to prevail." Otani tapped his finger to the table and lowered his voice even further. "In that regard, I do recommend that you visit the Cozad Apothecary before you leave for the next stretch of your trip."

"An apothecary?" Rakhmet furrowed his brows. "For supplies? You have already provided more than enough."

"For some information you were seeking. About that plant-based salve you were looking into." Otani tapped his finger again then leaned back, looking out over the crowd once more.

Rakhmet cleared his throat as understanding hit him. Whoever ran the apothecary had the information about the plant tribe that Otani had been searching for. The information that would give them the next step in the plan.

"They apparently have some very rare blooms that will provide the outcome you seek," his uncle continued, an offhand comment as he noticed someone across the room. He raised his hand and smiled, his eyes lighting up with delight.

"What do you know . . . Ah, please join us!" he called, beckoning two young women forward. They were dressed to the nines, decked out in glittering jewels and fine silks, and their smiles widened as they drifted toward them. One was a brunette with long waves falling across one shoulder and the other a blonde, her hair cut short in a graceful bob that curled around the edge of her patrician jaw.

They curtsied as they reached the table, and Otani stood to pull out a chair for each of them, giving introductions as they settled into their seats. "My dear nephew, this is Curra Desran, the daughter of a business partner of mine, and her academy mate, Imonella Artez."

"Well met, Curra and Imonella." Rakhmet nodded politely. He could smell his uncle's intentions from a mile away and suppressed the groan.

They tilted their heads sweetly as Otani struck up a conversation and responded with all the right answers at the appropriate moments. The girls were both philosophy students at the academy, having been raised by influential families in the region. Both the exact sort of girl that had the prerequisite breeding to help lead a kingdom one day, just like his own mother once upon a time.

Rakhmet tried to follow along as dinner was served and they all began to eat, humming with an affirmative or negative when prompted, but it bored him to death. All he could think was how their pretty little philosophies would fare in the face of the monster that lurked under his skin. They would never see him at his worst, so they would never deserve him at his best.

His head, his heart was full of another who was like him. Another whose inner fire burned as his did.

As much as she tried to hide it under the many layers of royal guard propriety, he and Hara were one in the same. Two birds of a phoenix feather, as it were.

There was an undeniable connection that had been forged between them the night she had become his oathed guard and it had only grown from there. That bond was the one he would uphold in the end.

As the evening came to a close, his patience had worn thin and he offered brief farewells as he made his leave. He promised to be in touch with his uncle on the morrow but didn't stick around, aiming for the stairs that would lead them back to their suite.

Hara had been quiet the entire time and it grated on his nerves. He couldn't even look at her when she was stationed behind him like that, and he felt his shoulders ease a bit as he glanced over to find her close. It was growing more and more obvious to him that he needed her by his side, not following in his footsteps.

They approached the double doors and he unlocked one, drawing them inside and closing it to block out the exhausting world outside. He braced both hands on the back of it and stretched his neck out, letting out a long exhale.

Hearing a chuckle behind him, he turned to find Hara smirking at him with her arms crossed. "You look like you're barring the door in case they come running for you."

He huffed, surprised by the joking gleam in her eye. "I'd beat 'em off with a stick if I could."

Her smile softened at the seriousness in his voice, and he took it as a sign to step forward.

"Hara, I—" He took another step toward her. "I need you to know something."

She retreated a foot as he advanced another, her brows creasing. "And what's that?"

"I will wait for you," he said, stopping a couple feet from her.

"What?" Her forehead wrinkled further.

"There's no one else for me." He drank her in. "It's you. I wait for none other."

"Rakhmet," she protested. "You can't."

"I will."

"It's madness." Her voice was harder, her anger with his stubbornness rising. She pressed him back, her palm flat against his chest, and he relented a step as she shifted forward.

"It makes perfect sense to me." He held up his hands as if to say *see? no tricks up my sleeve* then cupped her elbows. "I need you to understand this: I want you."

"Do you forget that I've seen you all these years? Chasing after everyone and anything? I will not be another one of your conquests!" she exclaimed, fury flashing in her gaze, and pushed him again. He yielded a foot but didn't let go of her arms.

"No," he growled, leaning into her space. "I will make you my queen."

Hara froze, her jaw popping open in shock as she swayed for a moment. "Wh-what?"

He stepped forward as she moved backward, a dance between two flames.

"I want you on my throne, in my bed, and by my side. It's you and me, Hara. There is no one else."

"You wouldn't," she murmured. Her eyes were wide as she read every inch of his face.

"I swear this to you," he vowed, moving so that her back hit the wall on one side of their parlor. "It is your name that is branded on my heart, has been for fourteen years."

He brought her hand to his pectoral and held it there as if she could feel the ridges of her name as it beat for her.

She shook her head in disbelief, brows furrowing. "I . . . I thought you would choose . . . It never occurred to me . . . There was no way . . ."

"Let me prove it to you. I can wait . . . I can—"

"You can't be serious, Rakhmet. I—"

He leaned in, drawing her to him as if getting her closer would help her feel his desperate heart, and brushed his lips against her ear. "Tell me you don't burn for me as I burn for you. Just say the word and I will never speak of this again."

Her frustrated exhale traveled across his collarbone and his skin prickled at the sensation, but she was silent as she fisted his now rumpled shirt.

"Tell me that there's no hope," he whispered. *"Tell me that you don't fear losing me as much as I fear losing you. Tell me it's not my name engraved on your heart. Tell me I'm not yours."*

"How do I know you mean it?" she demanded. "How can I tell this is real?"

Pulling back, he met her eye. "Touch me, feel me, know that I am flesh and blood."

He dropped to his knees in front of her, putting her hands on his cheeks. "Look upon me and know the truth. I will show you. I will wait for you, I promise."

His palms soothed up and down on the sides of her legs as she glared at him, but he caught glimpses of intrigue there too. He watched as she debated and questioned, the crease on the edge of her mouth deepening then flattening.

"You want to prove it?" she finally asked, dropping her hands from his cheeks to his shoulders and giving a shove. "Convince me."

She bent her knee, bringing her booted foot to the middle of his chest, but he caught it with a smirk before she could force him farther back. He held it still, testing her, testing him. For years and years, they had grappled and sparred, punched and kicked. Of course she was going to make him fight for it.

"Hara," he growled. "You're it for me."

Still gripping her foot, he brought his other hand to one of the slits in her tunic, trailing up until he reached the top of her pants.

"I realized it when we were stuck on that godsforsaken mountain," he continued, brushing his fingers against her warm skin. She let out a sharp exhale and her hand landed on his forearm, squeezing. "All this time, it's always been you.

"I've been a fool not to see it." He moved the hand holding her foot to her calf, massaging the tight muscles, and studied the emotions flickering across her face. "Because I am entirely at your mercy."

He kept working her long, lean leg and smiled as her brows relaxed. "I beg because I know that I've been unworthy. I know that I've fucked up too many times. But I am here, on my knees, desperate to prove myself to you."

Her grip on his arm slackened and he moved slowly, memorizing the curves of her hip bone and the coiled strength in her thigh. She was a masterful creature to behold, her tall frame corded with muscle and her eyes burning with want. A vision all his own.

"Prove it," she breathed, the breastplate rising and falling with her hitching chest as his thumb trailed over the front of her, just above where he truly wanted to touch.

"I want to taste you," he rasped, his heart pounding. "May I?"

Her fingers clenched around his arm, but she nodded, the challenge clear.

He gently set down her foot and tugged on the ties of her pants, his gaze never leaving hers as color rose in her cheeks, and a fever lit her from the inside. The fabric started to fall away, and he couldn't help but groan as the scent of her hit him. It was a musky sweetness that made him lick his lips, and he smirked as Hara's attention caught on his mouth.

Sliding one pant leg down then the other, he helped free her from anything that impeded him and soon found his hands on her bare thighs. He groaned again, the reality hitting him as he gripped her, and leaned his forehead against her pelvic bone, still hidden by the long tunic she wore. He breathed her in and shifted his hands until they reached the creases where her legs met her hips, his thumbs turning in toward the hottest part of her.

Her fingers dug into the fabric of his jacket, straining against his shoulders, and he vaguely realized he was still fully dressed. On his knees in a full suit, about to put his mouth to the woman that held his heart. But the thought fell away as he swept his thumb into her damp curls. Then, everything disappeared as he thumbed her slit, his calloused pad sliding through the building nectar, and she let out a long moan.

He felt the jerk go through her, her body reacting to his exploration of her, and he nuzzled her lower belly to soothe her. Her breath quickened and he pushed in farther, his finger breaching the slick folds. Pushing her tunic to the side with his other hand, he watched as his thumb separated her for him and he almost fell apart.

Glancing up, he marveled at her as she gasped and clung tighter to him. Her lids were heavy and her mouth was hanging open as she fought to catch her breath. She was coming undone in his hands, and it was like handling raw flame. He could coax her, urge her to burn.

He took away his hand and slid it to the back of her thigh, watching as her brow creased at the removal before shooting up again as he lifted her leg onto his shoulder. It fully exposed her secret core, and he smiled up at her as she swayed, using him for balance. He didn't break her gaze as he held her tight, his fingers digging into her ass to position her where he wanted, where he could move her, shape her, feed her flame.

Leaning in, he took a deep breath and waited until her full focus was on his mouth just inches from her. He let his jaw drop slowly open, her attention so complete that her lips parted to unconsciously mirror his, and then paused again, letting the tension build. His tongue extended to rest on his bottom lip, his whole expression open to her as he waited for the sign.

She choked in a breath, then another, and her hips twitched forward of their own accord, an impatient huff coming from the back of her throat. He fell forward in an instant, sealing his tongue to her, and they both moaned at the contact. Like honey, the taste of her flowed onto and into him and his eyes rolled closed in ecstasy. He dragged his mouth against her, tasting as if he hadn't eaten a morsel since her lips last touched his.

He licked her with abandon, losing himself to his frenzy. He had to consume her. He wanted to drink from her very marrow.

"Oh gods!" she cried out as he sucked her sensitive nub into his mouth, pulling as if she were the only sustenance he'd ever need, and her fingers threaded into his hair. He moaned encouragingly, the vibrations causing her to squirm. She clutched at him as her hips undulated against his face, her muscles trembling under his hands. "Good . . . good, that's it—"

As he sucked and kissed, her wetness covered his chin and dripped down his jaw as her gasps grew louder and sharper. He scraped his teeth against her clit and then latched on, tugging gently as she keened, her body going rigid. Her release was still barreling through her when he abruptly let go and swiped his tongue through her juice, slipping a finger inside her at the same time.

"Rakh . . . met!" Her moan turned into a scream as he plunged in, pushing his finger to the rough spot that he knew would make her see stars. He rubbed, unrelenting, as she was thrown into another orgasm.

Her body arced and her head thumped against the wall as she lost herself, a string of prayers and curses falling from her. It was the most gorgeous song he had ever heard, and his body grew rock hard at the sounds he was teasing from her. His own hips started grinding, a ravenous yearning flaming through him.

She consumed his entire focus, every inch of his being enthralled as he devoured her, and her cries turned into a panting stream that didn't end. Pushing her over another edge, he tried to hold on as she jerked in his grip, but she managed to wedge her foot against his shoulder for leverage. She kicked out, a blind surge of strength, and knocked him to the floor with a hard thud.

They both gasped as they tumbled, their limbs tangling together as she slid to the floor with legs that wouldn't hold her up. He ended up on his ass, his knees bent and legs folded, with her slumped in between them. Their chests heaved as they stared at each other, his lips dripping and red from her.

Her eyes were darting all over him, her expression caught somewhere between mania and deep-rooted satisfaction, and his heart pounded with pride. She looked like her world had just been blown off its axis as she struggled to grasp a cohesive thought.

"Fuck," she grunted and tried shifting. The foot she had kicked him with had ended up draped over the side of his lap and she attempted to fold it back into herself, but he caught it with his hand, halting her.

His other hand snaked out and wrapped around the back of her neck, pulling her in and laying a brand on her lips with his. Her immediate moan slipped past her filter as he kissed her with all he had, pouring his heart into her.

Breaking the kiss, he touched his forehead to hers for a brief moment then gave her some space to breathe. He scooted away, releasing her leg, and waited for her to collect herself.

She went from dazed to frustrated as she tried to get her legs to work, and he popped up to help her, holding out his hands. Scowling, she gripped them and hauled herself to a standing position. Her knees only knocked together once before she got them locked and glared at him.

"Don't look so smug," she rasped.

He fought the chuckle that arose, biting his lip to keep it in.

"I mean it." She shoved him. "This doesn't change anything."

"Is that so?" he murmured, curling his arms around her waist and dropping his head to nuzzle into the side of her neck. The sigh that molded her to him gave him all the answer he needed, but she braced her hands against his chest and pushed.

"You're still an idiot," she bit at him, and he couldn't help the laugh that threw his head back.

"Of course I am." He grinned at her, his smile turning serious. "But I'm your idiot."

She rolled her eyes, but she had to bite her own lip and look away as she extracted herself and stepped back. Crossing her arms, she cleared her throat. "Well . . . whatever . . . The point is, I should go to bed."

Her eyes shot to him and a blush overtook her face. "Alone, I mean."

His humor faded a bit as he watched her walls go back up between them. She was still protecting herself from something, but it didn't necessarily bother him. His decision had been made; he would wait. So he gave her a slight nod, letting her know that he was respecting her unspoken reluctance.

Seeing her shoulders relax a fraction, he couldn't help but add softly: "Tell me it's not my name on your heart, Hara."

Her gaze burned into him, setting every inch of him afire. His nostrils flared as he caught the scent of charcoal, and she couldn't hide the words that blazed behind her dark pupils, staying silent as her inner flame betrayed her.

She refused to answer, turning to grab her pants and boots from the floor and taking measured steps toward her bedroom door. He watched as she turned the knob, entered, and then closed herself in, all without sparing him another glance.

Standing there in the dark night, he stared at the molding around the threshold for several long minutes. It was gilded, a gold that matched the over-the-top furnishings, and its metallic sheen stood out in the shadowed room.

He nodded, a response to a question unasked, then retired, savoring the taste of her as he drifted into a deep sleep.

DAY THIRTY-ONE

When they had visited the Cozad Apothecary the next morning, they had learned that Pasha Cozad was a renowned herbal healer in Lythenea and secretly traded with the plant tribe for a very particular kind of red flower that only grew on Tabriara's lands. It was apparently integral to a tincture that alleviated the symptoms of a liver disease that was passed from some fathers to their offspring, and she was the only herbalist in the city who made the coveted medicine.

She had never given out the name of her supplier before, but she had owed Otani a great favor for protecting her interests from a competing healer's practice a few years back. So Rakhmet and Hara had soon had their hands on solid directions to reach the sacred village and had made a quick exit, thanking his uncle profusely for procuring them both the informant as well as two pack goats for their journey.

They had headed southward using one of the Twin Arches, the two bridges connecting the great riverbanks that flanked Lythenea, and had found the road that would take them deeper into the rainforest. It had taken them two and a half days, tugging their somewhat recalcitrant loads behind them as Hara avoided Rakhmet's eye.

A flustered blush would creep across her face whenever they did happen to accidentally lock together and she would huff, glancing away and checking the tightness of the straps holding her things to her goat for the hundredth time. But he would just smile to himself and keep quiet, not saying a word when he had awoke both mornings to a warm hand on his arm.

It was midmorning when he started to feel faint, his head reeling as they climbed a particularly steep portion of the path. The road had ended about eight miles back, turning into a foot trail that wove through the tangled landscape. Hara was in the process of hacking away some of the vines that covered their way when he stumbled and reached out to brace himself against his goat's flank. It bleated, surprised, as it craned its neck to glance at him, and Rakhmet swayed, trying to stay upright.

"Hara," he choked, and she spun at the sound. Her brows fell as she clocked him, sheathing her sword in a fluid motion and reaching out to steady him. He felt sick to his stomach as he doubled over, holding an arm across himself.

"It's my blessing." The croak turned into a moan as he tried to swallow the bile down.

"It's okay," she soothed. One hand rubbed his back and the other held him up as he tried to gather himself.

His heat left him like a fire doused in water and suddenly he was cold, so cold. He shivered and Hara pulled him closer, the warmth of her a stunning contrast to his chilled skin. Leaning into her, he groaned softly and burrowed further. She continued to murmur as he nuzzled her neck, his shaking arms clutching her to him.

He breathed deep, sucking in draws of her as his heart settled its panicked beat and gradually calmed, growing used to the sensation. The aching vacuum inside was no stranger to him. He had spent years trapped in its clutches, and the only thing holding him back from fading into that blank state of the living dead was the woman in his arms.

Her scent filled him like billowing incense and her flame licked his soul, keeping its ember lit. She held him together, her strength enough for the both of them, and she let him take what he needed as long minutes passed.

Clearing his throat, he finally pulled back once his legs felt steady again, but Hara kept her hands on his shoulders for a moment longer. She looked at him with eyes that knew him to his core, knowing better than anyone what had happened last time he had lost access to his blessing.

He supposed it should have been a relief to lose it all those months ago, after spending his entire life living a lie. Being free of his secret should have been exhilarating, but his power was the truest piece of him. It was woven into the very fiber of who he was. It was in his blood.

Without it, he was an empty mask. A vacancy of the soul.

He shook his head to get focused again and Hara stepped back, sensing the shift. He couldn't let himself dissociate when they were almost to the finish line. Waving them forward, he urged her on. They had more important things to do. He would just have to suck it up and keep his feet moving forward.

About half an hour later, the rainforest surrounding them grew eerily quiet and they both paused out of instinct. There was the rustle of leaves in the wind, but something was off. The path seemed unchanged, the expected overabundance of plant life protruding from all sides, but even the goats stomped nervously as their square pupils darted around.

Hara's shoulders bunched, both hands going to her divine weapons, but her fingers hovered above the pommels as she studied all fifty shades of green that stretched before them. There was a long moment, and then the snap of a twig came from a thicket of bushes ahead and to the right about fifty feet. It was deliberate, no additional cracks or obvious signs of movement following it.

He went for his own dagger, but Hara glanced over her shoulder and stopped him with a look. Instead, she pulled her zulfiqar and held it in front of her. A twitch to the side and she lit it, the flame sweeping up the edge of the golden blade, then snuffed it just as quickly. A simple demonstration.

"Praise be to the gods and goddesses who have granted their blessings upon us," she proclaimed, bowing over her zulfiqar before setting it on the ground in front of her. "Praise be to the blessed Plant Goddess and her beloved children. Their fire kin wish to rekindle our communion with them."

She drew her dagger next, holding it out as she did before. "The blessed fire prince and his guard wish to enter your sacred domain and offer our assistance. We come bearing information that we believe will be welcomed."

Setting the dagger next to her zulfiqar with another bow, she moved back respectfully and held her hands at her shoulders in a sign of nonviolence. Rakhmet mirrored her, raising his own and stepping out of the shadows behind her. They watched their surroundings as another long moment stretched.

He was about to ask Hara if they had been mistaken when a figure appeared in front of them about thirty feet away. They silently rose from the flora, their features obscured by multiple layers of natural camouflage. They were covered in dried mosses and leaves, and the browns and greens of their leathers made them near invisible.

They held a heavy crossbow in their hands and kept it trained on Rakhmet as they approached and stopped at a safe distance. No one moved as they stared at each other.

"How many in your party?" Their accent was thick, the vowels crowded in the back of their throat.

"Just us two," Hara answered.

"And the goats," Rakhmet added, jerking his chin in their direction.

The figure stared for another moment, then nodded at Hara's weapons on the ground. "Come."

They then turned and made some sort of hand motion that had four more figures rising from the foliage, one pair coming from the rear to take the goats' reins while the other two flanked either side of Rakhmet and Hara. They wielded a mixture of crossbows and swords, each weapon carefully decorated to blend in with the rest of them.

Hara picked hers up and sheathed them, letting them lead her and Rakhmet forward into another curtain of vines. The figure didn't cut them away though, but instead walked right into them. Their body parted the mass of tendrils and forged the way into a verdant sea.

They had no option but to follow as they delved deeper, the glossy leaves and pollen-laden blooms brushing against them like thousands of hands smoothing across their limbs. It seemed never-ending as they walked on and on, and Rakhmet started counting in his head to get past the feeling of vertigo. His hand instinctively reached out and Hara pressed her palm to his in reassurance, easing his nerves.

Eventually, light started to appear ahead of them, and they emerged into a large opening. A small village unfolded before them like a living tapestry, intricately woven into the fabric of the rainforest itself. Buildings with sinuous forms and organic contours rose from the earth as if they simply grew that way, their walls crafted from intertwining vines, living wood, and blooming flora.

They were brought to a pathway that meandered like a serpent through the village, paved with soft moss. There was a temple ahead that stood at the heart of it all, its spires reaching skyward, and it seemed to be made of ancient trees, crowned with blossoms that shimmered like precious gems.

Villagers were scattered here and there, wearing similar clothes made from natural fibers, and some of them stopped to watch their procession. Their gazes were curious but wary, looking between them, the camouflaged guards, and the two goats laden with packs. They all wore some sort of blade strapped to their hips, an obvious sign that they were ready to defend their home at a moment's notice.

They stopped in front of the temple and the lead guard motioned for them to wait as they entered the structure through the open archway. Rakhmet tried to listen to the soft conversation inside, but another curtain of vines blocked their sight and muffled any sound. The guard soon returned, however, and paused as if about to say something but was interrupted by the creaking of wood from above.

Rakhmet and Hara flinched back, their hands going to their weapons as the canopy above them started to shift and shake. The leaves parted and a thick vine fell through, landing next to the guard as they glanced up in anticipation. One pale foot then another emerged, extending into agile limbs that wrapped around the vine for purchase.

A young woman with a long mane of burnt umber hair came into view, her nimble hands lowering herself down to the waiting group. She dropped the last few feet, landing without a sound as she straightened and gave them a friendly smile.

"Visitors?" she asked, her accent very different from the guard who had spoken before. Her consonants were harsh, but the tone was mild, almost dreamy. It matched her small stature, the delicacy of her bearing a marked difference between her and the tall guard next to her. There was a scar that slashed across her forehead on the left side, and she wore the same camouflaged leathers.

"They claim to be the fire blessed and his guard," the muscled figure supplied, nodding toward Hara. "She wields an oath dagger."

The woman's green eyes blew wide, a look of delight blossoming as she clasped her hands together. "Oh, truly? How wonderful!"

Rakhmet and Hara exchanged glances, then he cleared his throat and stepped forward. "'Tis true. I am Rakhmet Pyrantus, the fire blessed heir and Prince of Zahar, and this is my royal guard, Hara Gamal."

"How lovely it is to meet you both!" she said in a singsong voice, moving to take his hand in hers. "I am Esia, the plant blessed, and this is my oathed guard, Nees."

"Well met, Esia and Nees." Rakhmet nodded at each with a relieved smile. "We come bearing information and assistance. We have much to discuss with you."

"Of course, of course!" She beamed, her luminous gaze sparkling. "The village of Curaco welcomes you! Please, come inside."

Looping one arm through Rakhmet's and one through Hara's, she ushered them inside the temple, revealing a large gathering space that was dominated by a circular table crafted from a colossal tree trunk at the center. It was covered in intricate carvings depicting the life cycles of plants, illuminated by lanterns containing bioluminescent specimens on the worn wooden walls.

There were several figures scattered throughout, engaged in hushed discussions that halted as soon as the trio of them appeared with Nees close behind. They seemed to be some of the elders of the village, all bearing evidence of the years in their wrinkles and age spots, and they studied the visitors with keen curiosity as Esia led them to the table.

She selected the seat next to Rakhmet as they settled in and leaned forward with interest. "Please, tell us of your journey. Are the fire blessed well? Do they suffer under the weight of the shadows too?"

"The shadows? Ah, yes. We have been calling it 'the corruption,' but I'm guessing you're referring to the energy that is blocking access to your blessing?" Rakhmet asked, glancing around the room to read everyone's reactions.

Brows furrowed and some nodded as Esia clasped his scarred forearm with a gasp. "Yes! Yes, that's it!"

Rakhmet hummed in understanding. "That is what brings us to you. Your tribe has not had contact with the outside world in some time, is that correct? You have not heard of the troubles that ail the blessed?"

"We sent someone out a few months ago, seeking information about the strange storms that brought the shadows, but were unsuccessful," Nees answered for her, standing to the side with their arms crossed. They had removed their helm and Rakhmet could now see their serious expression. Light, short hair capped their angular face, and Rakhmet could tell their lanky form had been honed into a weapon of its own accord.

"Yes, we heard about your inquiries. We have been searching for clues on the whereabouts of the temples because we believe many of them to be corrupted," Rakhmet continued. "There have been quite a few . . . difficulties afoot."

He launched into an explanation of what he knew concerning the initial discoveries of Kelah and Roe, including her mysterious appearance on Tusi Island and their subsequent clearing of the water temple. He explained that the Rutrulans had renewed contact with the fire blessed in Zahar afterwards and also detailed how his and his father's blessings had been stifled until Nasima had come to Zahar to help secure the fire temple.

Gesturing to Hara, he let her pick up the story as she filled them in on what had exactly happened in the temple and her discussion with Furaro. Murmurs started filling the room as she described the monstrosity they had faced, and Nees began pacing as she told them that, while the water and fire temples were now safe once more, the sacred plant, wind, sun, and metal lands were likely still infected.

"And on top of all of this, the country of Nalliendra is slowly taking over as much as they can," Rakhmet added. "They have been adamant in their desire to eliminate all blessed ones and have already conquered most of Frandae, if not all. They have supposedly claimed the Staroh and Metuit Seas as their own, even going so far as to attack one of our ships because they refused to let them board.

"My father has declared war against them and convened the Endrian Coalition of Rulers to protect the eastern South Endrian coast," he finished up. "Hara and I have come here in the meantime to assist you in clearing your temple and, hopefully, reestablishing contact with blessed Tabriara."

"Goodness, that is a lot." Esia sat back in her chair with a dazed expression.

"Are you certain that you are capable of clearing the shadows?" Nees asked, studying them.

"Well." Rakhmet glanced at Hara. "We intended to arrive here with a dozen of our best-trained guards, but we encountered some . . . unexpected obstacles. It is now just the two of us, but we have tried to restock with appropriate supplies. Our chances would be much better, though, if your tribe could contribute some fighters to the cause."

"Oh, of course, we'd be more than happy to come along," Esia was quick to offer.

"Ah, blessed Esia Ricina," one of the elders interrupted with a concerned expression. "Do you truly think that is best? It sounds quite dangerous and your blessing is silenced still."

Esia looked to Nees, whose lips thinned into a stern line but didn't offer an opinion, seemingly deferring to Esia's judgment.

"These . . . shadow creatures you speak of." She hesitated, turning to Hara. "What is your plan to expel them?"

"The ichor is particularly vulnerable to flame," Hara answered. "So we have brought with us quite a bit of explosives and other materials. The key to getting through the fire temple was clearing the way to the center, where the sacred crystal was, then defeating the creatures who guarded it."

"Do you have any understanding of the layout of your temple?" Rakhmet asked Esia.

"Only the top portion. We used to travel there to perform rituals, but after the storm . . . it wasn't safe anymore." She shook her head sadly.

"What do you mean?"

"There's a malevolent presence there now," Nees explained for her. "There is darkness lurking in the boughs, an evil that consumes all around it. It slowly took over the sacred forest. We have forbidden everyone from crossing its boundaries."

"Sacred forest?" Hara asked.

"Yes, there's a forest that surrounds the temple. The trees there are unique. They have their own ways of communicating to us." Esia sighed longingly.

"We can take you there to see for yourselves. Perhaps tomorrow," Nees added.

"That would be appreciated. We hope to get started on this as soon as possible. It's a race against time at this point." Rakhmet nodded.

"Rakhmet's blessing is dampened too," Hara explained, turning to the elder who had posed the question. "As was Nasima's when she entered the fire temple, but it was restored near the end of the fight. We anticipate that it will be the same for Rakhmet and Esia, if she decides to join us."

"The Esia Ricina is at the center of our village," another elder cut in, an older man with long gray hair hanging down his back. "She is the very fabric of our devotion. If anything were to befall her, we'd be bereft. Aimless."

"**The** Esia Ricina?" Rakhmet asked. "Is that your title here?"

"Yes." She gave a soft, almost sad smile to the elder who spoke. "That is what they call me."

"Are there no other blessed here?" Hara's brows creased as she began to understand the full impact of what they were asking.

"No, I am the only one. I . . ." She paused, taking a deep breath. "I do not know where the rest of my blood kin are. There are quite a few things I do not know. I . . . was not born here. It wasn't until about five years ago that I first arrived in Curaco and I don't remember much about my life prior. All I know is that I found myself crawling through the jungle alone, a deep-seated impulse driving me forward."

"Alone?" Rakhmet asked, surprised. "You don't remember anything?"

"No." She shook her head. "I have vague memories of being locked in a bedroom of some kind and needing to escape. I just knew I had to get away. So I ran . . . until I came across this village. They took me in. They understood who I was before I even knew."

"We immediately recognized her for who she was: our long lost Ricina. Our blessed one, finally come home," the older man continued with pride in his eyes. "Our tribe has struggled to persevere ever since we were forced into hiding centuries ago, but we had our blessed ones to guide us. Ever present yet never discovered. Tragedy struck, though, three generations back, when the Ricina at the time died protecting our lands from the Talegartians.

"Their council had been trying to make inroads into our forests, seeking out the rare flowers and herbs that grow here, but we held them back. Used what we could

233

to confuse and rebuff them, convincing them that there was nothing here they could want. Unfortunately, the Ricina sacrificed her life in the process without an heir to continue in her place."

"They believe that I come from another branch of the bloodline, one that fled after the council took over," Esia explained, her expression full of mourning.

"It was dark times without a blessed one to lead us." The elder frowned. "We barely held the village together, but our hope never wavered and our prayers were finally answered. Praise be to the gods."

The rest of the elders echoed him with a solemn, "Praise be to the gods."

"And there are no . . . heirs now?" Hara asked carefully.

Esia's face crumpled, her moss-colored gaze dimming. "No . . . no heirs yet."

There seemed to be more behind her answer, but Rakhmet could tell it was a sensitive subject.

"Well, if you don't want to risk yourself . . . ," Hara started to say.

"No," Esia interjected firmly, her jaw tightening. "I want to come. The sacred temple is mine to protect and I have been failing in my duty."

"How long has it been since . . . ?" Rakhmet asked, the elders murmuring their reluctance at Esia's determination.

"It's been eighteen months since the storm," Nees said, having stopped their pacing to stand at Esia's side like an unmovable tree. "We haven't crossed the boundaries since then."

"And you wish to come as well?" Hara asked Nees.

"Wherever the Esia Ricina goes, I go," they responded, their conviction solid.

"You said you were her oathed guard. What exactly does that mean in your tribe?" Her eyes flicked to Rakhmet as she posed the question before darting away again.

"It is an honor that has a long history in our culture," they answered gravely. "Ever since the first Plant Queen was chosen by blessed Tabriara, there have been oathed guards specifically trained to stand by her side and keep her safe from harm. While we did not have blessed ones for many years, the tradition carried on and I was selected at a young age to be a protector of the temple."

They looked to Esia and their expression took on an adoring quality to it. "Then our prayers were answered."

Esia smiled back at them, her face alight with the same care and veneration, and something sparked alive in Rakhmet's chest.

He rubbed his sternum and felt Hara shift in her seat next to him as she asked: "We have something similar in our country, but it's more for the royal family than specifically for the blessed. You spoke of an oath dagger earlier, though. What did you mean by that?"

"The dagger you wield." Nees nodded to Hara's waist. "It's an oath dagger. I recognize it as cousin to my own."

They unsheathed their own dagger from its holster and flipped it around, holding the pommel out to Hara. Her eyes darted to Rakhmet's for a brief second, her usual reserve fraying at the edges as wonder and bewilderment broke through. They had spent weeks looking for any clue as to what her dagger was, and here was the information they had been seeking in the most unexpected of places.

Hara took a hold of it and examined it closely. Without a doubt, it was as they said: a long-lost relative of the one sheathed at her side. She slowly drew hers out and set them side by side. They were the same length and color, but at the ends of the pommels sat an emerald on Nees's and a ruby on Hara's. One blade was engraved with trailing vines and flowers, the other with flame.

"You were not aware of the weapon you possessed?" Nees asked, catching Hara's stunned reaction.

"No, I . . . It was gifted to me by blessed Furaro in thanks for . . ." Her wide gaze jumped from Nees to Rakhmet. "He said the zulfiqar was for helping clear his temple, but the dagger . . . it was for my service as the oathed protector of the Pyrantus heir."

"That would make sense." Nees nodded. "You should have been given the dagger when you first oathed yourself to Rakhmet, but it seems as though it had been returned to the Fire God at some point."

"Likely when the revolution happened, when all of our records got sealed away." Rakhmet reached out to touch the fire dagger reverently.

"Did you complete the oathing ceremony once you came into possession of it?" the elder man who had spoken before asked.

"Oathing ceremony?" Rakhmet glanced up, his hand dropping to his lap. "No, I mean, we had the original ceremony a while back but no additional one."

"Then your bond is yet incomplete," the elder said. "The oath bond is one that transcends the usual connection between a guard and their ward. It will provide you with fortitude and power. A sacred tether that supports you both. Each oathed relationship is unique to those who are bonded, but most choose to take the other as a partner in every sense of the word."

"It is what has kept me rooted while my blessing is silent." Esia smiled at Nees. "They are my strength."

Hara was quiet, staring at the daggers in front of her and avoiding Rakhmet's searching look. This could be a game changer for them, but he was quick to snuff his excitement. It was clear she still didn't fully trust him.

Clearing his throat, he focused on the elder. "What does the ceremony entail?"

"It's a blood oath," the elder answered. "You must each cut your palm with the dagger and clasp hands to create the tether. Your blessing will be strengthened, like intertwined vines."

"I see," Rakhmet murmured. His chest burned at the thought of deepening his bond with Hara, yet he was afraid that she would deny him. He certainly wouldn't blame her for being reluctant to shackle herself further to him. As much as he tried to fool himself, thinking that he was capable of change, the fear still clenched his throat in a vice grip.

There was a brief silence, but Esia broke it by standing with an understanding smile. "This is a lot of information for all of us and I'm sure you are tired from your journey. Let me show you to the guest hut. Your belongings should have been unloaded by now."

"Right, thank you," he answered, rising as well. He dared a glance at Hara, but she still wouldn't meet his gaze as she resheathed her dagger. They exited, following Esia and Nees to the rear of the village, where they found the two goats tied to a post outside of a curved structure. They had been given some feed and were happily chomping away, not even raising their heads as the four humans approached.

Nees drew aside the leather curtain that hung over the doorway and motioned for the rest of them to enter before joining them in the darker interior. A few of the bioluminescent lamps gave them a view of simple furnishings lovingly carved from wood: a bed, a couple chairs, and a table. Woven grass mats covered the floor, and their packs had been set in one corner.

Esia turned to them, her placid expression a strange sort of contrast to the piercing recognition in her gaze. "I cannot thank you enough for your offer of support. You've brought hope that has been missing for some time now."

"Of course," Rakhmet answered automatically. "I understand how empty an existence it is to lose access to your blessing, and I don't wish it on any of us."

"Yes, well . . ." Esia looked at Nees, her lips curving into a soft smile. Something passed between them that lit a flash of envy in his gut, but he tried to swallow it down. "We will persevere and all will be well again. The gods look favorably upon us. You being here is evidence enough."

Rakhmet cleared his throat, the awkwardness of being hailed as the answer to their prayers making his skin itch. His eyes trailed to Hara once more, but she was studying the plant blessed and her guard as if they held the answers she sought.

Esia caught his look and her brows creased sympathetically. "We are in your debt, my fire kin. If there's anything we can do to return the favor . . ."

"Accompanying us into the temple will be more than enough. Please wait to thank us until we are able to return you to your village safe and whole," Rakhmet was quick to warn, the memory of Hara returning with scars turning his stomach. "There is no guarantee that we will be successful in our efforts."

Esia gave him a long look, her eyes suddenly seeming to hold knowledge beyond her years. "And yet, it is what we must do."

Rakhmet's lips thinned. "Yes . . . it is what we must do."

Esia dipped her chin in acknowledgement, the seriousness just a passing shadow across her face. Reaching out, she threaded her fingers through Nees's with a smile. "Come, let's leave our visitors to settle in. Preparations must be made, for tomorrow brings a new dawn."

Nees obediently followed her out, and soon, Rakhmet and Hara were left alone. They stood there in silence, the sounds of the jungle and people milling about the village filtering through the leather-covered doorway. Rubbing a hand over his curls, he paced distractedly to one side of the hut and shifted their packs around. All of their provisions were still there, organized exactly as they had left them, and he busied himself with triple-checking it all as he waited for Hara to say something. When she didn't, he finally gave up his pointless rifling and turned to face her.

She hadn't moved from where she stood, her eyes glued to the doorway and her hands clenching and unclenching at her sides.

"Well?" he finally asked, both eager and apprehensive to know what was going through her head.

It took a few moments for her to meet his eye, and when she did, his body heated at the fire he saw reflected at him. There was conflict, confusion, and fear. But there was also the barest hint of yearning that had his feet carrying him forward before he could form the thought.

"Please, Hara," he begged. "Talk to me."

A tremor went through her as she watched him approach and his heart galloped into a sprint, throwing itself against his ribs. He had to press a hand to his chest, a pathetic attempt at holding it in as the ache grew.

"Please . . . tell me what holds you back," he urged. "I'm in agony and I know—I know that you care for me. I can see it in your eyes. I know . . . Deep down, I know that you feel the same way. I've been a complete ass. I am not unwilling to admit that. I've made some awful decisions and I understand why you would be mad at me. But I've been trying, Hara. I've been trying to be a better man."

He stopped in front of her. "You . . . you make me a better man, and I'm laying myself at your feet. I'm telling you that I will listen. I will follow. Whatever you say . . . I trust your judgment. More than anyone, I trust you. You know me at my core, and I will do everything in my power to deserve you. I will give you everything I have. My heart, my crown, my blood . . . everything. It's yours."

Her chest stuttered with nervous breaths as her eyes flicked over his face, and he couldn't help but reach for her, his hands curling around her strong arms. He watched her throat bob as she searched for the words.

"I . . . ," she started, her voice soft and uncertain. "I always thought we were two sides of the same coin. When we were growing up . . . it felt like there was nothing that could come between us. We shared so much, and it just felt so natural . . . so inevitable. I thought that it'd always be that way, that that was just how it was to be an oathed guard.

"To be prepared to give up my life . . . to fight for you and protect you . . . it just made sense that we would be so attuned. I needed to be able to anticipate your moves, to step in at the right moment when it came down to it."

He leaned in, drawing her confession deep into his lungs, and her hands came up to rest on his chest as she dropped her eyes, unable to meet his needy stare.

"But . . . things changed. You started hiding from me, keeping things secret. And it hurt. I understand why you did it, but it still hurt. For the first time, I couldn't read your thoughts. I couldn't predict what you were going to do or say or even where you would be. You were erratic, irrational, angry . . . sneaking out, lying. I tried to reach you, tried to get you to talk to me, but then you lost your blessing and . . . it was like trying to pin down a ghost.

"I had to watch from afar as you faded away and I just felt so helpless. There was nothing I could do. You turned into someone I didn't know, and I was left with this . . . bottomless pit inside me, like something fundamental had been stripped away."

He exhaled roughly, pain lancing through him as he started to realize how bad it had been for her, and pulled her closer, one arm wrapping around her waist as the other cupped the side of her neck.

"I'm so sorry," he murmured.

She shook her head sadly then met his gaze again. "When we learned about the corruption in the water temple and the possible reason for your blessing being blocked, I thought that was the answer we had been waiting for. I thought, for sure, that we could go to our temple and figure it out and fix everything. But . . . it all went to shit. It was a complete nightmare. To have you injured like that . . . it broke something in me.

"I-I was so worried. I was frantic." Her gaze burned into him. "I ran toward any possible solution I could find. When the king asked me to go to Tusi, I jumped at the opportunity. I was desperate. All I could do was keep going. I was driven by a fear that haunted me, even when I slept . . . .

"I prayed . . . Oh gods did I pray." Her voice broke and he pressed his lips to her forehead, attempting to soothe away the pain, but she pulled back as her gaze hardened. "And then you ran right back into danger."

She pushed him away, extracting herself from his arms, and started pacing. "After all that, the solution you came up with was to put yourself directly in harm's way. I was shocked. After all that pain and uncertainty and desperation, you just decided to jump right back in. Not only that, but you were going to take innocent guards down with you. It was reckless and stupid and . . ."

Stopping her march across the space, she spun on him and pointed an accusing finger. "It was selfish, Rakhmet. You weren't thinking about anyone else but yourself. You were using it as a way to . . . to . . . I don't know, make up for your sins. But it wasn't right. You were running into it just like you ran into all those taverns and brothels and beds."

He winced, knowing exactly what she was referring to. All those years, he had been throwing himself into anything and everything as a way to avoid and distract. Some way to help him forget the sour sting of disappointment that had plagued him day and night. And she was right. His insistence on rushing off to the plant temple as soon as possible had been another attempt at trying to make himself feel better.

"And people died as a result of your hubris, Rakhmet. Good, honest, loyal people." Her bottom lip trembled as she forced the words out. "You put us all in a dangerously tenuous position. You gambled with our lives . . . and lost. And you wonder why I'm reluctant to give you my heart?"

His jaw dropped open, responses crowding his throat as he rushed to try and reassure her, but she held up a hand, cutting him off.

"If I give it to you, how do I know that you won't run right back into the flames with it? How do I know that you won't doom us both?" she demanded, her eyes flashing.

"Hara, I—" he croaked. "I promise you, I know better now. I've seen the damage I've done. I've learned from my mistakes."

"Have you truly?" Her jaw was hard, telling him just how much the hurt and anger burned her insides.

"Please believe me," he pleaded, reaching for her again. "Let me prove it to you."

He grasped her hands and placed them on his chest, urging her to feel the riotous beat of his heart. "We can take it step by step. I will show you how serious I am. I am yours as much as you are mine. You must know this to be true."

She wavered, her brow creasing as she found the truth in his gaze. "Rakhmet . . ."

"Please, Hara," he murmured again, drawing her closer to him. "I'll take whatever you give me. I've tasted your desire. I know that it's there."

She sucked in a breath of air, her cheeks coloring at the reminder as her lips parted slightly.

"You kissed me first. You lit this fire in me. Take whatever you want, I give it freely."

There was a long moment as he waited for a response, her wide eyes taking him in. Her chest heaved, countless emotions blazing through her, and he watched as a split-second decision was made.

In one swift movement, she fisted the front of his shirt and pulled him toward her as her mouth met his in a punishing kiss. She scorched him with her anger, bruising him as her lips battled his, and he let himself fall.

He lost himself in her, their tongues tangling and teeth clashing as if they were sparring. She gripped the back of his head, fingers yanking on his hair, and he wrapped himself around her. Digging into her curves, he molded her to him, and she came willingly as their bodies fought to seal together.

She moaned into his mouth, the vibration traveling down his torso and into his hips. Instantly hard, he pushed her backward and they knocked into one of the chairs, toppling it with a crash, but they didn't stop as she twisted and wrestled him in turn. They bounced off the table next, spinning out of control as their stumbling trajectory took them toward the bed.

Their feet got caught up and gravity took over as they landed half on, half off, the blankets sliding as they fought for purchase. He heaved them up, latching onto her thighs to hold her in place, and she started tugging on his armor and clothes. Her lips only left his for a moment as his shirt came off and her nails dug into his scarred skin.

She scratched him and he growled, sinking his teeth into her bottom lip as his desperate fingers worked to free her from her own layers. He fumbled with the straps, but he didn't hesitate. Gods, her skin was burning against his and he couldn't get close enough, but she rolled him onto his back before he could get there and pinned him down as she tossed her own shirt to the side. Shooting upward, he sucked her perfect breast into his mouth with a groan.

"Rakhmet!" She gasped, her head falling back, and her hips rolled against him as the muscles in her legs clenched tighter.

"My darling," he murmured into her soft skin. The tight bud of her nipple was wet as it slid across his lips. He nibbled and bit, leaving teeth marks on the tantalizing swell of flesh.

Flipping her over with a fierce shove, he devoured her as her encouraging pants filled the space and her nails continued to scrape across him. He tried to cover every inch, but she was impatient, hauling him back up to sear another kiss on his mouth. They both moaned, her hands finding the waist of his pants and jerking them down.

245

He tried to pull back in surprise, the speed at which things were progressing making his head spin, but she held on, keeping them lip-locked as she used her feet to pull the fabric off him completely. Breathing heavily, he grappled for control, but before he knew it, she had her hand wrapped around his thick shaft and was pumping him in a way that had him burying his face in her neck, his teeth sinking into her as he lapped at her pounding pulse.

"Oh gods." He moaned, completely undone. "Hara, I-I—"

Her thumb spread through the wetness gathering at his tip and his eyes rolled back in his head as she writhed, tugging her own pants down. He bit along her neck to get her attention and left welts from her earlobe to her jaw.

"Hara, please," he tried again. "Are you sure?"

Stabilizing himself on his elbows, he met her feverish gaze as skin met skin and she pressed against him. Her slick folds spread to accommodate his arousal, and he had to grit his teeth to hold himself back. She curled her hips, her clit rubbing along his ridges, and the sensation alone would've brought him to his knees if he were standing.

"Hara—" he choked, unable to catch his breath.

"Take me, I need you," she challenged. "Prove how much you need me."

"But—"

"Rakhmet, please," she cut him off. "Please."

"Gods," he groaned. His hips pumped forward of their own accord as he gazed down at her. Her dark eyes were shining with intensity, pinning him in place, and he gaped at the vision before him. She was everything to him in that moment. His hope, his dreams, his salvation.

"I love you. I love you more than anything." The words slipped past his lips. "You don't have to say it. I just need you to know. I need you to know what this means to me. You're it for me."

She inhaled sharply, her mouth dropping open in surprise, and the anger from before faded away completely. Left behind in its wake was an expression so full of awe that he felt his chest break open, his heart falling out and landing in her waiting hands. It was no longer a battle of wills, but a meeting of souls as he leaned down and placed a reverent kiss on her lips.

"My Hara," he murmured as she trembled underneath him. He nudged the side of her nose with his, the same soothing gesture she had given him all those weeks ago in that remote cave.

She melted, the softest sigh escaping her as he shifted and settled his weight. "Dear Rakhmet, I do fear losing you. I fear it the most."

Taking that as the sign he was waiting for, he positioned himself and groaned as he slipped inside. The world tilted off its axis and he had to still for a moment as he regained his bearings, the feeling of her clenched around him beyond anything he had felt before.

She moved against him, urging him to continue as her fingers dug into his back, so he thrust slowly, once then twice, finding a rhythm that had her moaning his name again. The sound was divine, her smooth skin sliding against him and her delicious scent filling his nose. It was so familiar to him and felt like home, here in her arms. It was exactly where he was meant to be.

Pumping, he drove them higher and higher, dropping kisses along every piece of her he could reach. He worshipped her with his body, whispering all the phrases of love and praise that he needed her to hear. She had to know that there was no one else except for her, nothing that consumed him in such entirety.

He seared every ounce of himself into her and she glowed from his light, her head straining back as cries fell from her lips. She twitched and jerked, losing herself to her spasms as she broke apart, but he just gripped her tighter and picked up speed. His grunts became gasping pants, his teeth bared as a second orgasm barreled through her, and his vision flashed as his release found him.

With one final surge, they fell limp as his arms buckled and he flattened her to the bed. They lay there breathing heavily for a stretch of time, limbs still intertwined with him buried deep within her, but she eventually pushed him off and he stretched out next to her as they stared at the mud-patched ceiling above them.

He turned his head to the side and studied the faint sheen on her skin until she met his gaze, her eyes darkening as her senses returned.

"I love you," he said again, reaching down to clasp her hand. He brought her knuckles to his lips and brushed a kiss across them, then laid their hands back down in the space between them. He didn't let go, though, holding onto her despite the growing wariness he saw in her face.

She remained silent, her attention going back to the ceiling, but he simply renewed his vow to wait. He would show her that he was capable of keeping her heart safe, whenever she decided to offer it to him. Whether it would be the next day, the next month, or the next year, he knew that she was worth waiting for.

DAY THIRTY-TWO

Morning came too soon, forcing Rakhmet to face the harsh reality outside of the bed where he and Hara had reached another level of understanding, for now. Yes, her hand had been curled around his bicep, but the minute her feet hit the floor, she slipped into her role of stoic guard, still refusing to let him glimpse the thoughts he knew were burning behind her dark eyes. That didn't stop him from asking the main question that had been plaguing him, though.

"What do you want to do about the oath bond?" he asked as they pulled on their boots and prepared their packs after a quick breakfast.

She looked up at him with an unreadable expression from where she crouched, dividing the fire starters and explosives into four piles. There was a long pause as she considered him.

"I don't know," she finally admitted. "I'm reluctant to do the ceremonial cuts before we head into the temple. We'll be putting ourselves at a disadvantage."

"They said it would make us both stronger," he countered, strapping on his weapons, "but I don't want you to feel obligated. I'm aware I've asked too much of you already."

Her dark eyes stayed on him for a long moment, passing emotions causing her lashes to twitch despite her best efforts to hide them. What had happened the night before was a heavy presence in the room and, even though he had vowed to wait for her, he couldn't help the yearning blaze inside his chest. He needed the reassurance from her more than anything.

Her attention dropped back to their packs. "I have always been willing to do what it takes to fulfill my duty to the Crown, you know that. I can give you my . . . support in this journey. I . . . I can give you my body. But I don't . . ."

She heaved a breath and forced it out, her reluctance clear. "I don't know if I can give more than that, Rakhmet."

Their eyes met again and a valley of unspoken words sat between them. He was asking too much, like he always had, and she was telling him no. He swallowed his dejection, trying and failing to turn it into acceptance, but a knock at the entrance to the hut interrupted them, and Nees entered through the leather curtain, giving them both an appraising glance. The guard was wearing heavier armor than the day before, clearly prepared to fight when they reached their destination.

"I've come to inquire about your supplies. You mentioned you brought some specific equipment?" they asked.

Hara nodded and waved to the piles she had made. "Half of these are for you and Esia, and Rakhmet and I will carry the rest. We should each be prepared to use them in case we get separated."

She then ran through a brief explanation of their functions, making sure that Nees understood when and how to use them, while Rakhmet stood by awkwardly. He couldn't help but feel a bit useless. Fire power was supposed to be his speciality, but he was reduced to using layman's tools like the rest of them. Rubbing at his chest, he fought to keep the self-disgust at bay. Now was not the time to let his imposter syndrome take the reins.

Luckily, Nees interrupted his spiraling and, after picking up the supplies meant for them and Esia, gestured for him to step outside. Rakhmet followed as Hara finished organizing their packs and was led to a larger hut on the northern edge of the village, where Esia was in the process of donning her own armor. She gave them a pleasant smile as they approached, incongruous with the somber mood of the scene around them.

It seemed as though overnight, villagers had come by to pay their respects to her, leaving offerings of flowers, herbs, nectars, and food at her doorstep, and there was a group of elders helping her into her protective layers with a sense of reverence that was almost overwhelming for Rakhmet. But Esia tolerated it all with aplomb, giving each and every villager a warm word or two as they kneeled to kiss her hands.

With the arrival of Nees and Rakhmet, they quickly finished up what they were doing and turned their attention to the fire heir, performing the same obeisance before retreating into the village. He cleared his throat as the last left, feeling like an interloper as Esia rushed forward and clasped his hands in hers.

"How fortunate it is to embark on this journey together, dear cousin." Her tone was calm and unhurried but her gaze was sharp, as if she could see through to the circling doubts inside him. *I understand* her eyes told him, even if the words weren't actually spoken.

"Thank you," he murmured. "I will be glad to have you by my side, cousin."

She glanced up to the treetops, tilting her head as if listening for something, and got distracted for a moment but didn't let go of his hands. Rakhmet looked to Nees, but the guard was standing by and attaching weapons to their belt as if this were totally normal behavior for her.

"We must get going soon," she said suddenly, turning back to him with an odd expression and patting his hands once before releasing them. "Is your guard— Ah, there she is."

Hara strode toward them with their packs, tossing Rakhmet's to him and dipping her chin in confirmation. "At your service."

"It will take us a few hours to reach the sacred forest, but we cannot take the goats with us. Are you able to carry everything you need?" Nees asked, stepping up to Esia's side protectively. They had wickedly sharp blades strapped all over their chest in addition to the swords and heavy crossbow at their waist. Between the four of them, they were armed to the teeth, yet Rakhmet still wasn't sure if it would be enough.

"I think so," he answered when it became obvious that Hara wasn't going to fill the silence. The only response she gave him was a tightening in her jaw that told him she was hardening herself to whatever came next.

With that uncertain announcement, they didn't waste any time as they strapped on their packs and exited the village using a path that led to the west. They waded through the same dense expanse of vines that shielded the village proper, then Rakhmet began to realize why the goats had been barred from the trip: because the path promptly disappeared as Nees guided them into the wildest jungle Rakhmet had ever seen. If he had thought the plant life was abundant before, now it was positively choking as they continued on.

They climbed over massive roots and ducked under thorn-clad limbs, navigating foliage that reached for them and snagged at their clothes. At times they had to squeeze through thin gaps between tree trunks and crawl through thick undergrowth, their hands sinking into the loamy earth. The change that came over Esia as they got closer and closer was obvious, her fingers trailing over the bark and leaves with tenderness and her expression becoming more and more distant, as if she were in her own secret world.

"You mentioned that you encountered difficulties on the way here." Nees interrupted their thoughts about an hour into the journey. "Was it from the council?"

"Ah, not exactly," Rakhmet answered, grimacing at the reminder of the lives lost because of his stupid decisions.

255

"We did get some resistance from the Talegartian ambassador we have at court, but he eventually permitted us access to this side of the mountains. The real trouble came from my own countrymen. It seems as though my father's and my intention to reinstate the elemental crowns was not received well by some. There was a warlord on the western border who attempted a kidnapping when he heard I'd be traveling through and slaughtered some of my guards. Hara and I barely escaped."

Nees considered this for a moment as they walked. "Do you think they have connections with the Nalliendran forces? They're the ones who are looking to suppress the blessed, yes? And if you've publicly declared your intention for the elemental crowns, you're likely now at the top of their list, especially as blessed who have the backing of an entire country behind them."

Rakhmet's eyebrows raised as he glanced at Hara for her reaction. "I hadn't drawn the parallel but . . . maybe you're right."

Esia looked back at him with a thoughtful tilt to her head. "I suppose that's how they'd want you to feel."

"What do you mean?" he asked.

"The Nalliendrans . . . If they wanted to give the impression that they were attacking on all sides, they might also be seeking to separate you from potential allies or at least prevent you from gaining more influence." She shrugged as Rakhmet gave her a surprised look. "All alone, you're not as much of a threat."

"That's quite astute." Rakhmet couldn't help but think of what his father had said when he had first learned of the potential connection between Nalliendra and the temples' corruption. He had said that to separate the blessed ones from their temples and their powers was a savvy move if they were indeed looking to defeat them.

Esia went back to staring at the foliage around them. "At least, that's how it felt for me . . . for us in the village. We don't have much power as isolated as we are."

"How . . ." Rakhmet hesitated. "How exactly did you end up here if you don't remember your past?"

She lifted a shoulder, her hand resting lightly on her belly. "I'm not entirely sure. I woke up in that room and knew I needed to get out, so I chose a direction and ran. I suppose there are things I must miss and I do get rather sad sometimes, but I've got Nees . . . and the other villagers."

Rakhmet hummed, reluctant to pry further as his attention was drawn to Hara again. His guard had been quiet this entire trip and wouldn't look at him for more than a few seconds, her lips thinning in an expression that told him she was processing her own shit and wasn't going to let him in just yet. She was making him wait, for good reason he was sure, and he had to respect that.

Eventually, they crested the edge of an enormous hill and came upon a section of forest that was decidedly apart from what they had been trekking through. Nees drew them to a stop as the landscape suddenly changed, the land dipping before them. It created some sort of crater, as if a giant being had pressed their thumb into the earth, and filling the indentation was an old-growth forest of towering trees that sent shivers down Rakhmet's spine.

Where there had been fresh, vibrant plants before, now they were hard and cold. Spiteful and malicious. Even the sun seemed to retreat from the darkness that cloaked their boughs, the wind deathly still. No sounds of animals, no rush of waterfalls. It was an entirely different world.

"Is it always like this?" he asked in a low voice.

"No," Esia answered in the same tone. "It was full of life once, a place of veneration and worship, but it has been ruined. Corrupted, as you say."

Rakhmet frowned as he took it in. Even Hara was shifting uncomfortably beside him, instinctively moving closer.

They watched as the shadows rippled, moving like billowing smoke through the trees, and Rakhmet palmed his flame dagger in one hand and a sword in the other, just to soothe his nerves a bit. Hara mirrored him and Nees as well. Only Esia kept her hands empty, gazing upon the scene with a look of deep mourning.

"Where's the temple?" Hara asked, her keen eyes trained ahead.

"In the center, about 300 feet in," Nees responded gravely.

There was a pause as they all took a breath, then Nees nodded at Hara, a silent agreement passing between the two guards, and took the first step in. Esia followed with Hara just behind and Rakhmet taking up the rear.

Their footsteps seemed too loud as they slowly progressed forward, the gloom pushing in at them on all sides. The trees themselves looked like they were carved out of stone, with only pebbles and gray moss under their feet, and every now and then, there was an eerie creaking noise that came from somewhere farther in. Rakhmet kept his gaze constantly moving and took in as many details as possible, his muscles bunching until his whole body was tense with anticipation.

The shadows gradually thickened until they could only see about twenty feet ahead, and even the tops of the trees were obscured, making Rakhmet's skin prickle in warning. His stomach soured with dread and his brows knotted, the unnaturalness of their surroundings telling him to turn around and run.

Then the moans started.

Esia was the first to notice, her head whipping to the left in alarm as she flinched backward with Nees moving to shield her just a second later. Hara's body instantly flexed forward and Rakhmet raised his weapons, going back-to-back with her instinctively. They hung there for a suspended moment, eyes darting around, until Hara drew in a sharp breath.

"*Wraiths*," she whispered, pointing her dagger to indicate the mass of blackness that was hurtling toward them with alarming speed.

Rakhmet's eyes widened, his lungs clenching tight as the air rushed from him at the sight. It was difficult to tell exactly how many there were. Ten? A dozen? More? They shifted together and apart, forming and reforming as far too many mouths opened and wailed at them with a resounding war cry. Nees immediately raised their crossbow and started firing, the bolts disappearing into their dark forms, and Hara flicked her arm to the side to light her zulfiqar. But he was frozen as he watched them approach in horror.

"Oh gods," he heard himself pray. "Oh gods, please protect us."

The sound was drowned out as the wraiths fell upon them, slicing with their razor-sharp claws, and that was his last coherent thought as his years of training took hold. His body lashed out, swinging his blades through their forms, and he heard the grunts of his companions doing the same. The wraiths grabbed at his arms and legs, drawing blood in shallow cuts as he winced, but he couldn't let it slow him down, so he gritted his teeth and threw himself forward.

A claw across his cheekbone and a swing of his sword through a shadowy torso. A spike of pain in his thigh and a jab of his dagger in a throat. A ripping tear on his forearm and a spin to the side with a well-aimed elbow to knock them away.

He saw Esia out of the corner of his eye, slipping in between the wraiths with subtle dexterity, and Nees cleaved them apart next to her. He felt Hara move behind him, her presence keeping him focused as he ducked and parried, and it seemed like hours, or maybe just seconds as he fought the thinning horde.

Knocked to the ground, he wrestled with a dark form until he was able to carve into its chest, and it dissolved into a puff of nothing as his companions finished theirs off. He jumped up into a crouch, ready to fight, but that seemed to be the end of it, the sudden silence filled with their panting breaths. His attention immediately went to Hara, but she was free as well, spinning in a circle as she scanned the trees for more.

It took them a moment to recover, their eyes searching all sides just in case, but it was still once more and Rakhmet sank to his knees to catch his breath. Glancing around, he found that they were all covered in slashes and cuts. Blood was running into Nees's left eye from a gash on their forehead, Esia was clasping her right arm with bloodstained fingers, and Hara had a swollen bottom lip that had busted open at some point. But they were all standing. That was good enough for him.

"Was that . . . What were . . ." Nees looked to Hara for an explanation, wiping a hand across their face and grimacing.

"Wraiths," she repeated, brows furrowing. "Those were wraiths. They guarded the corrupted fire and water temples too. But . . . there were more this time."

"They knew we would come," Rakhmet realized. "They were prepared for us."

"It seems that way," Hara agreed, her tone wary.

"How . . . ?" Rakhmet started to ask but was too afraid to finish the thought.

"I . . . don't know," Hara admitted.

"The temple should be sixty or so feet that way." Nees frowned, looking in that direction. "They know that's our destination."

"It will get worse," Esia said softly, halting their conversation. She stood there quietly, holding her arm, but wasn't looking at them, staring into the shadows. Her expression was almost apologetic, but there was a matter-of-factness that raised the hair on Rakhmet's neck. He couldn't tell if she could somehow see their future and her calm was an acceptance of their fate or if that serene tone was a sort of blind detachment from reality. Honestly, he didn't know which he preferred either.

Nobody said a word, unable to come up with a comforting response, and Rakhmet cleared his throat, busying himself with pulling medical supplies out of his pack as the two guards kept an eye on their surroundings. Soon enough, he had everyone patched up to the best of his ability and readied himself to continue.

This time, they moved even more stealthily. They were now on high alert as the occasional creaking they had been hearing before grew louder and a clearing in the heart of the forest was slowly revealed. Esia gasped, her hands covering her mouth, and the sense of foreboding thickened further as Rakhmet stared up at the enormous tree that dominated a desolate island in the middle of what seemed to be a dried-out moat.

The sunken earth, which looked like it had once held a vibrant underwater ecosystem, was barren and lifeless. Sprawling tendrils of black reached across the land, strangling everything in their path. Countless twisted bodies of fish and reptiles lay constricted next to dried-out husks of rodents and other creatures of the forest, their life force drained. Enormous bodies of crocodiles were scattered here and there, contorted and shriveled, and Rakhmet could feel his heartbeat pounding in his fingertips in warning.

The tree itself was a gnarled behemoth, its bark thick and sturdy, as if it bore the weight of untold centuries, with jagged branches that stretched out like skeletal fingers. Its boughs were leafless and creaked as they shifted ever so slightly in a wind they couldn't feel. The ichor emerged from its base, snaking across the dry moat and coiling around its massive roots like tight ropes, holding it in place.

It was a nightmarish tableau, and Rakhmet glanced at Esia to see tears streaming down her cheeks, leaving trails in the blood and dirt. Nees had stepped closer to her, placing a steadying hand on her shoulder as they looked on with despair, and Rakhmet moved away to give them some privacy as the two of them bowed their heads in silent prayer. Esia's shoulders shook as she cried and it pierced him, his eyes drawn to Hara next to him.

Her face was hard, her jaw set as she studied the corrupted land, and he could see the calculations running behind her angry gaze. She wouldn't even look at him, her hand clenching and unclenching around the pommels of her weapons, but her presence still soothed him, the fire within her the light at the end of the tunnel.

The stillness was soon interrupted, though, by another call of wailing wraiths, and Hara and Rakhmet spun to find them surrounding their group from all sides. It was another large horde, perhaps even more than before, and Rakhmet stumbled back in surprise, his boot catching on one of the roots protruding from the ground.

He swore, reaching for his crossbow, and started unloading bolts in every direction as Nees scrambled to follow suit, the two of them taking the lead as the women drew their blades and began picking their way backward into the dry moat. But they were quickly swarmed, and Rakhmet shouted as he was forced to the ground by several black forms.

Fighting like a rabid dog, he hacked his way through them until he felt warm hands hook under his arms and pull him upright. Hara yanked him toward the tree, taking a few blows from the wraiths as he found his footing, and then they fell into their automatic defense position, back-to-back with blades spinning.

Pain shot through the side of his face and left knee as he was harried, but he refused to yield, the shadows crowding around them like malevolent smoke. Blood streamed into his eye, partially blinding him, and yet he still struck out, jabbing, slashing, twisting, and carving, but his grip was slipping on his blades. From blood or sweat? He had no idea and was acutely aware of the lack of his blessing in a fight like this.

He heard Esia cry out from somewhere behind him and a pained grunt from Nees, but he couldn't even glance over his shoulder, too focused on the forms in front of him. Hara was the next to fall, her feet getting tangled in the gnarled roots weaving through the bed of the moat, but he was right there to grab her, throwing elbows and kicks to get her free.

Getting knocked about, he lurched side to side and willed his arms to keep going. He pushed the wraiths off him just to have more take their place, his fury matching theirs. He bared his teeth, resorting to growls and snarls that made him more animal than human, but he didn't have the luxury to care. He let the monster come out of him, ripping and tearing with tooth and nail.

It was a nasty brawl, one unlike any he had ever experienced, and they just kept coming until the four of them were backed into the base of the towering tree. He felt himself bump into something warm and solid behind him, smaller hands coming to brace against his shoulders to prevent him from crushing them into the trunk as he kept his blades swinging.

"You have to open the door!" Hara yelled over her shoulder, ducking a slash from one of the wraiths next to him.

Esia's response was lost in the din, but he felt her fumble for something and she shouted again: "It's not enough! I need—"

Whatever she said wasn't audible, so Rakhmet turned to help her, remembering the report from Tusi saying that both Roe and Kelah had had to channel a piece of their blessings into the door of the water temple to open it. Since half of the door had been broken at the fire temple, they had wondered if that was why Nasima had been able to open it on her own.

Running with his split-second decision, he slammed his bloody palm next to where Esia had hers pressed to the bark and felt a sucking sensation deep within him. It pulled from the very center of him, drawing a single ember from his banked fire, and the tree split open in front of them. Apparently, two were needed at this door too.

He fell inside with Esia, shoved by Hara from behind as the two guards closed in tight to block the entrance. They continued their defense as Rakhmet scrambled to his feet and searched for a way to close the door, finding the edge of the hard surface that had slid to the side. Throwing his weight against it, he pushed as Esia grabbed Nees and Hara and they slipped in just as the door slammed closed and plunged them into pitch darkness.

But it made absolutely no difference as he felt the wraiths materialize through the door and grab for him.

The lack of sight made things ten times worse, and he panicked as he lashed out, punching blindly. He heard Hara curse behind him as she yelled for Esia to light a torch then threw herself into the fray with Rakhmet. They had to resort to wrestling the fucking creatures, too afraid to accidentally slash each other, and they took blows left and right as he felt claws rake down his arms.

Light flared, suddenly illuminating the terrifying sight, and he instantly sunk his blades into the wraith in front of him then turned and helped Hara with hers. Nees was on the ground, panting as they finished off theirs, and then there were only two left as Rakhmet and Hara rushed forward. It took a few quick swipes, but finally they were alone once again.

He braced himself on his hands, his knuckles split open and his chest heaving from the effort as he scanned Hara for injuries. The flickering light showed stains of red flowing from slashes across her arms, neck, and face, but her expression was fierce and she met his gaze with such heat that it took his breath away all over again. There was an extended moment where he couldn't tear his eyes away from her, the look on her face speaking volumes.

But there was no time to process it as Esia cried out, rushing to Nees's side, and Rakhmet turned to find the guard struggling to stand, a deep gash pouring blood on their left thigh. They gave up and slumped to the ground as Esia pressed a hand to the wound to staunch the flow, her face creased in terror. Hara blinked, shaking herself, then flung her pack to the ground to dig out her med kit.

She was efficient as she cleaned the wound and her implements, the injury bad enough to warrant stitches, and Rakhmet had flashbacks to that night in the cave. At least they had more than enough supplies this time around so they didn't have to rely on boiling water to sterilize things, but it still gave him pause, his gut burning as he watched her swift fingers sew the torn flesh closed.

They couldn't waste any time and they all knew it, Nees keeping their jaw clenched through the pain. Rakhmet distracted himself by tending to his and Esia's wounds then urged Hara to stay seated after she finished with Nees so that he could clean and wrap hers too. After a lot of convincing, Nees finally accepted a single dose of redan flower extract to help with the pain, and then they insisted that they continue on.

They had stumbled into the hollow interior of the massive trunk, a space that was about ten by ten feet with some sort of ceremonial stone slab in the center. The black tendrils grew from the base of the slab, indicating that their route was likely underneath it, but the question was how to access it.

Esia walked around the room, carefully stepping over the branching black ooze, and examined their surroundings. "I'm not sure how to proceed downward."

There were no markings on the walls, but Rakhmet was caught by the carvings that decorated the stone. While there were the usual depictions of leaves, vines, and flowers, there were also clusters of what looked to be seeds or beans. They fell from spiny pods, spilling out into the surrounding flora, and tiny, engraved ants carried them to and fro.

"Do you know what these are?" he asked, pointing them out to Esia.

She leaned in and studied them, the easy expression back on her face, but the slight crease in her brow gave her emotional turmoil away. The curved shapes seemed to be smoother than the rest of the surface, and she gently ran her fingers over the worn stone.

"Ricina," she murmured to herself.

"What?" Rakhmet asked, unsure if he had heard her correctly.

She repeated the word more clearly, glancing over at Nees. The guard bent down and nodded, confirming her identification.

"It is blessed Tabriara's sacred plant," she explained. "It is how my blessing manifests. When I have access to it, I can produce them myself."

"You produce . . . beans?" Rakhmet asked, confused.

"Seeds," she corrected. "I can generate seeds and pollen, as well as control existing plant life."

Rakhmet didn't even want to know how that worked, eyeing her. Controlling flame felt a lot more explainable, but then again, maybe others found his blessing to be as mystifying as he found Esia's.

"How does that help us right now? You don't have access to your blessing," Hara asked, standing watch by the door.

"In the past, we've left offerings at the base of the tree to thank the Plant Goddess for her gifts," Esia said, circling it.

"Maybe we have to give this something more powerful," Rakhmet wondered out loud.

Hara glanced at the door then back to them. "Whatever it is, we need to get moving."

An idea struck him. "What about blood? Isn't that what the oath is all about?"

Esia tilted her head and considered him, then looked over at Nees. Some sort of silent conversation unfolded between them until the guard dipped their chin in agreement. Pressing her lips together, Esia unwrapped one of the bandages on her arm and swiped her finger through the drying blood then pressed it to one of the carvings.

There was a flicker of light, then the slab started glowing a vibrant green, the radiance trailing along the vines and flowers surrounding her bloody fingerprint. But it didn't spread far, only about a few inches in each direction. Esia started smiling in excitement and tore off another bandage, gathering more red liquid and pressing it to another cluster of seeds. The brilliance expanded farther, and she reached for another bandage, but Nees stopped her before she could tear it off.

Instead, the guard unwrapped one of their own and held out the wound for her to take what she needed. She placed a gentle kiss on their cheek in thanks, and together, they took turns offering the blood needed as Rakhmet backed up in surprise. Logically, he understood their eagerness, but it made him queasy to watch. It felt wrong, even though he had suggested it.

He had thought that it would've been a quick slice and all would be good, but as her red smudges slowly covered the slab and the green light grew brighter and brighter, it suddenly felt like too much of a sacrifice. He couldn't help but reach for Hara as his uneasiness increased, his hand finding hers as the plant blessed and her guard all but forgot them in their benefaction. Before long, the entire slab was lit up and cast-off bandages littered the floor.

With a great crack, the slab shifted and slowly slid to the side to reveal a descending staircase, and Esia clapped happily. She flung her arms around Nees in a celebratory hug, and Rakhmet glanced over at Hara, finding her brows furrowed in consternation. The look she gave him told him that she was as uncomfortable with the display as he was, so he squeezed her hand, clearing his throat and turning back to the smiling pair.

"We need to rewrap your injuries before we move on," he urged, trying to temper the disquiet in his voice.

Esia startled, glancing in their direction. "Oh yes, of course."

Her attention went back to Nees, and the look on the guard's face was pure admiration as they dug through their own pack and carefully bandaged both of them once again. The way they handled Esia was reminiscent of the reverence the villagers had shown her before they had left, and she herself almost glowed from the tenderness. It was awkwardly quiet as they did so, but Hara nudged Rakhmet to check out the hole they had created while she remained by the door, just in case.

The stairs went deep into the earth, a passage that was shaped by the twisting roots of the tree, but it was covered in ominous black tendrils, so Rakhmet reached for one of the bottles of fire starter in his pack and started pouring it out to clear the way. Once Esia and Nees finished their ministrations, they all backed up toward the door and covered their noses and mouths with their sleeves, then Rakhmet lit another torch and threw it into the hole.

The flames exploded upward, and thick smoke filled the room, but luckily the space was tall enough that most of it rose to the top, sparing them from the worst of it. With that done, they all crowded around the edges and looked down into the darkness. Their path was scorched but clear, and Nees was the first to step down with their sword held out in front of them.

Esia followed close behind with the first torch, lighting the way as they descended into the twisting passage. It followed the pattern of roots, occasionally branching out here and there, so they decided to keep to the main one, figuring that, like the other temples, the center room would be at the very bottom. As they went, they burned the tendrils away over time, but it didn't entirely go to plan.

First, they were fooled more than once, taking turns that terminated in dead ends and causing them to curse and backtrack over and over again. Even worse, some of these tunnels contained the massive bodies of what seemed to be monstrous worm creatures. They were about five feet in length and covered in chitinous plates with a stinger at the rear. Rows and rows of sharp teeth were seen in their gaping mouths, stuck open in their final throes as they had been wrapped and constricted by branches of ichor. Just like the enormous crocodiles outside the temple, they had been sucked dry, their twisted corpses creating an eerie underground catacomb. Rakhmet shivered each time they came upon one, wondering if that was the fate awaiting them.

Second, the ground they walked upon also proved to be treacherous in itself, as gaping holes appeared every so often, barely covered by dried-out roots that led to pits of wicked-looking spikes for those unlucky enough to misstep. Because the black tendrils seemed to suck the moisture out of everything they touched, shrinking the wooden roots and causing them to crumble from the barest of brushes, the traps were easy enough to identify, but it slowed them down even further since they had to use pitons and rope to swing themselves across each time.

The gilding on the lily was that they also encountered groups of wraiths here and there, but it was random and uncoordinated, as if they, too, were getting lost. Or maybe they were leading them on a wild-goose chase with all of their wrong turns. The blind leading the blind. It was impossible to tell as their path went on forever, sometimes turning left, sometimes right, and even rising and lowering at times. They were forced to use their rapidly decreasing stores of fire starter each step of the way in order to clear away the blackness, but the veins only got thicker and thicker and Rakhmet's mood grew darker and darker as they went on, the ichor creating its own ecosystem of sorts where it hung from the ceiling like heavy limbs.

A Descent

After hours of fighting their way downward, Rakhmet was starting to lose his mind, the last bottle of fire starter sitting heavily in his pack as he doubted whether they would make it. They still had their explosives, but they were afraid to use them in case they collapsed the entire tunnel in the process. It was too much of a gamble. Eventually, though, they came upon another stretch of ichor that blocked their path forward and Nees held their hand out for the bottle with a grim frown.

Rakhmet threw his hands up in frustration and paced back toward where they had come from, grinding his teeth as he tried to come up with some sort of reason to spare the last of their reserves. Stomping back and forth, he couldn't come up with anything and looked to Hara for help. Her face was just as drawn as Nees's was, though, and Rakhmet could see the writing on the wall. They had no choice.

He huffed again, stalling, and was just about to give them all an earful about their predicament when he caught the sound of moans coming from behind them.

"Fuck," he snapped. "More wraiths incoming."

Hara jumped into action, tugging his pack open without asking and tossing the bottle to Nees before readying her weapons as Rakhmet fumbled to load his crossbow. It was only seconds before he saw the mass of shadows round the corner from where they had come, and he started unloosing bolts until they were directly upon them and he was compelled to switch to blades.

"Gods, fuck, damn, shit, balls—" The curses fell from him as he threw himself forward into pure chaos, darkness filling the space as Nees lit the fire starter on one side of them and the wraiths overwhelmed them on the other. He choked on the smoke but couldn't stop for anything as the combined screams of his party and the wails of the creatures echoed around them, sharp claws and teeth digging into him.

He was thrown against the walls, wrestling masses he couldn't see, and was desperately wishing for his own fire as the resentment inside him threatened to swallow him whole, but he heard Hara yelp somewhere next to him, a demand that his shaking arms keep going. At a certain point, the only thing he could distinguish from the din around him was Hara's voice, and he continued to cut his way forward until he could reach her.

The smoke finally dissipated and he caught a glimpse of her, spinning blades between two wraiths harrying her with her lip curled in a snarl as Esia and Nees battled a handful behind her. Their way had been cleared and they were backing farther down the tunnel as he finished off the last one near him and rushed forward to aid them. He had no idea how many they had already downed and didn't know if he wanted to, the pain and exhaustion in his limbs telling a story he couldn't afford to listen to.

Stumbling, he knocked another to the ground and slashed until it was no more, then heaved himself to a stand as Hara threw him a grateful look and turned to help the plant blessed and her guard. All four of them were dripping blood, their bandages torn to shreds and chests heaving, but suddenly Esia and Nees disappeared from view, their startled shouts bouncing off the wood.

Hara gave a swiping cut to the one remaining wraith's throat, then spun and ran toward where their companions had been as Rakhmet followed her. Sliding to a stop, they found a deep hole at the dead end of the tunnel, about five feet wide with woven root sides like a basket, but where it led was too far away to see.

Esia's distant screams continued, her tone growing more and more panicked as Hara threw her pack to the ground and tore through it, pulling out a piton, hammer, and rope. Rakhmet quickly caught on and helped her hammer the piton into the side of the tunnel, making sure it was secure as they tied the end of the rope to it.

Hara didn't even spare him a glance as she shouldered her pack, sheathed her weapons, and started climbing down, her hands and feet moving in a blur. He followed her, and it only took a few moments to reach the end of their rope, but they could barely see the bottom. Flashes of black tore this way and that underneath them, Esia's terror tangible as it filled their ears.

Making a quick decision, Hara and Rakhmet's eyes met as she glanced up at him and he nodded. Her face tightened and then she abruptly let go of the rope, falling another fifteen feet until she hit the ground with a jarring thud, but she immediately rolled to her feet and drew her weapons. Just as she disappeared from view, Rakhmet did the same. The landing was rough, his teeth clattering as his bones protested, but the horrific sight that greeted him was more than enough of a distraction.

Twisting into a crouch, he didn't know what to focus on first. Hara fought two wraiths to his left, a writhing mass of black ichor loomed to his right, and Esia was frantically trying to cut what looked to be thick coils wrapped around Nees's torso just ahead of him. They seemed to be in the inner sanctum, from what he had heard about the water and fire temples, but he didn't even have time to get his bearings as something slammed into him from behind and pinned him to the ground.

Jagged teeth shredded his shoulder and he yelled, palming his dagger and wrenching it backward into whatever was on him. He managed to hit, the blade sinking in and giving him enough leverage to curl onto his side and force his opponent down with his bulk. It was another wraith, the shadowed hands grabbing at him as he knocked them aside.

He was fucking sick of these goddamn things and never wanted to see another after they were done with this, but he couldn't fool himself into thinking they had a fat chance in hell of that as he slammed his fist into its face over and over again, his fury overtaking him and wreathing hands and limbs in flames. It howled at him and he howled right back, hooking his dagger into its collarbone and cutting it clean through to the other side.

His weight hit the ground in its sudden absence, and he spun to face the mass that was slithering toward him on the right, his eyes going wide as he realized that it wasn't just a large trunk of ichor like he had first assumed but an enormous black snake. Its head was at least four feet wide, its shocking length coiled protectively around a tall shape in the back corner of the basket-like room and shining eyes trained directly on him as it towered.

With a pitiful croak, his throat clenched shut and a shudder went through him as he willed his bladder to not empty. He scrambled backward, shooting across the ground on his hands like a spooked crab, but was caught immediately by a tendril of black that turned out to be another snake. It wrapped up his arm with a hiss, the ichor burning into his skin and leaving welts in its wake, and he jerked to the side to fling it off as he realized that there were snakes literally everywhere.

They slithered across the floors and walls like animated roots, their oily black bodies tangling around the feet of his companions and constricting their movement. His heart rattled in his chest and bile rose in his throat. It was worse than he had ever imagined. It wasn't supposed to go like this. The tendrils weren't supposed to come alive.

Dancing away from hers, Hara managed to finish off the last wraith but was too late to catch the wide serpent body that latched onto her waist and yanked her upward to the ceiling. She flailed, her legs dangling as she worked on getting it off her. The stench of burning skin and leather was too much and Rakhmet gagged, seeing Esia get grabbed too as she fought to release Nees from theirs. With every snake they cut away, more took their place, and Rakhmet pulled his crossbow and started shooting as the largest snapped toward him.

Bolts sank into its flank and its arm-length fangs flashed in front of him as he threw himself out of the way, the huge mouth snapping just inches from his leg. He landed in another pile of writhing blackness, but he barely noticed the searing pain, pure adrenaline coursing through him as he watched Nees finally free themselves from the snake that had them suspended in the air.

They landed awkwardly, their knee giving out due to a clear break in the top half of their shin, but they kept lurching forward toward Esia, who was in the process of cutting through her own snakes. There was blood pouring down the side of her face and her vibrant green eyes were wide with terror, but there was an innate nimbleness to her movements, as if she had spent years rehearsing the dance. Rakhmet was impressed with how well she was handling herself. He had to admit there had been a twinge of reluctance when he had agreed to let her go with them. He hadn't been in the position to deny the support at the time, though, and based on what he was seeing now, it had been the right call.

Just as the largest snake reared up to snap at him again, Hara dropped from above and landed on its back, straddling it like a horse and sinking both blades to the hilt as it roared in fury and tried to buck her off. Rakhmet took the opportunity to slice at its exposed neck, cutting deep, but the stickiness of its body made it difficult to pull his blade out and he struggled to get it free as the monstrous creature writhed above him. Hara, too, seemed to be stuck, the ichor burning through her pants and stinging her skin as it thrashed side to side.

But Nees managed to get Esia free and spun on unsteady legs to face the large creature, drawing their own crossbow and studding it with more bolts to drive it back. The guard wobbled, bracing one hand against the wall to hold themself up with a vicious sneer twisting their face. It allowed Rakhmet to get free of it and grab ahold of Hara's leg to pull her off, her weight falling on him as they scrambled away. His hands slipped on her, the both of them rushing to get back to standing in the midst of more snakes coiling up their limbs and trying to bite through their armor.

Esia, seeing that there was a bit of distance now, reached into her pack and drew out one of their explosives. Lighting it with the torch that had fallen with them through the hole, she hurled it toward the monstrous form and called for everyone to brace themselves just before it blew a wide hole into the side of its body. The whole room shuddered, and it screeched, twisting and cringing as the ichor shifted to cover the wound like dripping molasses.

Emboldened, Hara followed suit and grabbed one of her own explosives, lighting and throwing it in quick succession. The room rocked again, bits of blackness flying every which way, and in response, another broad tendril dropped down from above and wrapped around her, pulling her away with a shout. Rakhmet was torn, glancing between Hara where she was pinned to the ceiling and the faintest green light that had started to emerge from the corner where the majority of the monster's body was curled. But he focused on what mattered, darting over to hack at the tendrils underneath Hara.

The snake took advantage of his distraction, its enormous tail slamming against him and throwing him across the room with a loud crunch as he hit a wall and felt his shoulder dislodge. Groaning, he urged his broken body to get back up just as Nees threw another explosive, this time hitting the creature square in the face and blowing away half of its jaw. The hit was so bad that the extra tendrils started receding in a panicked effort to replace what was lost and its infuriated eyes trained on the plant guard with vengeance.

More verdant light filled the space as Esia lunged to block Nees but was too late, the wide body of the snake wrapping around her oathed like a boa constrictor. It squeezed and Nees's agony was multiplied, the guard's limbs cracking under the force of its grip. The sound echoed, reverberating through Rakhmet's skull, and Esia started screaming, frantically slicing at the ichor as Hara dropped from above, stumbling over to Rakhmet. She met his shaken gaze, her expression aghast as she took in his injuries, and he saw the moment another decision was made.

Time slowed as she let all of her facades drop and he finally saw what she had been trying to hide: love, adoration, need, respect, honor. All for him. It was her heart, bared to him in this tenuous second as Esia's terror-stricken cries filled the room. The only way they were going to get out of this was if they tapped into everything they had.

She grabbed her oath dagger, slicing her palm as she reached for his then repeating the motion. The pain didn't even register, his entire focus captured by the woman in front of him. Chest heaving, he watched as their bloody skin met and a scorching jolt went through them both. Her fingers tightened around his and her head fell back, a look of ecstasy passing across her face as her eyes squeezed shut.

Power blazed through him, igniting his blessing with a resounding blast, and he felt his core heat to an impossible temperature. Gasping, he yanked her toward him and gripped her tight. His lungs filled with hot air, buoying him, restoring him, resurrecting him as an inhuman bellow tore from his throat. Vibrant red light clashed with green as he stood with her clasped to his chest, fire suddenly engulfing their bodies, but it didn't hurt, the flames licking their shredded skin and cauterizing their wounds.

He roared again, the feeling overwhelming as instinct took hold. Scanning the room through a red haze, his eyes landed on the snake as it crushed Nees's body in an unforgiving twist, the guard going limp. Esia's shriek intensified, her hands clawing at the ichor blindly as the green light surrounded her, coiling up her limbs like vines. Her hair rippled, flying behind her like a cape as her expression went from alarmed denial to hard, unflinching revenge.

Pushing Hara behind him, he guarded her with his body as he reached deep within and pulled sparking embers to his fingertips, his rings completely forgotten. They came

281

eagerly, ready to be released, and holding his limp arm to his stomach, he used the other to shape them into a massive fireball until it grew to an impossible size.

With a great heave, he hurled it at the snake and demolished a stretch of its body in a flashing explosion that rocked the room again. But he didn't let it stop there, harnessing the flames as they flew outward and pressing them back to the blackness in a fiery ring. He coaxed them, urging them to wrap tighter and tighter as they burned into its sticky corpulence.

The creature screeched louder, writhing as it tried to escape the heat, but Esia doubled down, tapping into her own power as her hands reached out to the ground and latched onto the woven roots, thrusting upward. Thick trunks pierced through the creature's body in retaliation, and the monster twisted as it cried out. It was being torn to shreds, swaths of ichor burning away with Rakhmet's fire while Esia continued her assault, her face tight with vivid hatred.

Hara simply held onto Rakhmet, her flaming fingers digging into his shoulder in solidarity, but it didn't take long for the heirs to finish off the creature. It dissolved into nothing, a forest of singed trees left in its wake as a sudden silence filled the space, broken only by their rasping pants. Esia dropped to her knees where Nees's body had fallen in a lifeless pile. Their torso was bent at an impossible angle and their head was hanging from their broken shoulders like a bag of rocks. It was a gut-wrenching sight.

Rakhmet doused the flames and rushed to her side, reaching for his cousin to comfort, but she shrugged him off with a fierce howl. Overwrought, she desperately attempted to smooth out her guard's form, bringing their joints back into alignment, but it was no use. The blank look in their gaze was enough of an answer for Rakhmet, and all he could do was look on helplessly as she fussed, blood and tears pouring down her cheeks.

Hara threaded her stained fingers through his as they stood there, but her attention was on the glowing crystal that sat in the corner of the room. Rakhmet startled as it flashed, and Hara automatically dropped onto one knee in a bow, her free hand touching her brow, lips, and chest in a gesture of reverence. His focus was drawn to the figure that emerged from behind it, an impossibly tall woman whose brilliant gaze was intent on Esia's shuddering shoulders.

Shakily moving into a kneeling position, he let go of Hara's hand to repeat the gesture for the Plant Goddess before them. But she glided over to her blessed daughter without glancing in their direction, the roots of the room sprouting broad leaves that supported her weight with each footfall. Leaves and petals floated from her moss-colored hair, the swaying movement knocking them loose, and constantly shifting tendrils of plant life covered her body like living armor. Her skin was a deep brown that reminded him of mahogany, and she laid a gentle hand on Esia's arm to still her jerky movements.

The plant blessed glanced up into the face of her goddess with surprise, choked sobs rising from her throat as she wept openly. Her whole body trembled, and Tabriara pulled her up, holding onto both of her arms to steady her, a silent communion blossoming between them. No words were spoken, but Esia broke down when she received the answer she didn't want, swaying under the weight of her grief.

Long moments passed as she mourned the loss of her guard, and Rakhmet wiped away the wetness that spilled over his own cheeks as he watched them then wrapped his hand around Hara's, bloody palm to bloody palm, as they remained on their knees. Eventually, Esia ran out of energy and fell into a numb quiet, sniffing to clear her clogged nose. It was only then that Tabriara locked her lustrous gaze on the two of them.

"Follow me, dear ones," she said simply then turned and led Esia by the shoulder toward the crystal, where a portal shimmered on the other side. Rakhmet looked at Hara for confirmation and she dipped her chin, telling him that this was the next step in their journey, so he got to his feet and followed.

There was a stunning flash of green, and then they emerged into a passage that was halfway between a corridor and a forest, similar to the curving tunnels of roots they had been traveling through before. The enclosed space was unlike anything they had seen, though, every surface covered in a riot of plant life, like a hallucinated terrain.

Flowering vines cascaded from the ceiling in vibrant hues of pink, purple, and gold, their delicate blossoms swaying gently of their own accord. The air was filled with the heady scent of jasmine and wisteria, mingling with the earthy aroma of damp soil, while moss-covered trees crowded the walls with gnarled branches twisting and intertwining like ancient guardians.

Exuberant bushes of all sizes lined the meandering passage, their lush foliage spilling out onto the path, but they politely shifted to the side as Tabriara led the way forward. Some bore delicate flowers that shivered when the Plant Goddess passed, while others boasted glossy leaves that stretched out to brush against her. The ground beneath her unfurled and contracted with each step but felt soft and springy to Rakhmet, carpeted with a thick layer of moss and ferns like a plush carpet.

As they moved deeper in, the air grew cooler and more refreshing, carrying with it the scent of fresh growth as well as earthy decay. Birds flitted among the branches overhead, butterflies danced in the air, and large, toothed fly catchers the size of tigers snapped at them as they passed, but eventually, they reached a pair of algae-covered doors that opened as the Plant Goddess stopped in front of them, her arm still wrapped around Esia protectively. They revealed a room that looked like the inside of a succulent, the walls a smooth green flesh, and two strange figures came into view. Their limbs were branches, the creak of wood audible as they moved forward on feet that spread like roots, and they were adorned with sheaths of vibrant fall leaves, their faces lined like bark.

Tabriara turned to Rakhmet and Hara, indicating the two beings with her free hand. "My healers will tend to you and then you will be retrieved. We have much to discuss."

"Of course, My Divine Majesty." Rakhmet bowed. "Thank you for your kindness."

One of the healers reached to take Esia, but Tabriara whipped her head toward them and hissed, the petals falling from her hair turning a bright red. "No, I will take care of my daughter."

The figure cringed away, their body language immediately submissive.

"Yes, mistress," they rasped, head bowed.

"Send someone to retrieve her fallen guard and prepare their body appropriately," the Plant Goddess added, then nodded at Rakhmet and Hara and turned away. She disappeared around the bend

with Esia, seeming to melt into the greenery, as one figure stepped forward to guide their patients into the room. The other exited into the hall, turning the way they had come.

Rakhmet didn't let go of Hara's hand as they were led to a grouping of metal tables, insisting on sitting together on one of them as the figure gestured for them to take a seat. They were handed two vials of shimmering gold liquid, and Rakhmet raised a brow at Hara in question, but she gave him a reassuring look and downed hers willingly. Her throat was illuminated for a moment as the potion slid into her and he watched as her wounds started closing, so he drank his next and felt a flush of healing energy course through him.

His shoulder snapped back into place and he groaned at the unexpected sensation, the other figure reappearing to take the empty bottles while the first gathered tonic and bandages that shimmered ever so slightly in the light of the bioluminescent algae that covered the ceiling.

"What are your names?" he asked, finding his voice as the pain ebbed.

They looked up in surprise as they arranged the supplies on another table, glancing at each other before answering.

"Hes, blessed one," the being on the right said, the voice a soft rush of wind.

"And I am Cyna, blessed one," the other added.

"Thank you, Hes and Cyna. Your assistance is appreciated." He nodded, noting the way their beady gazes darted away shyly.

"It is our honor," they said as one.

Silence descended again as they started peeling away Rakhmet's and Hara's layers, cleaning their skin as they went, and he was relieved to find that most of their injuries had sealed well, only leaving behind irritated scrapes and bruises. He was more tired than anything else, his muscles still aching despite the draft they had been given.

They were forced to loosen their grips on each other at a certain point, the healers checking their palms and wrapping them with gauze, but Rakhmet kept his gaze on Hara, memorizing her open expression. There were no barriers between them anymore, the relief and love in her eyes filling him with light.

She had given herself to him in the middle of that fight, flinging away her doubt as they bore witness to the brutal breaking of Nees. There had been no more room for hesitation in that moment, and she had reached across the divide to secure what they had both truly needed to survive, to thrive. A binding that fused them irrevocably.

The image of her emblazoned with his blessing, the gold bands of her uniform flashing, and her eyes igniting as they seared into his soul was what he saw when he blinked, and he couldn't imagine what Esia must be going through in losing her own oathed guard. No wonder she had been so desolate and desperate. It felt as if he were one half of a whole now and there was nothing he wouldn't do to keep it that way.

A Conversation

*S*oon enough, they were wrapped up and another figure was called into the room, one outfitted in plates of chitinous armor. Their brown hair hung in thick ropes, gathered into a ponytail with thorned vines, and while they had a more human-like appearance, their stern expression was tinted green.

Rakhmet thanked the two healers, Hara echoing his gratitude, then followed the armored figure out of the room and back into the wild corridor. They were led farther into the seemingly never-ending pathway that featured no other intersecting hallways, only doors scattered here and there, until they reached an enormous archway made from two trees that joined as one about ten feet above their heads.

Inside was a palatial hall, the ceiling again hidden by heavy boughs laden with leaves that were bigger than Rakhmet's torso, and in the center was the largest of them all, a colossal banyan tree with layers and layers of intertwined trunks. At its base was *a throne shaped from the surrounding wood and covered in glossy leaves in a dark purple-red color interspersed with the spiny seed capsules they had seen depicted on the stone slab to which Esia and Nees had pressed their fingerprints.*

The guard motioned for them to proceed to where Tabriara sat upon the throne, following a raised path of large, mossy stones that parted two ponds littered with lily pads on either side. Esia was perched on a mound of grass and wildflowers to the goddess's left, watching them approach with drawn eyes. Despite the evident sadness in her gaze, she looked as healthy and repaired as the two of them, which brought a breath of relief to Rakhmet's lips.

Once Rakhmet and Hara reached them, they dropped into another kneel, giving a gesture of reverence as Tabriara dipped her chin in acknowledgment.

"My dear children, I am thankful for your service and wish to offer you my immortal gratitude for your loyal duty," she intoned from her seat and gestured to Esia. "My daughter here has told me of your journey and the messages you have carried from my kin. There is much afoot."

"Yes, My Divine Majesty." Rakhmet bowed his head. "My oathed guard here has spoken with the Fire God himself, and the sun blessed, Roe, and moon blessed, Kelah, met with the Water Goddess. We are on a mission to right the wrongs that have unjustly divided us."

"Indeed," Tabriara answered, pausing as she looked them over. Her expression was unreadable, and Rakhmet snuck a glance at Hara to see if she, too, was picking up on the odd chill that made his skin prickle. Hara met his eye, and the subtle twitch of her brow told him it wasn't what she had been expecting either.

Rakhmet cleared his throat and refocused on the goddess. "Yes, we are honored to perform these duties for the divine Crowns. Praise be to you and your kin."

"Praise be to the divine Crowns," Hara murmured in response next to him.

There was a long silence, as if Tabriara were testing their patience, her time much more infinite than theirs. Curiosity burned in his throat, but Rakhmet held his tongue. Minutes passed as they kneeled there, her gaze piercing through them, but eventually, there was a rustle of leaves from above and one floated down to land in her lap.

The goddess picked it up and studied its surface, seemingly reading something, then passed it to Esia. "It seems as though Hazu, Dishiru, and Urkus are yet disconnected from us. Where do you plan to go from here?"

The goddess named the Sun, Wind, and Metal Gods, referring to the sacred lands that had yet to be cleared, and Rakhmet shifted uncomfortably. "Ah, well, we are still looking for clues as to the whereabouts of their temples. We know the sun temple will be somewhere near Aepol, but it is a treacherous journey and those seas are currently patrolled by Nalliendran forces. We have convened the Endrian Coalition of Rulers and sent several battalions to the eastern coast, but I haven't heard news on the success of our efforts yet."

"Ah, yes, Nalliendra." The goddess hummed. "The thorn in our side that Hecatah warned of before we lost contact. They have set their sights beyond Frandae?"

"They have been seen patrolling both the Staroh and Metuit Seas and attacked a Zahari ship a little over two months ago. We are aiding Nasima as much as possible in her efforts to push them back."

"Keeping the water blessed busy, I am sure. Where are the sun and moon blessed?" The goddess's gaze darkened as she tilted her head.

"They are expecting a child and are unable to travel so they are staying close to home for now."

Tabriara hummed again, looking down at Esia next to her. "So it falls on the shoulders of the fire and plant heirs."

Rakhmet didn't know what to say in response, letting her statement hang in the air as another long pause filled the room. Their disadvantage without assistance from the other blessed was something that had become patently clear since leaving Zahar, but he couldn't fault their reasons for remaining on the island. They had to take care of their own, didn't they?

"We must work with that which we do have." The goddess rose from her seat and approached Hara, gliding on leaves as they unfolded for her. "Oathed Hara Gamal, Royal Guard of Prince Pyrantus, you wield powerful gifts already I see."

Hara shivered next to him, pinned by the goddess's undivided attention.

"Y-yes, My Divine Majesty," she managed.

"More weapons you need not, for you are a formidable one of your own, my dear child." Tabriara stopped in front of her with her hands clasped by her waist. "Instead, I offer you something much more valuable . . . knowledge."

Hara swallowed, her eyes burning with anticipation.

"The blood oath has been completed and you are now inextricably connected to your prince; I can sense the threads that bind you. That will support you well in your future journeys. Yet, heed my warning. All blessed must secure an oath in order to stand at their full power. Only then will we be able to triumph." Her chin dipped, her expression growing hard. "Dark days are ahead. We have only seen *a fraction of the evil that lurks in the shadows. They play with us like mice caught in the claws of a bored feline.*

"I cannot see where the other daggers are, nor can I grasp the full picture of what you will face. There are forces out there taking great care to remain hidden. However, I can tell you that two are in the domain of the Water Goddess. She has heard their call, and yet dormant they still remain. Know this, the blessed must come together as one. Division will only lead to weakness. We have seen the effects of such this night. Learn from this terrible lesson." She gestured to Esia, who bowed her head as fresh tears spilled down her cheeks.

Rakhmet opened his mouth to say something reassuring, but the goddess lifted a hand to stop him.

"Rakhmet Pyrantus, blessed son of Furaro, answer me this." Her brilliant eyes landed on him, cutting through him like sharpened emeralds. "With your oathed by your side, what will you do?"

"I . . . I will lead my people and fight to end this division. Usher them into a new era of cooperation and advancement without hiding who I truly am." He glanced at Hara and remembered their conversation in that small jungle inn. "I want to invest in my people, feed and nurture and support them with everything at my disposal."

"Through what means?" she asked as a bead of nervous sweat trickled down the back of his neck under her scrutiny.

"I will help my father, and when I become king, I—"

"I see no other king here." She opened her hand to indicate the room around them.

His breath caught in his throat. "But my father, he—"

"Your father did not journey to the plant tribe. Your father did not enter unto my sacred temple. Your father did not risk life and limb to clear my land of corruption. Your father did not secure an oath to a guard of true worth," she stated, her chin rising.

"M-my Divine Majesty—" he tried again.

"Your father is. Not. Here," she gritted through clenched teeth, crimson petals falling from her hair. "You are."

He was stunned into silence, his jaw dropping open at the implication the goddess was laying before him. He couldn't possibly . . . To usurp his father like that . . . It was— It was—

Tabriara lifted a hand and the leaves above them shifted once more as a thick vine fell to her side, the enormous leaf unfurling like a scroll. Inside was a golden crown encrusted with rubies and fire opals, shining like a beacon as he blinked rapidly in confusion.

He had heard of Roe, Kelah, and Nasima receiving their respective elemental crowns, but he had assumed that he would be delivering the fire crown to his father after all was said and done. He wasn't king, only second in line. He was supposed to follow in his father's footsteps; that was the proper order of things. It was too soon. He wasn't ready.

"Furaro is proud of you, my dear child," she said, waving her hand and coaxing the leaf to hover in front of him. There was a slight shift in her expression, a wry press to her lips. "He sent a missive the moment my temple was freed, demanding in his usual way to know the details of what unfolded."

"I-I am supremely grateful, blessed Tabriara, but I couldn't—"

"Do you dare doubt our divine judgment?" she hissed at him, her eyes glowing with intensity. "Do you not dream of a different path? Do you not burn for more, child? Our eyes see much. We are not blind to your mortal yearnings. We hear the prayers that are whispered to us. Do you know what murmurs have reached my ears since the channels of communication have been opened once more?"

He shook his head dumbly, too afraid to say the wrong thing.

"They whisper of a fire heir, powerful beyond belief. A blessed son who has delved into the darkest depths of humanity, befriending those who others would deem unworthy. A scarred fighter who has

yet to be defeated, earning the respect and loyalty of those he leads. A spark of hope in a hearth long gone cold, a steadfast flame in the heart of his people."

Rakhmet sat back on his heels, the pieces falling into place. Where he thought he had been fumbling around all those years, he had been learning and experiencing things those at court would never touch in their lifetimes. He had been broadening his understanding of the world around him and probing at what lay underneath the polished surfaces that only reflected what the privileged few in the palace wanted to see. He had not only been educated in the ways of the monarchy and kinghood, but alongside the common man as well. He knew better than his father what life was like for the regular, everyday individuals they were meant to lead.

She waited as his wide gaze dropped to the crown in front of him, an entirely unexpected path materializing. Had he not been speaking of breaking the generational patterns that bound him? Had he not been itching for a way to build something new? Was this his chance?

Glancing at Hara, he found her dark eyes burning with pride and a smile on her face that was equal parts awed, encouraging, and full of knowledge. She was telling him that it was possible if he were to only reach for it, and in that moment, he truly saw her as his queen. A royal guard rising to the station of royalty, one with the practical know-how to keep him focused and grounded. One that knew him through and through.

His hands reached out and shaking fingers wrapped around the golden flames. Bringing the crown to his head, he positioned its weight as his skin burned. His inner fire suffused him with warmth, like settling next to a fireplace on a cold night, and a deep knowing took up residence in his gut. He had been found worthy. The gods had decreed that his love and affection, power and ambition, and

295

training and preparation surpassed his father's, and he was being given the chance to step toward his destiny with divine sanction.

"Thank you, My Divine Majesty. My gratitude is beyond words." He dipped his head in a shallow bow, giving another gesture of reverence.

"Do not disappoint us," she intoned, her expression cooling.

"In life and death, I am your humble servant," he vowed.

"Before I move onto the next, I wish to grant you a boon that will support you in a time of need." The goddess flicked her wrist, her hand closing around a small container summoned from thin air. She held a box made of woven grasses out to him, and he lifted it from her grasp. Opening the top, he found three seeds nestled within a folded leaf.

"Swallow one when you face your greatest test and my assistance will grant you the strength you need to see it through," Tabriara explained. *"There is one for each of you. Guard them well."*

Rakhmet nodded, closing and tucking the box away in his pocket.

"With that said." She turned to Esia and held out her hand. *"Come, daughter."*

The plant blessed rose from her mound, tears still staining her cheeks, and padded over to her goddess with drawn shoulders, her grief all-encompassing. Guiding her with a gentle touch, Tabriara brought her to her knees at Rakhmet's side.

"My gift for you, my dear one, may not be palatable, but it is necessary." She locked eyes with Rakhmet before continuing, *"You must guide her through the darkness. It is my divine decree. Do you understand?"*

"Of course, My Divine Majesty," he answered, brows furrowing. He was willing to do what was asked, but her tone made him uneasy.

296

Engraved On A Heart Of Flame

The goddess refocused on her blessed one, her eyes glowing brighter than before. "Something has been stolen from you, something vital and sacred to us all, and I wish to restore it. I wish to set you on your fated path and right the wrongs that have been committed. The way may be obscure and difficult, but never forget your power that is seeded within.

"The fortitude is yours, and remember that without remorse, without shame or guilt, nature feasts on the bodies that fall to the test of time. Their bones sustain our growth. That is how it has always been and always will be. Pay no heed to the maxims of mortals, daughter, for you are a force to be reckoned with. Go forth and claim what is yours by right. You have earned it and paid for it in blood."

Esia started trembling next to him as she gazed up at Tabriara with wide-eyed devotion, and Rakhmet reached out instinctively, his hand curling around her elbow to steady her.

"Evelaine Peonille, blessed daughter of mine, I grant you . . ." The goddess's hand landed on her forehead. ". . . your memories."

Rakhmet flinched as a radiant green light flashed around Esia—Evelaine?—and her head fell back as she inhaled sharply, overcome by the gift. Two verdant beams emerged from her eyes, a sudden expulsion of energy that had him dropping her elbow in alarm as her gasp turned into a wailing scream.

"Noooo!!" Evelaine shrieked, her hands flying to her temples and squeezing as her nails started leaving indentations in her pale skin. "NonononoNOOOOO!!!"

Her body convulsed, a visceral reaction to the return of her memories, and Rakhmet glanced at Tabriara in horror as her shouts echoed in the cavernous space. The goddess had simply stepped back, though, her face a mask of somber understanding as she watched her blessed twist and scramble to get away from the long-lost images bombarding her.

"NOO!!" Evelaine yelled, her face losing all of its former dreaminess as her whole demeanor transformed in front of them. Her brows became sharp angles, the planes of her cheeks creating a stark, vicious mug. "Th-th-they took EVERYTHING!!"

Rakhmet's hand found Hara's as the plant blessed struggled to her feet, staggering away from them. She bent forward, her body folding in on itself, and her muscles grew taut across her limbs, then her fists dropped to her sides and she bowed backward as a vengeful war cry exploded from her.

It pierced straight through Rakhmet's chest, and he caught the moment she twitched, her fingers splaying as a cloud of pollen erupted from them in a great blast outward. He reacted before the thought finished forming, pulling a shroud of flames over him and Hara in an instant as the spores eclipsed them in a rush. Their sight disappeared, the bright light of his fire the only thing he could see as the plants under their knees bulged and swelled in abrupt jerks.

He pulled Hara against his chest, the ground quaking from the sheer force of Evelaine's fury, and intensified his flames to protect them both as her screams mixed with the roar of his blessing. Jarring thuds and slaps rocked them from side to side, the impacts of things falling and moving all around them as they clung to each other.

It went on for long minutes, her howls echoing through his head as her voice grew hoarser and hoarser, but he kept feeding their protective shroud, pouring everything he had into it. Eventually, though, it quieted and the ground stilled, and Rakhmet carefully let his blessing fade. The view that greeted them was astonishing: plants torn from the floors and walls, the pond water sloshing as it settled, Evelaine fallen in a heap to the side, the natural order disrupted. Her shoulders were shuddering, distraught weeping shaking her body with fingers twisted around clumps of tangled hair that hid her face from view.

Rakhmet glanced at Tabriara, standing where she had been with a crease in her brow, untouched by the ravages of her blessed daughter. "Should we . . . ?"

"I will take care of her," the goddess murmured, her glowing eyes never leaving Evelaine. "Go, rest. All will be well."

"Yes, My Divine Majesty." He dipped his head, his hand still tight around Hara's as they stood.

His feet were impossibly heavy, but he forced them to hold his weight as he paused for a moment, his heart urging him to comfort his cousin in some way, but Tabriara held up her hand. "You have done well, blessed son. Leave us."

He rubbed his free hand over his curls, then nodded and turned to exit with unsteady steps. They were met by the figure in armor outside the archway, their face giving away no reaction as they led them farther down the corridor to another inconspicuous door covered in greenery. They opened it and gestured for them to enter, then shut it and left them in silence once again.

It was a lavishly appointed bedroom, the silk wallpaper decorated with enormous images of blooming flowers in vibrant oranges and reds. The floor was laid stonework with soft moss growing in the cracks, and the furniture resembled the trunks of trees, a large chandelier of green crystal illuminating it all with a gentle glow. It was disarmingly soothing after the storm of fury they had just been subjected to, and they stood for a moment at the threshold, getting their bearings.

"Well then." Hara spoke first.

"Well then."

She pulled him to the couch that was in the center of the room and they fell into the velvet cushions, still holding onto each other, as Rakhmet began to realize how utterly exhausted he was. The protective fire he had summoned in the throne room had depleted him entirely and he leaned back with a long sigh, rubbing the bridge of his nose as Hara poured them each a glass of water from the pitcher on the wide table shaped like a lily pad.

"Do you think she'll be okay?" he asked, his head propped on the back of the couch as he turned to look at her.

"I . . . I think so," Hara replied hesitantly, folding one leg underneath herself and angling toward him. "She has displayed strength beyond what I expected, to be honest."

"That is very true."

She played with his fingers in her lap, squeezing the callouses and pads. "We will look after her. It's the least we can do considering . . ."

"Yes," he agreed, the images of Nees's broken body flickering through his head. The sound of Evelaine's cries. The crumpled anguish that had distorted her face.

"I couldn't . . . I can't lose you like that," he rasped, bringing her hand to his lips.

Hara nodded, her expression sad. "I understand, truly I do, but we don't know what the future holds for us."

"We will make it, I promise," he swore.

They were interrupted by a knock on the door, and a servant entered with a tray full of food, setting it on the table in front of them before bowing and leaving them once again. Rakhmet's stomach let out a fierce growl, and Hara twitched her lips to the side, smirking at him as he forced his body upright with a huff and started digging into the heaping piles of roasted vegetables, tossed salad, and grilled frog legs.

"I mean it, though," he continued as they ate. "I will ensure that doesn't happen to us. We will be more prepared."

"*Do you intend on going to the next temple, then?*" *she asked warily. Her eyes strayed on the crown that lay heavily on his brow, and he could sense her apprehension.*

"*I think we have to, Hara. We have to stay united. You heard what the goddess said.*" *He hated dragging her into danger again, but what choice did they have? She was arguably the most experienced fighter on their team now, having survived two temples. And gods knew he wouldn't let her journey into another without him by her side.*

"*Yes, I know.*" *Her gaze hardened.* "*But we have to do more research first. We don't even know where the next one is unless we want to go against Nalliendra and try for Aepol.*"

"*No, we need to remain at the rear of this war. Gain allies, grow our forces, then attack once we have more blessed on our side. Maybe after Roe and Kelah's baby is born. There's five of us now, and we can make sure that they all go through the oathing ceremony too beforehand.*"

"*Do you really think that will be enough? I doubt Evelaine will be willing to oath someone else so soon.*"

"*Yeah, Evelaine . . . she may be our weakest link at the moment, but we can take care of her in the meantime. And maybe . . . maybe she won't be able to go through with it, but we'd still have five blessed, four oathed, the ECR forces, as well as whatever navy Nasima's able to muster between now and then. Do we know when the baby's due?*"

"*I think it should only be a couple of months now.*"

"*Good, that will give us enough time to prepare. We can give them, what? Three months after the birth to wean the child then see where we're at. I know we're on a time crunch, but maybe we can find out where the metal and wind temples are in the meantime.*"

301

"We can't be sure, though. We have no idea what's going to be waiting for us in Zahar." Hara frowned. *"Your father . . ."*

"Yes." Rakhmet sighed. *"That is an unknown variable at this point. I . . . I honestly don't know how he's going to react to all of it."*

They fell silent as Hara eyed him with a slightly bewildered look.

"Rakhmet," she whispered, *"you really intend to go forward with this? With . . . us?"*

He leaned forward and clasped her hands. *"Yes, a thousand times yes, Hara. I told you, I will make you my queen. I will have you by my side and on my throne. I love you."*

"The court," she protested, *"they won't approve."*

"You have more than proven your worth, my love. If they can't see that, then fuck them. Our country needs someone like you to help lead, especially now. We are at war. Who better to share the crown than a tried-and-true fighter?"

"Rakhmet . . . I don't know."

"I was chosen by the gods to be king above my father, and yes, I'm still grappling with that, but we have to trust their judgment. They know what they are doing. It is their divine right. They granted you their boons because you earned them, Hara. They saw the love and affection, power and ambition, and training and preparation in you that I've known was there for the last eighteen years. They love you as I love you, and as our people will too."

"I never intended . . . This is something that was never in the cards for me. I was trained to be a guard, not a queen."

"Things need to change, Hara. We both know this. The Crown has been stagnant and repressed for too many generations, following the same path year after year after year. And where has it gotten us? Divided and mistrustful and blind. We can do real good here."

"You truly want to help our people? You think it can be done? There are centuries of precedent we are going against. It's not going to happen overnight." She looked like she wanted to believe him, but her dark eyes were nervous.

"You've heard the stories. The fire heir, the folk hero prince. I . . . I think I can use it, use the role they've spun for me. This is the chance I've been looking for, my opportunity to take hold of my destiny and direct it forward in my own way, not in the one that was laid out for me. I was stifled before, muzzled and prevented from doing anything of true importance. Now, I can shape our country into something better, something worthwhile. And I want you by my side as I do it.

"I know . . . I know I'm asking a lot, again. You never signed up for this, and I'm not going to lie to you and say it's going to be easy. There will be people at court who try to stop it, you will be subjected to malicious rumors and gossip, and we will have to constantly watch our backs. It's one thing to raise a guard to the position of Nesu Medjay; it's another thing entirely to raise a guard to the position of queen. To become not only the leader at my side, but my wife, my partner in all things, maybe even the mother of the future king . . . ."

Hara let out a choked breath, her eyes blowing wide, and he stumbled to get the words out. "If . . . if any of that is too much, I would understand. I don't want you to feel like you're being forced into it. I would never . . ."

He faltered, his throat clenching. "I would never accept anything from you that wasn't freely given."

Overcome by the sheer emotion in his gaze, she stared at him in wonder, her lashes fluttering, and there was a beat of silence between them as her mouth opened and closed. Her dark eyes shone as they

303

took him in, and he found himself holding his breath as he waited for her answer.

"Gods help us, I will follow you wherever. I would be honored, my king," *she finally whispered as light blazed through his chest in relief.*

Placing both hands on her cheeks, he drew her forward and kissed her softly. "My queen, do you forgive me for all I have done?"

"How could I not, Rakhmet? I've been yours for years. I just didn't want to admit it. I was so mad at you, but back there in the temple . . . you stepped up and did what was necessary. You could've thrown yourself into helping Esia—and I would've understood if you had—but you made sure that you . . . that we would make it out of there alive first. I showed you my heart and you didn't run into the fire with it; you protected it. You didn't choose to be a martyr. We lost so much, but we didn't lose each other."

"I never want to lose you," *he whispered.*

She leaned into him as she finally let herself go. No more hesitating, no more doubts, no more questions, she kissed him with everything she had. He returned it and then some.

When they finally pulled away, he swiped a thumb across her cheek to dry the tears that had fallen. "Please don't cry for me, my love."

"I cry because I am overjoyed. I had lost all hope that we would be this bonded again. After everything . . . I love you. I always have," *she murmured, her bottom lip trembling as she smiled softly.*

He kissed her, tasting the saltiness on her lips, and pressed his own vows of love into her skin. "I will cherish you for as long as I live and ever after. My heart is yours."

"Good, please don't fuck this up." *She laughed, her voice thick.*

He grinned, his lids growing heavy from the exhaustion plaguing him. "I promise I will do my best."

She stared at him, her dark gaze full of warmth that soothed his weary body and soul as she pulled him to stand and walked him to the bathroom carved out of green crystal. Setting him down on the edge of the enormous bathtub, she turned the faucets on and kneeled in front of him to untie his scuffed boots. She carefully undressed him, tossing aside his welted armor and bloody clothes before dealing with her own.

By the time the tub had filled, they were both down to their bare skin, and he languidly drank her in as she helped him settle in the steaming water. A satisfied groan escaped him as she climbed in after him, and his hands gripped her slick hips. Even though there was more than enough room for the both of them, she stayed close and reached for the cloths that were stacked neatly on the shelving to the side.

"I've got you, my love," she murmured, tenderly wiping away the dirt and blood and sweat, and his blinks grew longer and longer as he relaxed against the back of the tub. As she hummed under her breath, he trailed his fingertips across her curves and memorized each swell and dip. He knew that he would recognize her even blindfolded with his hands tied. His soul would sing to hers even in the blackest of nights, for they shared a bond that transcended everything he had ever known and everything he would ever know from this day forward. He felt the surety of it in his very bones.

He must have dozed off a bit because after a while, he was roused by the sensation of her fingers in his hair, rubbing suds through it. He groaned again and tilted into her hold. She chuckled softly and he smiled at the contentment that flickered through him at the sound.

"I've always admired your curls." She sighed as she rinsed them out, and he cracked an eye open to glance sideways at her.

"Really?"

"*Really.*" *She nodded, a thoughtful grin curving her lips.* "*My hair never could hold a curl to save its life, no matter how many times I tried. But yours are effortless. They bounce and sway with every step, as if they have a life of their own. It adds to your charm.*"

"*Huh.*" *He returned the grin, craning his neck to look at her fully. He reached out a finger to wrap around one of her straight, wet strands.* "*But I love yours. It's always so sleek. Makes me want to run my hands through it and feel how smooth it is. You keep it hidden away in that bun of yours, though.*"

She rubbed a thumb across his bottom lip as she stared at him, her warm body pressed against his side. "*Well, I suppose I don't have to wear it like that anymore. It was more for convenience than anything else. I didn't know you cared one way or another.*"

"*Oh, I cared, more than was appropriate. More than I probably realized, honestly.*" *He bit down softly on the pad of her thumb.* "*I always sought you out, no matter where we were or whom we were with.*"

She chewed on her own lip, pure love suffusing her expression, and the ease between them made his heart soar. "*My attention was always on you, even when it didn't seem like it. Even when I desperately didn't want it to be.*"

He chuckled, knowing that telltale lip curl all too well, but a huge yawn caught him as his mouth stretched wide.

"*Alright, let's get you to bed, my dear.*" *She laughed and stood, the water sluicing off her toned limbs as she held her hands out for him.*

"*Only if you come with me,*" *he mumbled on the exhale, the words warped by his exhaustion.*

"*Always,*" *she promised, drawing him out of the tub and grabbing towels for the both of them. Drying them quickly, she got him to the bed and laid him down as his breath grew deeper and deeper. He forced himself to stay awake until she slid in next to him and nestled into his shoulder, wrapping her arms around him as another yawn cracked his jaw with its strength. The last thing he was aware of before sleep took him was her hand pressed against his bare chest, holding his heart in her sure grasp.*

DAY THIRTY-THREE

The first thing that came to him was the sound of birds chirping, then the rustling of leaves and a distant rumble of thunder as his fingers instinctively flexed around a warm body next to him. Cracking his eyes, Rakhmet was greeted by a mixture of browns and greens as he realized that he was staring up at the enormous branches of the tree temple that stood at the heart of the plant tribe's sacred forest. Seemingly overnight, the foliage had begun to recover from its former barrenness, new buds sprouting with enthusiasm from every surface.

Turning his head, he found Hara curled around him, her lips slightly parted as she slept soundly on the bed of soft moss that cushioned them. He smiled, his scarred hand coming to brush along her hairline, and kissed the tip of her nose as she started to stir. Her breath was quick as she jerked awake, but her alarm quickly dissipated as her gaze landed on him, and she returned his grin with a look that told him she was enjoying waking up in his arms as much as he was in hers. His heart sighed in relief.

But harsh reality soon returned, and he shifted to find Evelaine on the other side of them, nestled next to a still form that was lovingly wrapped in vines like a mummy. His stomach dropped at the sight, a frown creasing his brow as he sat up and swallowed the regret that burned in his throat. They would be returning to the village with one less in their party, and he wasn't looking forward to the outpouring of grief he knew would follow.

His movements caught the attention of Evelaine as she awoke in a rush, her hand splaying outward to land on the form next to her. She flinched away, a cry falling from her as her face fell and she scrambled to her knees. Her chest heaved as she came to terms with what was in front of her, her jaw grinding as her expression hardened.

Her sharp gaze flicked to him and Hara, where they sat silently to give her the space she needed, and her lips thinned even further in anger. She was a completely different person from the day before. Where there had been an easy dreaminess, there was now a harsh vitriol that threatened to lash out at the slightest provocation.

"Are you okay?" Rakhmet asked, breaking the quiet.

Evelaine cleared her throat but didn't answer, her attention going back to Nees's body.

He waited but she remained mute, so he glanced at Hara for help. She lifted a shoulder, not knowing what to say either. With no other direction given, he stood and awkwardly gathered his pack, noticing that they were all

310

wearing refreshed clothes and armor. Both his and Hara's chest plates bore engravings of phoenixes in flight, their wings sprouting flames at the tips, whereas Evelaine's featured a large leaf and spiked seed cluster.

When Evelaine still didn't move, he slowly approached and crouched on the other side of the body. "We're going to have to move them somehow. How about Hara and I . . ."

Her red-rimmed eyes latched onto him with a ferocity that made him recoil as she hissed at him, "No, they're **mine**."

"Ah, well, of course." He glanced at Hara, who had come up to his side with her own pack. "No one's doubting that, but they're going to . . . be a heavy load, and the terrain is uneven and—"

"I'll take care of the path," she gritted between bared teeth. Even her features had changed, turning angular and stark to match the rigid consonants of her accent. "I have my blessing back now."

"Okay, but we can handle the body while you—"

"I said **I** will do it." She grabbed the oath dagger that had been carefully laid on top of Nees's chest and pushed herself to a stand. Hoisting her pack, she strapped it on and tucked the blade into the belt at her waist.

"Ah." Rakhmet hesitated. "Are you sure? We are more than willing to—"

"I. Will. Do. It," Evelaine snarled at him.

Rakhmet's brows jumped as he stood, startled by her aggression. He looked to Hara again for help, but she was standing to the side, gazing at Evelaine with an expression

311

of deep sadness as the plant blessed looked at the trees above them and raised her hands.

Tendrils of green emerged from the branches and lengthened into long vines that reached down and wrapped around the prone body at her feet. One by one, they lifted the dead weight until it was hovering about four feet off the ground, and then Evelaine turned around and coaxed a few of the growths to attach to her shoulders so that Nees was anchored to her.

Rakhmet and Hara looked on, astonished, as the plant blessed began walking forward, away from the tree temple and back the way they had originally come. The body floated behind her as she kept her hands out, drawing more and more vines to them as if there were a procession of thin, verdant pallbearers carrying Nees to their final destination. She didn't even spare them a glance as she continued on, the vines crumbling away in her wake once their duty had been passed onto the next ones that grew to take their places.

"Gods above," Hara murmured next to him, and all he could do was nod, performing a gesture of reverence before he even realized what he was doing.

That was how it was the entire way back to the village as Evelaine cleared their path, forcing trees, shrubs, and thickets out of the way as they walked in grim silence. The thunder also began in earnest about half an hour in and lightning licked the lush canopies above them, causing Rakhmet to flinch each time it hit. The memories of the accident at the fire temple were still too fresh, and his only solace was keeping his fingers resolutely threaded through Hara's, his eyes never leaving the green form that

312

was carried in front of them and the tense back it was attached to.

But the storm only grew fiercer as they went, until Evelaine was forced to create another layer of woven branches to shelter them and catch the bolts that pierced through the upper boughs. It was like nothing he had ever seen before, as if the environment surrounding them were the clay and Evelaine the sculptor, with full control over the shape and form it took. The landscape was entirely at her beck and call, hers to carve and mold. At times, he even had to tap into his own blessing and quell the flames that flared in the wake of the most powerful strikes.

It was more instinct than anything else, his mind too busy considering whether he would react in a similar way if Hara were to be taken from him. Would he be as inconsolable as Evelaine? Would he insist on throwing himself on the pyre to follow his oathed guard into eternity? Without finishing what he had set out to do? Leaving his parents to struggle in this war without him?

He shuddered to think of the destruction that he might leave in his wake and tightened his hand around Hara's, as if that would protect them from the same fate. Tabriara had said that Evelaine must right the wrongs that had been committed and claim what was hers by right, but what did that mean? What memories had she been shown? Had she lost more than just Nees?

The questions crowded his lips, but Evelaine was clearly in no mood to answer them, and as much as they burned within him, he knew it was not the time to push her. He had to give her time and space, practicing the patience that he had been carefully cultivating over the past month.

He had enough to worry about when it came to how their return trip to Zahar would play out.

What would his father say when he showed up at the palace with the fire crown on his head and Hara by his side? Would his father challenge him? Gods, he desperately hoped that it wouldn't turn into a knock-down, drag-out argument for the ages. How could they question what was decided by divine decree? And in terms of Hara? He was the new Fire King. His word was now law.

What a weird thought.

He kept repeating it to himself, hoping that with enough repetition, it would feel more natural, more solid, but he had a feeling it was going to take a while. Gods knew they would have more than enough time to stew over everything on their way back to Zahar. It would be, what? Another two months to get there?

His attempts at planning were interrupted by their arrival at the village, the curtains of vines eagerly submitting to Evelaine's will as they passed through the final barrier before emerging onto the moss-covered path that led them to the center temple. And what an arrival it was, the villagers immediately freezing in the middle of their chores as they caught sight of the stern plant blessed followed by her precious green bundle.

Gasps filled the air and they all fell to their knees as she passed, not even acknowledging Rakmet and Hara. He could hear the sobs as they rose up behind them and, internally, he cringed, but he didn't let his discomfort show as whispers of *The Esia Ricina* and *Nees, the Oathed* scorched his ears. He only squared his shoulders and followed the procession to its bitter end.

Evelaine didn't even pause as she strode into the center building, the vines attaching to every surface to keep the body aloft before carefully depositing it on the massive circular table. The elders scrambled to stand, caught unaware as whatever conversation they had been having stuttered to a halt. They looked to Evelaine with horror in their eyes, trying to understand what was going on.

"Esia R-Ricina . . ." The older man from before hesitated as Evelaine threw her pack to the ground. "W-what—"

"You will give Nees the burial they deserve, is that clear?" she ordered, meeting each of their wide gazes with a hard look.

"Y-yes, of course, we will honor their noble sacrifice, but Esia Ricina, you must—"

"No," she interrupted. "The Esia Ricina must also be mourned, for she is dead as well. Or rather, she was never here to begin with . . . . I was never her."

The elder looked confused, his gray eyebrows knotting together as he struggled to take in the change that had come over her. "But—"

"I am Evelaine Peonille, daughter of Elemona, a plant blessed who once lived and worked in Risten, Tirdan Republic."

The elders' jaws dropped open, murmurs of surprise escaping their lips.

"That is where I wish to return," Evelaine declared in the stunned silence.

"But Es— I mean, Evelaine," another elder cut in. "You must lead the village. We need you."

"No, you don't. This is not my home. You were perfectly able to survive on your own before I arrived and you will

315

be fine after I leave." She crossed her arms, indicating her immovability.

"Evelaine," Rakhmet tried, his voice respectful. "I understand your need to return home. Truly, I do. But wouldn't it be better to come with us to Zahar first? Perhaps find someone to lead in your stead in the meantime?"

Her cold green eyes locked on him. "No. My duty is to my blooded family, not to these villagers who I've only known for a handful of years and certainly not to a fire blessed who I only met two days ago."

He blinked, caught off guard by her harsh determination. "But we could go with you. We need to stay together. That's what blessed Tabriara told us."

Evelaine looked away, her attention going to the body lying on the table before them. "I am thankful for what the Plant Goddess gave me, but she also said that I needed to right the wrongs that stole everything from me. That is what I intend to do, and I can't wait around any longer than necessary."

"Th—the blessed goddess s-spoke with you?" The older man clutched at the back of one of the chairs, looking like he was about to fall over from all the information that was coming at him. "What happened? What did she say? Is the temple restored?"

Evelaine huffed. "Yes, your precious temple is cleared. There are no more shadows to trouble you anymore. We killed them all and some . . . some of us died in the process. Is that good enough for you? Was their 'noble' sacrifice worth it?"

"Oh, thank the go—" the elder started to say but halted as Evelaine spun back to Rakhmet and Hara and pointed an accusing finger.

"You lied! You didn't tell us it would be that dangerous. You said there would only be a few wraiths. We were outnumbered by far!" Her lips curled as she snarled at Hara in particular.

"Hey now—" Rakhmet stepped forward and put out his arm to block Hara.

"It was far more than anticipated, that is true," Hara cut in calmly, her dark gaze on Evelaine. "There were a handful of wraiths at the water temple and about a dozen at the fire temple, but I counted over thirty yesterday. They are catching onto us. They knew we were coming."

"This is all your fault! If we had known—" Evelaine advanced toward Hara, ducking around Rakhmet's arm to get into her face.

"This is the work of a force beyond our control. You heard what she told us. There are things at play that even the gods themselves cannot see," Hara replied, her tone still even as Rakhmet grabbed Evelaine's shoulder to pull her away, but Hara held up her hand to stop him. "You have the right to be angry, you have all the right in the world, but getting mad at us isn't going to fix anything. It's not going to bring Nees back."

"Fuck you and your fucking noble platitudes!" Evelaine spat, her fists balling at her sides. "They're DEAD because of you!"

"No, they're dead because they chose to go into that fight, knowing that they might not come out of it. They're dead because there are forces out there who are strategically and systematically taking out the blessed ones and everyone they love. Just ask Kelah, who lost her entire family to the Nalliendrans, or Nasima, who lost her mother to the storm that tore apart their island and brought the corruption to their temple."

"I don't fucking care about Kelah or Nasima or whoever the fuck! I care about the people who share my blood, about Nees who was blood-oathed to me, and I care about my grandfather and m-my—" She choked on her words, unable to finish the sentence. "If they're even still ALIVE!! I've had everything, EVERYTHING taken from me and I'm going to do whatever it takes to enact my revenge and save the people who are left!"

Her chest heaved as Hara's brows creased in understanding, and Rakhmet took the opportunity to step in again. "Evelaine, come on, this isn't—"

"NO! Fuck you, fuck your oathed guard, and fuck this village!! You all are NOTHING to me!" Evelaine turned on her foot and stormed out of the temple, tense silence descending as a few of the elders tried to stifle their startled sobs.

Hara met Rakhmet's eye, her expression telling him that she was fine, just worried about Evelaine, and he nodded in response before turning back to the elders who looked a little worse for wear.

"Ah, well." He cleared his throat. "I'm sorry that we could not have brought better news to you, but be assured that the sacred plant temple and surrounding lands are indeed free of corruption. The plants have already begun healing and evidence of new growth was seen this morning."

"Th-thank you, blessed fire heir," the older man murmured, his face distraught. "How ever can we repay you?"

"It's not necessary. Your gratitude is welcome and your village has paid more than enough." He bowed his head toward the form on the table. "Our deepest sympathies are with you. Please know that the Zahari Kingdom and the Fire Crown will do everything within our power to support you whenever you need us."

"Blessed be the Fire Crown. We are forever in your debt." The elder approached and clasped Rakhmet's hands, laying a kiss on his knuckles then turning to Hara and doing the same. "Could you please tell us of what happened at the temple? Is the Es— I mean, Evelaine truly leaving us?"

Rakhmet hesitated but complied, carefully telling them of their journey and subsequent interactions with the Plant Goddess. He made sure that the facts were conveyed but also left out the details concerning the return of Evelaine's memories. He didn't want the tribe to think any less of her, despite the performance she had just given. Grief took many different forms, and he couldn't fault her for lashing out. It was just unfortunate that she would alienate those who had supported her for so many years. After all, he did know what that was like.

He finished by telling them that he would do as much as he could to convince Evelaine to at least come to Zahar first so that she could grieve in a safe and supportive environment, maybe even meet with the other blessed and find some sort of solace in their companionship. In response, the elders dipped their chins one by one and

319

slowly lowered themselves to their knees as they echoed: "Blessings be upon you and yours, may the gods guide us."

"May the gods guide us," Rakhmet returned as Hara repeated it softly, her hand finding his once more. "We will leave you to your . . . ceremonies and will come by in the morning to say our farewells."

They nodded as they got to their feet, and Rakhmet and Hara turned to exit, looking to find their way back to the guest hut that they had been given before. The scene in the village was bleak, though, the villagers having gathered around the outside of the temple in their collective mourning, and Rakhmet couldn't pass by them without giving his condolences to each and every one. They stared up at him from their knees, their teary eyes full of respect, and he was soon crying along with them, moved by their veneration.

Finally, they made it to their hut and briefly greeted the goats that were still tied to the post before escaping inside to the darkened interior, dropping their packs at the foot of the bed. Rakhmet sank onto one of the chairs and held his face in his hands, letting the tears run their course as Hara sat beside him and rubbed his back.

"Gods," he said eventually, sitting back and scrubbing his face clear. "That was a disaster."

Hara hummed, catching one of his hands and threading her fingers through his. "In some ways, yes. In others . . . you did well, Rakhmet."

He stared at her. "You're amazing, you know that?"

She smiled. "So I've been told."

"I love you."

"And I you."

There was a long pause as he tried to wrangle his thoughts. "What are we going to do now?"

"Well, first we need to head back to Lythenea and send word to your parents." Hara glanced toward the door. "I think we'll be able to convince Evelaine to go with us that far, but once we get there . . ."

"Who knows what will happen," Rakhmet finished.

"She's going to fight us every step of the way. She's really hurting."

"Yeah." He sighed. "What do you think our chances are of convincing her to come with us to Zahar?"

"We can try, but . . . I don't know. She seems determined to go her own way and we might just have to let her."

"We'll be losing a valuable ally. We're just right back where we started."

"Not exactly." Her eyes dropped to his pack. "You're king now, Rakhmet. We are oathed, and the plant temple is free again. Those are huge accomplishments."

He exhaled roughly. "You're right. I just . . . wish we had more."

"More than being king?" Hara teased, her lips curling in a smirk that had him leaning forward to kiss her. He couldn't get over how right it felt to finally be able to express his love for her like this. It felt as natural as breathing. He wanted to hold her in his arms for days on end.

"You know what I mean." He smiled, sitting back. "We need all the blessed on our side that we can get."

"That's true, but we will be stronger once Roe and Kelah are able to travel again. Plus, there are more blessed out there. We'll find them."

Rakhmet pressed his lips together, knowing that she was right. He had to focus on the advantages they did have. "Speaking of, I think I want to keep the whole king thing secret until I get a chance to talk to my father face-to-face. I don't think it will go over well if he learns of it through a pigeon message. There's too much to explain."

"I think that's the right move, especially along with the news of, well, us." Her expression grew a bit shy, and he loved the way her cheeks pinkened as she looked at him.

"I'll have them make you the most dazzling crown of them all, studded with every jewel in the royal vault." He grinned at her.

She rolled her eyes. "You know that's not the point. We're supposed to be investing in the people, not gilding ourselves further."

"Of course, of course, my love. What would I do without you?" He brought her knuckles to his lips and kissed them. "You'll be a wonderful queen. Our people will love you as I do."

"Let's cross that bridge once we get to it." She laughed. "First, we have to get back home in one piece."

"True," he acceded. "Should we go back through the mountains? Do you think the roads will be safe enough?"

Hara hummed, thinking. "I'm not sure. I'm wondering if we should go by water instead. I haven't been able to forget about the comment that Nees made about Nalliendra possibly making inroads into the border towns. It's very possible that they are taking a multipronged approach just as we are. They might be craftier than we're giving them credit for."

"I think they are definitely craftier than we initially thought. Remember when my father said he was worried about how they found out where the temples were in the first place? I didn't really think anything of it at the time, I was too focused on the issue of the plant temple, but he was right. How did they find them?"

"I wonder if they're torturing the blessed they find for information. If they came across some that knew about Tusi, that would make sense, but how did they find out about the fire and plant temples? That information has been hidden for centuries, unless they have eyes and ears looking for clues all over just as we are. That would support Nees's theory that they are more infiltrated than we are aware of."

"Do you think we have spies in the palace? People who could've overheard our plans for the temples?" Rakhmet was struck by the possibility.

"No, I don't think so because we didn't start talking about the temples until after your blessings were dampened. We didn't even think about the connection until we received word from the Rutrulans." She thought for a moment. "If anything, maybe there are spies in the temple in Kemet. They're the ones with all the old records."

"I'll launch an investigation once we get back. It's worth at least looking into," Rakhmet agreed. "But you're right, returning by water might be the best bet. We'll have to go around the entire continent, though."

Hara stood to rifle through her pack, pulling out a map they had chosen from the items provided by his uncle and opening it on the table between them. Trailing her finger along the edges of South Endrian, she calculated out loud:

"Going south through the Jikan Pass will probably take about forty days? Give or take. But going north through the Somansian Canal would take a bit less. Maybe thirty-six? It would take us right past Tusi, though, if we wanted to stop in and talk with Nasima."

"That might be a good idea. We should update her on everything we've learned as well as meet with Roe and Kelah if they're available. I'd definitely feel better having spoken with them personally. I feel so disconnected from them with all of our messages going through the Rutrulans."

"I did meet Roe briefly while I was there. He seems like a good fighter and he obviously cares a lot for the people on the island. I think he grew up with Nasima and Cas, so I'm sure there's some sense of loyalty between them all. That will be helpful if we ever have to fight together."

"Speaking of Cas, do you think she would want to be Nasima's oathed?" Rakhmet hadn't even thought that far ahead, but it seemed like an obvious match.

"Based on how they were looking out for each other in the fire temple, I would bet on it." Hara sat back and considered him. "Blessed Tabriara did say that there were two daggers on Tusi but they were dormant. It would make sense that one of them would be the water dagger, but what about the other?"

"If I had to guess, I would say either the sun or the moon, considering Roe's and Kelah's presence there, but who knows? They didn't say anything about that when you were there?"

"No, but we didn't get much of a chance to talk beyond the one dinner with Roe. She said that each blessed needs an oathed, so I wonder if they would need to find their own. Or could they be each other's?"

"I have no idea, but it would benefit us to stop at Tusi and inform them at the very least. I trust they can figure out the details on their own. All I know is that we need to take advantage of any and all chances at being stronger. I don't want to lose anyone else. That was . . . awful." He leaned in to cup her face. "I won't lose you."

"We can prepare and take our time." Hara tilted into his hand, her gaze soft.

"I love you," he murmured. "More than anything."

"I love you." She sighed. "With everything I have."

He kissed her, taking deep draws from what she was so readily giving, and she pulled him closer. Shifting to the edge of his chair, he wrapped one hand around the back of her neck and one around her waist and she sighed again, her warm breath caressing his skin as she leisurely tasted his lips.

The sensations she urged from him were a world apart from anything he had ever experienced before, light filling his sternum until he swore it burst from him to envelop her in his glow. But she was right there, matching his fire with hers, and he felt the molten gold cover his heart protectively just as he was covering hers. They were bound, she and him. Utterly, irrevocably, and most ardently.

His fingers threaded through her hair and freed it from the top bun she had woken up with, the metal band falling to the floor with a gentle ting. Her silky lengths curtained her shoulders, brushing against his knuckles as he buried his hands deep within them, and she laid reverent kisses on his scars. Shuddering, he held her as her lips traveled down his cheek and onto his neck, worshiping every ridge and swell.

"These are beautiful. You are beautiful," she murmured, and his heart soared, the flames of their love burning brighter and brighter.

He pulled her back and looked her square in the eye. "You, my love, are everything to me. Everything."

She smiled, her grin radiant as she beamed at him, and he fell further than he had ever thought possible. His love for her was endless, an eternally burning fire that seared into the very core of who he was. Her name and hers alone was etched into the gold plating of his heart for all time.

Clutching her to him, his hands dug into her thighs as he picked her up, carrying her to the bed and laying her out before him. Her dark hair fanned behind her on the rough-spun bedcover and her smile didn't waver as he tugged the boots from her feet and loosened the ties around her waist.

He took his time admiring as he stripped her bare, kissing every inch of her luscious brown skin and muscled limbs. From her graceful neck and strong shoulders to her peaked nipples and flat stomach, her rounded hips and firm thighs and the patchwork of old scars scattered along her calves from all the years sparring with him and other guards, she was utterly perfect to him.

She moaned as he explored, loosening his own armor and clothes until the heavy leather and fine fabric was soon gone and their hot skin was sliding against one another's. Her wet mouth found the scars on his arm and she peppered him with tender kisses as he sucked on a nipple, her breathy sighs turning into gasps that made him thicker and thicker with each passing second. His hips were churning of their own accord, impatiently pressing into the bed while he traveled down to her core.

"So good . . . ," she breathed as his tongue disappeared into her damp curls, and they both groaned at the sensation.

Her own hips urged him on, undulating underneath him as he drank up every drop of nectar that gathered there, and her nails bit into his shoulders. He licked and sucked and nibbled the delicate flesh, then drew her sensitive bud into his mouth for a fierce pull. Pants turned into cries of ecstasy as her head fell back and her body spasmed, her legs kicking blindly.

He drew himself up her body, his chin dripping with her juices, and settled between her legs, his length rubbing in her slick folds. Grabbing his face again, she yanked him to her lips, tasting herself as they bruised each other with their passion. He couldn't hold back any longer, entering her with a sharp thrust, and she gasped into his mouth.

"My love," he gritted as his hips started pistoning. "My love, my love . . ."

"Yes." She keened, her fingers digging into his hips as she wrapped her long legs around him. "Always and forever."

"Always and forever," he repeated, lifting his head to gaze into her burning eyes. The bed, the room, the village, his worries about the future, it all fell away as they stared at one another and he moved in and out, in and out. All there was was the two of them, and that was all that mattered in that moment. "I am yours, Hara."

"Yours, my good Rakhmet," she returned, kissing him with such promise that it took his breath away.

THREE DAYS LATER

After storming out of the central temple in Curacu, Evelaine had pointedly ignored all of the villagers who had looked to her with tears in their eyes and had sequestered herself in her own hut, alone. She hadn't even bothered to open the shutters, choosing to sit in the dark where she couldn't see the cold items that had belonged to Nees sitting untouched around the space, and stewed over the sequence of events that had stripped her to the bone. Her long, tangled locks falling into her face, she had sat for hours and tried to come to terms with the aching chasm in her chest.

The pain was unreal, beyond anything she had ever experienced, and she had certainly suffered far more than her fair share in her lifetime. The truth was, she wasn't a stranger to agony. Her life had not been easy, and while she had had a brief respite from her nasty history thanks to the amnesia that had wrapped her in a soft cocoon for five years, the ugly memories of her harsh upbringing were back in full force.

Esia had been a fanciful illusion, a dream-filled existence that had smoothed her rough edges and given her a glimpse at what life could've been like for her. But she knew better. She knew what was waiting for her in the Tirdan Republic. Misery, desperation, bitterness.

Vengeance.

By dawn the next day, she had taken the oath dagger to her hair and chopped it all off in fierce cuts, returning it to the more manageable style that she was used to. As Mistress Satine's top assassin, she had preferred to keep her hair short. It didn't hinder her movements nor give her opponents anything to grab as she slipped past them, slashing their throats before they even realized. Plus, it was easier to wash the blood out that way.

The elders had looked on in shock as she had followed Rakhmet and Hara out of the village, their goats in tow. She had refused to give them any kind words, knowing that if she had opened her mouth, her poisonous anger would have spilled out and crushed their preciously held fantasies of who their plant blessed was. But she had never been theirs to begin with.

She had learned long ago that, with the exception of her grandfather, she was the only one she could truly trust. Having grown up as the bastard child of a courtesan, she had had to fight for her survival from a very early age. Luckily, her mother's employer had taken a liking to her and taken her under her wing after Elemona had died from a bad case of pneumonia when Evelaine had only been ten.

The Mistress had seen potential in her after she had made herself useful by working backstage, balancing high up on the grid and working the ropes during the brothel's nightly burlesque performances. Her slight stature and nimble limbs had been valuable, aiding her in being able to slip in and out of tight spaces unseen and unheard. It was truly a transferable skill set. Once she had come of age, the Mistress had placed her under the tutelage of her top assassin at the time, and by the time she had turned eighteen, she had outpaced her trainer.

It seemed like lifetimes ago, but Evelaine's body had remembered everything as she spent days trudging alongside Rakhmet and Hara through the jungle toward Lythenea. She had proved as much in their doomed journey into the plant temple, yet her skills had not been enough to protect Nees from their tragic fate. While she had certainly dispensed death as easily as the card dealers that populated Mistress Satine's great hall, losing Nees had ripped something vital away from her.

She had grown to love her loyal guard in the five years she had spent in the village, and her shattered soul was dark as pitch as they arrived in the glimmering coastal city, its graceful curves rising above them and proclaiming its importance to the world. Sneering at the gaudy opulence, she silently judged the shining stone structures and elaborate decorations. Why should they have all these riches at their disposal while thousands went hungry elsewhere?

The starving desperation that came from not knowing where your next meal would come from had been her constant companion after her mother had died. She had been expected to work for her room and board like everyone else—no one got a free pass under the Mistress's roof. So she had scrimped and hustled, making every coin that she had earned count as she had tried to save enough to get out and start a life of her own. But her employer had been adept at her manipulations, keeping her staff under her thumb just enough to keep them dependent on her.

It hadn't been until she had met Mason that her fortune had started to turn, but she couldn't bring herself to linger on that thought as Rakhmet and Hara handed their goats over to a guard standing outside a palatial inn that choked Evelaine with distaste in the Aerie District. They waved Evelaine inside with them, obviously not wanting to leave her to her own devices for fear of her taking her leave of them once and for all, and she grimaced but followed, knowing that she at least needed to stay on their good side until she could fill her pockets with enough of their coin to pay for passage home.

Rakhmet spoke with the starry-eyed attendants behind the front desk, and soon they were being escorted up a grand staircase toward a pair of gilded doors that opened into a parlor with doors on either side. Hara immediately started surveying the rooms, presumably checking them for threats like the loyal oathed she was, and Evelaine rolled her eyes as she dropped her pack on the floor with a huff.

It drew a side eye from Rakhmet, who was reading over a letter that had been handed to him by the attendant before she had left, and Evelaine made a halfhearted attempt to swallow down her irritation. He and Hara had been giving her space throughout their trip, but she could tell that sooner or later, he was going to ask her questions that she didn't want to answer. While she had to admit that she had been impressed by the way they had handled themselves in the temple, it didn't mean that she trusted them by any means. She pulled a more impassive expression onto her face and stalked to the window, glaring out onto the street below as he read and Hara finished her inspections.

Eventually, Rakhmet cleared his throat and broke the silence. "My father says that they've received word in Zahar that Kelah has had a vision of the metal tapestry. It seems like that is the temple we will need to find next."

Evelaine looked over her shoulder at him. "Tapestry?"

Rakhmet glanced at Hara, who had come up beside him, and there was some sort of unspoken conversation that passed between them before he answered, "Kelah, the moon blessed, is granted visions by her goddess of a tapestry corridor. She had a vision of the water tapestry before going to the water temple and then another of the fire tapestry when Nasima, the water blessed, left to come help us with the fire temple. Most recently, she had one of the plant tapestry."

"I see," Evelaine said, dusty and forgotten memories blooming inside her.

"That means we either need to find clues regarding the whereabouts of the metal temple or somehow track down one of the metal blessed, preferably both." Rakhmet turned to Hara. "Do you have any idea where to start?"

"We'll have to ask Nasima when we stop by Tusi and see if they've heard of anything. But we might just have to wait until after the baby is born, then we can spread out and do a more thorough search."

"What baby?" Evelaine's stomach churned at the word, her hand unconsciously landing on her own belly.

"Kelah and Roe, the sun blessed, are expecting a child . . . in about two months. It shouldn't be too long now," Hara answered, her gaze subtly dropping to where Evelaine's hand was pressed.

Evelaine quickly dropped her arm. "Right."

She vaguely remembered them saying something about that when they were in Tabriara's throne room, but she had been too dazed from losing Nees to comprehend what was going on. Bitterness crept up her throat. From what she had heard so far, she wasn't taking a liking to these other blessed they kept referring to who seemed to have everything figured out and yet hadn't been there for Evelaine when it had truly mattered. If they had been in the plant temple with them . . .

"I know you've already said that you want to return to Risten," Rakhmet said, interrupting her thoughts. "But I really think it would be better if you joined us in Zahar first. You can meet the other blessed and we can—"

"No," she shook her head. "I've made my decision. I'm going to Risten. I need . . . There are people there that I'm responsible for and I've been away for too long."

"Are you sure? We could go with you, protect you, after we gather our forces and—"

"I said no," she gritted between clenched teeth. "I just need money and then I'm leaving."

Rakhmet looked surprised despite the clear conflict in his gaze. "Money? Oh, uh, sure . . . of course."

He glanced at Hara, who frowned but opened her own pack and rifled through it to draw out a pouch of coins. Evelaine could see from across the room that it was bulging and it choked her. The thought that they had been carelessly carrying around a fortune that would've bought the freedom of a good third of Mistress Satine's staff? There was nothing she could do to hide her sneer of disgust.

Hara handed it to Rakhmet and he walked over to Evelaine, holding it out to her as he studied her sour expression. His brows furrowed and he ran his other hand over his black curls. "Truly, Evelaine, we are on your side. Whatever you need . . ."

"This is more than enough," she said, taking the pouch and weighing it in her palm. Yeah, this would buy more than she had ever imagined and then some. Her plans started clicking into place. "I'll also help you out with your problem, then we can call it even."

"What problem?" he asked hesitantly.

"The metal blessed. I happen to know one."

"What?!" Rakhmet and Hara both exclaimed.

"I grew up with one in Risten. We were close once. I'll see if I can track him down."

Rakhmet stared at her wide-eyed, trying to determine if she was telling the truth, so she kept her gaze steady and honest until he relented, glancing back at Hara with a relieved look. "That would be amazing, Evelaine. It would really help us out."

"You got it." She casually saluted him with her free hand. "So we're good? I can head out?"

His dark eyes darted back to her. "Ah, sure, but . . . I was hoping that, ah, you would stick around for a bit? We can have dinner with my uncle. He wanted to—"

"Nah, I'm not one for the warm and fuzzy family shit. I appreciate it, but I'd rather get going." She ducked around him and headed for her pack, stuffing the pouch deep inside it. The only time she had ever caught a glimpse of that much coin before had been in the Mistress's office, and even then, her employer had made sure to hide it from sight the moment anyone walked in her door. Evelaine would have to be very careful with how she handled it, but she had some promising ideas unfurling in the back of her mind.

"Uh, well, please do send us word when you get to the Tirdan Republic. We'd like to know that you arrived safely," Rakhmet said somewhat helplessly, watching her strap on her pack with a worried crease in his forehead while Hara stood by silently. The guard's arms were crossed, and while her face was carefully blank, Evelaine could see the suspicion lurking in the back of her keen gaze.

She pasted on a cheery smile, trying to assuage them as she backed toward the double doors of the suite. "Sure thing. Don't worry about me. I can handle myself."

Her heart was pounding in anticipation. She could tell that they didn't want to let her leave so she was trying to slip out before they came to their senses and stopped her by force. But neither of them moved and she took hold of the opportunity that was right in front of her, gripping the doorknob and opening it to step over the threshold.

"Wait." Rakhmet held out a hand to stop her and she grimaced internally. She was so close . . . .

"I, uh." Rakhmet's hand dipped into his pocket and drew something out. "Take these."

On his palm lay three silver coins and her brows furrowed in confusion. Why would he offer her three measly coins when she already had a pouch brimming with more than enough money? Was he trying to pull something on her?

"These, ah . . . I know they don't seem like much, but they helped me when I needed them." He hesitated, seeing the suspicion on her face. "I just . . . Sometimes you need a bit of reassurance when things seem bleak. Even if it's only three silver coins."

He cautiously walked forward and held them out to her as she studied his expression for any hint of manipulation. But he seemed to be genuine, so she delicately picked them up as if they might bite her at any second, her muscles tensed and ready to bolt if needed.

"Uh, thanks," she said, her eyes darting between him and Hara uncertainly.

"Yeah, ah, well, take care of yourself." He rubbed his now empty hand over his curls, a nervous gesture. "We'll come see you soon."

"Yeah, sure." She nodded one last time, catching sight of Rakhmet locking eyes with his guard and having another one of their silent conversations, then closed the door behind her and swiftly made her way down the stairs and out of the inn. Once she was in the fresh air again, she stuffed the coins into her pocket and breathed deeply but didn't relish her freedom just yet. She needed to put distance between her and the figures she knew would be watching her disappear into the streets from the window as quickly as possible.

Keeping her pace even, she wove her way through the crowds and aimed for the docks at the bottom of the city.

It was nearing sundown, and she knew she had to secure passage on a boat before nightfall. If she delayed at all, the chances of Rakhmet and Hara coming to look for her rose exponentially, and every fiber of her being needed to get out and away because gods only knew what had happened in her absence.

A little over five years ago, the Mistress had sent her to the port city of Werthine on a mission to track down Nydas Sutherland, a coastal mob boss that had been intercepting and stealing shipments of drugs meant for the brothel. It was another line of business that kept the Mistress's pockets lined, her patrons blissfully content, and her courtesans willfully complacent. With multiple shipments missing, Evelaine had been dispatched to fix the irritation posthaste.

It hadn't been difficult to find him, his boastful cronies unknowingly leading her right to their secret headquarters nestled away in a seemingly derelict warehouse in the shipping district. She had spent several days watching their comings and goings, learning their patterns and movements. When she had been certain she would find Nydas relatively unprotected, she had infiltrated the building with all the stealth of a mouse and found her way to his office.

What she hadn't been expecting was the number of traps installed in the room when she had entered and interrupted him in the middle of a meeting with five of his henchmen. Usually, her targets were either too arrogant or stupid to invest much in their defenses, but it seemed as though the mob boss had insisted on multiple layers of protection when she had assumed that he would simply rely on his men to defend against intruders. Despite her years of working her way up to become one of the most feared shadows of the night in Risten, it had been her undoing.

Perhaps her reputation had preceded her and Nydas knew who he would be tangling with when he had started stealing shipments from the Mistress. Perhaps her confidence in her abilities had gone to her head. Either way, she had been immediately pierced upon crossing the threshold with two long javelins that had emerged from holes in the walls before she could even react. One had struck through her right thigh while the other had ripped a gash in her left arm as she had tried to twist away.

Striking out in retaliation, she had instantly called forth her cloud of poisonous pollen and had pushed it in the direction of the five men that were up, armed, and aiming for her, but it had made no difference as Nydas had pulled a lever on the desk next to him and a wall of thick glass had dropped down from the ceiling. It had separated them, saving the men from inhaling the toxic spores as they had rapidly drawn cloth masks over their noses and mouths in preparation. Another step forward and her foot had fallen through a hole that had been covered by the rug and her ankle had been caught in a toothed bear trap as she had howled in pain.

She had tried to pull her leg free as the cloud had dissipated around her, but soon the glass wall had been raised once again and the men had studded her with crossbow bolts, forcing her to the floor as alarming amounts of blood had poured from her. Making one last attempt to wrap them in her vines, she had managed to capture three of them, but the remaining two had broken away and rushed her. She had flailed, knocking them away with everything she had left, yet one had a piece of doused cloth ready and had pressed it against her face. It had smelled rank, the overwhelming scent of chemicals filling her nostrils as the sedative had taken hold.

She remembered locking eyes with Nydas, a satisfied smirk stretching across his pockmarked face as he had gazed upon his prize. The final thought she had before she had lost consciousness had been one of revenge, but all of it had faded into nothing. The drug they had used had stolen every memory, every recollection, every dream, every treasured face that she had once held dear.

Because of them, she had not only lost the last five years, but her entire life.

Now, she was going to enact her vengeance if it was the last thing she ever did.

FIN.

Bonus Chapter:
Six Weeks Later

Hara leaned her elbows on the railing of the merchant vessel they had bought passage on to ferry them from Melatius to Zahar, the home that, at her darkest moments, she had been afraid she would never see again. They were so close she could smell the familiar spices drifting from the food stalls dotting the shores and hear the occasional call of a barker advertising their wares. She felt it all seep into her bones like a soothing balm, easing some of the tight anxiety that had been choking her ribs for months.

But she couldn't relax just yet. They still had to face the former king and handle whatever reaction he would have to the news that not only did Rakhmet get chosen by the gods to be the new Fire King, but he would be installing his oathed guard as queen by his side. Her stomach flipped at the thought. She hadn't yet gotten used to the idea, it almost seemed like a fever dream, yet Rakhmet had demonstrated his resolve time and time again.

She had never seen him so sure of anything before. It was hard to believe that she had inspired such staunch determination in him. Her, the child of two palace guards who had never aspired to rise to the station of royalty even in her wildest dreams. It was like a tale out of the books full of fantastical lore that were read to children at their mother's knee.

When she glanced over her shoulder, her eyes were instinctively drawn to the regal figure at the head of the ship speaking with the captain. His confidence had grown in leaps and bounds ever since he had wrapped his hands around that crown of flame, and it shone from him like a beacon. He no longer needed to act the role, a facade that only she had been able to see through. He embodied it.

Everyone around him responded to him like moths to a flame, flocking to him and gazing upon him with wide-eyed respect and veneration. The tales of his heroics had traveled far and wide and the masses fell to their knees with gestures of reverence everywhere he went. Treating them all with understanding and compassion, he had made a point of stopping to give a kind word to each and every one. It took them forever to get anywhere that way, but no one rushed him.

Their time on Tusi had been the only respite from the fanfare with the people there treating him as one of their own, like he was family, as they sat around the large wooden table in Ohn and Rochelle's home and discussed everything that had happened. The Rutrulans had readily renewed their support of the Fire Crown and Roe had immediately followed suit once he had arrived at Yerbe a day later. Rakhmet and Hara had even traveled with him to Kartok in order to speak with Kelah in person, her due date fast approaching.

It had been comforting to strengthen their relationships with the other blessed, hearing from Kelah firsthand about her visions of the tapestry corridor as well as informing them of what they had learned concerning the oath daggers. Kelah had gasped when they had explained what Tabriara had told them, ordering Roe to retrieve the dagger that she had apparently found after the shipwreck she had survived all those months ago.

Clearly, it was cousin to the one Hara carried as well as the blade that had been displayed on the wall of the armory in Yerbe. The Rutrulans had always thought of it as a ceremonial dagger, one that hadn't been used for anything other than decoration in centuries, but upon further inspection, it was nearly identical to the others. The moon dagger featured engravings of cypress with a smoky gem on the end of the pommel, whereas the water dagger had coral and a brilliant sapphire.

Cas had immediately volunteered to go through the oathing ceremony with Nasima, her blue eyes earnest and bright, and for Kelah, a villager introduced as Zan had stepped up with fierce conviction. Hara had been heartened by the obvious bond between Kelah and Zan. It would be a great boon to them when push came to shove, and Roe had stood in witness to the palm cutting with pride, clear approval shining in his gaze.

Both Nasima and Kelah had experienced impressive boosts to their powers, Nasima summoning ice-cold water from inside herself with a mere thought and Kelah calling forth the vivid light of a full moon as her eyes had glowed like stars, and it had honestly been a relief to see their plans coming together. They now had three blessed on their side with their oathed who were more than willing to join them in coming battles, as well as a sun blessed who had been gifted the ability to instantly revive any blessed who happened to die in the heat of fighting. Roe's abilities wouldn't help any oathed who happen to fall, like Nees, but Hara had the feeling that she and the other oathed were willing to take that chance if it meant that their blessed could see it through.

They'd had to alter their timelines a bit, though. Rakhmet's cheeks had pinkened when Brishna had chided him for assuming that three months would be enough to wean Roe and Kelah's coming child. She had told them that it would be at least six months, if not longer, so Rakhmet had agreed to look further into what they had heard of the metal blessed in the meantime. It would give them a chance to track down Evelaine and hopefully convince her that they would all do better together. The Plant Goddess's order to stay with her and help her had haunted them each and every mile that took them farther and farther away from the plant blessed. They had promised everyone on Tusi that the moment they were able to settle things back in Zahar, they would head to Risten and fulfill their duty to the goddess. Hara was almost optimistic about their chances, but she was also well aware that they had a long path ahead of them.

Nalliendra had backed away from the eastern coast of South Endrian once the ECR ships had started their patrols, but word was coming in from the north that wasn't as favorable. It seemed as though they had simply reoriented their sights elsewhere, even going so far as to make landings in North Endrian to ransack coastal towns. Those who had fled Zahar to the north when the Pyrantuses had announced their intention to reinstate the elemental crowns were now rushing back to the kingdom alongside droves of foreigners, choosing guaranteed safety under the Fire Crown over the death and destruction that Nalliendra promised.

Rakhmet's father had been keeping them as informed as possible via pigeon messenger, but only so much could be conveyed in the short-form scrolls. Most of their insights had come firsthand from Nasima and Roe, who had their own networks of informants feeding them news across the seas. No one knew what was happening in the countries that had already been conquered, though, and that was what was most worrying. But they had to keep focused on one step at a time, and today that meant confronting the former king and organizing the transfer of power, hopefully with minimal upset and interference.

Hara sighed, her attention going back to the docks as they approached the royal slips. There were at least a dozen guards there waiting for them and one by one, they dropped to their knees with the expected reverence as Rakhmet and Hara disembarked. Breaking from protocol, Rakhmet helped her into the carriage first, a move that caused many an eyebrow to rise in surprise and a hot blush to overtake her cheeks. She still wore her royal guard uniform and divine weapons at her waist (even if she now wore her hair in a long braid that Rakhmet liked to stroke when they were alone), but the respect Rakhmet was showing her was definitely outside the norm.

They rode toward the palace in silence, her heart pounding in her ears and Rakhmet's hand wrapped around hers. He squeezed her fingers in solidarity and gave her a smile that told her he would stand by her no matter what, but she couldn't get her lips to curve in response, the nervousness overtaking her body too powerful to ignore. Eventually, though, she found herself climbing out of the carriage and walking through a line of more kneeling guards toward Uma, who beamed at them in pure joy at the threshold, greeting them with her own gesture of reverence as well as a great big hug once the towering doors were closed and they were provided a bit of privacy.

"Your Highness, our happiness is beyond measure to see you return." Her smile creased the skin around her tear-filled eyes. "And Royal Guard Gamal, it is likewise that we welcome you home."

"Thank you, Uma. It's an immense pleasure to be back," Rakhmet responded, his own gaze misting for a moment as he held her at arm's length and grinned, but he soon shook himself and waved her on. "Please, take us to my father and gather my mother. We have much to discuss."

"Of course, Your Highness. Right away," she said, breaking into a brisk walk and leading them through the winding hallways toward the king's study.

Hara tried to control her breath as they went, forcing her reserved facade into place with much effort until her reliable stoicism was firmly set and ready for anything.

Rakhmet had let go of her hand but he kept pace with her, not letting her fall behind to her usual guard position, and it was that subtle act of support that had Uma side-eyeing her with a curious look. But she kept her expression impassive and refused to give anything away as the royal manager stepped aside and they were let into the study.

Rakhmet's father glanced up from where he was writing correspondence at his desk, jumping to his feet with a surge of energy and wide eyes as he rushed forward and embraced his son with a choked greeting. "My dear Rakhmet, oh my son, how good it is to see you."

Hara stood to the side while they murmured to each other, each rubbing at their cheeks as tears fell, but the former king soon turned to Hara and reached out to grasp her hand. "Thank you from the bottom of my heart, Royal Guard Gamal. Your loyal stewardship of my son has been above and beyond your duties, and we are immensely grateful for your valiant efforts."

"It has been my pleasure, truly." She bowed her head in thanks, not sure how to properly address him. She kept her words short to be safe and glanced at Rakmet to help her out.

He gave her a subtle nod and dropped his pack by the chairs that sat in front of his father's desk, a satchel that he had pointedly kept by his side every step of their return journey because inside was an item that would change their lives forever. "Father, please sit. We have much to tell you and Mother once she—"

He was interrupted by the two doors of the king's study flying open and banging against the walls with a loud crash, all of their heads turning to see his mother fling herself over the threshold with a frantic expression. Her chest heaving and tears streaming down her cheeks, she ran for Rakhmet and threw her arms around him with a sob as he caught her.

"Oh my dear, my dear, my dear . . ." She cried, her voice thick with emotion. "My dear boy."

"Mother, it is so good to see you." Rakhmet spoke into her hair, clutching her close.

They stood like that for a prolonged moment, her shoulders shuddering as she touched his face and ran her hands over his arms, assuring herself that he was flesh and blood in front of her. But eventually, she pulled back and looked over his shoulder at Hara as well, giving her a grateful albeit wobbly smile.

"Thank you, Royal Guard Gamal, for bringing our son back to us. We cannot thank you enough."

"Of course." Hara simply nodded, unwilling to say more for fear of misstepping.

Rakhmet cut in, catching the hesitation that followed her words. "Mother, please sit. I must tell you both of our . . . story."

His father took his place behind his desk and his mother chose one of the chairs in front, leaving the other for Rakhmet as he sat. He glanced over his shoulder and used his eyes to indicate that he wanted Hara to stand next to him, not behind, as he launched into an explanation of their journeys. She kept her expression neutral as the former king gave her a curious look, but he was soon distracted by the tale as Rakhmet told them of what had gone down at the Hapimose estate, their treacherous travels through the mountains, how they found the first small village and made their way to Lythenea, and meeting up with Otani at the Aerie Auberge.

He told them of arriving in the plant village, meeting the blessed and her guard, and learning of the oath daggers before heading to the temple. He detailed their encounters with the wraiths and the state of the tunnels as they found them, his father's brows furrowing at the news that the defenses had increased exponentially compared to those at the fire temple. When he continued on to what had happened once they reached the central room and the consequent death of Nees, his mother gasped and covered her mouth at the gory details.

Then he paused, his attention darting to Hara briefly before he cleared his throat and described the plant healers and their conversation with Tabriara. She gritted her jaw in anticipation, but he spoke of Evelaine receiving her memories first, choosing to go out of order, and then paused again. Bending down, he retrieved his pack and set it in his lap, unopened.

"See, the thing is . . . in thanks, the Plant Goddess gifted me the Fire Crown." He reached inside his pack and slowly drew it out, the golden flames and red gems catching the light. His mother's eyes widened and his father leaned forward in awe, holding his hand out to his son in anticipation. But Rakhmet didn't move, just met his father's gaze with a steady expression.

"Father," he said carefully, "the goddess gave **me** the Fire Crown."

The former king blinked, his brows falling in confusion, then blinked again. The silence wore on, the two men staring at each other as realization dawned. A series of emotions crossed Rakhmet's father's face, from surprise to disbelief to affront.

"What?" he demanded, planting his palms on his desk and rising. Hara almost reached for Rakhmet's shoulder but clenched her hands at her sides.

Rakhmet's thumb rubbed the curve of the crown in his hand, a protective move that didn't escape his father's notice. "Blessed Tabriara and blessed Furaro have deemed me the new Fire King."

His mother gasped again, her eyes darting back and forth between her husband and her son. "Wh-what does that mean?"

"I am now king," Rakhmet declared, his voice low in an effort to not anger his father further, and Hara's heartbeat quickened.

Another long moment passed as the former king leaned his weight on his desk, his gaze searing as he studied his son. His body language was threatening, but Rakhmet did not cower. He didn't even stand to confront him. He just sat there with his head held high, letting his father know that he meant what he said as Hara's heart pounded in her ears.

When no one moved, Rakhmet raised one hand. "Must I demonstrate?"

His father's expression grew stony but he nodded once, a jerk of his chin that indicated his challenge. The small movement was louder than a shout and Hara held in her wince.

With a flick of his wrist, Rakhmet's hand was enveloped in flame and his father stumbled back in surprise. His attention went to Rakhmet's other hand, which was still holding the crown in his lap, and then back to the fire.

"Where are your rings?" he asked, amazed. Both Rakhmet and his father had always had to rely on the flint and steel in their rings in order to generate fire on their own, and the former king had been able to use his powers without striking his rings together in front of the court when asked by Ambassador Risais only because he could draw from the torches that had already been burning on the walls around the room.

"I no longer need them," Rakhmet explained, his gaze holding his father's as he stood. With another quick movement, he snuffed the flames and then slowly placed the crown upon his head. "I am the Fire King, as decreed by the gods."

He stepped back to stand next to Hara as his father's mouth opened then closed, then opened and closed again. Hara forced herself to breathe evenly, giving nothing away as she slowly counted in and out. But eventually, the older man's expression softened and morphed into pride touched by a hint of sadness.

"Well then," he murmured in astonishment. "My son, the king."

He came around the side of the desk in halting steps then stopped in front of Rakhmet and placed his fist over his heart, Hara almost reaching for Rakhmet again as he imperceptibly swayed in relief. "May his honored reign be prolonged, peaceful, and prosperous, gods willing."

As he bowed, Rakhmet's mother also popped to her feet, fresh tears flooding her cheeks, and rushed to place her own fist over her heart to echo: "May his honored reign be prolonged, peaceful, and prosperous, gods willing."

"Gods willing," Rakhmet repeated, dipping his chin in acknowledgement as Hara murmured it as well. He then glanced at her and reached out his hand to clasp hers as her stomach flipped, her fingers trembling in his. "Furthermore, I have chosen my queen."

At that, his mother gasped again and her knees went limp as she fell back into her chair, and his father instinctively grasped her shoulder to steady her. Her shaking hands covered her mouth, and they both looked at Hara with utter shock.

Hara's heart was aflame, her fingers tightening around Rakhmet's as heat licked her clenched throat, but she didn't miss the words he uttered next:

"Hara Gamal will be my queen, my partner in all things. She is to share my heart and my throne. She will be by my side, in life and in death. I swear this on this day and forevermore."

"Oh gods." His mother gasped and his father's jaw dropped open.

"But Rakhmet . . . are you sure?" the former king questioned, his wide gaze darting between them. "This is entirely unprecedented."

"My heart is hers and hers mine. I have never been more sure," Rakhmet vowed solemnly, and in that moment, Hara could see the king inside of him. Gravitas dripped from every syllable and demanded the respect he was due. It was a world away from the playboy prince that had been chasing after every distraction available, running from the duties that were expected of him in fear. He had stepped into his destiny, taking control of the threads that wove his path, and he was doing it his way. With love, compassion, understanding, and hope for a better future.

"He is my king," she said, a smile curving her lips as she nodded to his parents. "And I am his queen, in life and in death."

His father stared at her for a long moment, his eyes fully taking her in for the first time. He had never truly looked upon her as she had always been in the background, an accessory to his son, but now, he studied her with a keen, searching gaze. What he found, she could not say, but it seemed to be enough as he started to grin, his lips stretching across his face to show his pearly whites as a laugh escaped him.

"Well I'll be . . . ." He chuckled. "A warrior queen, bestowed gifts from the gods themselves and loyal to the Fire Crown through and through. I can't think of a better choice, my son."

Rakhmet's mother smiled at that, pushing herself to a stand and clasping Hara's free hand between hers. "My brave daughter-in-law, it is an honor to welcome you to our family."

Hara's heart expanded to an impossible size and her vision grew fuzzy, warmth spreading through her. The former king clapped Rakhmet on the shoulder and his mother wrapped an arm around Hara as they all leaned in for an embrace. She murmured her thanks and they theirs, not a dry eye in the room as they stepped back and placed their fists over their hearts.

"To the great Fire King and his warrior queen, may their reign be prolonged, peaceful, and prosperous, gods willing," they said together, bowing as Rakhmet looked to Hara with a blaze burning in his dark eyes just for her. It spoke of long days and hot nights, senseless arguments and enthusiastic reunions, a winding path ahead of them that would take them to the darkest shadows and the brightest lights. All with him by her side, never to be parted.

ACKNOWLEDGMENTS

I always leave writing these acknowledgements to the very last minute, because, like Rakhmet, I find it difficult to put into words the depth of gratitude that exists in my heart for the people who support me. I truly would not have gotten as far as I have without the enthusiasm and encouragement of those around me, from close friends and family to connections and acquaintances I may only speak to once every couple of years.

Thanking my book team is the easy part: I would completely flounder, not knowing where to put my commas, em dashes, and ellipses, without my amazing editor Norma Gambini. My incredible formatter, Samantha Pico, is also invaluable. Without her, this would simply be a manuscript, not a book. Thank you as well to my cover artist, Carlos Ortega-Haas. I have very much enjoyed watching his rise to internet stardom over the years and am honored that he still takes the time to collaborate with me.

Furthermore, I am immensely grateful for my beta reading team: Sarah Madden, Aiden Murray, H.P.T., and Austin Valenzuela. They are the brave souls who lead the war against my imposter syndrome and, without fail, always make me laugh (and cry) with their feedback and comments.

More indirectly, I would like to thank the dozens and dozens of authors, business connections, and colleagues who remind me that to write and publish a book is no easy feat (let alone doing it three times). I am what they call an "ex-gifted kid". High-achieving is my base minimum, and it's both a blessing and curse. On the one hand, I am damn good at what I do no matter what I apply myself to. On the other, I often don't recognize and/or value my efforts since excellence is simply an average Tuesday for me. I am my own worst critic and don't always give myself the credit my results deserve.

But the people around me remind me that my achievements are worth celebrating and I could not be more thankful. Without them, I wouldn't get any sleep, tossing and turning and overthinking everything. My anxiety and self-doubt would run the show, and I'd be a very sad Claire. So thank you, thank you, thank you, from the bottom of my heart.

GLOSSARY:
GODS & GODDESSES

Dishiru | God of Wind

Temple somewhere unknown.

Blessed Bloodline: unknown

Furaro | God of Fire

Temple near Zahar, a desert city in South Endrian. Known as the Fire God, his power controls all forms of flame, and he lives in a palace surrounded by a source of magma. His tapestry features a phoenix and a flaming tree.

Blessed Pyrantus Bloodline: King Rakhmet Pyrantus and his father, Pharosos

Gamarna | Goddess of Earth

Temple somewhere unknown.

Blessed Bloodline: unknown

Hazu | God of Life

Temple near Aepol, the northern pole in North Endrian. Known as the Sun God, his power is the gift of life and healing, and he is married to Hecatah. His tapestry features a sun, a tree of life with interconnected roots, and two lions with the wings of an eagle.

Blessed Sintal Bloodline: King Roe Sintal

Hecatah | Goddess of Death

Temple near Supol, the southern pole in Brindt. Known as the Moon Goddess, her power involves overseeing the death process and the passage of ghosts and spirits. She is married to Hazu. Her tapestry features a moon in a winter landscape with a cypress tree and two owls in flight.

Blessed Makaanis Bloodline: Queen Kelah Makaanis

Sirenia | Goddess of Water

Temple on Tusi Island, the northernmost of the Bourisian Islands to the east of South Endrian. Her power controls all forms and bodies of water, and she rules over all marine creatures from her palace at the bottom of the ocean. Her tapestry features an expanse of coral, crowned by a crab in a sea of green and blue.

Blessed Rutrulan Bloodline: Queen Nasima Rutrulan and her grandparent, Ohn

Tabriara | Goddess of Plants

Temple near the village of Curacu, east of Lythenea in Talegartia on the western coast of South Endrian. Her power controls all forms of plant life, but her special plant is the castor bean. She rules from her palace decorated with a cacophony of plants, and her tapestry features a red-purple leaf and spiked seed cluster.

Blessed Peonille Bloodline: Evelaine Peonille

Urkus | God of Metal

Temple somewhere unknown.

Blessed Bloodline: unknown

GLOSSARY:
MORTAL COURTS

The Makaanises
In the past, they protected and honored the Moon Goddess's sacred land and temple near Supol, the southern pole in Brindt. There is a single blessed one per generation and they can see, speak to, and command spirits as well as see between the veils.

> *Moon Queen: Kelah Makaanis*
> > *Partner: Roe Sintal*
> > *Oathed Guard: Zandira Gwendi*
> > *Mother: Molla Makaanis (deceased)*
> > *Father: Beret Makaanis (deceased)*
> > *Brother: Lienn Makaanis (deceased)*

The Pyrantuses
They protect and honor the Fire God's sacred land and temple near Zahar, a desert city in South Endrian. There are multiple blessed ones per generation and they are connected to and can wield all forms of fire.

> *Fire King: Rakhmet Pyrantus*
> > *Father: Pharosos Pyrantus*
> > *Grandfather: Diemani Pyrantus (deceased)*
> > *Mother: Oyah Pyrantus*
> > *Oathed Guard and Partner: Hara Gamal*

Advisors: Viceroy Emat Nehitet, Vicerah Nerfera Semitep, Viceroy Nikat Tuthakht, Vicerah Duae Setaemtir, Viceroy Kay Ramsey, Viziera Niankha Hotep, Vizier Desher Sekhem, Viziera Meruka Kagemni

Ambassadors: Arad Shivash (from Gheseruti), Tellis Risais (from Talegartia)

Other Members: Nebehet Tuthakht, Inenekah Hotep, Khenti Kagemni

The Rutrulans

They protect and honor the Water Goddess's sacred land and temple on Tusi Island, the northernmost of the Bourisian Islands to the east of South Endrian. There are multiple blessed ones per generation and they are connected to and can wield all forms of water.

Water Queen: Nasima Rutrulan

Oathed Guard and Partner: Cassandra Mertusa

Mother: Charo Rutrulan (deceased)

Father: Jameson Wulf, Captain of the Golden Inquirer

Grandparent: Ohn Rutrulan

Spouse: Rochelle Willan

Other Members: Dumadi Tongse, Annisa Tongse, Arika Tongse, Kai Tongse

The Peonilles

In the past, they protected and honored the Plant Goddess's sacred land and temple near the village of Curacu, east of Lythenea in Talegartia on the western coast of South Endrian. There are multiple blessed ones per generation and they are connected to and can wield all forms of plant life as well as produce poisonous seeds and pollen spores.

Plant Blessed: Evelaine Peonille

Mother: Elemona Peonille (deceased)
Oathed Guard: Nees Rasa (deceased)

The Sintals

In the past, they protected and honored the Sun God's sacred land and temple near Aepol, the northern pole in North Endrian. There is a single blessed one per generation and they can wield healing abilities.

Sun King: Roe Sintal
    Partner: Kelah Makaanis
    Daughter: Venara Sintal
    Mother: Osmia Sintal (deceased)
    Other Members: Brishna Reconi

DISCOVER MORE IN THE NEXT BOOK OF THE THREADS
OF DESTINY SERIES!
Coming Halloween 2025

Photo by Holli Margell

Claire E. Jones | Existential glitter bomb. Dog mom. Bookworm. Romantic. Nerd. Creative AF. Dancer. Only child. Goof. Introvert. Blonde. Artaholic. Entrepreneur. Clairvoyant. Homebody. Prochoice. Philanthropist. Stoner. Intellectual. Visionary. German. Lithuanian. Welsh. Pansexual. Millennial. Intuitive. Liberal. Prounion. Humanitarian. Pegan. Pagan. Witch. Anti-capitalist. Seattleite. Former Midwesterner. Pisces Sun. Pisces Moon. Leo Rising. Mercury in Aquarius. Five planets in Capricorn.

CONNECT ONLINE
www.claireejones.com
@clairjoyance

Milton Keynes UK
Ingram Content Group UK Ltd.
UKHW040254291024
450401UK00005B/20